# The Betrayal Path

by

B. Van Norman

i

Wilf, for his faith.

Susan, for her love.

ISBN: 9780986856914

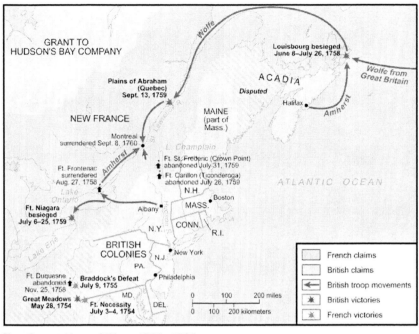

## THE NEW WORLD, 1757

# 1

He had lost Ledrew somewhere in those foetid alleys. The cutlass slash in his shoulder had left him only one option. Useless in a fight he had run through the shadowy streets to the night beach where men should have been waiting. In the moonlight he could see the English frigate far out, an easy swim for a healthy man, impossible for him. Soldiers' boots pounded the cobbled street behind him and suddenly there was no choice. His shoulder searing, he dived into the Mediterranean's dark waters.

As he struggled, strength ebbing too quickly, through the surf the moon exposed him. A rattle of musketry from the shore sent a spray of lead into the water around him. He felt stinging in his legs as miniballs peppered them. He tried to keep swimming but his legs were useless. Finally he lay quietly in the water allowing the pull of the tide to take him out, hoping it would drift him toward the frigate. He did not want to die out here, drowning in warm, black water. He could feel himself sinking, allowing the drowsiness to overwhelm his will to live.

A splash and a squeal of oarlocks brought him back to consciousness. Then he heard English voices and strong, rough hands laid hold of him hauling him up over wood gunwales.

He had only enough energy to mumble one word to the sailors. "Ledrew?"

A face appeared in front of him.

"T'other one, sir? Aye, we got 'im an 'alf hour ago. 'Twas 'im made us come back for you."

"They're shootin' again, Tom," a frightened voice cut in.

"Let's be off then! We done our share for this night."

The skiff hauled out toward the frigate, sped by the fear of its oarsmen, taking Alan Nashe away from Marseilles.

*** 

With time his health improved, the wounds healing due to the competence of the frigate's surgeon and his own youthful energy. Alan Nashe was ordered home, congratulated on his escape, and sent on recuperative leave. Just that.

Nothing more. War had been declared with the French, but Nashe would be out of it for some time. Just as well. He'd been in the snake pit of espionage far too long.

Finances for his 'time away' were courtesy His Majesty's Paymaster General and supplemented by his success at the gaming tables of Bath. Nashe had always considered the pay of a Royal Marine officer somewhat less than suitable for his needs, thus the move to Bath.

The city was a centre of Georgian fashion. The baths, in existence since Roman times, were rediscovered by a new society. Patched, powdered, and rouged, bedecked in the finest lace and velvets; they listened to Handl's newest on the Esplanade, lolled in the sulphurous waters of the Pump Room, and gossiped over the latest scandals. It suited him well.

In Bath he was a peaceful man. During the days he would read: Fielding, Smollet, Pope. The nights were for the tables: pharaoh, whist, the roll of dice. Club Arthur rang with his successes; his new-found profits renovated his apartments and he even took a mistress, Isabel Wishfort, a courtesan of the gaming tables.

Still, a part of each day was spent on necessities: horsemanship, shooting, fencing practice, regaining his strength and honing the skills he would need when he left this paradise of pleasure.

For despite his best efforts to blend in, there was something that set Nashe apart from the others. Handsome in a dark, brooding manner, he looked older than his twenty-six years. It was in the way he held himself, in the hard eyes, and the abandon about him, and all the powders in the world would not cover the thin, jagged scar that wended its way along his right jaw. That scar, and iron nerves at the table gave him a reputation he had not at all intended.

In a few months his recovery was complete. Yet with it came unexpected monotony. Nashe was soon bored with his triumphs, with the spring rains, and especially with Mrs. Wishfort. He wondered if the war office had forgotten him.

The conflict with the French was going badly. Prussians, under King Frederick, had been contained by France; one of many huge battles on the continent. The Duke of Newcastle committed English ships to the fray and an unprepared England paid for it dearly. The British lost their naval station on Minorca and with it control of the Mediterranean. It seemed nothing could stop France's conquests.

Nashe knew if the war continued his talents would be called upon. He would be ready. Yet had he known then the nature of his future assignment and the effect it would have upon him, he would have thanked His Majesty very much, asserted that he had done his duty, cashed his commission in the Royal Marines, and despite the war ended his service to King George II.

But he did not know where and why, only who would send him.

When the letter came he accepted it.

## 2

The letter came shrouded in mystery. Indeed, an exasperated Mrs. Wishfort informed Nashe the messenger had taken great pains to hide his identity and had actually refused to stay to tea. Nashe left the letter unopened avoiding Isabel's inquisitive glances and shut the door politely behind him.

The letter was wrapped in oiled silk and bound tightly with a sealed ribbon, with no marking on the seal. Its author had taken precautions against its being covertly opened. The words were succinct with no salutation.

'Your presence is required immediately upon receipt. Please make your attendance, early evening of the date given below, at the summer house of Brigadier Lord Howe, Bath.' The remainder of the note contained the address of the house and the date. The note was unsigned but beneath it, in a postscript, 'Attire: dress uniform.'

The postscript was initialled: 'OF.'

"More and more curious," Nashe pondered aloud. The initial was that of Brigadier Offingham, his commanding officer. Nashe knew the man well and cryptic notes were not his style. He decided the postscript was not to be taken lightly.

After an early light supper, he dressed. Booted to the knee, scarlet tunic with silver piping and polished buttons, rapier in a black leather scabbard, Nashe peered into his glass briefly admiring his martial costume then laughed at his vanity. He left the apartments and took a carriage to the suburban home of Lord Howe.

He was not shown the drawing room upon arrival. Rather, he was escorted to the stable yard. A courteous major appeared and led him to a waiting carriage. The carriage was shuttered.

It was nightfall when the carriage finally rolled to a stop. A stiff and somewhat irate Nashe climbed down, curtly saluted his escort, and was taken into a well-guarded mansion concealed from the road by an alder grove. In the dusk it frowned forbiddingly. Nashe entered and was met with a deft salute from a tall, unsmiling sergeant-at-arms. Without a word, Nashe was conveyed through cold, lofty halls hung with faded battle flags. At a set of oaken doors he halted, surrounded now by six of His Majesty's Marines.

There they stood: the sergeant, Nashe, and the six gleaming guards for close to an hour. No one sat; indeed, there were no chairs. No one spoke.

A colonel who stepped through the doors to greet Nashe interrupted their vigil. Nashe recognized him: Widdifield, an old style soldier with no admiration for modern society and especially its young rakes (he had two daughters). Yet now he smiled at Nashe.

"Pleasant trip, Captain?"

"Not exactly, Sir."

"A little discomfort, yes? You're accustomed, I gather, to more plush surroundings."

"You might say that, Sir."

"Well, time you adjusted, young man. The Spartan life, the great out-of-doors and all that. Good luck among the heathen, old boy."

Then Widdifield, uncharacteristically cheerful, showed him into the room beyond the mysterious doors. As Nashe entered he was greeted with a gruff command to be seated, a suggestion he immediately ignored. Having glimpsed the inhabitants of the room, he stood to attention.

There was Lord Howe, of course, he'd expected that; but he noticed too the indomitable Admiral Saunders, one of England's best naval commanders; the great Jeffrey Amherst, Britain's most respected general; then a colonial officer by his blue uniform and finally, Offingham, looking very, very nervous.

But most surprising were those who sat behind a table piled with folders: Lord Cumberland, deputy chief of strategy for the King's council, and, unbelievably, the supposedly ousted William Pitt, former prime minister of England. He did not appear ousted now, thought Nashe; in fact, he seemed in control of this meeting.

Nashe began to think conspiracy. It would explain the men here, Offingham's nervousness, and the fact that Pitt ran the meeting.

"Please step forward, Captain," Pitt beckoned. He was smiling.

Things were no longer curious. Things were becoming alarming indeed.

## 3

"Now I realize, Captain Nashe, this little get-together has all the earmarks of a plot," Pitt began, "but rest assured that is not the case."

The room stiffened at the reference.

"I must apologize for the precautions, Captain...the carriage and all..."

"Quite all right, Sir, though somewhat unorthodox I believe," Nashe returned.

"Yes, well, from what I gather you are rather an unorthodox young man yourself, Captain," Pitt smiled. The remainder of the men did not.

"Yes, Sir."

In the ensuing pause, Nashe felt Pitt's eyes searching him. This was a man accustomed to sizing up others. His look had not been subtle; it had not been meant to be.

"Now we have little time, Captain, so I'll just skip the pleasantries for the moment and we'll address the business at hand. Amherst?"

Major General Amherst appeared everything Nashe had heard: disciplined, rugged, a committed soldier. He acknowledged Pitt with a brief, "Sir," and waved Nashe to a chair near the desk.

"Sit down, Captain, you'll be here a while."

"Thank you, Sir."

"I trust, Captain Nashe, after you're 'time away' you are ready to rejoin active service? I gather you have kept up some semblance of fitness other than the use of the dice hand."

"I am aware, Sir, of the war with France."

"This briefing," Pitt interrupted, "will have little to do with Europe. We consider this war to be of a much different sort from those of the past, both in its scope and its aims. This will be a world war, Nashe, and we intend to fight it on all fronts, and win it."

For the first time in months, Alan Nashe was no longer bored.

"I'll just review the basics," Amherst continued. "The French have developed an extensive empire worldwide: India, parts of Africa, assorted islands in the South Seas, and in the Americas a place called Kanata which they have named New France. We will dispense with discussion of all but this last, for that is our primary concern."

"Here it comes..." Nashe muttered, recalling Widdifield's smiling face.

"I beg your pardon, Captain?"

"Nothing, Sir. Rather a bad habit of mine."

"A very bad habit, Nashe."

"Yes, Sir."

"Now if we may return to the business at hand. In recent years, traders in our American colonies have pushed westward to expand their trade. The French, however, seem to believe that they, and they only, have jurisdiction there. A ridiculous idea, but one they take rather seriously."

"Sir," Nashe addressed Amherst, "you refer to New France, America and Kanata when you seem to be discussing the same place. As you know I have little knowledge of the colonies..."

"Essentially, Captain, New France is the theoretical holdings of France in the Americas. But perhaps Colonel Schuyler could provide you with a more detailed description." The man dressed in colonial uniform approached with chart in hand, when he spoke his voice was rough with the sound of years of battle.

"This is a map of America as far as we and the French have explored it, Captain Nashe. You must understand that the land is huge, greater than all Europe. The point being: we have thirteen loosely knit colonies on this eastern coast reaching up to our northernmost port of Halifax. France claims everything west of them. Their land stretches right from New Orleans to the far north of Kanata, as the natives call it."

"That seems the devil of an area to hold, Sir. Or have they the troops?"

"Damn it, man, they haven't one tenth our population!" This was obviously a sore point with the colonel. "But they have their forts. And from those forts they have raided our northern borders for years. They send savages against isolated settlements: burning, massacres, scalping."

"They refuse to meet you in open battle?"

"You don't understand, Nashe. This is not Europe. These men live in the forest appearing where they're least expected, desecrate everything in their path, then melt back into the bush."

"Can you not follow them?"

"How? A thousand miles of forest and rivers? You could lose an army in the forest, be half a mile from your objective and never know it was there!"

"I see..."

"Thank you, Colonel," Pitt murmured. "Gentlemen, I think it time for a little supper. Captain Nashe, you will dine with us."

The supper, an affair of cold lamb and cheese, was brought in on Georgian silver, the punch was doled out and the men partook in small, quiet groups. Nashe sat alone. No one, not even Offingham, deigned to speak with him. He was left to his thoughts, pondering the mysteries he would find in this strange, raw new world.

## 4

With trays cleared and the claret passed round, the meeting reconvened. Nashe looked to this segment with some trepidation. He wondered if it were possible to refuse. He considered it somehow doubtful.

"You can see from the chart, Captain," Amherst began brusquely, "the French fortifications. Louisbourg to the east; in the west is Fort Duquesne; Niagara and Frontenac guard the St. Lawrence river and on Lake Champlain is Fort Carillon protecting their southern flank. Finally in the centre, Montreal and Quebec, both fortified cities on the St. Lawrence and the keystone to their defence."

Amherst paused for breath and Pitt, a finger tapping his chin, interrupted.

"Captain Nashe," Pitt's voice rose slightly, "what we intend is to invest this system by force of arms, blockade the St. Lawrence river with naval units, and eventually take their capitol, Quebec. The campaign is to begin this next year when we have transported enough British regulars to our colonies. How many, Loudon?"

A red-fleshed bear of a man stood amid the gathering. His voice was as big as he was: "Thirty thousand, Sir!"

"The campaign will not be a quick one. There has been fighting for four years now, Nashe. We have learned some hard lessons." Pitt looked across the room and all eyes stared at the floor. Obviously something had gone amiss.

"Offingham," Pitt declared, "I believe it is your turn now."

Nashe had become fond of the old Brigadier. Offingham was tolerant, provided one achieved results. And this was why the man performed the duties he did: overseeing the networks of spies that served as the eyes of England.

"These forts are a result of the fur trade, something of which I'm sure you've been part." The Brigadier's innuendo on the current rage in beaver hats seemed to pass above the others. But from the corner of his eye Nashe caught the faintest glimmer of a smile on Pitt's lips.

"The French have expanded in search of more fur, as have we; thus the conflict. In '54, a young fellow named Washington was sent to warn the French out of disputed territories. He was careless. There was a skirmish. A French officer named Jumonville was killed. The French claim he was on a peace mission when Washington ordered the attack. Unfortunately, Washington was captured and the fool signed a paper admitting the crime!"

"Brigadier," Amherst cut in, "if you could keep to the matter at hand..."

Offingham stiffened. "In '55 we succeeded in capturing the French commander, Dieskau. He was replaced by a Marquis de Montcalm."

Amherst again interrupted. "We need to know the troops we will face, the fortifications we must besiege, and a great deal more concerning French leaders. And it seems," he glanced disparagingly toward Offingham, "our present network has broken down. You are to remedy that. But more to the point, Nashe, we are sending you because your dossier, which I might add is none too impressive, indicates you are fluent in French and French custom and that you are an inveterate gambler, the last of which is significant in light of your assignment. A certain official of New France, their finance minister to be exact, is also a high living, decadent fool who just might be taken advantage of. A fellow named Bigot."

"We have availed ourselves," Offingham resumed, "at the cost of a life some rather unique French trade papers and placed your name to them. You are to be a Scots fur trader, an entrepreneur. You'll be supplied with a goodly amount from His Majesty's treasury that should, along with your new characterization, put you in touch with the people you wish to meet. It is left to your discretion as to how you use it, but for God's sake, man, don't lose it at the tables. It's all you will get!"

Nashe was quickly warming to the plot.

"Don't underestimate these people, Captain," Schuyler seemed to anticipate Nashe's lightened frame of mind. "They are not simpletons. Their officials have gained their positions in Quebec through intrigue at the French court. And I have seen the remains of men they considered spies."

"Nevertheless," Offingham added, "you must get as close as possible to these people."

"But how do I communicate?" Nashe questioned.

"The network there is in fragments. You are to help the head of that network rebuild. We think he hasn't been captured but the situation has us at a loss."

"And who is this man?"

"His name is Ledrew."

"Jeffrey Ledrew? Good God, Sir..."

"The same," grinned the old Brigadier. In Marseilles Ledrew and Nashe were the perfectly balanced team: Nashe creative, unorthodox; Ledrew quietly efficient. The Brigadier was confident they would be again.

And in the spring of 1757, as Alan Nashe boarded ship at New Rochelle, he was confident. Simple colonials, he was sure, were no match for his training and skills. And he would be with his former partner.

And in thinking this, Nashe made his first mistake; ignoring the warning of Colonel Schuyler.

## 5

It was the worst seven weeks Nashe had ever encountered; an awful voyage, long and bitter: the weather cruel, the ship pitching. And then there had been the murder.

A few of the more experienced sea hands were not completely immobilized. The crew, of course, and some men, including Nashe, seemed to bear the crossing with stoic doggedness. These passengers would gather of evenings at the captain's table. Captain Gilbert, starved for civilized discussion, encouraged the men to conversation over the sliding crockery and spilled food that served as supper. They discussed Voltaire, the Ancients, commerce, war, anything that came to mind. And amid that varied group Nashe found himself watching carefully one particular individual. The man was employed with the Ministere de la Marine, France's colonial office. His name was Trémais, Claude Querdisien-Trémais; a minor official in the bureaucracy.

Trémais was a short, plump, mild mannered character. His appearance, the kindly round face and the hair going to pepper and salt, reminded Nashe of a village merchant. Monsieur Trémais played the simple soul well, but Nashe was accustomed to players of roles, and soon decided to investigate.

A quick excuse from the table as Trémais was in the midst of discussion, a slip of the lock on his cabin door and ensuing search of the room indicated Trémais was no minor functionary. The man was an inspector-general, highly placed in the ministry. His orders had been hidden away in a secret compartment of his trunk; easy prey for Nashe. And those orders were intriguing indeed. Trémais was to investigate the financial affairs of the colony, paying special attention to Intendant Bigot and company. There was some suspicion of embezzlement or at very least, incompetence. Trémais was to pose as a minor official taking his post temporarily under the Intendant's auspices. This was not considered suspicious as Trémais had indeed been a trade officer in Quebec some six years past.

The man had lived there. Now he was returning. Trémais had been empowered, should he find it necessary: to assume control of the Intendancy, send Monsieur Bigot to Paris for trial and re-vamp the finances of the colony.

A man to be reckoned with, thought Nashe, and cultivated for information. Nashe considered the irony: two spies on the same ship drawn to the same destination, both with the same man in mind, each suspicious of the other. For Trémais had attempted his own search as well.

Nashe had made certain the inspector would find little more than fur trade attachments and hints of Nashe's rapacious character. A few letters carefully, but not too carefully hidden, his trading papers, a note of introduction and some rather large sums of gold louis would, he knew, intrigue the man. But the more incriminating tools of his trade no man, at least not one of Trémais' calibre, would discover.

Nashe relaxed then. He should not have.

One evening the sea was particularly vicious, spray flying in great washes over the ship. The captain was tired, the meal sparse, conversation flaccid. They all retired early that evening. And that early retirement led Nashe to his cabin and trouble.

As he entered he was smiling, a joke at the table half remembered. The smile disappeared as he found his room turned upside down and in the midst of the shambles a wiry sailor who snarled and lunged at Nashe.

He was on him in a second, scratching, gouging, his knee driving into Nashe's groin. Nashe doubled over with the pain and met a fist to his face. He fell back helpless. A knife flashed from the sailor's belt, the blade snaking toward Nashe's throat. Nashe desperately brought up one foot just in time to kick at the sailor's face as he lunged. Blood gushed, the man fell, the knife clattered under the bed. But the man rolled and was up like a cat, wary now as Nashe too rose.

The ship rolled throwing them both off balance. The sailor bounced off a wall and attacked. He was not quick enough. Nashe chopped down with both hands as the greasy head met his stomach. The man dropped. Nashe's knee smashed into his face. The sailor grunted and fell like a stone to the deck, his head cracking hard against a locker. He tried once to rise, then his eyes rolled up into his head and he collapsed, unconscious.

Nashe hobbled to the door, opened it and listened for an alarm. He heard nothing, the storm too high for anyone to have heard anything. As his pain subsided he returned to the sailor.

In moments Nashe had brought the man around, groaning, trying to feel the back of his head. He could not. Nashe had pinioned his arms.

"Good, you've returned," Nashe growled pulling the arms upward. The sailor's head reeled forward and he howled in pain. Nashe shoved his face into a pillow. "Now I have a few questions."

A string of muffled epithets directed at Nashe were as amusing as they were varied. This man was tough; he understood pain. Still, Nashe knew he would talk.

"Alright, my friend, I know what I am and have no need of your reminding me," Nashe muttered. "What I do not know is who you are, or more important, who sent you. Trémais?"

Another curse answered him and Nashe brought the arms up further.

"I suggest you concentrate, friend. All I ask is the name of your master and you're free," he jerked up on one arm to make his point.

"I don't know. I don't know!"

"Quietly. Who told you to search my cabin?"

"For God's sake let up. I don't know I tell you!"

Nashe snapped the left arm at the shoulder. Before the man could scream Nashe covered his mouth and held him until he stopped convulsing.

"This will not end until I have answers, friend. They don't pay crippled sailors."

The man was beaten, his eyes panicked. He nodded and Nashe removed his hand.

"An agent from Gradis and Son at Bordeaux. He told me to find out about you."

"Why?"

"I don't know! He paid me ten louis."

"Who are you to report to in Quebec?"

"I don't know."

The right arm was pushed to his neck.

"Cadet! Joseph Cadet! Commissary at Quebec! For God's sake my arm!"

"And who is this Cadet's master?"

"I don't..." the arm went up again, "Bigot! The Intendant! His company is Gradis and Son. Bigot!"

There was little else he could get from the man. Nashe released the arm and stood over him.

"So, my friend, what is the penalty for theft on this ship, eh?!

That second of carelessness was almost Nashe's last. Again the groin, the man's good hand smashing up into him and Nashe was writhing on the floor. But the sailor was injured and slow to rise. Nashe reached for the knife in his boot. And through mists of agony saw his throw was accurate, the blade suddenly in the sailor's throat. The man clawed at it, gouts of blood gurgling from his mouth, then he fell.

Nashe fought the pain that convulsed his body. He wrapped the man in a velvet cape torn from his rack of costumes, then dragged him up to the deck careful to leave no blood trail. The storm still raged and no one was in the open. Nashe dumped his burden overboard. Burial at sea, he thought, grimacing as another rush of pain took him. A sailor washed away in the tempest. There would be no questions. Nashe made his way slowly back to his bed and collapsed there in unthinking agony.

But another man lay on his bed that night deep in thought. Claude Querdisien-Trémais had investigated strange noises, had seen Nashe with his burden and for the first time in his forty-three years, was completely perplexed.

## 6

The sun wafted above the tree-lined cliffs that rimmed the Quebec Basin. The Celebre had spent the night at anchor waiting the morning to enter the Cul-de-Sac, the city's harbour. The morning air was brisk and surprisingly cold for late May.

Somehow they had come upon land. The ship had slipped the Atlantic's cold grasp directly on the doorstep of Louisbourg. Captain Gilbert, Nashe considered, would make a fine addition to the Royal Navy. They remained a few days to provision and repair. Nashe idled the time away with Trémais touring the great fort's defences. The ramparts were a mile in circumference: great thick walls with huge cannon facing the sea commanding each avenue of approach. The French well understood the import of this isolated, gale-blasted fortress. It controlled access to their new world.

The place seemed impregnable.  Nashe doubted whether the English campaign could survive a defence such as this.  And this, Pitt had reiterated, was the keystone for invasion.  Take this bastion and then starve the French out of their colony.  There was only one weakness to the plan: how to take Louisbourg.

Then the ship had departed west toward riviere St. Laurent, around the Gaspé and on up the tremendous river stopping at Ile aux Coudres to take on a pilot.  It took days until they heaved to at the northern tip of Ile d'Orleans and then, the river pilot commanding, made their way up the treacherous strait called the Traverse.  It had been dusk then and grey, lowering clouds had obscured any view of their surroundings.

Now the morning sun dawned slowly, by degrees, illuminating the stage upon which Nashe was to play out his role.  And an incredible stage it was.

The Basin itself was huge; a near lake encompassed by cliffs a hundred and more feet high.  At its southern end the river narrowed between two massive pillars of land to a mere thousand yards in width.  And there, commanding the narrows, glowering down on the Basin from its towering, ominous bastion: Quebec.  In the distance its church spires, the walls of its fortress, the quaint, crowded harbour at its base were miniatures in contrast to the huge mount rearing up from the river.  If ever nature had created a stronghold, this was it.

"Cap aux Diamants, an impressive sight is it not?"  Trémais joined Nashe.  "The city has existed for a hundred and fifty years.  Jacques Cartier explored this river.  He found the Cap two hundred years ago.  He thought it was made of diamonds, it so sparkled in the sun; must have been a morning like this when he first came upon it."

"Was it?"

"Was it what, my dear Nashe?"

"Diamonds."

"Alas, no...quartz.  But the place has value in other ways now.  Cartier would have been happy."

"I see what you mean," a subdued Nashe replied.

"A man named Champlain was first to build here: below the Cap there, near the harbour.  He nearly starved to death that winter, forced to leave in the spring.  But something drew him back, thank God, and now we have this."

"What is that fortress on top, at the edge facing us?"

"The Governor's palace: Chateau St. Louis.  Beside it is the Bishop's palace.  They flank the Cote de la Montagne, the road up from the harbour."

"You know this place well."

"I lived here some years back. It fascinates me, Monsieur Nashe. I admire the men who made it."

"It's a damn fine fortress but how is the trade?"

"Ah, Nashe, I should have realized. The mind of the merchant is not on the past, but on profits and women and wine and the future!"

"Trémais, you are a man who understands men."

"Still, the Cap aux Diamantes... a beautiful and fitting name is it not? I like to think it the portal of all New France. Once through this gateway you sail for weeks upriver and through inland seas. This is a new world, Monsieur, a world of forest that stretches away beyond imagination. Trees exist here like grass blades in Europe. And the forest is a strange place. When you enter it, it swallows you, closes behind you as if it were a grave. It has been the grave of too many men," he paused a moment lost in some private reverie. "It is a savage place, Alan. The only matter of any account is survival. You will find here, my friend, that a great many men, both brown and white, have learned the laws of the forest. But I forget myself," Trémais' mood turned suddenly, "forgive a romantic bureaucrat his nostalgia. Look, we enter the Cul-de-Sac!"

The Celebre swung into the harbour nestled at the foot of the cliff. In the brisk dawn the place was bustling with activity. Bateaux and long rafts rustled and bumped against each other accompanied by the songs and occasional curses of men loading and off-loading. Nashe could not resist one more despondent look at the fortress towering two hundred feet above. Then he turned to business.

"Why is the harbour so busy this early?"

"In the colony everything begins early. Even Governor Vaudreuil holds audience at seven in the morning. Night falls fast in this land and there is much to be done in a day. Besides, the night is for pleasure is it not?"

"And what are those men loading, over there?"

"Monsieur Nashe, you spite me," he remonstrated gently. "You know I'm aware you are a trader. Those men prepare to leave for the pays en haut, the interior. The sooner one leaves the more fur he returns with."

"I confess, Monsieur Trémais," Nashe countered quickly, "that I am a trader in name only. I have papers from the Compagnie but I am new to all this. I hope to expand my enterprises and learn."

"That is best in anything, Monsieur," Trémais was polite, convincingly appropriate in his response. "To learn one must begin at the beginning, eh? You must journey into the forest then. Perhaps I might accompany you?"

"Perhaps. But I admit, Monsieur, that the city itself is as close to wilderness as I wish to venture. My blood is too thin, I think, for gambols in the wild."

"Nonsense! You appear quite in health to me and the diversion would educate you."

"Perhaps I am wrong to assume that Quebec is uncivilized?"

"You are indeed mistaken, Monsieur. It may not be Paris but it contains the necessary comforts, some of excellent quality. You will find the ladies quite accomplished and beautiful, and the men can be the epitome of wit in the right company. Naturally the peasants and artisans of the Lower Town are considered somewhat boorish, and the winters are very long and cold, but I believe you'll come to appreciate this city."

Nashe was unsure of the double entendre in Trémais' final words. It was the way in which they were spoken more than what was said. Nashe decided to be wary.

"Of course I shall. I know it."

"Good. Now let me acquaint you with the lay of the city," Trémais seemed more than willing to be of assistance. "As you can see the city is really two. The Lower Town includes the harbour, traders' maisons and warehouses, and shops and assorted diversions which I am sure you will come to enjoy," his eyes twinkled a little. "Above, on the Cap itself is the Upper Town containing the fortifications, redoubtes for the garrison, churches and the Ursuline convent, private homes and the like where one may attend most exceptional soirees."

"Monsieur Trémais," Nashe interrupted, "perhaps knowing the city as you do you would consent to assist me in finding accommodations. I confess an ulterior motive, Monsieur," half-truth was better than lies, "I need information. And you appear the most informed man I am likely to meet."

The mask of conviviality fell. Trémais' eyes hardened. The question had had its desired effect. In a brief second of calculation Nashe had garnered a wealth of information. He decided then to watch this man carefully, and reverted to his masquerade.

"My friend, I am in need of lodgings; such an ignoramus as I would fall for the smooth talk of sailors, and I do not wish to tarnish myself so soon in a brothel."

God help the French if this were an example of their inspectors-general, Nashe thought. I've read him like a book.

"I beg pardon for my lack of manners, Monsieur Nashe." Trémais regained his composure. "But regrettably I've been taken advantage of before. I would suggest my own lodgings but I'm not sure they would satisfy the Monsieur's tastes."

"Nonsense, my friend, if there are apartments near yours so much the better."

Trémais seemed very pleased.

"Then permit me, Monsieur Nashe, to partake of a glass with you before we go ashore. Unfortunately, there is a law here which, in order to prevent the spread of disease from Europe, requires an inspector of the Amirauté to board ship. We will not be allowed ashore for two hours yet."

"In that case I accept the invitation gratefully."

The two men went below while the inspector and his officers boarded ship. Some of them indeed searched for signs of disease. Some of them, for something else. By the rail where Trémais and Nashe had been standing a smartly dressed young subaltern bent quickly to retrieve a kerchief. Inside the cloth was a parchment. He read the note and quickly reported to his superior. A bateau was soon dispatched to shore. In it was the young subaltern. He was escorted in haste to the mansions of Monsieur Bigot, Intendant of New France.

## 7

Henri Savrebois, Inspector of the Amirauté, took his job seriously: he had lost a daughter three years back to the smallpox that came with some new arrival and swept like a plague through the natives, catching in its wake many whites as well. Savrebois did not want another such occurrence in his lifetime. He was careful in his search. Yet he mumbled to himself as he worked. The colonial officers under commandant Daine only got in the way. But they too, he realized, were looking for vermin. The first ship always held in its bowels some spy, or criminal, or other unwelcome individual. The inspector thus scoured this ship even more thoroughly, found nothing, and signalled the shore.

Four great bateaux filled with harbour voyageurs quickly launched, tied onto the ship and with a great show of power towed it alongside the quay.

For this was by no means an ordinary ship. As it nestled into its berth hundreds began to converge upon it. They came walking from the Lower Town, riding in carioles down the steep winding ways from the Upper Town, they had paddled in from the forests and parishes spotted up and down the river and found their ways here, to Quebec harbour: rich mingling with poor, nobility with farmer, artisan and voyageur, each yearning for news of France, of new fashions, noble scandals, of war... news from the world.

For half the year Quebec was isolated from that world. Ice formed on the river, the ships stopped coming, and no one would dare make the thousand mile overland trek from Louisbourg. In effect, the capitol of New France was cut off to survive on its own. But the hibernation was not unpleasant, the magazins beneath each house kept everyone in food, the entertainments of winter were many and varied, and families and friends grew close.

Nevertheless, winter did not kill curiosity, and these vibrant souls still felt strong ties with the mother country. So they came by the hundreds to mingle in front of this first contact: to receive their letters, open their imported packages, and talk to the passengers just arrived.

This was the scene greeting Nashe as he appeared on deck. He had passed a comfortable time with Trémais over some excellent Madeira and cheese. The conversation had filled Nashe with a sense of wonder. He had come upon a land of strange contrasts: a world of the forest and the salon, of the war dance and the minuet. It was, he admitted, far more complex a place than he had initially thought.

But there was business to be done and so Nashe put aside his thoughts and retired to his cabin early enough to make his arrangements. He knew he must look the part. First impressions would be the most lasting. The practice allowed him freedom if the façade were suddenly dropped. Everyone looked for the young peacock that they well recognized. They never looked for a disguise, and they never saw through one.

Thus, ensconced in his cabin, Nashe prepared: powdered periwig, blue-black patch just large enough to be noticed on the left cheek bone, white silk blouse with a fall of Rouen lace, beige hose complimenting brown crushed velvet breeches, cape and tricorn each inlaid with gold. He bespattered his fingers with expensive rings, his neck with a gold chain and the cross of Catholicism, his waist and feet respectively with a soft leather belt and shoes with touches of brass. He then donned a beautifully balanced and very expensive rapier - thirty two inches of the finest Damascus steel in a gold inlay scabbard – and grasping a slender onyx cane, made ready to present himself to the cream and rabble of New France.

Trémais joined Nashe on the gangway. He raised his eyebrows as was his habit and muttered something about God protecting the women of Quebec as the two descended into the crowd. Besieged by questions, they accepted their baggage and ordered a barouche. The carriage moved slowly along the wharves, giving time for one and all to observe its passengers, then turned up the Ruelle de la Place and entered Place Royale, the market square for the Lower Town.

They were proceeding nicely when they decried a rattle of drums and saw soldiers invading the square, pushing people aside, and barking commands. Nashe noted the black facings on white uniforms of troupes de la marine. Colonial troops, used to police the city. But these swaggering buffoons acted too little like soldiers for Nashe's liking. He liked it even less as one burly sergeant bullied a family out of the way. Nashe stepped down from the barouche and approached the man, tapping him lightly on the arm with his cane.

The big sergeant turned slowly to the source of admonition. The tugs of a somewhat agitated Trémais had no effect on Nashe as he faced the bully. Nashe noted the man's size, had a brief moment of doubt, and then smiled it away.

"Oh, ho," the sergeant snarled, "it seems we have a gentleman in our midst. Sacré, comrades, could this be the fop from France?" News travelled fast here, Nashe thought, something to be remembered.

"Of course," the sergeant continued, "the Monsieur is aware of all the piss-cutting manners ever invented in our beloved mother country. He concerns himself with not spitting in the street and being kind to little dogs. Why look at the costume! Have you seen the like, eh?" He reached out meaning to tear the cloth and a second later was writhing on the cobbles, his wrist broken; the short work of Nashe's cane.

A crowd gathered quickly as soldiers rushed to their comrade's aid. Two of them joined their friend on the street: one with a cracked skull, the other blood flowing from his mouth. A small cheer emanated from the spectators. Nashe glanced toward Trémais. The older man was looking on, mouth agape;

18

the eyebrows higher than Nashe had yet seen them. Then the quick tread of more soldiers' boots turned Nashe away from him.

"Would the Monsieur care for assistance from a poor man, but one who shares his sentiments?" Nashe glanced at a young voyageur beside him. The face looked vaguely familiar but Nashe was at a loss to know why. He put aside curiosity as three more soldiers advanced: two of them, wary now of his cane, turned on the voyageur, the other, more foolhardy, charged Nashe like a bull. And seconds later the three were down. The voyageur had dispatched his men as quickly as any trained combatant. Nashe's interest stirred. But he could not place the thick, black moustache and thin, tanned face.

"I suggest, my friend," Nashe grinned at his companion, "that you make your way out of here as fast as your feet will carry you. I've placed you in some jeopardy with the law. I apologize, and thank you. Have you always had that moustache?"

The click of a musket hammer ripped his eyes away from his new-found ally. A soldier stood ten feet from him, taking aim. There was little Nashe could do but stare down the gun's black muzzle. The barrel shivered as the man began to squeeze off the shot. Nashe waited for the flash and white heat of the ball. He could do nothing but smile.

## 8

The spit-fire of the musket did not come; instead, a commanding voice froze the soldier to immobility. Nashe breathed again. Soldiers ran past him. He glanced around to see his ally melt into the crowd, the soldiers pursuing.

"The captain is asking you to follow him, Nashe." Trémais was speaking to him. Nashe realized he did not know how much time had passed. "The captain, we are to follow." Trémais took his arm and led him behind the officer. Trémais stared at Nashe oddly.

"Where did you learn to defend yourself like that?"

Nashe could have cursed. He damned his ego realizing what he had done, causing conjecture of the wrong kind; not at all what he'd intended. He smiled at Trémais, his mind searching for an excuse.

"Why, Monsieur Trémais, I have traded in foreign ports before. One learns to protect oneself amid the scum of harbours."

It was a lame excuse, and Nashe saw clearly the indignation on Trémais' face.

More soldiers surrounded them as they walked, less an escort than a guard. The crowd around them buzzed. Questions flew like birds. A thousand rumours filled the square and there was a rush toward the caleche the two prisoners were approaching.

"I'm afraid, my friend, you have placed us in rather an awkward situation." Trémais spoke softly.

"My apologies, Trémais, a poor method of launching myself as a respectable businessman."

"No doubt you've established yourself as a dangerous man with whom to argue. But things, I think, will prove more intriguing. The man who saved your life was none other than Intendant Bigot."

The guards brought the two men before the calèche, and as they halted, Nashe glimpsed the man who was his objective. Lounging on piled cushions within the two-wheeled carriage was a personage of incredible contrast. Perhaps the ugliest man Nashe had ever seen, his body was short and squat, the face flaccid, cold grey eyes, the mouth a mere line, and his nose aquiline. He looked every inch the middle aged, dissipated rake.

Yet he had countered nature's lack of generosity with his own. His chunky hands were flawlessly manicured. He wore an ornate, brocade coat glistening with gold inlay. His surroundings were immaculate. The caleche was of polished oak, its horses a matched pair of blacks with obvious lineage, and the cane he held a striking work of craftsmanship. Everything about Bigot bespoke tasteful, luxurious living.

"Now young man," his voice rasped, "your clothing indicates breeding, but does that include a set of manners?"

"Monsieur..." Trémais attempted to intercede.

"My conversation is with this gentleman here, Monsieur. I will see to you later. Meanwhile, I suggest your mouth remain shut, or I shall have it shut for you. Now, young man, do you have a name? Can you explain this foolishness? Speak up, Monsieur!"

Nashe's thoughts raced to find a suitable counter. No ordinary answer would do. He had to be convincing to shore up the tattered masquerade.

"Monsieur Bigot, as you are no doubt aware, I have just arrived on business from France. I find life in France degraded enough and had hoped to discover at least one small remaining bastion of manners in which to conduct my affairs. Yet on disembarking without, I might add, benefit of a porter, I found myself jostled by a group of villainous bullies who, though dressed as soldiers, are clearly a gang of moronic ruffians masquerading in uniform!" Nashe noticed his guards' looks more threatening. "On being manhandled by a sergeant, I tried to reason with the lout. Yet the fellow seemed intent on soiling both my character and my costume and so I was forced to strike. I was about to be shot down in the midst of this barbaric village when the only man of reason I have yet had the privilege to meet, yourself, Monsieur, put a stop to it. For that, I thank you. But I make no apologies for curbing the behaviour of your troops." He ended with a sniff and produced a japanned snuffbox as if to solidify the argument. Bigot was taken aback.

Nashe congratulated himself. Now, as long as there were no further mistakes.

"But, Monsieur, how is it you know my name? Did you not say you had just arrived?" Bigot's amusement increased with each breath. Nashe countered with as much disdain as he could muster.

"Monsieur Bigot, though merely a merchant, I do not consider myself completely dense. Even in France we have heard of the reputation of Monsieur Bigot for taste and a certain flair. I took notice of the insignia on your carriage indicating to me that you were either the Intendant himself or a rather foolish impostor. Thus, Monsieur Bigot, I arrived at the knowledge that such a man as you must be yourself. Simple, really. And, I should add, my companion here informed me a few moments ago of your identity." Nashe smiled.

Bigot appeared pleased with the praise. He leaned his thick neck out of the carriage to take a closer look at Nashe.

"I see Monsieur is a man of wit. But I am afraid your first glimpse of our city has been an unfortunate one. We are not the savages our cousins in France believe us to be. Yet before I introduce you to the more civilized elements of our society, Monsieur, I must again inquire as to your name."

"Nashe. Alan Nashe. I come as a fur trader and student of the finer pleasures. Here, Monsieur, are my credentials and all necessary papers. I trust you will find them in order."

"No doubt I shall." Bigot nevertheless peered carefully at the papers scrutinizing each page. "Nashe...rather an interesting name..."

"Unfortunately, I had the fate to be the son of a Scotsman living in France. My mother, who was French, did as much as possible to remove any taint." Again the snuff and a lace kerchief to put the point across.

"I see." Bigot smiled through yellowed teeth. "But you did take rather a chance, Monsieur Nashe, with your pompous attitude."

Nashe decided to play his trump. "I am a gambling man by nature, Monsieur Bigot, and sensed I must appeal to you as a man of bearing."

"I could just as easily have had you imprisoned."

"Monsieur, as in cards, one must be aware of the stakes of the game and the hand one holds. At the time, I had nothing to lose and no cards to play."

Bigot was captured. He leaned his squat frame toward Nashe, lowering his voice to more intimate tones. "I, too, have a passion for the tables, Monsieur. Perhaps we might meet in future to enjoy a leisurely game. Nothing, of course, like France, but we do enjoy our entertainments. Alas, I do miss France. Perhaps you could be persuaded to share what news you bring at a small soirée I have planned."

"An honour, Monsieur. I will need a few days rest and for my affairs, a rather dreary crossing you know."

"Of course, of course. The event is not to occur for three weeks, Monsieur Nashe. In three weeks, we expect a little surprise on the next incoming ship. The party will be a celebration."

"It will be a pleasure, Monsieur Bigot. Incidentally..."

"Yes?"

"Might I inquire as to the ruffian who assisted me? Has he been arrested?"

"Unfortunately not, Monsieur. He would have been brought here by now were that the case."

Nashe sighed softly with relief. Recognition had come slowly. The smile on his face betrayed a hint of irony.

"You find the matter humorous, Monsieur?" Bigot's voice portrayed displeasure. Nashe cursed himself again.

"Of course not, Monsieur, though considering the situation I can only side with my ally. I smile at my own lack of manners. I have been so preoccupied with my fight for survival that I have completely forgotten to present to you my travelling companion, Monsieur Trémais, a man who, providing you do not throw us both in gaol, has come from France to take a position in your government."

Surprisingly, Bigot recognized Trémais. Nashe made a mental note not to underestimate the man. The usual greetings ensued, papers exchanged, and Bigot bid them adieu. He also insisted on lending some rather surly soldiers to assist in moving them to their lodgings.

Nashe and Trémais resumed their journey. As they approached their destination Nashe was pleased with himself. He had turned the tables on his error, had already met his prey, and ingratiated himself into the clique that would be so important to his operation. He whistled a Scottish lilt to the great delight of Trémais as the two proceeded from the carriage to their lodgings: a fine suite of rooms for each man on Rue St. Anne, in the Upper City.

## 9

The ensuing three weeks were hectic for Nashe: settling in, hiring men, and accomplishing matters essential to his role. Most immediate: to build his business. Had he taken more time, appeared to relax in the least then someone, and there were many men of trade here, would have wondered at his inaction.

And so each morning at dawn he would leave his rooms in the Courvier house and proceed to his offices on the wharves. It was a brief, bracing walk along Rue St. Anne and down the twisting way of Cote de la Montagne. From there he turned along Sous le Fort, through Place Royale on to St. Pierre, the centre of the business district. Sometimes he would make other excursions down the city's narrow streets, interested in their sights, slowly comprehending the city's layout, but these were infrequent diversions. He worked twelve hours daily putting his fledgling company in order. There was time for little else but the brief supper each evening and then dog-tired to bed.

Trémais, who was busy with his own duties, nevertheless proved an invaluable advisor. He insisted on using his contacts to assist Nashe in finding offices. He suggested the best clerks and notaries. He introduced Nashe to the right people. Trémais mentioned he had never seen a new business receive such support from the usually harried Compagnie officials. Someone, Trémais would grin knowingly, was behind this; someone with a great deal of power.

This became more apparent when Nashe was introduced to Jean Baptiste Chevalier. Chevalier offered Nashe space in his maison, a warehouse on the Cul-de-Sac. Nashe could hardly refuse. But Trémais was taken aback by the offer. In a highly competitive business, he explained, the offer bordered on unbelievable. These men staked their all in the fur trade. They grew rich through their ruthlessness. And, as Trémais told him, their cunning knew no bounds.

As trade with Europe grew lucrative the most powerful traders had formed la Compagnie des Indes Occidentales in the hope of gaining a monopoly. Each new merchant was forced to pay for a license to trade: the quart, twenty five percent of the merchant's revenues. If this price was not paid then government pressure was brought to bear. Intendant Bigot was the official responsible for the law and indeed, it was rumoured the man held a primary share in the Compagnie.

So evolved renegades, the coureurs du bois: men who traded illegally with the natives. A strange, tough hybrid of men outside the law. If they were caught they were brought to trial occasionally; more often they were found scalped or mutilated. Natives were usually blamed. They were very convenient.

Nashe, of course, had no wish to be known as a renegade. He delivered his papers faithfully to Joseph Cadet, commissary general for Quebec, and quickly received his license. He'd been taken in hand by Cadet, chief of Bigot's Grand Societé of gentlemen. It was only later, at a meeting of the fur merchants, that Nashe recognized the animosity his fortunes had created. The greatest trade houses were there: Chevalier, Fornel, Leduc, Barbel, the Perthuis house, Gosselin and others. Nashe had a time of it remembering names. Yet there was one of whom he made special note: a trader who, like himself, had just begun business. His name was Charest, and what made the man so notable was his obvious envy of Nashe and an altercation during the meeting.

Cadet, stinking of strong drink and garlic, had decided to offer Nashe the basics of the fur trade. His voice slurred.

"Now young...er..."

"Nashe, Monsieur."

"Of course, young Nashe! You see there are many, many types of fur, all marketable in Europe: otter, martin, fox, bear, even wolf...but the one that makes the money, eh...our entire raison d'etre, is the beaver. Four livres per pound, my boy! I know the trade. I know the beaver. Castor sec or castor gras makes little difference to me. It all sells!" Cadet's voice had become loud and boisterous, commanding the attention of the room.

"I'm afraid I am an ignorant trader, Monsieur," Nashe patronized him.

"Simple! Simple..." Cadet seemed to have forgotten what he was saying. It took a moment for him to recover. "Ah, castor sec is dry fur as it comes from the animal. Castor gras is greasy fur having been worn by the natives before trading. Indeed, some say the gras is the better fur, having been aged by the oils of a man. I prefer the soft feel of the sec, the purity of it."

"And how does one tell the difference, Monsieur?"

"No need to worry, good fellow. Soon you'll discover the feel of good fur for yourself, but until then trust your notaries. Men to be trusted, I say... men to be trusted. Did I tell you some of them once worked for me?"

"It seems Monsieur Nashe owns a number of advantages," Charest interrupted. "Perhaps, Monsieur," Charest peered at Nashe, "you might instruct me in your methods of business?"

"I have been lucky," Nashe replied curtly.

"Indeed, Monsieur, or is it the rumoured wealth you've brought?"

Cadet, disliking the turn of the conversation, departed. Nashe faced the infuriated Charest.

"Perhaps if your manners were better you might enjoy the same opportunities."

"You should watch yourself, Nashe. I am not alone in my distaste for this... bribery, I smell."

"If you believe rumour then that is your choice. As things stand I have little time for it. I have a business to run."

"Take care, Monsieur; I am not a man to trifle with."

"And neither, Monsieur, am I. Good day to you. I will not say it has been a pleasure."

Despite the altercation with Charest, Nashe felt his masquerade was impeccable. He'd established himself: his business running smoothly and his voyageurs close to embarking for the interior. Still he wondered at the treatment he had received. Had he become Bigot's hobby, a spring amusement, and when would those debts be called?

His other business had proven less fruitful. The voyageur from the street had not yet come forward to establish contact.

Then a third piece of business arose.

## 10

In the streets of the Lower Town, people engaged in their morning commerce. It was a good day, bright and cloudless. Nashe knew it would be hot later on. Down toward the river, past the fishmonger with his aged horse and cart of fresh fish, the harbour voyageurs were loading the boats. They were a hardy lot, muscles bulging beneath coloured jackets, the different hues vivid in the sun. They wore beads and feathers, jerkins and oft-patched trousers and each possessed the bright wool sock caps called tuques, the badge of their calling. These were robust men, accustomed to hot sun and frozen winters; good men with whom Nashe would talk and curse and share their sun-warmed ale. Though he employed them, he knew he was not their master. These men would never be servants.

They sang as they loaded Nashe's supplies on his boats. They seemed not to have a care in the world; until suddenly the singing was stopped by shouts of alarm.

Nashe turned in time to see two of his men tossed like kittens into the river. The cause of their displacement stood, legs straddling the dock, like a great tree having suddenly grown there. Close to seven feet tall and half that broad, the colossus was costumed in buckskin and furs. He looked shoddy: his clothing slept in, bathed in, lived in for weeks; but of all the colourful garb that morning this man appeared a veritable rainbow. Feathers, beads and trinkets swayed to the giant's rhythm as he walked. Even his beaver cap sparkled with quartz dust. Nashe nearly laughed aloud at the glistening apparition but quickly thought better of it.

Jammed into a wide brass-buckled belt were a tomahawk and a huge hunting knife. Two hands, each the size of a man's head, rested on the weapons. He had no need of them. Nashe's voyageurs gave way as mice avoid the cat. The great man cursed in a voice that seemed to come from the earth itself as he strode toward Nashe. Nashe's right hand moved slowly to his pistol butt. Then he saw that the man was smiling.

"Sons of muskrat bitches!" The giant shoved another unfortunate into the drink. "When Vadnais comes to call no one interferes, eh!"

Nashe's chief notary tugged at his arm, the bespectacled clerk was quaking. "Please, Monsieur, you must get into the bateau. This man is dangerous." The notary's loyalty was beyond question for he stepped into the path of the giant.

"What is it you wish, Monsieur Vadnais?" the little man squeaked. "Monsieur Nashe is busy at the moment..."

"Piss-headed runt!" Vadnais growled and the notary was tossed easily over a loaded boat into the river. "Now where in the name of the Great Beaver is the owner of this wreckage?"

"I presume you are looking for me, Monsieur," Nashe stepped forward somewhat warily. "My name is Nashe, and I am the owner of this, what you term, wreckage."

"Eh? Well...good! I have decided to speak with you on matters of business."

"Then first I must know your name, Monsieur," Nashe returned, "and the right you claim to come upon my dock, wreak havoc, and then demand to do business!"

"My name is Vadnais." His voice rolled up from the mighty stomach. "Many simply call me The Owl. That is because I am so wise and far seeing. The forest is my brother, the wind and the rivers my pathways, and the great inland lakes are my ponds! But now I come to you, Monsieur, to demand work. These company asses have tied you in knots and I propose to rid you of them!"

"And I propose, Monsieur, to remove you from my dock!"

"But this is no way to begin the best of friendships, eh? After all, you are new to this land and do not realize my value."

"How you could consider that we could be friends is beyond me."

"The cub has spunk." Vadnais chuckled aloud to no one in particular. Then his tone changed slightly. "Monsieur Nashe, perhaps I have come upon you too rashly. I had hoped you would permit me to help you gather more fur than you could believe imaginable."

Nashe nearly choked. The man was an agent! Ledrew, he decided, had outdone himself. Nashe gave the countersign.

"You have access perhaps to a new tribe of natives?"

A clerk intervened.

"Excuse me, Monsieur, but this man is a coureur wanted by the Compagnie." The clerk skipped nimbly backward at Vadnais' glare. "Monsieur, you must not listen to a criminal. He is a Métis, a mere half-breed and..."

A great fist smashing into the man's face terminated the rest. Though the man was not killed, Vadnais had been gentle, he would never again please his wife with what once had been a winning smile.

"Twist the goddamned Compagnie! I speak to Monsieur Nashe on business. Be there any more who would interfere?" The question was obviously rhetorical. "Now, Monsieur Nashe, do you listen or do I take my secrets elsewhere?"

As he tried to read the giant's face, Nashe played for time. Vadnais would make a powerful ally, or a formidable foe. A long scar crossed diagonally from his right eye to his chin, clearly no childhood accident. His eyes were as piercing as a hawk. Nashe desperately needed time to think.

"You must be aware, Monsieur Vadnais, that I am a lawful trader associated with the Compagnie and so subject to its rules and advice."

"Otter balls, Nashe! I'd thought you an intelligent man. There are no rules saying a man may not discover new trade grounds, or tell him what guides to hire to get him there!"

"I am always ready to consider new possibilities, Monsieur, but you come to me without reference and your manners..."

The barrel chest heaved, and Vadnais took a frightening step forward. "Beaver dung on my manners, Nashe! Be you a fool who measures a man's worth by manners? Mon Dieu, you're a greater fop than I thought. References you say? What have I just given you!" he shouted, turning to leave.

"This new trade ground...has it been explored?" Nashe chanced the second recognition.

The reply came quickly and partner to a smile: "Only by the Ouendat and the sun." Vadnais had met the sequence. "Ah, Nashe." The giant seemed to tire of the game. "Thus, I am hired, eh?"

Nashe motioned Vadnais to follow him along the quay to his offices. It was all he could do to keep up with the fellow, his strides nearly two of a normal man. Vadnais filled an office chair, straining it with his bulk. In the confines of the room he appeared doubly formidable.

"Now we have done with these silly codes, Nashe. I see you do not trust me. Well, these are bad times, and I'm not what you expected."

"I had assumed from the code I'd be meeting a merchant."

"My name is Owl." The man smiled whimsically. "If we are to labour together, we should be on more familiar terms, eh?"

"Of course...Owl. I assume you have some message for me?" Nashe decided to keep his guard up. He was not ready yet to be familiar.

"Still the suspicion, eh? I suppose that must be expected. I deliver you this, Monsieur: tonight there is to be a party. Oh, none so great as our beloved Intendant's goose-cursed affair, but a fine party nonetheless. You will find it at Le Roi David, a tavern in Sous le Cap. I do not expect a personage of your exalted position to accompany me, but if you will merely walk by the place at eleven this night you will come to learn much of the fur trade." He rose to leave. "You are new to the country, Nashe, so I'll tell you this tavern, as all taverns here, is marked with sprigs of evergreen over the door. Bonjour,

Monsieur Nashe, and please change your perfume; it smells and bothers the animals."

With that he was gone, ducking through the door so as not to take the building with him. Nashe remained in his chair concerned by this turn of events. A stranger in Sous le Cap, he'd heard of it, could end up too conveniently dead. There were a great many footpads in Quebec. The dark, twisting streets of the city's slums were perfect for ambush. But Nashe had little choice. The contact would have to be made.

"Stupid profession to have chosen anyway," he muttered as he left the office. He met Chevalier that afternoon for a sumptuous luncheon of wine and cakes in the simple world of business. And that afternoon too his voyageurs departed for the depths of the forest.

## 11

A moonless night, raining, a soft mist soaking through to the bones, Nashe shivered as he made his way along the slippery cobbles of the Upper City. He had been walking half an hour now trying to evade the man following him. Nashe hoped he too was shivering as he led him through a neighbourhood of narrow, twisting streets. Occasional lanterns, their thin rays reflecting off stone walls, provided some illumination, but mostly the streets were dark. Nashe wandered down the steep hill of Rue St. Francis toward the bastion on Rue Sur la Ramparte. At first he had intended on melting into some deep shadow, allowing the man to pass by and so into ambush, but the man who followed him was experienced and knew these streets well. He kept a distance and almost never revealed himself.

Nashe decided on another stratagem. Stretching his patience to the limit, he spent the next fifteen minutes strolling the vicinity of Sur la Ramparte, always keeping within a small radius of his target, the Canoterie gate that led to the Lower Town. As he walked, his onyx cane tapped to the rhythm of his footsteps. He set the rhythm, unhurried, hoping his shadow would follow the sound, and come to depend upon it.

He turned up Rue St. George when he judged the man had lost sight of him. Then quickly he lifted the cane and sprinted to his left along Rue de Lavalée. He ducked quickly into an alley. He froze as the familiar shuffling footsteps passed nearby. But the boots walked more quickly now, then began to run back and forth, searching, their owner listening intently for the familiar tap of a cane. He heard only rainwater guttering down the incline. When the boots quickened, desperately running back up St. George, Nashe permitted himself a sigh of relief.

The streets were deserted. The guards at the top of Canoterie were at cards inside their hut. The heat of their wood stove made them all sleepy. They saw no sense in patrolling. On such a night what was there to guard against? Even their sergeant agreed as he stepped outside to relieve himself. He never saw Nashe. The rain-soaked figure was already down the mountain road and invisible in the cliff's shadow.

Rue Sous le Cap was a forbidding slum directly beneath the Cap. A filthy place, not even the rain could clean it. Sewage guttered down its earthen streets creating a quagmire from the mountain's run-off. On one side perched the dilapidated houses and infested alleys of man, on the other was the great, grey face of the cliff. The street was pitch dark.

Shivering in the shadows of Le Roi David, Nashe awaited contact. Within the tavern, the party Vadnais had spoken of was a riot of song and cursing. Every so often another inebriate would pitch through the oaken door splashing into the street, find his bearings and weave away singing, cursing, or struck dumb from cheap wine. The warmth and cheer of the tavern were a far cry from the gloom outside.

When he first heard the sound, he did not believe it. Almost a part of the rain, it was close to him already: the familiar shuffle of boots. Nashe fought a moment of panic. His shadow had somehow found him again, or had known where to look. Nashe's hand slid to the hilt of his cane. Ears judging the miniscule sounds of stealth, he steadied himself, knowing what was to come. He had faced other men in similar places. This was his battleground. Still, how could the man have found him?

And he was not alone. He was playing the bait, shuffling along the muddy street. Nashe could almost smell his fear. The other was hidden, a scraping sound from a recessed doorway. The stiletto withdrew from its onyx scabbard. Nashe took two deep breaths and lunged into the street.

In this fight it would be speed that won. He relied on his ears to tell him the hidden man's movements and was on the bait like a striking game fish. He used his precious seconds well, feinting left as the man's hand swung at him. The hand held no weapon. Nashe had anticipated the tactic. His opponent's other arm came up knife in fist. Nashe arced down with his own knife. There was a slicing sound, then the clatter of metal on cobbles. His assailant howled. Nashe dropped low avoiding the second man's rush.

A raucous chorus erupted from inside the tavern. No one heard the wails of the fingerless villain rolling in the mud. Nashe leaped across the street and was crouched in readiness, grimly anticipating the huge form of Vadnais. But the man he faced was not Vadnais. Nashe caught a glimpse of a feral face and two feathers dangling from greasy, braided hair. He had never fought a native. He had little time to think about it.

The man swept down with his knife. Nashe parried and pulled back avoiding the upswing of the other hand. A tomahawk glanced off his thigh just missing his ribcage. He'd never fought an axe before.

The man possessed speed and uncanny accuracy. Nashe retreated, parrying, dodging, falling back, and then found himself trapped against the tavern wall as the native parried a last desperate lunge then swung high in a vicious arc. The tomahawk buried itself in the wood where Nashe's head had just been.

It stuck there. Nashe, beneath it, thrust his knife at the warrior's belly. Incredibly, he missed. The man was gone. Nashe's blade sliced rain, a foot caught it and it flew into the gutter. Nashe tried to plan. Something. Anything. This was no ordinary opponent. Whatever had brought him into the city had not dulled his savage edge.

Nashe closed in, grasping the man's arms. Legs and feet shifted quickly, trying for the trip or the groin. The two seemed engaged in some weird dance, grunting, straining, and reaching in a dance of death.

Then Nashe stumbled, swinging his back to the native. It was a dangerous gamble, and he fought like the devil to keep his footing. The man pressed his advantage. But Nashe had been waiting for just this response. He swung his weight to one side and tossed his opponent over his shoulder. He heard the man's breath rasp as he landed. The weapon flew from his hands. Nashe kicked at the defenceless head. But again the target was too quick for him.

In an instant the native's arm encircled Nashe's neck. A knee punched into his back. His breath was gone; the knee had seen to that, and the arm choked off his air. His foe forced Nashe's face into the street trying to drown him in muck. Nashe fought wildly to turn his head up. There was no air. He was drowning, helpless. Here, in this awful place, he would die.

And then the arm was ripped from his neck. His breath came in great, tearing gulps. He rolled looking up. Vadnais stood like a mountain above him

31

holding the native over his head. The man screamed as Vadnais hurled him against the cliff side. Bones shattered.

The last thing Nashe heard was tavern voices singing, harsh and warm, and licked with wine. Then everything was dark.

## 12

The voice was familiar. He wished he could remember how he knew it. The voice seemed very distant. A calm voice, so familiar. "Take this, Alan. You'll feel better."

The blur of a glass before his eyes; it felt like stone on his lips. He took a long drink expecting cool water, and instantly sat up sputtering into consciousness. The brandy was fire in his throat. And then the voice came clear. A man with long, unkempt hair and a great black moustache was half smiling at him. But Nashe saw past disguise now, past the hard, bright colours and sweaty odour. Beneath this strange veneer was Jeff Ledrew. A friend in a land of harsh enemies.

He felt a sharp pain in his right thigh, and then remembered the axe. His head felt the size of a gourd, and as delicate. He did not remember hitting his head. And there was the flickering ache of abrasions and a bruised kidney, the result of the native's knee. Nashe decided he was luckier than most for his gift of being more stupid than most. He tried to sit up. His friend was smiling, relieved. Nashe took another drink of the brandy.

"Good God, Captain Nashe, you look as if you'd been hit by a tree!"

"All the more reason, Captain Ledrew, for a further sample of your brandy."

"Of course." The brandy was poured. "Owl brought you here and we patched you up. I thought for a moment we might lose the honour of your company, permanently."

Nashe lay on a cot in a simple room illuminated by a guttering oil lamp that succeeded for all its smoke in causing more shadow than light. He noticed a rough table, two stools and a stove. By the door, Owl Vadnais stood, his huge arms crossed over his chest.

"I thought they'd been sent by Vadnais," Nashe murmured.

"Owl? He told me you didn't trust him," Ledrew answered.

"Just who the hell is he, Jeff?"

Ledrew changed to English, his words very serious.

"Until he leaves, don't insult him, even in jest. He could kill you quicker than you could blink."

Nashe returned in French, "Then I must thank you, Monsieur Vadnais, for saving my life. And I apologize for mistrusting you this afternoon."

A grunt was his answer.

Ledrew spoke instead, "By the way, Owl recognized the man who tried to kill you. An Abenaki. Known murderer."

"I will find the one who got away," Vadnais interjected. "He will tell us what this is about."

"Then look for a man with no fingers on his left hand. I think I might have left the thumb."

"I see you haven't lost your style," Ledrew murmured.

"And you as well," Nashe grinned. "Since our battle in Place Royale, I knew something was up."

"So you recognized me." Ledrew half-smiled. "I thought you too busy saving honour and limb to notice. Of course I should have known you wouldn't skulk in by night in a canoe."

"And you," Nashe replied, examining his partner, "is all this... costume necessary, Jeff?"

"In this, yes," he murmured, and then he turned to Vadnais. "Are you leaving now?"

"Yes. But Jacques will be at the door outside."

"You think that necessary?"

"Yes."

"Owl will find this man. We think it may have been business, Alan."

"You mean they would kill me for trade?"

"I would watch my back were I you," Vadnais said. He glanced at Ledrew then departed, leaving the door slightly ajar. Nashe noticed a second man on the other side of the door.

"Well, I was lucky he arrived when he did, Jeff."

"What do you mean?"

"Vadnais. Owl, or whatever he calls himself. He came just in time to save my neck."

"He was there all the time, watching from the roof."

"What!"

33

Ledrew looked grim: "One thing you must know about Vadnais: he is a careful man. I suppose he assumed you would handle the situation. I'm afraid I've built you up a little much once I'd asked Offingham for you."

"You? You asked for me?"

"I thought you knew. At any rate, I told Owl a little about you. It seems he was watching you to learn something. He is a man," Ledrew grew solemn, "who loves to learn."

"Bloody hell! I could have been killed while that colossus sat up there taking notes!"

"When he recognized the Abenaki he jumped. He knew the man was a killer."

"Abenaki or leprechaun, that great bastard could have helped me sooner. I am his ally, aren't I?"

"In a sense, yes," Ledrew murmured again and then changed his tone. "Now we need to talk. I have little time. Are you up to it?"

"If we're going to conspire, Captain, I'll trouble you to replenish my cup."

Ledrew poured brimming tumblers. The two sat facing each other over the lamp. And while they talked, Owl Vadnais prowled the night hollows of Quebec. For all his size he moved with the stealth of a cat. He searched for a man with no fingers.

## 13

With Vadnais gone, Ledrew seemed to relax but remained somehow aloof. A year had wrought changes in him. There was harshness to him now, a brooding darkness Nashe had not seen before. He was thin and gaunt and his eyes were dull beads in a lined face.

Ledrew's voice was blunt and almost emotionless, "I'll tell you a little of my own network, but it won't do much good. I've been unable to infiltrate the upper echelons without risking the whole operation. I've tried to make up for it in the field."

"Your effectiveness is questionable, Jeff. Offingham has almost no information. He's worried."

"Really." Ledrew seemed strangely antagonized.

"Where are your agents?"

"Out there, most of them. Coureurs, some natives, a few soldiers I've bribed. They roam and report what they've seen in their travels. Most of them have no idea what's important and what is not. So they inform me of anything unusual, and I go out to investigate. I spend most of my time on these chases."

"Can't you find men who are better trained?"

"I'm doing the best I can." Ledrew was annoyed.

"Perhaps I can help."

"You can. Be quiet and listen! I've decided it best to divide the system, you and whomever you might recruit at the top, myself, and the existing group providing the base. The go-between is Vadnais. You must trust him completely."

"He'll give my information to you?"

"Yes. When I'm within reach he will know where I am."

"But mostly you'll be in the forest," Nashe muttered glumly, "out of reach. Not like Marseilles."

"Don't judge until you understand it!" Ledrew snapped.

"You think we'll lose this war, don't you."

"We're losing it now," Ledrew answered quickly. "English colonials can't fight this kind of war. The French can, and do. Since Montcalm arrived they haven't lost a major engagement. Our people thought Fort William-Henry impregnable; the French besieged and took it in a week."

"How are the French regulars?" Nashe put an end to his partner's conjecture.

"Varied. I've seen battalions of Guyenne, Artois, Languedoc, La Reine, Royal Rousillon. And I've heard talk of importing artillery, though Lord knows why. It can't be moved through the forest."

"I know why."

"How can you? You've been here only three weeks."

"I know, but I have information for you, and if this artillery element proves true then I think Offingham may be right."

"Whatever are you talking about?"

"He believes we have a double playing both sides. There is a campaign planned for this theatre. I think this artillery is defensive. I think the French have been fed our intentions."

"Perhaps they simply outguessed us. Montcalm is noted for that."

"Nevertheless, look into your people."

"A double agent?"

"You doubt what I'm saying?"

35

"Offingham is an ocean away! How do you think Montcalm got his reputation?"

"You're sure you can trust Vadnais? He's an outlaw."

"Don't be a fool. If he were a double, you'd be dead now. I'll look into it, but you stay out. Only Vadnais and I know of you."

"And someone else." Nashe asserted.

"That attack came from one of your competitors. It's happened before, this kind of thing. Now I must finish." Ledrew seemed agitated. Nashe let the matter stand. If there were a double agent the man would be found. Ledrew's character might have altered, his skills had not.

"Along with the regulars, the troupes de terre, there are colonial soldiers, the troupes de la marine, under the naval department. They are sent from France to serve as a sort of home guard. When their service ends they receive property here. Most of the citizens here are ex-soldiers. They make up the third military force, the militia. Every man from sixteen to sixty belongs. They form companies according to their parishes. As bush fighters no one can touch them. But in formal battle they're useless. They're so undependable Montcalm won't include them. He keeps them for scouting, skirmishing, transport. Relations are not good between the European and colonial officers. You might use that to some advantage."

"Indeed." Nashe pondered the possibilities.

"And there are other weaknesses," Ledrew continued, "more substantial. Corruption. It's widespread, especially in military supply. Joseph Cadet has fingers in every conceivable pie. The man is completely self serving."

"I know. I've met him."

"A drunken lout from what I gather."

"You gather correctly."

"But he has power. No one can touch him. Versailles considers this place a backwater."

"I'm not so sure."

"You've heard something?"

"More than that." Nashe explained his recognizance of Trémais. "He seems to have been given considerable power."

"If he isn't found dead in the river, Cadet knows how to protect himself. And I still maintain France cares little. The French are winning here, but that's because of Montcalm. If he had enough troops, the thirteen colonies would be eleven by now. I've heard he's expecting reinforcements, but that's rumour."

"So if they don't get troops, and our campaign launches, Montcalm may run out of men."

"But the forest is in the way."

"We may come up the river."

"Impossible. The French know it. We'd never pass the Traverse without river pilots."

"But Offingham told me..."

"Offingham. Offingham! What in hell does he know! Do what you want, Alan," Ledrew muttered. "It's obvious I've failed according to him. The subject is closed."

And that ended it. Ledrew mumbled a brief goodbye and left the room taking the man at the door with him. Nashe was left to find his way home. With a shrug, he extinguished the lamp and left for the dark of Sous le Cap.

## 14

Ledrew's rumours of reinforcements proved true. Five ships arrived. They were filled with troops, new conscripts for the troupes de la marine, a few French officers, and cannon. Nashe watched from his dockside office as a squadron of gunners disembarked, and after them fifty great guns were offloaded. His suspicions were confirmed. The armament of fortress Quebec was beginning. And Ledrew had indeed had the misfortune of recruiting a double agent. Things did not bode well for the English.

As always, the troops were marched into the Upper City to parade on the Place D'Armes. The huge square was, in peacetime, a market place. Its grassy expanse formed a natural forum for the city's inhabitants, bounded on one side by the Chateau St. Louis and opposite, the huge Recollet monastery; all major thoroughfares converged on the Place. But now it served its primary purpose, the Place D'Armes, the military square, and it was lined all round by grey-clad recruits of the French régime.

Hard-edged colonial officers inspected the troops to replenish their companies. In four days, the troops would be gone, dispatched to their frontier posts. But in those four days there would be celebration, the new officers greeted at soirées, card parties, and the culmination of it all, the Intendant's Ball. It became apparent through the excited chatter of merchants' wives and the immense preparations throughout the city that this was to be the highlight of the season. It was a highlight for Nashe as well.

To this point, he had socialized, of necessity, primarily with businessmen. And though merchants were important to the colony's commerce they were not the men who conducted its political affairs. Nashe's next hurdle was to gain acceptance with the nobility and military leaders. Few merchants were admitted to those ranks. He had to ensure he was one of the few. He hoped he would be skillful enough, or lucky enough, to attract someone of high office. As it turned out he was lucky, and even before the ball.

As the final recruits marched away and curious spectators dispersed, Nashe felt a gentle tug on his sleeve; the subtle greeting of Chevalier. The wealthy merchant had brought a friend. The fellow was about Nashe's age, a short and swarthy major. He wore a perfectly fitted uniform with the gold facings of a staff officer. His dark, frank eyes and pleasant smile exuded intelligence. Nashe was intrigued.

"Permit me," Chevalier began, "the honour of introducing Sieur Louis Antoine de Bougainville, aide-de-camp to General Montcalm. The major here has expressed some interest in meeting you, Alan. Perhaps you've heard of him?"

Nashe had indeed. Bougainville was the son of a French notary and despite his youth had already established himself as a renowned scholar. He'd lived in London for a time, where Nashe noticed his rising star. The young Frenchman had been honoured with a position in Britain's Royal Society of Science. By the time they met, Bougainville had completed his book on integral calculus.

The major proved as pleasant as he was brilliant. The two men, through Chevalier's further words of introduction, discovered they shared a common interest in modern authors. In the current anciens-moderns conflict both had read the classics and both expressed the desire for new ideas closer to themselves.

They retired to Nashe's apartments where they enjoyed a luncheon of smoked eel and coffee, and a long discussion on the merits of the English author, Fielding. Chevalier seemed pleased he had brought two such young minds together. His experienced eye showed him the birth of a friendship. It was the motives he missed.

This was an opportunity Nashe would have been a fool to let slip. Bougainville was his ticket; if he happened to like the man, then so much the better. And Bougainville, too, enjoyed the company of the young merchant trying so hard to be sociable. Nashe was rising quickly in the fur trade. And though Bougainville could never be part of that bourgeoisie, he could make some money through a subtle partnership. It was decided the two of them would attend the Intendant's ball together. As they parted company late that afternoon, each was smugly pleased with himself at his good and fortunate find.

*** 

On a dusky evening three days later, Bougainville met Nashe and Trémais outside their apartments on Rue Ste. Anne. His carriage was polished to its finest and Bougainville himself, dressed in full regalia, lounged in the rear with a bottle of full bodied wine.

They turned down Rue des Jardins passing across from the Basilica of Notre Dame and wheeled onto Rue de la Fabrique. Past the Hotel Dieu and on down Rue des Pauvres they drove through the gate at St. Nicholas. Descending the hill to the St. Charles shoreline, a brief trot along Rue St. Vallier brought them to the Intendancy walls. They passed quickly through the narrow gate and into the humming courtyard beyond.

Dozens of glittering carriages were parked within the grounds. Nashe caught glimpses of liveried footmen and heard the roll of drums at the central entrance. Soldiers in dress whites lined the drive to the doorway. The Intendancy palace was a long, ugly building, three stories high with a clock tower above the main doors. Nashe guessed the building contained at least fifty rooms, and Trémais added that beneath the main floors were storage vaults for government supplies. Few people were allowed there, he continued, and a great many dearly wished to discover their contents. Bigot was suspect. Since his appointment as Intendant, he had attained immeasurable wealth, too much to be gotten honestly, some said.

A white and gold Fleur de Lis shimmered proudly at the peak of the tower as they pulled up to the entranceway. Nashe prepared himself as they alighted from the carriage, adjusting his brocade, inspecting the polish of his leathers, tightening his cravat. He expected much of this evening. But he knew he would have to work for it.

## 15

It was not Versailles. It was smaller. In the ballroom powder blue walls were bespattered with portraits and landscapes in great gilt frames that shone in baroque perfection. Nashe noticed a work by Lenfant, and later he discovered a small treasure by Vermet in a vestibule. Ceilings glittered with chandeliers, their crystals reflecting soft candlelight. Leaded windows peered out over sumptuous gardens to the quicksilver flow of the St. Charles River.

The gathering itself was delightful, filled with the smart dress whites of officers, the velvets and satins of country seigneurs, and the stunning fashions of their ladies. Nashe decided that Trémais had not over-stated the attributes of Quebec's belles; they were graceful and mannered as they flowed through the room in soft streams of silk, their smiles stars in the candlelight, their faces flushed and soft. In the harsh inspecting eye of day they might have been different, but here and now they were dreams. Their characters seemed to have changed with their costumes: perfect manners, perfect dress, and soft flirtatious sensuality.

Bigot himself received the guests as they entered. The Intendant remembered Nashe, joked of their first meeting, and invited him to cards after supper. Beside Bigot stood a petite, lovely girl whom Nashe decided was the man's daughter. She was introduced as Mme. Angélique Péan. Nashe was intrigued and as the three friends strolled Bougainville filled him in.

"You are taken with la belle Angélique, my dear Nashe." The major was smiling. "A truly exceptional woman, is she not?"

"Indeed. She is his daughter?" Nashe queried.

"And how would a ripe old boar like that," Bougainville whispered, "produce such a specimen of beauty? No, my dear fellow, she is not his daughter. She is his mistress!"

"Dear God!"

"No doubt. Be warned, my friend, certain ladies' favours are reserved. Express your amorous interests elsewhere. The old boar has tusks."

"Very poetic, Antoine." Nashe was handed a drink. He noticed the glass was Venetian crystal. "But it is the chase that brings one to happiness, is it not?"

"There are many pathways to joy, my friend," Trémais interrupted dourly, "and not all of them lascivious."

"Too true, Trémais, too true." Bougainville smiled ironically. "I myself am interested in the world of integral calculus; this mundane clatter is beneath me."

"Meanwhile," Nashe returned with a grin, "the mundane will suffice."

"Alas, my friend, the soul is governed by the senses. The perfumes I breathe take my spirit, and I am lost to corruption."

Trémais shrugged disapprovingly at the morality of modern young rakes, and while explicating the values of the pure life, a passing matron of uncommon beauty suddenly took his interest. He followed without so much as a goodbye to his companions.

"It seems Trémais has sighted his happiness for the night." Nashe chuckled. "He is a wise man. Tell me more of these untouchable ladies."

"Quite simple, really. I'll not waste breath couching it in polite terms. Women are at a premium here. There are few of them and they know it. The best of them, married or not, are taken by power. Thus form the chains of love knots, the perfect example being Angélique. She is the Pompadour of this colony, the reigning sultana. Her connection with Bigot gives her power. Her husband, the cuckolded Monsieur Péan, is a confederate of Bigot. He cannot argue so he takes advantage. His mistress is the wife of his business partner, Penniseault. Penniseault enjoys the favours of the good Mme. Varin. Varin, in turn, comforts himself with some other lady and so on down the line."

"And what of you then," Nashe probed. "You have power, no doubt. Whom have you attracted?"

"Alas, Nashe, I, too, have fallen to the best, or you might say the worst of all. Madeleine Duchesnay is my torch. She dallies with men, my Madeleine; then she discards them. Unfortunately, I have been cast on the pile of useless cards. She has not taken my soul, my friend, but my heart is hers forever."

"Is she here? Point her out to me."

"She is not. But she will be. Her father is a stalwart seigneur who takes a dim view of these functions. He has a house in the city, on St. Louis just at the edge of the Place D'Armes, though in summer he takes his family to his estates outside Quebec. He does not appreciate his daughter's social hobbies, but she will not let him miss this one. Of that I am sure."

"I would like to meet this Duchesnay."

"You would even more like to meet his daughters."

"He has more than one?"

"Two. Different as sun and moon. Madeleine is a magnificent sun. The other, Reine Marie, is younger. Seventeen, I believe, and so much the subtle beauty of the moon. She is stunning, Nashe. Madeleine has not affected her yet. I hope she never does."

"And why, do you suppose, I would be interested in her?"

"Because she is beautiful, and you are a student of beauty, I think. But I warn you, my friend," Bougainville sounded only partly in jest. "I would duel for that girl's honour. She, if anyone, deserves it."

"It sounds as though you love them both."

"I do. I love the whole family. They are the stuff that makes this land. But for me, I am too brash for the moon; the sun's glow on my face blots out all other light. Though it burns, I accept my fate."

"I do hope with all this talk of burning, there is some salve to alleviate the pain, Monsieur." Mme. Péan joined them.

"Indeed, Madame, the ointment stands before me," the major returned, "and I am cured."

"Why thank you, Monsieur Bougainville."

"Antoine, please. And may I be permitted to present a recent discovery of mine." Bougainville chuckled. "Monsieur Alan Nashe, newly arrived to this country."

"I have heard of you, Monsieur Nashe." Her soft eyes studied him. "I must say I am not disappointed. Now if you two gentlemen will enjoin yourselves to the dance, I intend to display both of you on my arm tonight."

"Enchanted, Mme. Péan," Nashe smiled. "And may I say that in meeting you this dreary frontier once again has become liveable."

"Monsieur, your tongue matches your notability. Indeed, it appears since your arrival you have made life intriguing for a number of ladies of my acquaintance. Bonne chance, Monsieur. I'm sure you will enjoy yourself. And Antoine, you will have my hand for the first dance!"

As she fluttered away, she passed through the bustle and approached the conductor of a small orchestra at one end of the room. Then a loud voice commanded the room to attention.

"Mesdames et Messieurs! Louis-Joseph, Marquis de Montcalm, Gozon de Saint-Veran!"

The entire room wheeled, Nashe quicker than most, to catch a glimpse of the famed commander. Surprisingly, he was a man of small stature: his uniform simple, bearing none of the ostentation so favoured by French generals. And why not, Nashe mused. Montcalm was winning; there was little need for exhibition.

42

He descended the steps accompanied, not with the usual retinue of officers but by a stately woman richly garbed and of obvious breeding. She was a head taller than the general.

"Mme. de Beaubasin," Bougainville commented. "His confidante, a remarkable woman. But look, my sun and her family!"

On the steps behind the general appeared a dour, clearly wealthy older couple. They dressed conservatively and little appreciated the stares that came their way. But it was not they to whom the eyes were addressed. Beside them stood two of the most enchanting creatures Nashe, in a life of looking, had ever seen. And Bougainville had been right, as different as sun and moon.

Madeleine Duchesnay was in the prime of life. Her golden hair seemed to shimmer in the soft light. She was bedazzling, her satin gown a deep scarlet and cut so low as to give men of little strength heart trouble. She was a sun. A perfect face, full pouting lips, eyes that matched the glimmer of her diamonds, and a small scarlet patch just beneath the high, delicate cheekbone.

Every eye was on her and she knew it. Every person there revelled in her breathtaking beauty. Everyone but Nashe for he had glimpsed the moon.

Whereas the eldest basked in attention, the younger girl held shyly her mother's arm. She was slim. Her gown was conservative, a light summer colour enhancing the porcelain flesh. Her hair was raven, that glowing black with auburn highlights that seemed to make it never the same with each look. Beneath, was the face of an angel, glowing complexion and liquid eyes, dark and mystic. She leaned and whispered something to her mother; the older woman smiled and nodded. Then Nashe watched as the girl glided, (the only description he could conceive of) down the stairway and disappeared into the press. As she went, she caught sight of Bougainville and smiled toward him.

That smile transformed Nashe. He looked to Bougainville and saw the man nod his head in empathy. He gazed about the room, barely noticed the people around him, and then again caught a fleeting glimpse of her. He looked at her with that idiot vision of one who has, in a moment, fallen in love.

## 16

He was drawn to her as a tide to the moon. He was not alone. Nashe despaired of meeting her when Bougainville, noticing his face, started forward. His rank passed him easily through the flow of junior officers, with Nashe in his wake. The two men received embittered glances as they approached the Duchesnay clan.

"Good evening, Monsieur Duchesnay, Madame, ladies..." Bougainville had eyes only for Madeleine. "Permit me the honour of introducing Monsieur Alan Nashe. Monsieur Nashe...Monsieur Duchesnay, Mme. Juchereau Duchesnay, Mesdemoiselles Madeleine and Reine Marie."

"An honour, Monsieur Duchesnay," it was all Nashe could do to take his eyes from the raven-haired beauty. "You have a delightful family, Monsieur, as I'm sure you are aware."

"Indeed," was the gruff reply.

"You must excuse my husband, Monsieur Nashe, his manners reflect his disaffection for these soirées. He is here on command of the ladies in the family."

As the older woman spoke Nashe noticed Bougainville slipping away with Madeleine. They were laughing together, but it was clear the girl was not sincere. Frequently that evening, Nashe caught her eyes on him. Bougainville, if he noticed, said nothing.

"You are the young man just arrived from France," Mme. Duchesnay continued. Reine Marie was smiling at him. "Monsieur Chevalier has spoken of your ventures. You are, I gather, adept at your business."

"I am a mere apprentice, Madame. Monsieur Chevalier is too kind."

"Perhaps you will pay us a visit, when we return from the country in autumn, of course."

"I would be delighted, Madame. Monsieur Duchesnay, I believe the dance has begun. May I have the honour of your daughter's companionship?"

"Naturally."

It was obvious that Duchesnay was accustomed to requests for his daughter. With a brief and hopeful, "Mademoiselle?" Nashe took the girl's hand. She nodded and they assumed their places on the floor.

The orchestra might have been bad, mediocre... magnificent. Nashe barely heard it. Instead, he revelled in her face as it lit with pleasure through the intricate steps. She possessed grace and delicacy in the dance. When she spoke her voice was soft but surprisingly husky.

"Monsieur Nashe, you must look about you. You'll fall over someone," she laughed almost musically.

"Your pardon, Mademoiselle, I seem to have lost my manners. They disappear in my study of a perfect partner."

"Study not so intensely, Monsieur. But it is pleasant to see the renowned Monsieur Nashe is really a boy at heart."

"Renowned?"

"You've been subject of considerable gossip. I'm almost afraid to be seen with you. It is rumoured you might be a pirate. The mysterious trader who runs from France..."

They circled each other in the dance.

"I'm afraid the rumours are quite out of place, Mademoiselle. I am a simple merchant. I have a great deal to learn of this land. Perhaps you would consent to be my teacher?"

"So quickly, Monsieur? Remember I am very young and quite unused to the designs of men. You must be careful of me, Monsieur Nashe, you may break my heart."

"I apologize for my forwardness, Mademoiselle. I am a simple creature in the face of such beauty."

"Humility, Monsieur? A far cry from the man I saw in Place Royale." Her quip was answered by the astonishment in his face. "Surprise? You were the centre of attraction. And a very fine show you were. Monsieur Daine, I have heard, now insists on more rigorous training for his troops."

"You were there?"

"Of course. Who wasn't? It was the first ship of the year."

"Then I apologize doubly, Mademoiselle. My behaviour was barbaric. The entire incident is regrettable."

"On the contrary, I found it quite refreshing. There is more to you, Monsieur Nashe, than the simple merchant."

"You are mistaken, Mademoiselle. I was quite lucky."

"You will not fool me, Alan Nashe." The familiarity of his name from her lips pleased him. She returned his look with a smile. "I've known fops from France before; you are not one of them."

"Indeed, Mademoiselle..."

"For heaven's sake, Monsieur, I have a name. And you have heard me clearly speak yours. Will you embarrass me at my own forwardness?"

"Reine Marie..."

"I knew you could do it. Isn't that more pleasant?"

"Yes..." For once Nashe found himself lost for words.

"Good. You may stop dancing now, Alan. The music ended some time ago."

With a jolt, Nashe halted his prancing progress to find the orchestra silent and the entire room smiling smugly. She looked at him with an amused grin. Then Bougainville shouted from down the line something about 'dancing masters' and the crowd laughed as one. Nashe coloured scarlet. But then Reine Marie leaned forward kissing his cheek. Her demonstration of favour rescued him.

"I must dance with some others," she whispered, "but perhaps you and Monsieur Bougainville would join my sister and me for supper."

"Mademoiselle, I embarrassed you..."

"Oh posh! Will we see you at supper?"

"If you wish...Reine Marie."

"I wish it very much." She winked at him slyly and was gone.

Nashe became the butt of that evening's humour. Strangely, he found that his error had welcomed him into the folds of society. It was as if they had all been waiting for some sign of human weakness from him. As he danced and drank and acquainted himself with the various parties that evening, he found ready smiles awaiting him. He would introduce himself as 'Nashe, the dance master', and each group would laugh with him and invite him into conversation. Nashe had been accepted.

*\*\**

Supper was announced late in the evening and the party repaired to the banquet hall. Tables groaned with tourtieres, capons, pork, pastries, and delicacies of every nature. Each person took heaping plates and retired to one of the tables set about the room. Servants in silvered livery poured a continuous flow of wine enhancing a feast fit for kings.

Nashe found a place reserved for him beside Reine Marie. A despondent Bougainville sat opposite.

"My sister has decided to take her meal elsewhere." The girl was radiant. "So I have the company of the two most amiable men at the ball. The other ladies are positively green. And yet Monsieur Bougainville appears not to enjoy my presence." She leaned forward and brushed her lace handkerchief against the sorrowful major's chin.

"My sun has set," Bougainville sighed.

46

"What on earth are you talking about?"

"The Major ruminates on his plans for travelling the world, Mademoiselle. He wishes to follow the sun on its journeys."

"Oh posh! Monsieur Bougainville is merely feeling sorry for himself. There are other ladies in the room, Antoine. Eat your food, you'll feel better."

Bougainville sighed again but with gusto attacked his plate.

"I, on the other hand, Mademoiselle..."

"My name, Monsieur?"

"Reine Marie. I am a follower of the moon and its cycles. The moon to me is the most beautiful presence imaginable," Nashe intoned, smiling across at his vivacious friend. Bougainville stopped chewing long enough to chuckle through his food.

"Is this some sort of military code, Messieurs?" She pouted. "Remember, I am a mere country girl."

"Mademoiselle is not so simple as she protests." Bougainville regained his wit. "After all, she forgets that I have been part of her conversations. On the ways of the world even her sister listens to this country lass!"

"I'm afraid my sister is considerably more informed than I on certain ways of the world, Monsieur. That kind of knowledge is not my idea of fulfilment," she muttered.

Supper was enchanting: the food excellent, the old fiddler entertaining and lively, and Nashe's new companion proved best of all. The lady's intelligence matched her beauty. Occasionally, Bougainville would rise from his torpor to add to the conversation. Nashe had rarely enjoyed himself more. But the time passed and was over too soon. On a brief signal from her mother, Reine Marie reticently prepared to leave.

"But why?" Nashe was crestfallen. "The evening is young."

"Father doesn't like gambling. We were fortunate just to have been here this long."

"Will I see you again?"

"Why, Monsieur Nashe, you sound so intense."

"I'm sorry. I just...Is it possible to call upon you?"

"I believe my mother has invited you. I hope you will accept."

"But that isn't until the fall!"

"I am sorry, Alan. I do as my father bids. One of his daughters must. I've had a very nice evening. You may kiss my cheek."

Nashe did so, noting the subtle fragrance of sandalwood, a rare bouquet for a rare flower. And then she was gone with her parents. Madeleine, he noticed, remained.

"It appears, my friend, you are close to falling in love." Bougainville smiled across the table. "I wish you more luck than I presently enjoy with her sister."

"I've never met anyone like her. How can I thank you, Antoine?"

"Be careful how you go, Alan. Remember, that one is precious to me."

"And to me, Antoine. That is the woman I will marry."

"You frighten me, Monsieur.." Bougainville smiled.

"I frighten myself...a little," he murmured, then turned to his companion and smiled in return.

## 17

Meal completed, the guests returned to the ballroom that, to the delight of all, had been transformed into a casino. Velvet covered tables in royal blue held stacks of cards, dice, and the inevitable buckets of iced wines. Tobacco smoke guttered up from some of the tables as a few men settled seriously into their games.

Nashe was directed to Bigot's private table. The squat Intendant rose with some difficulty, and as he took Nashe's hand, the latter noted the eyes of a gambler measuring his opponent. Even as they engaged in the introductions, it was clear Bigot intended to see what Nashe was made of at the tables this night. With compliments and small talk finished, Nashe took his place, noticing that at each of his opponents' places lay only gold louis, and by the number of coins in front of them, they played for high stakes. This would be another kind of test, he realized.

As the cards were dealt, the conversation he had interrupted resumed. A bombastic fellow was holding forth across from him, the brother, Nashe discovered, of Governor Vaudreuil. Nashe listened a moment, decided the man was a fool, and studied his cards.

"Then where in God's name is this famous English soldier you speak of lurking? The ones we encounter fight like shopkeepers!"

"You should not grow overconfident, Rigaud," Bigot answered patiently. "The naval blockade is beginning to cause difficulty."

"Typical of them, I must say: English lurking like cowards on the ocean. We can run their pitiful blockade Bigot, but to defeat us they must come upriver. And then they are in for a few surprises!"

"Be that as it may, without further reinforcements...."

"And what need have we of reinforcements? If Montcalm knew the value of colonial troops the war would be over by autumn!"

"I concur, Rigaud. But those troops must be supplied. We cannot make musket balls of cedar."

"When I took William-Henry," Rigaud boasted, ignoring the fact that Montcalm had commanded the operation, "we had a mere handful of supplies. And the English cowards still gave up!"

Bigot had had enough. He changed the subject smoothly, addressing Nashe. "So, Monsieur Nashe, you have come from Europe. And how goes the war there?"

"The Prussians, I gather, are stopped. The English of course have no army worth fielding..."

"God help 'em if they knock on our door!" Rigaud enjoined.

"But the entire matter is beyond me." Nashe touched a kerchief briefly to his lips. "For the life of me I can't see the bother. So long as trade is strong I am content."

"Indeed." Bigot smiled ironically. "I gather, Monsieur, that your voyageurs are off and all is well with business."

"I hope so. It has run so smoothly I think I have some benefactor to thank for clearing my way." He looked at Bigot meaningfully.

"The benefactor must have good reasons whatever they may be. It is your bid, Monsieur Nashe. But perhaps your mind is on other affairs tonight. Affairs of the dancing heart, perhaps?"

The joke was well taken. The men at the table laughed sympathetically. All men have known at one time or other the distractions of the heart.

Nashe lost, not heavily, but enough he could tell to disappoint the Intendant. He received the gentlemen's condolences and excused himself to wander among the tables. The play was extravagant. Nashe remembered Trémais' analysis of the carefree attitudes of the colony's noblemen. He had not underestimated. Gold flowed freely from hand to hand, as did the wine. Nashe noticed couples slipping off to the gardens, laughing together on their moonlight walks by the river. He envied them.

And then he saw Bougainville leave, but not for the garden, and certainly not on an amorous adventure. The major's face was grim. He moved quickly toward a recessed door. Nashe decided to follow.

He found himself in a small anteroom in the midst of a heated argument. A number of people were trying, with difficulty, to ignore the altercation. But the opponents' voices were so harsh that no one could pretend not to hear.

"I tell you again, General, that as governor I am responsible for strategy. You, Monsieur, are to confine yourself to military tactics. That is my mandate; your orders from the War Department inform you of that!"

Pierre François Rigaud, the Marquis de Vaudreuil, looked much like his brother: tall, pompous, a face sagging from luxury. He stood a head taller than his opponent and was dressed in the glittering trappings of power. He wore a Croix St. Louis on a shoulder sash as though the ostentation would add to his grandeur. Nashe instinctively did not like the man. It was clear Montcalm shared his sentiments and returned the argument vehemently.

"I do not question your position, Governor. I merely believe you misunderstand the need for defence."

"Damn defences, man! Attack! My colonials have proven time and again how easily it is done. Let us take New York, and hold it!"

"Monsieur Vaudreuil, the forces you speak of are minor, their assaults mere skirmishes. An army cannot be supplied over five hundred miles of trackless forest. We could never hold our advances."

"And so your answer is to hide behind a string of forts and make piddling little raids. No way to win a war, Monsieur, no way at all. And your preference for French regulars makes clear your defensive attitude. My soldiers are quite unaccustomed to this, General. They begin to wonder what they're being paid for."

"Your troops, I admit, accomplish their raids. But what happens when they meet the English, and mark my words, Monsieur, they will someday meet them, in formal battle?"

"Ten men who know what they are about can hold off an entire troop in the bush!"

"But they can't stop them. Eventually the greater numbers will break through."

"Damn you, Monsieur, you have a niggling answer to everything!"

"Because it is my occupation to do so, Governor."

During the altercation a heavyset woman continually interrupted Montcalm's speech with sighs and clicks of her tongue. Distracted, Montcalm nevertheless attempted to ignore her rudeness. Finally she spoke, and when she did her voice was imperious. "My husband has lived here all his life, Monsieur Montcalm. You have visited little more than two years. Permit me to observe, General, that you have little right to question our strategy."

Montcalm's temper betrayed itself in the growing flush of his face. Rather than look at the woman, he addressed Vaudreuil. "Monsieur Vaudreuil, I admit to being a novice in New France, but surely my successes say something for my capabilities. This is not a fit discussion for the present time."

"Beaver dung, Monsieur! This is the perfect time for it! You and your so-called professionals have come here expecting us to bow to your reputations. Well, we too have reputations! And none of your victories, Monsieur, could have been accomplished without the aid of my colonials!"

"Too true...too true..." the woman muttered.

"Permit me to say, Madame, that war is not a fit subject for women."

"She has every right, General. You are here at our service."

"And no adept servant by any means," the governor's wife murmured the insult just loud enough to be heard.

Bougainville stepped forward attempting to extricate his general. He was too late. Montcalm responded to the woman's challenge. He would not look at her. His address was aimed at Vaudreuil, but its meaning was clear. "Then permit me to say, most humbly, Monsieur Vaudreuil, that were Mme. de Montcalm, my dear wife and a noblesse by birth, were she here at this moment, she would as any self respecting French gentlewoman, refrain from talk of war, and refrain from interrupting the conversation of gentlemen! My wife understands decorum, Monsieur. When she knows nothing she keeps her counsel!"

As he finished, the woman's breath caught in her throat. She tried to speak but could not. Her face coloured. Then, expelling her breath in a great 'whooosh' she stomped away. Vaudreuil was livid.

"Be assured, Monsieur, I will take you to task for this... this effrontery to my wife. Be assured as well that Versailles will be informed and demand your resignation from this post. Indeed, Monsieur, if I have my way...from military service!"

He too departed quickly following the footsteps of his wife. Montcalm was nearly purple. It took all that was left of his tattered self-discipline to refrain from answering the ridiculous threat. Bougainville took his general's arm and tried to calm him. Noticing Nashe, he led the older man toward him. The three retired to a corner of the room.

"I'm afraid I rather took a turn on that one, Antoine." Montcalm was still shaking. "He's a damnable fellow, really. Ignores the English build up. Damn the man! Damn his ever-interfering wife!"

"I'm sure the incident will blow over, General. These tiffs have occurred before; this was no different."

"Still, I lost my temper. If only I could get on with my duties. Why in heaven's name will the War Department not give me control?"

"Politics, Sir."

"As usual."

"Yes, Sir."

"And who is this young man, Major?" Montcalm was settling down. "A friend, I hope."

"Indeed, Sir. This is Monsieur Alan Nashe, a new trader to the colony and a man of fine taste and good manners. I believe you may have noticed him in the first dance...with Mlle. Duchesnay."

"Ah, yes." Montcalm's mind shifted from his troubles. "You seemed quite taken with the girl, Monsieur Nashe. One can hardly blame you. She is a treasure."

"Indeed she is," Nashe responded.

"I do hope you will not judge my character by this unfortunate incident. Ridiculous really."

"No need for concern, General. I've encountered similar problems myself," Nashe responded. He and Bougainville explained Nashe's riotous arrival at the docks. Montcalm laughed heartily and appeared to relax.

"Well, that seems to make two pigs in the poke, Monsieur Nashe. I do hope we shall meet again. I am much in need of stories like yours. But now I must retire. My day has not been a good one. Major, please see to my carriage. Au revoir, Monsieur Nashe. It has been a pleasure."

Bougainville accompanied his general home, and Nashe discovered that Trémais too had departed. He was left to his own devices. He drifted back through the casino, chatting with various people. His mind was not in it. Even when Madeleine began a flirtation with him he found he could not respond. He asked her of Reine Marie, his questions evasive but nonetheless constant.

Madeleine became quite disgusted with Nashe's fixation, told him so, and left for more promising pastures.

And so Nashe walked home. It was a long walk but the night was clear and his thoughts kept him occupied. He had heard Montcalm speak of an English build up. There was no doubt now of a double agent. And then the animosity he had witnessed between the colony's leaders...that could be taken advantage of.

Nashe went to bed, exhausted from thought and the long walk. He dreamed of dancing, in moonlight.

## 18

For Reine Marie Duchesnay summer was a long and listless season. From the promontory by the river she could see Quebec, a scant four miles across the great Basin. More and more her family found her there lost in some secret reverie. She would not be persuaded to divulge her dream. Yet they knew. They had seen it before in Madeleine. The city so clear on a summer's day beckoned her.

But her father hated the stench of its gutters and the clouds of flies they attracted. He despised the hot stickiness of its streets. For him country breezes touched of pine were enough. His seigneury was a healthy and pleasant place far from the mobs of the city.

His family had settled this land a hundred years past: one of the ancien families, along with the d'Iberville and the de Longeuil clans; respected and revered. They had pioneered here. They had come to stay. They had fought the Iroquois and the winter's starving bitterness. They'd brought others from France, peasants mostly, running from feudal chains and offered them freedom. They had seen the beginnings of trade and had fought off more than once the cunning English. And they and their children had come to love this land as devotedly and passionately as they did their catholic God.

As a youth Antoine Duchesnay had prepared himself for his responsibilities. Like his peers he had taken to the forest, learning the huge, shaggy land. When he had returned to marry he'd worked his father's land and improved it. He was proud of his work; the third generation of his family, he knew he had not betrayed his father's and grandfather's dream.

Yet his was a new generation, not limited to forest or farm. Duchesnay found knowledge in books. And his reading gave him a new outlook. He wished his land to become self-sufficient. Though he loved France he loved New France more. And so with his knowledge he became a counsellor for Quebec. But Versailles was an ocean away. It did not understand his land. With growing frustration he began to limit his city visits to winter months.

But his daughters enjoyed the benefits of a rich, respected family: education at the Ursuline convent, the best of horses and carrioles, the freedom of their father's seigneury, fashions from France, and the devoted love of their parents. They owned the spirited liveliness of Quebec accompanied by the manners of Paris. They had seen the mysteries of the forest from birch bark canoes and the mansions of France from coaches. Both girls had been sent to Paris, at their mother's insistence, for two years to further their educations. And that occurrence had changed Madeleine.

For the elder sister Paris had been a revelation. When the two returned home Madeleine had defied her father and remained in the city. She rose with Angélique Péan as the latter rose with Bigot. In France she'd learned the arts of the sexes. She applied them here. She used men, abused the family name, and her disconcerted father finally admitted defeat and gave her up as lost. He loved her still, but there was nothing to be done. At twenty-two she was old for a decent marriage. It concerned him. But it never bothered Madeleine.

And so the father looked to his youngest. She became his jewel. And indeed she developed into a gem attracting many admirers, each of whom was abruptly discouraged by a man who wished the best for his daughter. But Mme. Juchereau, a woman of no mean intelligence herself, in turn insisted that he curb his instincts and allow the girl her life. It was plain to see Reine Marie was becoming a woman. It was obvious she was beautiful. Mme. Juchereau carefully explained to the dubious Antoine that their daughter was no longer a child. And that was why she spent so much time gazing across the St. Laurent toward Quebec.

Since the Intendancy ball she had thought often of Alan Nashe. Yet she knew so little of him, and what she did know came second hand through the letters of her sister. Her sister's words were full of him. She'd seen him often at soirées and card parties as he was accepted into society. Madeleine said more than once that she was intrigued. And for the first time in her life Reine Marie thought of her sister as a rival.

And so Reine Marie wanted more than ever to leave the slumberous Beauport. She pined for the coming change of leaves that would signal autumn; for then, and only then, would her father consent to return to Quebec.

\*\*\*

And the summer was long too for Alan Nashe. With Bougainville's friendship he had entered Quebec's society and the familiar dissipations he'd known at Bath. And there were new pleasures: canoes on the St. Charles, picnics below the cliffs on the beaches, sailing in the St. Laurent basin. The war was far away to the south and, apart from military dispatches, few noticed. According to Bougainville, who always seemed to know, the English were losing. And Nashe himself had confirmation: Ledrew had not returned. Nashe listened to the stories of French victories and continued the slow work of analysing Quebec's defences.

As autumn approached familiar faces returned to the city. The seigneurs came in from the harvest and officers began returning from war. Nashe attended more parties, flirted with a good many women and continued, in private moments, to ponder Reine Marie. He hoped he would catch a glimpse of her. He never did. Antoine Duchesnay, he was told, was always last to return.

He never asked of her openly. But Bougainville, though he joked of it at times, was a man too sensitive not to comprehend.

## 19

Late September and two men rode horses through the St. Louis gate and onto the Abraham Plains. The early afternoon was bright with a touch of autumn crisp. The men's horses were loaded with panniers of food and wine. They took the Chemin Royale, the King's Highway that followed the river toward Montreal. And then they left the road cutting cross-country to their destination: a woody copse above the river at a little cove called Anse au Foulon. As they arrived, children skittering among the blackberry bushes met them. Picnic blankets littered the ground. Nashe and Bougainville dismounted, set out their provisions and joined the crowd.

They saw each other simultaneously. For a moment they simply stood there, and then the girl approached Nashe. Bougainville enticed the men around her away to a game of quoits, spicing the offer with a wager. And the two were alone. Quietly, her eyes lowered, Reine Marie Duchesnay spoke first.

"So, Monsieur Nashe, we meet again, and even before you have come calling."

"But I have been to your house in town, Mademoiselle, more than once."

"To visit my sister," she pouted.

"To hear news of you, Mademoiselle."

"Monsieur Nashe, you do remember my name..."

"Reine Marie," he smiled. "I could never forget. But the summer has been so long I thought you would not remember mine."

"Long? Why it has simply flown by, Monsieur."

"Indeed, I think you've forgotten my name," he chided.

"Alan. I thought by now some graceful lady would have stolen your heart."

"One has."

"Oh."

"Do I detect disappointment? The lady is you, Reine Marie."

"But, Monsieur," she smiled at his seriousness. "Are you a trustworthy man? Or will you simply take my heart then fly off to some other corner of the world?"

"Reine Marie," he remained serious, "this playfulness, is it merely entertainment? I must know..."

"Slowly, Monsieur. This intensity may be but infatuation. I too am afraid."

"You admit the same feelings?"

"We must go slowly. Wait a little..."

"For my part, at least, there is no doubt. But I'll do what you think is best."

"Then smile, Monsieur Nashe. Where is that dashing cavalier I find so attractive? Ardent lovers can be so boring!" She laughed, bringing him back to earth. "We shall be friends a while. Oh, all right, more than friends. And we shall see what will occur."

"Mademoiselle, you are a stone." He smiled.

"And you, I think, are as constant as the changing breeze."

"I protest. I am a paragon of constancy."

"That's not what I've heard."

"Heard?"

"You think my interest so fleeting? I have made an investigation of you, Monsieur. Does that satisfy your ardour?"

"I am devastated with pleasure."

"And how is this chicken?" She giggled mischievously.

"I wonder I can cope with the intensity of your love."

"Silly man. A young woman must not pine away from love...but grow fat and have babies."

"Not too fat."

"Do you think me forward, Alan?" Her tone became shy and serious. He wanted so much to embrace her then. Instead, he answered lightly.

"I dislike conservative women, Mademoiselle. Thank God you are not one of them!"

"So it's a trollop you want?" She grinned.

"Can I say nothing without an attack?"

"You may counter attack, Monsieur...or surrender." Her last words came soft and deep. She leaned toward him like a wary deer. He kissed her. She pulled away glancing about for curious eyes.

"I surrender," he whispered.

"If you do so without a fight, Monsieur, I shall be quite bored!"

"Then I attack!" he shouted, stooped, and threw an armful of leaves in her hair. She laughed and grasped another bunch and then they were in a leafy, multicoloured shower. Her eyes sparkled. Her laughter was like soft bells.

"Young man," a gruff voice interrupted, "perhaps you might release my daughter so that I may have a word with her." Antoine Duchesnay stood above them. He did not look pleased.

Nashe scrambled to his feet trying to apologize. Duchesnay ignored him, took his daughter's hand and guided her off. Nashe was left alone in a pile of dead leaves, looking a little foolish and feeling devastated. Then summoning courage different from that which he usually knew, he followed them. He found them at their carriage.

"Monsieur Duchesnay, permit me the honour of apologizing for my behaviour," he said stiffly. "It was only in playfulness I assure you."

"Oh, posh!" the girl interrupted. "It has already been made very clear to father that nothing sinful occurred."

"Mind your tongue, daughter!" The older man's face flushed. "There are people about...ears."

"I'm aware of that, father. At any rate, Alan, I've received assurances from father that I may be courted, with proper chaperones, and he is only too happy to make your acquaintance." She nudged the older man none too gently, and he extended his hand.

"I must have it from you, Monsieur, that your intentions toward my daughter are honourable. I have lost one of my girls to society. I don't intend it to happen again."

"I assure you, Monsieur Duchesnay, that my feelings for Reine Marie are completely respectable. I realize this seems a trifle unconventional."

"You seem a bit of a fop, Monsieur," the older man cut in. "I do not much care for half-men."

"Father, for heaven's sake be civil!"

"You note, Monsieur Nashe, I am not a strong parent. I once believed the male species to be dominant. Experience has taught me otherwise. I am no match for the women about me."

"Indeed, Monsieur, your daughter is no ordinary woman."

"And I hope you are no ordinary man, Monsieur. If so, you will live to regret it."

"My intentions as I have said, Monsieur, are..."

"Will you two stop! I am perfectly capable of making my own decisions. My honour is mine, Messieurs. Now I suggest you two become friends; you will probably be seeing a great deal of each other. Monsieur Nashe, I invite you to join my family for lunch."

Duchesnay gave in with a defeated bow. Nashe shrugged his shoulders. The three of them joined Mme. Juchereau, and amid a repast of hard-boiled eggs, salt cucumber, and cold chicken, the luncheon turned into a warm affair.

Through autumn the two saw much of each other. On crisp, frosted mornings they walked the town, and evenings they attended suppers with friends. They laughed often together, playing that game of learning each other, of wanting to know. And, of course, they became, to their amusement, the object of gossip—the young merchant and the beautiful, magnificent ingénue of Duchesnay.

Nashe maintained the occasional nights of gambling, keeping his connections ripe, but his days were filled with her. They returned often to Anse au Foulon. She showed him the cliff side as it dropped so steeply to the river. They explored its copses together, and together they found the tortuous path that led down the precipice to the cove itself. And that placid cove amid high treed cliffs became their sanctuary away from the gossip and eyes, a private place owned by them, as only lovers can own that which they claim.

Bougainville often served as their chaperone and performed the task impeccably. Often he would disappear, leaving the two alone while he would stroll along the river and frequently return with bouquets of wildflowers for Reine Marie.

They did not make love. Their honesty would not allow them. For there were shadows to contend with, mysteries both withheld from each other. Nashe, of course, could not give her the truth. But she too held some darkness, some depth within her that would not be plumbed. And so both lied of their pasts, each trying to believe the other, both knowing somehow and for some reason they were destined for mere half love.

But for that, the autumn was heaven. Until a man named de Vergor returned from the war.

## 20

Indian summer faded into the rawness of late fall. Leaden skies promised winter and with it the return of the voyageurs. They travelled down the intricate network of rivers wrapped in the forest's shroud; single canoes at first, then small parties under the watchful, close moon, gliding through hoary October days as the jays screamed in trees and the squirrels chattered madly as they gathered their winter's hoard. The convoys grew, passing mountains of coloured light: maples rustling golden, sumac like rubies, russet oak, and the dark evergreen of unchanging pine. At pre-arranged rendezvous they met huge bateaux and forty-foot cedar canots du maitre. On wide beaches they stacked their bales into regulation hundred twenty-pound ballots. And then fleets continued down the St. Laurent shooting the rapids at Lachine laden with tons of cargo. And slowly the north winds stripped trees of their colours and each night's hoarfrost reminded the men they were coming home. The season had come to its end.

Its end was Montreal and the annual fur fair where merchants, natives, and voyageurs met in a grand trading auction. From the first morning mists into the evenings, they bartered bales for gold or guns, or more sensual comforts. The half-savages had come home from the forest alive and with their profits. Now was the time for brief idleness—for selling, for drinking, for brawling, for love.

Nashe travelled upriver as a guest on Chevalier's private sloop. No hard paddling for him, he drank wine with other merchants and spent his time observing the passing scenes. Along each bank through the trees one caught glimpses of steep Norman roofs, smoke curling from their clay chimneys, or mills working by fast flowing streams that emptied into the river. Occasionally he caught sight of a great manoir belonging to some rich seigneur. Each seigneury began at the river and then stretched back long, thin acres to end suddenly at the forest edge. Should a man have two sons he divided his property—two more narrow strips so that each son would touch the river. For the river was their road.

Occasionally, there would be a church and a cluster of houses denoting the centre of each parish. And once, halfway through the voyage, they passed Trois Riviéres, the smoke of its smithies' furnaces mingling with the overcast. And always, forever it seemed, was the forest.

Finally, Nashe glimpsed the gloom of Mont Royal, the mountain in mid-river commanding the island upon which nestled Montreal. Roughed out of forest, dominated by its mountain, it had once been a native village. Now it was a garrison town, its populace four thousand strong. It was a walled town; not very long ago it had been the frontier.

The streets were crowded with artisans, women in lace coats, soldiers returned from the south, the hardy woodsmen, and natives. Chevalier explained the different nations: Micmacs, Abenakis, Delawares, Shawanoes, Nipissing, Ottawa, Ojibwas, Huron, and Tuscaroras; Chevalier was surprised to see some Mohawks from the south and Menomonies from the far west—Oneidas, Mohegans—so many Nashe was at a loss to discern the differences among them.

As they passed through the crowds and onto the wharves, Nashe saw stacks, tonnes, mountains of furs baled high; so high they made little canyons between them. Nashe walked these alleys amid more fur than he thought could have existed. And each fur meant a death. Nashe realized this occurred every year, had done for more than a hundred. He shook his head heavily wondering then when the land would be wrung dry, when it would no longer answer the human call for fashion and necessity. But even as Nashe pondered this, a great voice rang out and drove the thoughts from his mind.

"Come along you moose-mating beaver turds! You think that's any pisscutting manner to stack bales? Let Vadnais show you the trade, you sons of stinking muskrat bitches!"

Nashe followed the booming noise to its source. It had been a long time. They hugged each other like brothers, Nashe gasping for breath at the end of it. A strange alliance, he thought, born of fear and the need to trust at least one man in an alien land.

"Well, my fine, gentle, brilliant employer; all the more so for hiring the great Vadnais! Did I not tell you your success would begin with me? The best and finest of beaver, the subtlest of martin, the damned biggest haul of fur you could pray for!"

"I find the great Vadnais has not lost his confidence." Nashe laughed. But more than fur was on his mind. For a moment he forgot himself. "I thought you were with Le..."

The alert tongue of Vadnais covered him quickly.

"With the Blackfoot in the great western mountains? Nonsense, Nashe! How could I leave you to these imbeciles?" Vadnais waved arrogantly toward the gathered notaries. "Someone had to be sure these half-skinned, beaver-fucking voyageurs of yours would work! And besides, I wanted to see you again, my friend."

The giant led Nashe through bales of fur to examine three fine ballots of otter. As they flipped through the furs Vadnais dropped his voice and spoke quickly.

"I was with Ledrew three weeks ago. Things are difficult on the border. He's gone to Albany. I think he's beginning to feel the strain. He knows the network is in confusion."

"When will he return? What am I to do?"

"Nothing. No orders. As I said, there is confusion."

"What do you think I should do?"

"Carry on as you are. Gather your facts. Meanwhile," the great voice boomed again as the notaries began to gather, "you must pay your dung-heaped quart to Varin. He is Bigot's bloodsucker here. I suggest your teat-licking notaries get on with their work and account your profits. And your profits will be great! So tonight you rest, and tomorrow night Vadnais will show you the town's pleasures, eh! Of course, you are rich now, so you will pay. I drink brandy with spruce beer to wash it down. Be prepared to spend a great deal! In addition to my other attributes I am the greatest drinker this side of the Atlantic!"

## 21

Despite the joys of the fur fair the city was tense; citizens kept bolted doors and primed firelocks. They had reason too, for just as the fair reached its height, the young cavaliers returned from war.

They were a careless lot, boy-men of the gentry swaggering half drunk and cocky. They were a strange hybrid--snuff and gunpowder, lace necklets and tomahawks, their courtly manners concealing a reckless abandon. After the gore of border wars, they were careless of life; they had seen too much death. Their war had receded for the winter, but they were not yet ready to stop.

The tavern was thick with acrid smoke from too many pipes and cheap oil lamps. It was a rough place—hard packed earthen floor with barrels and planking for furniture. The big room was filled to bursting. Men bent over rough-hewn tables talking, cursing, and singing with the fiddler who sawed in his corner.

Nashe entered the tavern accompanied by Vadnais and a young cavalier named Joseph de Longeuil. He was seventeen, slim and toughened by war, an ensign in the troupes de la marine; he possessed a frank smile and his eyes observed everything. Vadnais and he, despite their diverse social stations, treated each other as equals. Each of them had been to the forest. Each had learned to survive its green realm. Nashe envied the quiet bond they shared.

They made their way to an empty table. Around them, drunken laughter and sudden arguments split the air. And as they took their seats, they were accosted by a shout that seemed more insult than greeting. It was Charest at a table next to them, and with him were two boisterous companions. One, Nashe recognized, an ugly, gat-toothed trader named Leduc. The other he did not know, but the fellow was as striking as Leduc was plain. Duchambon de Vergor, a colonial captain, was blond and possessed a face so handsome it would, Nashe decided, turn a great many heads at Bath. But the man greeted Nashe with a cold, brutal sneer. Nashe noticed de Longeuil stiffen as he was introduced. It was clear from their looks the two possessed an obvious, mutual dislike. As soon as they sat, they started on one another.

"I see Monsieur de Longeuil," de Vergor began, "has brought with him a great bear to serve as protection. He's so seldom seen in the company of mere commoners."

"Perhaps Monsieur de Vergor has not seen me because I have been to war. When does Monsieur de Vergor go to war? Perhaps he awaits another posting," de Longeuil countered. De Vergor blanched; de Longeuil had touched a nerve.

"Is there an insinuation I should understand more clearly, Monsieur?" de Vergor returned. His hand drifted to his sword.

"Not at all, Monsieur. Only that, in the form of yourself, Acadia's loss is our gain."

"Watch your tongue, little one. You are not too young to have it removed!"

"And who will accomplish that, Monsieur? You? You have already accounted your bravery at Beausejour."

Whatever he'd said, de Longeuil had passed the line of decorum. De Vergor's rapier was half out of its scabbard when Vadnais' huge hand gripped the captain's forearm. De Vergor grimaced in pain.

"Monsieur de Longeuil should be thinking of drinking rather than battle," he muttered. "Monsieur de Vergor, I have ordered you a tumbler of brandy. Accept it from the purse of a humble coureur and sit down. We have no need of duels, Messieurs."

De Vergor slowly took his seat. Nashe did not like the look of things. He noticed the three men huddle at their table. Occasionally, one of them would peer at him. Nashe edged closer to his companions, wondering what had just happened.

"The man is a coward, Alan." De Longeuil was trembling with fury. "Three years ago, he was given command of Fort Beausejour in Acadia, an important location, but he was there only for profit. He cheated the garrison of everything: food, ammunition, everything. The English marched on Beausejour. Its men had nothing left to defend it. De Vergor surrendered without a fight. He made arrangements to be returned to Quebec. The deal did not include his men. We lost seven hundred to the English, not to mention Acadia!"

"Quietly, Joseph," Vadnais interrupted, "the man may be a coward, but he's dangerous nonetheless."

"If this is well known," Nashe argued, "then why was the man not cashiered?"

"Bigot," de Longeuil spat. "Vergor is one of our beloved Intendant's cronies. He faced a court martial but Bigot got him off. Bigot is, of course, in charge of justice."

"Military?"

"Colonial. He had the trial moved to a civil court. From there it was easy."

The conversation was disrupted by a drunken shout from Charest.

"Perhaps these fine gentlemen would consider a game of dice?" he challenged.

"And will Monsieur de Vergor be playing?" de Longeuil replied.

"Of course, Monsieur."

"Then I shall not."

"Then perhaps Monsieur Nashe would care to join us," Charest said. "Or does Monsieur Nashe reserve his play only for ladies?"

The sudden shift took Nashe by surprise. Mildly, he asked Charest what he meant.

"Why nothing at all, Monsieur, only it is well known that you have a penchant for enjoying other men's women."

"I've no idea what you're talking about, Charest."

"Perhaps I may fill you in, Monsieur Nashe," de Vergor rejoined from his seat. "It's become common rumour that you are attempting involvement with a girl named Duchesnay. Consider this advice a warning to end the affair. She is taken, Monsieur, though she is too young yet to realize it. She is already in love."

"I think that should be up to her, Monsieur. The two of us have no business discussing it. And as to the game, I'm afraid I share de Longeuil's sentiments. I will not dice with you."

"Then possibly Monsieur Nashe would care to try his hand at targets?" De Vergor smiled.

"Targets, Monsieur? I know nothing of the game."

"I shall teach you, Monsieur."

"I believe the argument originated with me, Monsieur," de Longeuil interrupted. "I claim the game first. And I know it very well!"

"Then I wager the greatest breakfast this mud hole of a town has to offer!" shouted his antagonist.

"Done!" De Longeuil answered before Vadnais or Nashe could stop him. Suddenly, a knife was vibrating between de Longeuil's spread fingers, the blade buried an inch into the table. Nashe reached for his own blade but was deterred by a quick look from Vadnais.

"Permit me the honour of offering you the first throw. My knife," de Vergor pointed vaguely toward the weapon. De Longeuil, smiling, slowly withdrew the blade from the table and stood. The two men backed away from each other until they each reached wooden pillars supporting the roof. Nashe looked to Vadnais for explanation.

"Two knives. Each man throws both, his and the other's, and comes as close to his target as he can. First man to draw blood loses; first to dodge a blade also loses."

"What prevents them from killing each other?"

"Honour," he said flatly.

The first knife flashed through the smoky air and Nashe saw it quivering two inches from de Vergor's left ear. The man remained smiling, his upper lip curled into his teeth. The second knife hit just below the first. Then de Vergor ripped the two from their wooden beds and returned them, one above de Longeuil's head, the other thrown poorly clattering to the ground.

They threw, and threw again, and each time Nashe felt his muscles clench as the blades blurred through the air. Razor edges came so close that at times Nashe was sure blood would come.

And finally it did. De Vergor's throw opened a slice at the base of de Longeuil's neck. The young cavalier smiled broadly as he felt the trickle of blood.

"I believe you are in debt for one breakfast, Monsieur. And for my two friends."

"I did not specify your friends in the wager, Monsieur." De Vergor was livid. "Monsieur Nashe, perhaps we might target for breakfast, and the honour of a certain lady."

"Monsieur," Nashe returned, "I'm afraid my skill with the knife is far less than what I've seen here. You would be placing yourself in great danger."

"Ah, but I have heard, Monsieur, of your fabled abilities with a walking stick." The captain sneered. "Perhaps that skill extends to the rapier?"

Nashe had enough of this baiting. Without a reply, he turned to his tumbler and drank. The pistol shot split the air and shattered the cup in his hand. The room fell silent. He sat quite still, allowing the shock to wear off before he turned to the source.

De Vergor blew smoke from the gun's frisson.

"Monsieur de Vergor," Nashe began softly, "I dislike the manners of certain men I have met tonight. I dislike their false boasting and idle warnings. I dislike men who smile when they are afraid and draw pistols when they do not mean to kill. But far greater than these, Monsieur, I despise this horrid waste of brandy which you have just perpetrated. I propose then to duel with you, for no reason other than repayment of this shattered cup. Rapiers; first to draw blood."

The tavern convulsed in a welter of betting as the two men removed their coats. De Vergor's skill was known; the foppish merchant had little chance. The two touched swords.

De Vergor was skillful indeed, but within the first minute it was apparent that Nashe was a good deal better. The betting increased in intensity. Nashe played his opening carefully, reading his opponent, finding his weakness. De Vergor's thrusts were not aimed simply at drawing blood; he thrust more than once for the vitals. Nashe parried deftly, inviting an opening. De Vergor repaired quickly his weapon snaking toward Nashe's belly. Nashe parried once more and reached in to nick the man's chin.

The duel should have ended. But de Vergor had other ideas. He cursed wildly and attacked, furious now. Nashe retreated, parrying each vicious slash. The crowd cheered him on, enjoying de Vergor's frustrated lunges. Nashe could easily have killed the man. Everyone knew it. Instead he used a Sicilian parry and de Vergor's blade flew from his grasp coming to rest under a table.

For a moment, de Vergor gaped at his empty hand. Then he bent and withdrew a knife from his boot. Nashe dodged as the weapon flew. The blade caught his shirtsleeve pinning him to a beam.

The room exploded into a brawl. Men crashed over chairs and headfirst into tables. There were no sides; pent up drunken energy and the bloodlust of the duel had infected everyone. The source did not matter. De Vergor tried to get to Nashe through the crowd. Vadnais came to Nashe's aid freeing his pinioned arm; de Longeuil was running and grinning and bringing his coat. His companions pushed him toward the door, Vadnais clearing a path with his fists. They leaped into the cold, brisk night. Laughing boisterously, they made their way toward their lodgings.

"It seems you have used a rapier before, Monsieur Nashe." De Longeuil could barely control himself. "We now share a mutual enemy. Nothing is more important to Duchambon de Vergor than his idiotic sense of superiority. And you've made a mockery of that tonight! Mon Dieu, it was like the cat and mouse!"

"It seems he was already my enemy."

"Your rival at least."

"I'm not sure I understand you."

"She did not tell you?"

"Reine Marie?"

"Yes. Before the business of Beausejour, she and de Vergor were betrothed. Her father ended it when the scandal broke. But they still see each other when Vergor is home."

"I had no idea."

"I wish she'd told you. I believe she is still attached to him somehow."

"Now I wish I'd killed him."

"Had you done that, Monsieur, I would never again have spoken to you."

"And why not, my friend?"

"The man still owes me breakfast!"

## 22

In November bitter north winds swept up the St. Laurent and into the Basin assaulting the promontory of Quebec. Ice formed on the river. The last ship had long departed with its cargo of furs. Quebec was once again trapped in winter's isolation.

The snow when it came fell in huge flakes. It was beautiful at first, drifting down as silver butterflies, making the land a white, magical place. But then came the first of the blizzards and the air was opaque with icy blasts. After a month there was eight feet of snow. Families and friends sat by their fires in small, warm groups. Nashe could not believe the world could become so incredibly cold.

Winter interrupted the war. In the forts men struggled simply to survive. They gnawed greedily on pemmican and dried apples, drank the suffocating rations of hot pea soup, and prayed for an end to it.

Ledrew had not returned. Even Vadnais had begun to worry and set off south in search of him. Nashe found himself with little to do. For him there was only the awful intensity of that first winter, and the wintering heart of Reine Marie.

For a while he had not been able to see her: the weather and trade keeping him away. And when finally he returned he noticed a change in her. She seemed distracted, almost disinterested. It was not that she would not see him. She was simply preoccupied. At times she would be affectionate; there were glimpses of her autumn feelings. Occasionally he caught her looking at him strangely, a dark mystery in her eyes, and then she would look away, to her new companion...to de Vergor.

Nashe found himself painfully fascinated with his plight. In her company de Vergor was transformed. No mention was made of Montreal. The captain could not be faulted in his manners. He was decorous to the extreme. Nashe came to feel resentment.

Antoine Duchesnay did not like de Vergor. And with Reine Marie occupied Nashe discovered the older man's study. They enjoyed each other's company. Were it not for his problems with the daughter, Nashe would have been the most satisfied of men.

One particular evening Nashe uncovered the depth of Duchesnay's feelings. As the two took their habitual seats on either side of the hearth the older man leaned forward, his hand on Nashe's knee.

"Are you in love with my daughter?"

Nashe was surprised by the man's bluntness. All he could do was respond in kind.

"I am."

"This then is why you torment yourself by coming here? And what do you propose to do with de Vergor?"

"What can I do? Obviously she loves the man."

"Bah! The girl doesn't know what love is. She is infatuated; has been on and off for some time. He seems to have some power over her, more than attraction I mean."

"But what of his feelings for her?"

"He plays with her. He plays with all women."

"They seem very close."

"Listen to me, Alan. In this country there are very few of us. We depend on each other for comfort, for company, even survival. We live in a harsh land. Reine Marie and Duchambon de Vergor have been acquainted since childhood. Naturally they share common interests. Once they were engaged to marry. I withdrew my permission for the marriage. Do you know why?"

"I was told of the court martial..."

"The man is empty! He has no conscience. In youth he was different. But Bigot and his cronies have influenced him. The same thing has happened to Madeleine. I watch, and can do nothing."

"But surely there must be some recourse?"

"Our children are taught independence when they are very young. They must in this land. Only a few years ago and even now at the edges of the frontier a father, a mother, an entire family can be lost: frozen to death, dead of starvation, murdered by natives or the English. I taught my daughters that independence, but did not foresee the disease that grows in our midst, this careless living. This is what destroys New France. This is what has taken Madeleine, and de Vergor. There is a devil within them now. I pray the same will not happen to Reine Marie."

"Surely she can see de Vergor as others do."

"She sees the man as he once was; ignoring his fraudulence. She lives a fantasy. If I should place stones in her path she might become like Madeleine. So I wait, and hope. I tell you to do the same. Whatever hold de Vergor has upon her, my daughter loves you. She has not recognized its depth yet, but I'm sure it is there. If it were not, my friend, you would not be here tonight discussing affairs of the heart with me."

Nashe left that evening without saying goodbye to Reine Marie. The old man's words troubled him. Nashe was a man unused to inaction and unaccustomed to love. Yet here were both. And though Duchesnay's advice had been clear, Nashe knew he could do nothing while living the lie. He'd come to admire the man, to trust Bougainville as a friend, to love Reine Marie. But it was for nothing. He was their enemy. And should any of them discover his true identity, he had no illusions what they would do.

The wind was bitter cold that December.

## 23

Always de Vergor was with her. Nashe tried to stay away yet found he could not despite the circumstances. Each day made him more desperate until finally he resolved to call upon her, to force some decision from her.

He planned the visit for early morning when he'd be sure of seeing her alone. He was shown into a parlour by a somewhat surprised maidservant, given coffee, and told to wait. Mademoiselle would see him shortly. She entered the room in a simple housedress. Her beauty took his heart like a hand.

"This is a strange sight," she was smiling. "First you deprive me of your company and suddenly appear at this ungodly hour. I'm barely out of bed."

"I apologize, Mademoiselle. I thought it necessary to call upon you at this time, before you became too busy."

"So formal, Alan? Is there something wrong?"

"Surely you know there is."

"Duchambon," she murmured, her smile disappeared.

"It seems I've been displaced in your affections. I simply wish to know whether I should continue my addresses to you."

"Alan, I am not my mother. There's no need for this formality."

"Have you an answer for me, Reine Marie?" Nashe's heart was in his throat. The girl settled on a divan close to him.

"There is something I haven't told you, Alan. Something I should have long ago."

"I know already. Your father told me."

"He has not told you all."

"What else is there? De Vergor has no claims on you. None of this is necessary if you love me! I remember once knowing you did. I ask you now to choose."

"If you will only let me explain..."

"There is no need for explanation. I will not sit by and be made a fool!"

"And what do you mean by that, Monsieur?"

"Will you give me an answer?"

"I will not be bullied, Monsieur! You don't understand my situation. You only want to make me cry. I will not cry. I will not!" Her lips quivered mocking her assertions.

"What are you talking about?"

"You would never understand. Once I thought you might. You're no different from other men after all!"

"I'll listen. It's just de Vergor..."

"Posh! It's not him. It's your pride! The great Alan Nashe who might have any woman he likes is suddenly jealous because his chosen woman has independence! I will not force you to listen."

"Then you've made your decision."

"Yes."

"I should leave."

"I don't want you to."

"You will continue to see de Vergor?"

"I must."

"Why? What is this hold he has on you?"

"You don't understand!"

"Then for God's sake give me your explanation!"

"I can't...now. Not after what you've just said."

"Then I must leave. Goodbye, Reine Marie."

"Alan?"

He closed the door softly behind him, her plea unheeded. He stood by the door for several minutes. He heard her crying. For a moment he thought of returning but his pride would not allow it. He did not go in to the woman he loved.

He resolved not to speak of her again, to hold his feelings at bay and return to the life more familiar to him.

\*\*\*

From their separate viewpoints, both Vadnais and Bougainville noticed Nashe's despondency. And each dedicated himself to the cure. Vadnais offered Nashe the rustic pleasures of the Lower Town. Nashe became comfortable in smoky rooms, eating tourtières and drinking beer or mulled wine, speaking with the men of the river.

He joined their hunting parties, scarce a mile from the city in sudden, endless forest. He found silent places there, evergreens mantled in white, bare hardwoods cracking in the wind, everything grey and deep green ice. He learned to track, to follow deer spoor. He learned to wait silent in the cold by a clearing watching the doe come first, sent by the wily buck. He watched her feed, then waited longer, and finally the big quick brown of the buck. He learned the single shot to the heart, to skin and dress the animal. And in all of this he made his decision. In spring, he would go to the forest away from Reine Marie and closer, he hoped, to Ledrew.

But Bougainville too propagated cures in hours of conversation. In these times Nashe despised himself for using the man both as friend and unsuspecting informant. For all his exceptional intelligence, Bougainville was too trusting. Nashe loved this in him, and used it. He hoped when the war finally ended the two could remain friends. For despite the obvious odds against it, Nashe believed Bougainville would understand. If any knew duty, it was Bougainville. If any understood destiny, it was he.

## 24

His intelligence, charm, and rank admitted Bougainville to every social circle. But his heart and soul were with the military. It was his duty to care for Montcalm, and Bougainville took pains to assure the general's comfort.

Trémais had departed for Montreal that winter. Nashe did not know why. But Trémais had graciously given over his apartments to the French major until his return. Bougainville was more than pleased to leave his rooms near the barracks. He took Nashe with him everywhere, trusting him as a brother. Nashe accompanied the major willingly. He, too, knew his duty.

The fruits of this friendship bloomed late in January. It began with Bougainville banging on Nashe's door one early morning. Nashe awakened too suddenly suffering the effects of a drinking bout with Vadnais the previous night. The cheap wines of Le Lion d'Or possessed a bitter aftertaste. He crawled out of bed to the door, opened it, and Bougainville brushed him aside as he strode into the room far too cheerful for Nashe's liking. Nashe had a splitting headache.

"Aha!" The Frenchman laughed. "It appears my young Scot has been into his cups! Well, no doubt the renowned Bougainville has a cure."

Nashe groaned and lay on a divan. Bougainville bounced around the room in excitement.

"Exercise, my dear fellow! Exercise for the weak and wicked body. A stiff refreshing walk, a snowball or two in the face, some luncheon, and you'll be good as new, ready for the day's challenge!" Bougainville drew his rapier with a flourish; the flash of steel nearly blinding Nashe. Bougainville thrust and parried with various objects in the room. Nashe did not get up.

"Not taken by the adventure, Monsieur?" Bougainville grinned and lunged at a pillow. "Surely the famous swordsman will rise to this occasion!"

"Sit down, Antoine! Please, get me some tea."

"But of course. Tea and cakes! Yet what is the sense in preparing them when they already await? Up, my friend! Dress. Today you meet your nemesis. Today is my revenge!"

"Whatever are you talking about? Antoine, I never believed you took your fencing so seriously."

"Ah, but you will not fence with me today, Monsieur. Today you meet a master. One who has been asking for you."

"And who might this hero be?"

"A surprise, my friend. Today you'll receive a lesson on the sports floor. Now dress yourself. We mustn't keep this fellow waiting. He's a lovely man but he has a quick temper. Ah, this is a fine, fine day!"

Nashe was rejuvenated by the crisp morning. Bougainville's pace was brisk. The latter fulfilled his promise of snowballs. Nashe retaliated. Four

72

small boys joined the fight popping over the walls of the Jesuit College. The two men returned their fire, admired the aim of the young apprentices, and beat a hasty retreat up Rue des Jardine. They turned down a narrow side street next to the gate of the Ursuline convent.

"The house of Beaubassin," Bougainville announced, and Nashe knew then whom he was to meet. He cursed his riotous night and resultant hangover. This would be an important meeting. As they waited an answer to their knocking Bougainville explained.

"He lives here when in Quebec. He has a wife and six children in France, but France is far away and time passes slowly here. Madame is a formidable woman. I have no idea if they are lovers. I do know they've become inseparable friends. She is very wealthy and life here for a soldier, even his, is expensive."

A footman answered the door and led the two into a great vestibule at one side of which rose an ornate staircase. The rooms through which they were led possessed pale pastel walls and frescoed ceilings, the sunlight washing over delicate paintings or fine walnut furniture. They passed through the kitchens and across a courtyard. One wall of the yard served also as the bastion of the Ursuline convent. They entered a stable. Once inside, Nashe discovered the stable had been converted into an exercise hall. He noticed the hard floor swept and polished with dung until the earth was like marble. A huge fireplace took up one end of the hall, a fire crackling hotly within. The remainder of the room was bare but for a wrought iron table and chairs near the fire. On the table were cakes, brandy, and hot tea.

Surrounding the table were five men and a woman. The men wore no coats. A glimpse at their cork-tipped weapons and thick moose hide coverlets indicated they had been fencing. The woman swept toward Nashe and Bougainville, taking the latter's hand. She was tall and gracious and possessed a deep, resonant voice, a voice accustomed to giving commands. Mme. Beaubassin was indeed formidable.

She made introductions. The first man Nashe met was Brigadier de Levis, second in command of regular forces in New France. He was in his mid-thirties, a tall man looking every inch the noble house to which he was born. The second was Colonel François Bourlamaque. He was older than de Levis, a steady, cool man with a handshake as strong as a trap. His greeting, Nashe was to find, was typically reserved. The following two were both dressed in colonial uniform. The first was Coulon de Villiers, the man who had

73

defeated Washington at Fort Necessity three years past. The other was Charles Jacques de Longeuil, older brother of Joseph. He greeted Nashe not with a bow but a great, encompassing bear hug.

"This is the man, General. This is he!" De Longeuil was exuberant. "This one— claims my brother— is the best swordsman he's ever seen!"

"Indeed." Montcalm smiled across the table. He'd waited until the end to be acknowledged, knowing Nashe would remember him. "So, Monsieur Nashe, we meet again as I promised, and under superior circumstances. Mme. Beaubassin was quite beside herself that you would consider me a fool."

"It is an honour, General. And I should think the man who holds the British to their farm fences would never fear to be thought a fool. Mme. Beaubassin, I thank you indeed for the privilege of your house."

"But it is my privilege, Monsieur. Now I have a true swordsman within my walls. Indeed, Messieurs, I claim Monsieur Nashe as my champion." She smiled at Montcalm.

"Alas, I am usurped." The general returned the smile. "My sword is of no further use in this house. My wife will be devastated at my emasculation."

The men roared at the pun, but the redoubtable Beaubassin would not be taken so easily.

"Indeed, Monsieur Montcalm seems not only to have lost his sword but his manners as well."

"But, Madame, a simple soldier who lays his life, his sword, at your feet and then is cast away? Are the ladies of New France so cold?"

"They are, as you know, very warm indeed. As I am sure too, Monsieur Nashe is aware. How goes it, young man, with the daughter of Duchesnay?"

"It is gone, Madame." Nashe tried to keep a steady face.

She recognized her error. Bougainville saved the two any further embarrassment.

"Madame, Messieurs, enough of this patter! Swordplay, Messieurs. I crave the martial arts!"

"A fine suggestion, Major." De Levis laughed. "Perhaps Monsieur Nashe would consent to an altercation with me."

"Monsieur Brigadier," Bougainville shouted, "with all due respect to your rank and your gracious family, you are a tactician, not a swordsman. Why even I have turned your hand more than once."

"Agreed, Monsieur. There is only one true match here. Between the new Beaubassin champion and the old. General, will you prove your mettle?"

"I fear I must, Gaston, or be turfed into the gutter. Monsieur Nashe, will you engage?"

"With pleasure, General. Though I may not be enough for you today."

"Ah, yes, I knew it." Bougainville had obtained a drink. "Our Scots friend will plead the effects of last night's wine. Regrettable but useless, Alan. You are beaten today, sick or not."

"What is your method, Monsieur Nashe?" the general inquired.

"My teaching is Spanish."

"Really. Mine is Italian...Sicilian actually."

"I begin to fear you, Monsieur Montcalm." Nashe smiled.

"A good general brings fear in advance to his enemy. I am old, Monsieur Nashe. Not so quick as I once was."

"Still, General, when one understands the method, speed is not always the best weapon."

"It sounds as though you have studied well, Monsieur."

"Have at it, Messieurs," Bougainville enjoined. He sat beside Mme. Beaubassin. "Did I not love books and wine so much, Madame, I would be your champion myself!"

"Sweet Bougainville," she replied quietly, "look at Montcalm. You've brought a man to make him happy today."

## 25

The two men touched swords in the salute and stepped back to their en garde positions. Then circling the floor, they began to test one another: short thrusts, quick parries. Nashe soon realized Montcalm a proficient swordsman but, correct in his self-evaluation, not so quick as he once must have been. Nevertheless he possessed adroit skill in the parry. Each blade manoeuvring against him found it blocked and turned aside. In that careful, measured defence Montcalm owned an uncanny patience. He forced his opponent to become impetuous.

Nashe pressed his attack, forcing the general into retreat. Suddenly Nashe crossed, shifted and reached for the red heart painted on Montcalm's coverlet. In that moment his sword tip was turned and the wily general had just as quickly tucked in and touched Nashe's own painted heart. Bougainville roared his approval; the others applauded the match. Mme. Beaubassin presented her general a glass of brandy.

Later, as Nashe watched Montcalm in a match with de Levis, he recalled what he knew of the general. The man was a marquis from the south of France. Bougainville had mentioned he owned estates near Nêmes. He was forty-six years old, but fit and confident. He'd joined the army at age fifteen, heir to an indebted estate. Apparently he was a learned man, a scholar of sorts, with knowledge of Greek and Latin. His favourite subject, Bougainville more than once intimated, was history. He impressed Nashe. His small stature, the keen eyes and his animated, vehement personality belied the master tactician beneath. Yet Nashe had seen his other side in the argument with Vaudreuil. Montcalm had a weakness.

The duel having ended, Nashe consoled the vanquished de Levis: "The general is a dangerous man, Monsieur. He has a knack of knowing where his opponent will strike. He has made us both into fencing fools."

"And that is precisely why," de Levis returned with a smile, "our general controls so deftly this thousand mile border. The English thrust and are parried. The English think, and he knows their thoughts."

"I fear, Gaston, you overestimate my skills," Montcalm enjoined. "There is the little matter of Roger's Rangers."

"Irregular troops will not win this war, General. You worry too much."

"Still, they wreak havoc. They damage morale."

"Of whom do you speak, Messieurs? Are they English?" Nashe did not wish to seem too interested, but this appeared a natural opening. "I intend travelling to the frontier in spring, General. Will it be secure?"

"He really means will his profits be secure," Bougainville broke in; the men laughed. Apparently they were prepared to accept Nashe.

"They are bushrangers, not unlike our own militia. The leader's name is Rogers," de Villiers explained. "His men know how to live in the forest. They strike unexpectedly and disappear. They leave much blood in their wake, Monsieur."

"They're an indication of things to come." Montcalm seated himself. "We must plan now for the future, Messieurs. We must solve our problems locally before we meet the enemy."

"Local problems, General?" Nashe's innuendo received not even the flicker of an eyelid. Montcalm turned to him speaking frankly.

"Monsieur Nashe, you are aware of the animosity between myself and the governor. Vaudreuil believes his colonials better suited for this type of warfare than trained regulars. Unlike our two companions here," Montcalm smiled at de Villiers and de Longeuil, "the governor has become obstinate on the point. The governor is technically the supreme commander in New France; I am merely his general."

"The man is an idiot," de Levis cut in. "His prejudice creates a rift between our officers and their colonial counterparts. The situation is abominable!"

"And the crux of all of this is we know the English are coming," Montcalm continued, "and most likely this year. It appears Versailles finds our little corner of the world unimportant in their scheme of things. The English disagree. I expect a major offensive by spring."

"There must be a way of making the governor understand. Surely if he listened..."

"That is of no consequence," the general answered. "The problem of the governor is not our first priority. There is also the matter of supply. De Villiers, time for our business."

De Villiers responded immediately. "Because supply is controlled by the Intendancy we're forced to deal once again with Cadet and Varin. We have suspicions that much of our material is being sold for profit. We've spoken to Monsieur Bigot and he is investigating. But he thinks we exaggerate. After all, it was he who hired those men."

"And thus we come to you, Monsieur Nashe," de Levis said.

"But what can I possibly have to do with this, Monsieur?"

Montcalm smiled. "Despite your fencing skills and obvious charm, we did have another reason for inviting you here. Please accept my apologies for our subterfuge. De Villiers, will you explain?"

"Monsieur Nashe, in the past weeks we have held a number of meetings such as this. To each has been invited a merchant we felt we could trust. Each of them has been sworn to secrecy. Apparently our trust was well placed, as you seem not to have any inkling of this. May I inquire, Monsieur, how many vessels, large or small, you actually own?"

"Why offhand I'd say six bateaux, some rafts, perhaps twenty canoes. But why..."

"Because the English are going to advance. We must be ready for them. We cannot depend on Cadet and Varin, thus we turn to the merchants."

"To serve in supply?"

"Precisely. We ask that you retain in port one third of your large vessels through the trading season. We realize this will eat into your profits but

Monsieur Bigot has assured us that each man who volunteers will pay only a ten percent quart on his furs rather than the regular tax. Thus, we hope to make the scheme reasonable to our businessmen."

"Not to mention, Monsieur Nashe, that this is for the benefit of France," Montcalm interjected. "How do you feel about it?"

"Of course, I agree. But how do you know the English are planning an offensive?"

"Along with fifteen thousand troops, the English have sent Lord Howe to their colonies. The present commander, Abercromby, is inept. Howe is the best the English have. And he is here, training colonial troops and adapting his regulars to fight a forest war."

"How can you know this?"

There was silence around the table. Nashe cursed his impetuousness. Then he noticed Bougainville turn to Montcalm. The general nodded. Bougainville turned back to Nashe.

"I know you well, Alan, and I trust you. But before this discussion goes further I must ask you on your honour that nothing you've heard in this room will go beyond its doors. Nothing."

"Of course, Antoine. I'd assumed that already." The lie came easily. Nashe could not believe his luck. To have reached his goals so quickly, to be taken so easily into their trust...then Bougainville continued.

"To answer your question, we have an agent who works for us as well as the English."

"He is Bigot's man," Montcalm added, "and the Intendant is very secretive. Thus, we have no idea of his identity. But Bigot has a system of counter espionage second to none, Monsieur."

When the fencing continued, Nashe did not engage, blaming his hangover. He sat at the table appearing to watch the proceedings. But the whirling blades and shouts of the duellists went unattended. He had to find Ledrew. Ledrew was in danger. Perhaps, Nashe considered, his friend was already dead. Yet Nashe could do nothing. Nothing, but wait for Ledrew...or find him.

## 26

Christmas blew over in a blizzard, isolating inhabitants beneath its ice and snow, huddling together close to their hearths. But in January the storms withdrew and the weather turned pleasant leaving banks of fluffy snow higher than a man. Rue St. Louis filled with pedestrians wrapped in furs smiling about their business. Rue St. Jean was filled with sleighs. There was almost a holiday spirit; food was plentiful, the war far away, and this winter beauty seemed created for the collective pleasures of Quebec.

The astounding concept of the sleighing expedition arose from this festive atmosphere. Monsieur Bigot and friends announced a delightful journey one hundred and sixty miles from Quebec to Montreal through the wonderland winter had conceived. Ostensibly, the visit was to be on business. Governor Vaudreuil was wintering upriver. The treasury would finance the excursion.

Nashe's personal invitation was a playful card embossed with silver trees and a sleigh. He accepted. He saw nothing wrong with including himself in this lavish depletion of the treasury. Indeed, he reckoned, one English agent might spend enough to save the lives of twenty English soldiers.

Familiar faces were gathered around him: Bigot and Mme Péan, her husband and his mistress Mme. Penniseault (Penniseault had been sent on a mission to Fort Duquesne; he was not expected back until spring) Chevalier, Joseph Cadet and his wife, de Vergor made his appearance, Rigaud, the d'Iberville brothers and a host of others. Along with twenty sleighs and numerous sledges to haul the supplies, Nashe noted a number of cooks, valets, and retainers. This party would be an expensive one. And Bigot, having the time of his life, organized everyone.

They drew lots for travelling companions, two men and two women to each sleigh. As he watched the pairings, it became clear the fair Angélique had her hand in the draw, and had already decided its outcome. Bigot, the Péans and Mme. Penniseault shared the lead sleigh. Bougainville and Nashe were put together with Mme. Terese de la Naudiére, a hostess of some repute to whom Bougainville had recently directed his attentions. Nashe wondered who his partner would be. He had not long to wait. She approached with all eyes upon her. She wore a shimmering martin coat and her smile rivalled the winter sun. His partner was Madeleine Duchesnay.

He could do little. The choices had been made. Nashe dubiously took his seat beside Bougainville, opposite the ladies. Warm bricks had been placed at their feet and huge bearskins covered them. Servants on horseback delivered panniers of spirits up and down the line as the caravan made its way through the St. Louis gate.

Madeleine was breathtaking. Mme. de la Naudiére proved equally vivacious. Bougainville, Nashe noticed, appeared of two minds. Yet it was clear Madeleine was not interested in him, so he turned his attentions to more fruitful fields.

They began their first bottle.

The journey was taken in easy stages, their first night's stopover Point aux Trembles as guests of a seigneur Hamel. Their host served a sumptuous meal of pea soup, smoked eels, and moose meat, and then plied them with coffee and brandy and Bigot's favourite refreshment: melted chocolate in hot milk. The dinner was long and congenial, most of the revellers happily drunk. Afterwards there was more drinking and card playing. No one seemed ready to sleep.

During the games Nashe left for some night air. He felt a strange attraction to the simple quiet of the farm. It surprised him. He thought of Reine Marie a moment then someone touched his shoulder.

"Looking at the stars, Monsieur Nashe?" Madeleine was smiling at him. "The brandy has made you meditative."

"I find I enjoy the peace of this place."

"You astound me, Monsieur. You seem the last man to seek solace in rural calm."

"Alas, I may dream, Mademoiselle."

"You miss my sister, yes?"

"I don't believe that a fit matter for discussion..."

"Oh, posh!" The familiar exclamation disturbed him. "I understand your feelings, Monsieur. You are not the first to fall for Reine Marie. But she is a child, Alan. You and she are not the same measure."

"Still, I can't help but think of her."

"You begin to sound like a plot from Molière. Forget my sister. There is much more there than you understand, and much you wouldn't like."

"You and your sister share a penchant for mystery. I've heard her say the same things."

"Then you would do well to regard them. I'll make you an offer, Alan. I will see to it that my sister receives you on our return. If you still feel inclined, perhaps the matter may be sorted out. I do, after all, have some sway in the scheme of things."

"You would do that?"

"On one condition."

"Oh?"

"On condition you treat this journey as your holiday. Dispense with your sour thoughts, Alan. Drink, eat, gamble, and enjoy yourself! I refuse to be accompanied by a dour lump. Entertain me! I had hoped to see the famed Alan Nashe in his prime on this excursion. You were, after all, my choice for the sleigh."

"Mademoiselle, what can I do to thank you?"

"Meet my condition."

"Agreed," he smiled.

"Good. Now let us return, and you may treat us all to your charms. Who knows, Alan, perhaps this week will become the best of your life."

"It's beginning to be already."

"I like you, Monsieur. You intrigue me."

She kissed him lightly, her fingers brushing his hair. Suddenly his spirits ran high. Thoughts of Reine Marie buoyed him. Madeleine remained by his side through the evening. They drank too much, they sparkled with wit and though meaningful looks passed among a select few, Nashe took no notice. He was drunk and looking to the future.

## 27

Breakfast was eggs, hot tea, and rum. Nashe was still drunk, a lusty carelessness in him. It appeared that Bougainville and the redoubtable Naudiére had consummated last night. The two were glowing, eyeing each other overtly. Nashe felt a touch of envy, his sensibility clouded by rum, and when Madeleine began another of her flirtations with him he responded. They drank a great deal more. Bougainville and Naudiére began to ignore them wrapped as they were within each other. Beneath the mounds of fur in the sleigh Nashe detected slight movements and noticed sudden ecstasies in their faces.

Madeleine noticed too. Leaning toward him she whispered that she was cold and in need of added coverings. She pouted as she observed the revels opposite them; a soft finger traced an outline on his neck.

"You are cold as well, Monsieur."

"Not at all."

"Yes, you are. Come close and get warm."

Nashe did not think. The soft invitation drew him near her. Her body was warm under the furs. She took his hand.

"One kiss, Alan, for payment of warmth. Have some rum."

He drank deeply, the liquid fire spilling from the cask and spreading through his veins. And then her lips were there, and he took them. Her mouth was full and moist, and the kiss lasted longer than he had intended. Then she kissed him again her tongue rushing inside, touching his. He responded drunkenly pulling her toward him. His hand moved, guided by hers, and he felt the smooth warmth of a naked thigh. He began to pull away.

"Alan, what can it hurt?"

"Mademoiselle, you know my situation."

"Things change, Alan, with the simple touch of a hand."

And then her fingers brazenly tickled up his leg. The palm of her hand rubbed gently at him, the fingers filling the spaces between the buttons of his breeches. Suddenly she pulled hard and the buttons snapped away and her hand was inside, exploring, touching his abrupt hardness. Nashe succumbed, befuddled by pleasure. In the light of day, in the sleigh, under the bearskins concealing them her hand began to move him. He glanced quickly over at Bougainville and saw the major wrapped in a long, drunken kiss. He looked down to where her hand was. The furs' thickness betrayed hardly a movement.

Then she changed her touch, no longer delicate but quick and purposeful. Bigot passed by shouting drunken greetings, and Nashe shouted back, and Madeleine laughed and made a fist around him. Their eyes met and held each other and all there was were eyes and mouths and the sheen of sweat he felt come to his forehead. His essence poured into her hand. She took it and with his hand still on her thigh she spread the warm viscosity over her skin. The only betrayal of passion was a wry, satisfied smile. Nashe had been captured.

That night in Trois Rivières they stayed in the manoir of the iron works master. Nashe thought the man's name was Franquet. He could not be sure. The alcohol haze had disturbed his reason, and all was a pleasure mist.

He bedded her that night. Her body was full and magnificent, her flesh creamy and like rare silk. It delivered its promise.

The following night they roomed at an inn close by the river. Vaudreuil and his friends had come up from Montreal to join the revels. There was a masquerade. Everyone knew each other. Everyone pretended not to. Nashe left early following Madeleine's signal.

She had ordered a bath to her room. By the fire the two of them, naked, sponged each other, the hot scented water flowing from their fingers dribbling seductively down their legs to the floor. They made love with abandon, and then sponged the heat from each other with cooling water; its perfumed droplets civilized them. And finally voluptuous, intoxicated sleep wrapped them together beneath thick blankets, the fire dying, its embers reddening the room.

***

Nashe awoke quivering. Twisted, dry dreams had made his sleep fitful. The awakening was a panic, his mind recalling Reine Marie. In the dawn light, he saw Madeleine. She was asleep. Her flesh had the grainy look of dissipation. The woman would never be ugly, but other things showed in that sleeping face.

Here were two empty vessels in a bed: beneath lust was nothing, worse than nothing, desperation. In those raw morning moments, Nashe realized what he had become. He felt the irony of his double life. He'd accepted this role thinking he could play it. He was no longer playing.

The role had taken him.

A soft, almost imperceptible tapping roused him from bed. He walked unsteadily to the door standing naked, his ear pressed against the dark oak. He waited. Again the tapping. He pulled the door open a crack and peered out. What he saw took his breath away.

"Trémais?"

It was not the man Nashe remembered. He looked exhausted, his eyes ringed with blue, the lines on his face etched deep.

"A servant informed me I'd find you here. What in God's name are you doing?"

"I wish I knew, my friend."

"Get dressed quickly; meet me at the end of the hallway. There is a linen closet..."

"What's happened?"

"Be sure you're not seen."

He was gone. As Nashe dressed he glanced toward the bed. Madeleine was half sitting, smiling at him, one perfect breast peering out from a corner of the sheet. She had the look of a satiated cat.

"Leaving?"

"I need some air."

"With your friend? Who was it?"

"A servant. I left orders last night to awaken me early."

"You will return?"

"No."

"I see. The carousal has ended. The bright Alan Nashe now pretends to be respectable. You are not that, Monsieur. You will never be that."

"I know."

"I only hope my sister won't hear of this. It would break her heart."

And then he knew. The whole episode had been an entrapment. And the brilliant, sophisticated Alan Nashe had walked into it like an ignorant farm boy. She lounged casually on the bed. He turned and left. As he shut the door, he heard her laugh. The sound was hollow, the hollowness of a sun in eclipse.

It was a dim storeroom; a narrow window allowed some light. Trémais was crouched by the door. In the half-light he looked even more bedraggled.

"What's all this about, Claude?"

"I'd heard you were part of this little diversion. It became necessary to see you."

"But why? What's happened?"

"First, I have a question."

"What?"

"Why did you kill that sailor aboard the Celebre?"

"How did you..."

"I saw. Why did you do it?"

"I caught the man stealing. We fought." Nashe retreated to his usual half-truths. "He fell and struck his head. I am a trader, Claude. I would have been ruined. I panicked."

"You are hardly the kind of man who panics. Now tell me the truth or you'll die where you stand." Suddenly, Trémais shoved a pistol into Nashe's belly. It was wrapped in cloth to muffle the sound of its firing. "I have no time for games. Tell me who you are and why you came to Quebec. I will use this, believe me, if I don't get the truth."

"Is that why you searched my cabin?" Nashe played for time.

"And why did you search mine? Surprised? You were very careful; someone has trained you. Now what is your business?"

He had underestimated Trémais. It was becoming an unfortunate habit. The pistol's hammer clicked back.

"I am an agent," Nashe muttered bluntly.

"I thought as much."

"I was stationed in Marseilles. Counter espionage. Finding English spies. No one was to know of my transfer here, not even the military. The sailor discovered my identity. He had to be disposed of."

"That answers a great deal: the fight in Place Royale, the way you handled it; Bigot's nurturing you, setting up your business. He knows of you?"

"No one was told of my assignment."

"The day we landed I left a message on the ship. I thought you might be an English agent. Thank God I'm wrong." The gun pulled away. Trémais produced a small, sealed packet.

"What if he believes I'm English?" Nashe whispered, struggling to keep panic from his voice.

"Bigot is a much more intelligent man than I, Alan. Had he suspected you'd have been arrested or killed by now. I've learned a great deal about the Intendant. He is ruthless. I fear him."

"Why?"

"It's too long a story to tell now. You are the only man I can trust. You've not been corrupted yet." He paused. "Economically at least. This packet contains documents. Important documents. They concern Cadet, Varin, Franquet, a host of scheming villains. I want you to hold it for me. If I should disappear or be found dead, take the packet to France. Don't send it. Take it. What I have here is much more significant than a few English spies."

"What is this about, Claude?"

"I can't tell you. The letters are encoded so they're safe for you to handle. Should anyone read them they would see only a will and some letters to my wife. Tell no one you've seen me. There's an address on the packet. If it becomes necessary, deliver it there as quickly as you can. Only there can the code be broken. I'm sorry to involve you in this. I would not do so were it not of the utmost necessity. Should your wench question you say you've simply been out for a walk."

"I'm not going back there."

"Indeed...rather late for that decision is it not?"

"Claude..."

"Go. Be careful. There is more treachery in this place than you know. I hope I'll see you again, Alan. I hope in better times."

Nashe watched as Trémais made his way down the back stairs of the inn. When the man had disappeared, Nashe retraced his steps around the corner past Madeleine's doorway. De Vergor stood there, looking straight at Nashe, his lips curled in a sneer of contempt. Nashe felt a sudden almost painful urge to crush the brutal, handsome face into blood and bone. Instead, he walked on. He did not look back.

He obtained a horse from the innkeeper. Without packing, he departed. The sun was an ugly, red disk in the morning grey. Nashe turned his mount north, toward Quebec. The morning was very cold.

## 28

He'd been four hours riding when the weather changed. Clouds obscured the sun. The land became lifeless, colourless. Snow fell. First it came in huge flakes that stuck to the shoulders then melted. But soon the flakes became swirls, the air grew biting cold, and the falling snow so thick his vision could not pierce it. Nashe and his mount were caked in a mantle of soft, encompassing white. The horse plodded through mounting drifts, and Nashe frequently steered it to the sides of the road where coloured poles marked the way. To miss those poles meant losing the road.

The solitude gave Nashe time to think. He would rather not have, his reflections ridden with disgust. He was confused as well at the turn of events. What could Trémais have found that could be so important? Nashe renewed his intent to find Ledrew. There was so much information now. Without Ledrew he was lost. Vadnais might know; if Vadnais could be trusted. He liked Vadnais, respected the man's rough ways...but he liked as much Bougainville, Montcalm, Chevalier, and the De Longeuil brothers...and all of them were his enemies. Alone in the snowfall, Nashe began to feel helpless.

His meditations turned to Reine Marie. He resolved to tell her the truth, all of it. Perhaps she would forgive him. Perhaps they could be free, away from subterfuge and war, far into the forest. Ridiculous. He ended the dream before it controlled him. The girl was French. This huge, incredible land was French. He was the alien. He began to think it better if the snow would fall forever burying him in its feathery coldness. He gazed at the drifts lining the roadside. Then suddenly the drifts moved.

Immediately, he was surrounded. Seven tough partisans, their green uniforms caked with snow, levelled muskets at him. The men looked uncommonly vicious; bearded faces lined with the marks of hard living.

"A very fine animal, friend," one of the bandits spoke to him. His French held a queer accent. "And you appear richly dressed for such a lonely journey as this. So why in the name of the beaver is a chevalier travelling the road without servants? The roads are dangerous this time of year, friend."

"I am a fur merchant, Monsieur." Nashe disliked the man's tone. "With pressing business in Quebec. Your rank and regiment? I don't believe I've come across that uniform before."

"No doubt." The man laughed coldly. "This regiment is one you're unlikely to see in Quebec."

"If you are bandits, or deserters, I have very little of value. I am new to the country and certainly not a wealthy man."

"You are of no importance. It's your fine horse we crave."

"Get this over with, Isaac, there might be patrols," another of the vagabonds intruded. The man spoke English! A squad of English soldiers in the heart of New France. Nashe understood then why these men looked so hard. They were two hundred miles from safety.

"We are in somewhat of a hurry, friend," Isaac spoke again. "If you will dismount..."

"Not if you intend to kill me, Monsieur."

"I claim the scalp," another man shouted in English.

"Shut up, you fool!" He was answered in the same language. "We got meat and a prisoner. This might be helpful to the captain."

"The captain said no prisoners."

"But he meant no peasants. This one's a far cry from that."

"But..."

"If he's not wanted, I promise you'll get the hair. Agreed?"

"Done."

The soldier reverted to French addressing Nashe in more threatening tones. "Dismount. You're coming with us."

As Nashe's feet touched the ground, he was pinioned by two burly soldiers and expertly searched by a third. These men took no chances. They found his pistol, wallet, and the packet given him by Trémais. Nashe heard a shot. He turned to look. On the road his horse lay kicking the last of its life away. Another shot and it was still. Then one of the soldiers took an axe to it, butchering until only a bleeding carcass remained. Nashe was sickened. He muttered to the man named Isaac. "Is this mutilation necessary, Monsieur? Some warning to other innocent travellers?"

"We need food and your animal has provided us a day's rations. Now shut up, friend, and if you value your tongue let it not speak until asked. A flick of the knife and you'll be tongueless."

Nashe thought the better of argument. His neck was roped to the belt of a soldier, and he was given snowshoes. Where these men were going there would be no pathways, and a man could sink to his neck in snow. A toboggan was hauled from the roadside trees. The soldiers heaved the carcass onto it. The remains of the horse were thrown aside to be buried by snowfall. Nashe noticed four men join the group, two from each direction along the road. Then the line of men plunged into the forest. Apart from Isaac's gruff commands no one spoke.

They crossed the St. Laurent's frozen waste and turned southeast. All day they plodded through snowfields and patches of forest. Nashe wondered how they were not lost. There were no landmarks, yet Isaac led his men purposefully on.

Dusk was simply a lessening of light, the grey-white turning to grey, and then dark. They were on a ridge and below in a ravine Nashe saw campfires winking up through the trees. They meandered down a pathway to the valley floor. By their fires, Nashe estimated at least a hundred men were encamped. A hundred hardened English partisans in the centre of French territory. Nashe was pleased to know such men were his allies. He knew now by whom he'd been taken.

And then the party split up, Nashe continuing with Isaac and two guards toward a small tent in the midst of the encampment. The tent's interior was smoky and cold. A few stumps served as stools, a pile of spruce boughs in one corner made a rough bed. Nashe noticed six scalps strung from a pole. They were fresh, the blood still drying.

And then he faced the deadly stare of the man who owned the grisly trophies; frigid, black eyes. His voice was flat and cold as a winter storm. "You are a trader," he muttered.

"Yes," Nashe replied to the man's broken French. "And you are English Rangers."

"My name is Rogers. Perhaps you've heard of me."

## 29

Now you have two simple choices," Rogers continued. "You may refuse to co-operate, in which case your hair will end up drying with those." He gestured to the scalps. "Or you may answer my questions, after which you'll be taken to Albany."

Nashe knew the latter promise was empty. These men travelled fast and hard; tough, merciless soldiers who would not be slowed by the flailing of an ill-conditioned civilian. Talk or not, Nashe knew in a matter of hours he would be dead. He decided it was high time to end his masquerade.

"Then I suggest, Captain, that we conduct the interview in English." Nashe reverted to his native tongue. His captor's face betrayed a flicker of confusion. "I have much more information in my possession than you could have hoped. And I give it to you willingly."

"You speak English very well, trader."

"I am an English agent. My name is Nashe. I'm a captain in His Majesty's Marines sent here on assignment. The mission is secret. No doubt, Captain Rogers, you have not heard of me."

"This story could easily be fiction, Mr. Nashe. A great many Frenchmen have lived in England, a great many more understand the language. This could be a ploy."

"Then question me."

"The answers might be lies."

"You're a cynical man, Captain. I suggest you keep me prisoner then, and take me to Albany. If Lord Howe is there he will vouch for me. If I am killed by your men, Captain, and the Brigadier discovers it, your entire head might yet hang from the self-same pole as these...trophies."

"You are an informed man, Mr. Nashe, to know of Howe's posting. You are also very foolish. My head will hang nowhere unless it is caught by the French. I know not who you are, but at present you are my prisoner."

"And my agent, Captain." A voice came from the tent's open flap.

Ledrew stood in the opening: hardened, unkempt, and swathed in furs against the cold. His face was creased and cracked from the harsh climate; his moustache had grown to a thick matted beard. He looked exactly like the men surrounding him. There was no smile for Nashe as he approached him. Ledrew had become a stranger.

Rogers seemed to respect him. On Ledrew's orders the tent was cleared of all but the three of them. Ledrew informed Rogers of Nashe's identity and his mission.

"Well, gentlemen." Rogers seemed intrigued. "I suggest we contribute each what we know."

"If I might prevail upon your hospitality, Captain, your men have given me a long and arduous journey. Have you a spirit with which I might restore myself?"

"I apologize, Captain Nashe. My men carry only essentials. Spirits are unnecessary. We have some melt water and tea. That can be my only offer."

"Tea then. Just how well equipped are your men, Captain?"

"As I said, simply," Rogers answered having ordered the tea. "Each squadron is assigned a sledge. Each sledge contains only what we need: bearskins, spare clothing, kettles, axes and ammunition. Enough for the squadron. We hunt and ration."

"You receive no supplies?"

"From where?"

"I see."

The tea arrived. Nashe thankfully restored himself with a hot mug.

"I will tell you what I've found. I hope, Nashe, you can confirm. The French are ensconced in their forts. It seems, gentlemen, they're running out of food. Up and down the system, every settlement we come across, there is nothing to steal. Everyone is rationed. Are they indeed out of food, Nashe?"

"Not in the circles I travel. But the colony is rife with corruption. You hear rumours of it everywhere. Jeff, you remember that fellow Trémais I told you about?"

"Yes."

"He's a government inspector sent to investigate these rumours. He seems to have found something that frightened him. And he is a man not easily frightened. I know little about it, but he believes I'm a French agent. He gave me a packet of letters documenting his discoveries."

"I've seen it. The soldiers brought it with your belongings. It appears meaningless."

"It's in code. I doubt we can crack it. I believe it's a very private code."

"Then you'd better keep it."

"Good. I've heard, Captain Rogers, some talk of the populace having trouble."

"They're hungry alright. And so are we. We've even had to raid military supplies. It's not something we like to do often."

"Then our plans for the spring might come to fruition," Ledrew broke in. "Pitt's offensive is beginning, a three pronged attack, gentlemen. A push on Louisbourg, Fort Duquesne, and Carillon. If the French are ill-prepared we might have them."

"I thank God bloody Abercromby's been relieved," Rogers muttered.

"Indeed. These are new men...good ones: Amherst to Louisbourg, Forbes to Duquesne, and Howe with Abercromby to Carillon. All of this is completely secret."

"Not so secret." Rogers frowned. "It seems our friend here knows of Howe."

"That's not possible!" Ledrew was astonished.

"I'm afraid so, Jeff, and there's more to it than that. I've infiltrated the military command, even to Montcalm," Nashe grinned.

"How, in heaven's name?"

"It doesn't matter. The fact is the French are more than ready for spring. They know of Howe and expect some kind of offensive. They've not been idle."

"How is this possible?"

"I've been trying to find you to tell you. The French indeed have a double agent. Apparently he works for Bigot. I think you're in a great deal of danger."

"I've been to Albany, through the network, all over. That's why I've been gone so long. There is a leak, no doubt, but I can't find it."

A soldier entered the tent and whispered to Rogers. Rogers left without a word.

"It must be someone highly placed. Is there no one you suspect?" Nashe queried.

"There is one. I was on my way back to investigate him."

"Vadnais?"

"Good lord, no. Whatever gave you that idea? Vadnais hates the French bureaucracy with a passion. No, it's not him."

"Who then?"

"A trader named Charest. He arrived just after you."

"But he's not part of your network. I was told this agent worked both sides."

"I've heard Charest was involved in something before he came here, in Europe. Perhaps Charest knows of you."

"Then maybe I shouldn't go back. He could have said something to Bigot."

"No!" Ledrew exclaimed. "You're too valuable now. Bigot's suspicions must have been allayed. Otherwise you'd be dead now. He works very quickly."

"Trémais told him about me."

"But you said Trémais was a government inspector. Bigot will suspect him far more than you. That answers it. Bigot likely thought you were an agent in the beginning. When he found out about Trémais, and he will have, he began to suspect Trémais more than you, thinking perhaps the inspector was leading him on a false trail to keep him off his own back."

"That makes sense."

"I'll see to Charest."

"I can help you."

"Don't be a fool! You're the only one in Quebec now whose identity isn't under suspicion. The men in my network don't know you; Bigot has let you pass. That is, no doubt, why you were given so much help in trade. Restitution for a past mistake."

"Still I think I should..."

"Stay out of it."

"Can you get this information to Albany?"

"I'll send it with Rogers. I must deal with Charest."

Rogers returned, striding into the tent. He seemed strangely animated. "Gentlemen," he announced, "we march!"

"But it's midnight."

"My scouts have returned. We go to Yamaska."

"That's more than thirty miles."

"Nevertheless, Captain Nashe, we have a party awaiting us. And we will not be late." Rogers was almost smiling.

## 30

They waited in the morning damp for an hour, the cold seeping through the thickest of coats into the bones, freezing. None of the forty men moved. They lay prone behind hillocks on either side of the road. They had marched all night, sweat transforming to frozen crystals, their beards icy from their breath in the Arctic air. They had come to this place near the village and prepared their ambush. A sharp, high whistle cut the dull air. Forty hammerlocks clicked into place; forty shoulders seated gun butts. Rogers spoke quietly past Nashe to the man beside him.

"Pass the word— the officer and two soldiers."

Word was passed. Nashe heard the neighing of a horse. A small column of soldiers rounded a turn into view. They escorted three large baggage sleighs.

Nashe felt the man beside him tense.

Six soldiers, ten drivers, and a young officer at their head, each with his shoulders shrugged, collars up, the frigid damp in every man's veins. Nashe imagined them dreaming of garrison fires and hot food and rum. And suddenly Nashe noted passengers on the sleighs—women, likely the wives of the drivers, seated beside their men. Not one of them looked up as they passed the hillocks. A driver smoked a pipe. Nashe could smell tobacco as the man passed below.

Nashe turned to Rogers. "There are civilians, women! What will you do?"

Rogers simply stood and shouted.

"Shoot!"

Forty muzzles flashed, and amid clouds of smoke and the reek of gunpowder everyone died. No thought. No hope. Only two soldiers and the officer at the head of the column were spared. The officer's horse reared as he turned. The soldiers dropped their weapons and raised their hands. The officer panicked, spurring his horse away. The animal galloped wildly, its rider bent low over its neck, whipping, spurring, and racing into distant safety. He was out of range. He was clear. Gone. Then two puffs of smoke and a second later two sharp reports. Man and animal died in their tracks plunging to the road, skidding on the frozen road, splashing into a snow bank.

Two fur clad miniatures appeared in the distance. They waved. Nashe saw knives glint in their hands. They walked purposefully toward the bodies. Then Nashe turned to the gully below where men hacked at the scalps of the dead. There was gore on their knives and strings of flesh. They were quick about it, experienced in their work.

The two survivors were trussed together, their eyes like saucers. The baggage train was pulled off the road. The slaughter had taken two minutes.

Nashe looked at Ledrew. His face was a stone. Rogers seemed annoyed.

"We should have had that officer, Sergeant."

"Yes sir. He might still be alive."

"He is not. Prepare the sleighs. We leave in five minutes."

"Sir." The burly man went about his business. Nashe was incensed. He strode up to Rogers.

"Those were not just soldiers, Captain. You've killed women! And now you allow this mutilation?"

"The men must be paid something, Nashe. Scalps are worth money back home."

"This is not warfare, Rogers."

"I suggest you save your judgements, sir, until you've seen the French at work."

"Regular soldiers do not behave..."

"We are not regulars, Nashe. We are vengeance. The French pay, in kind, for what they've done to us. I've left two horses, some food. I suggest you and Captain Ledrew depart from here. We go no further north, and you're close enough to make Quebec on your own."

"That, Captain Rogers, will be an unmitigated pleasure."

"You've a lot to learn, Nashe. This is not Europe."

Ledrew had already mounted. As they took to the road, Nashe glanced behind. Where there had been life there was nothing. The Rangers were gone. Only slow freezing, grey clad carcasses lay on the road, their blood turning to scarlet ice. It began to snow again. Rogers would be pleased, Nashe thought; his work would lay undiscovered until the spring.

*** 

It was a two-day ride to Quebec. They decided to travel together as far as Batiscan. They could not remain together after that for to do so would raise suspicions. As they rode, Nashe attempted conversation. He was rebuffed. The man who rode beside him had changed. He remained locked in a grim, secretive silence which Nashe could not comprehend. Nashe resigned himself to that silence. The year had been very hard on Ledrew. When he finally chose to speak, it was just outside Batiscan. It seemed an effort for him to be civil.

"I will look after Charest. Keep your distance from him."

"Of course."

"Stay with your circle of contacts. You've established yourself. Don't risk more."

"Have you seen much of that while you've been here?"

"What?" Ledrew said flatly.

"Scalping."

"I don't want to discuss it."

"What's wrong, Jeff?"

"I do not require your sympathy, Alan."

"I only meant..."

"It doesn't matter what you meant. You'll never see things from my point of view."

"What do you mean?"

"You don't like Rogers."

"The man is a savage."

"And yet for all the differences between you, the two of you are alike."

"I take the comparison as an insult."

"Take it as you like. Do you remember Marseilles?"

"I have the scars to remind me."

"In Marseilles, we used people. Innocent people. We twisted them for our own objectives. What do you think has become of them now? Sometimes I can't sleep for thinking."

"They were the enemy. It wasn't our choice."

"You are doing it still, in Quebec."

"Just what are you trying to say?"

"Just that you and Rogers are much alike."

"This is getting us nowhere..."

"Yes," Ledrew murmured flatly. "Goodbye then. I'll see to Charest."

Ledrew spurred his horse toward Batiscan. Nashe was left to himself then, with the wounds his comrade's invective had scored. He realized Ledrew was right. He thought of Reine Marie, of Bougainville, of the many he'd twisted for his designs. Rogers and he were indeed the same. They had chosen their lives. Unhappy lives. Men bound, for whatever reason, to duty.

Nashe shrugged his shoulders and spurred his horse. There would be no more running, no soul searching to soothe the pain. He knew what he was now. On that frozen road outside Batiscan, Nashe resigned himself to his affliction.

**31**

The days became warmer, and with the new warmth, cracks appeared in the river ice. Sap stirred in sugar maples, but their buds knew better and refused to swell. The forest and city streets were patched with dirty snow. Low clouds hovered over the mountains, and a cold mist seemed always to touch the tops of pines. There was dull rain and sharp morning frost and then snow again, and winter showed it was not yet finished.

But to the lofty spirits of Quebec's privileged classes the false spring brought new life, signalled by the Governor's annual New Year ball. It was time for new gowns, for fashion and wit, and the carelessness that comes of temperate climes. The ball was hosted in Chateau St. Louis, the fort transformed from its military demeanour into a festive, lantern festooned gala. There was dancing and copious food that belied the rumours of shortages.

Nashe danced, drank little, and stayed to the company of Bougainville. The major never mentioned Nashe's sudden departure from the sleighing trip. He well understood the reason but was far too sensitive a man to broach the subject. The two joined a group gathered in an anteroom of the Chateau. Among them were faces familiar to Nashe: de Levis, de Longeuil, some junior officers of his acquaintance, and finally, Montcalm. The Governor's Ball gave them fleeting pleasure. Other matters were at hand. These men faced a long and unpleasant season.

"So the scourge has ended," Montcalm pronounced. "My congratulations, Monsieur de Longeuil. Was he among the dead?"

"I have no idea, General. No one bore any markings of rank. If he did escape he was one of the few. Nearly all of them were killed."

"Where was it you found him?"

"East of Montreal in the mountains. They took their final stand on a mountain top."

Bougainville turned to Nashe.

"Rogers' Rangers. De Longeuil trapped them."

"When?"

"A week after you left the sleigh ride."

"He became too confident," Montcalm held forth. "Still, he was a sign of things to come. We no longer face farmers, Messieurs, and we must be ready. I myself intend to reinforce Carillon. When they come, I think it will be for our centre. I'll depart in April for Lac Champlain. De Levis will remain in command here. He seems better able to get along with our illustrious governor than I," Montcalm smiled, and then turned to Nashe.

"I trust, Monsieur Nashe, you recall our agreement?"

"I do indeed, General. I am at your disposal."

"Good. Then I suggest, Messieurs, we partake of this excellent wine. To the King, Messieurs, and victory!"

Bigot entered the room. The ugly Intendant was amiable; he smiled distinctly at Nashe.

"Messieurs, this hiding away from the ladies has created some consternation. The war will wait, no doubt, and I've been sent to enjoin you to the dance. In particular you, Monsieur Nashe. A certain young lady seems eager to see you. Here is her note. I accept no payment for my service, Monsieur, but later I will exact the toll at cards. I feel lucky tonight. Messieurs, will you follow me?"

Nashe remained behind the group to read his missive. The ink was still moist on the paper. It said simply: 'On the terrace.' The note was signed: 'RM'.

He had tried to avoid her since his return, stayed away from common friends, from the places where he might see her. Yet he had still been unable to quell his feelings. As he passed through the double doors of the terrace his heart was in his throat.

The St. Louis terrace perched atop the edge of the Cap. Below, the lights of the harbour winked placidly and against those dim illuminations, on the deserted terrace, Nashe saw the silhouette of a woman. She wore a cloak against the night chill, and as she turned, her pale complexion took his breath away.

"Hello, Alan." The voice betrayed a note of uncertainty. "I was afraid you wouldn't come."

"I've missed you, Reine Marie," he murmured quietly.

"And I you."

"Forgive me. I'm a proud fool."

"As am I. I should have given you the truth long ago."

"The truth should not hurt me."

"When I tell you, you must try to understand. I thought I knew love. I did not."

"Does this have to do with Vergor?"

"Yes."

"Then there's nothing to tell. I understand what happened."

"But it isn't just that, Alan. He has something of mine I wish dearly to have returned."

"Do you love him?"

"No. Once he was a good man, Alan."

"Must we speak of him?"

"I must tell you the truth."

"Then so will I. You deserve to know the man you only think you know."

He held her at arm's length, searching her eyes, preparing an answer. But he could not find the words. At that moment Nashe realized Ledrew had been right. He was a soldier, and to tell this woman before him the truth would jeopardize everything. He could not trust her. He loved her, but he could not trust. She was French. She was the enemy. Loving, beautiful enemy.

"I love you, Reine Marie. You are more to me than anyone has been or ever will be. But I cannot give you the truth. Not now."

"Then I'll wait. I can hope one day to understand. But I must..."

"No. I, too, will wait, and the day will come when we can both be honest."

"I pray it comes tomorrow."

"Tomorrow may be a long way off."

"I'll wait, Alan. I love you..."

He crushed her to him, savouring her, knowing soon she would be lost to him. It was cold on the terrace; the winds from the Basin were damp and chill. The clock passed midnight. It was a new year.

## WILDERNESS, 1758

## 32

Spring arrived; April rains persuaded the crocus to rise from its mud bed. Good weather meant an early start for the trade expeditions and greater profit returns in the fall. The merchants kept busy from dawn to dusk plying officials for dock space, setting routes for their voyageurs, supplying the hundreds of canoes that would leave from Quebec and Montreal. Each man was assigned his position on a canoe, supplied with corn meal, salt meat, a little rum and tobacco, and given a modest advance on his shares. These men would paddle from break of day long into each twilight, forty five strokes per minute, with only one or two rests each day; long enough for a meal and a pipe. They were hefty, barrel-chested men possessing phenomenal endurance, the strength to paddle a thousand miles in loaded canoes, and the cunning and knowledge to survive in the bush.

With spring, the army too made itself ready. By April's end the cliff's edge bristled with cannon. Now the gunners worked on the shore batteries: Batterie Royale at the mouth of the harbour, Batterie Dauphine to the east near Canoterie. From the beach they could fire the thousand yards across the strait between Quebec and Point Levis. Nashe watched the huge guns being emplaced, the earthen redoubts built and strengthened. Nothing would bypass those guns, he realized. They marked the gateway to the western world, and that gate would remain shut.

And as the troupes de la marine returned from winter garrison, Montcalm's strategy was clear. He replaced his colonials with rested, disciplined regulars for the summer campaign. Companies of these troupes de terre lined the docks daily awaiting embarkation. They had trained through the winter on the bleak stretch of the Esplanade. Now they were posted to the frontier, to Frontenac, Niagara, Detroit, and Carillon—professionals prepared to halt the advance Nashe knew, and they knew now, was inevitable.

Nashe became a member of the committee for the civilian supply plan. Bougainville was more than pleased at Nashe's taking a hand in the work. He explained everything to his friend, feeling that with comprehension would come increased dedication to the cause. They spent time in evenings after their work at a quiet tavern on the corner of Rue St. Georges.

It was late, the candles guttering low. The keeper of the house had left them with a small supper of tortiere, some salt cucumber for desert and an ample truncheon of burgundy. Both men were tired. Bougainville had loosened the high, gilt collar of his uniform. Nashe, in more comfortable costume, slouched in his chair. Their voices were barely a murmur in the empty room.

"The general is leaving at week's end," Bougainville pronounced. "There is nothing more for Montcalm here. He and the governor have been at odds to no end this past week."

"Things are worse between them?"

"Without de Levis as go-between the two would not even be speaking."

"You're leaving as well, with Montcalm?"

"No. He expects Howe to lead his best men up Lac George and into the forest."

"Yet you're not going with him?"

"There are other things to attend to. The western sector must be reinforced. I'm going by ship with Bourlamaque to resupply and deliver more troops to Frontenac and Niagara. We can't afford to lose the lakes. Pouchot, the engineer, is at Niagara now rebuilding its defences. Bourlamaque is to inspect them."

"Then you will be there for the campaign."

"My dear Nashe, you hardly expect me to be absent from my general at his moment of greatest need? After the inspection, Bourlamaque and I will journey cross-country to Carillon."

"But that's through English territory."

"Not English. Disputed."

"Still, it will be dangerous."

"We are travelling with picked men and a guide who knows that land like I know this tabletop."

"Native?"

"French. A trader named Joncaire. He and his brother have a trade post near Niagara. We should be at Carillon long before the English come north."

"The area will be infested with Rangers, Antoine."

"My friend, if one is careful one is invisible in the forest. You know so little of this land. Perhaps you should travel with us, at least to Niagara. You've spoken of following the fur trade to its source. This is the perfect opportunity!"

Unsure whether Ledrew would need him in Quebec, Nashe left his options open. He knew it would be good for him to see this war, but Ledrew had given him orders. He told Bougainville he would consider the offer provided the major would ascertain that his life would not be in jeopardy. Bougainville smiled ruefully. "Surely, Alan, your life is not so fragile as you believe. And, yes, you will be safe."

"Good. I'm a trader, Antoine, not a soldier."

"Consider it then. De Levis will leave just after I do. He stays in Quebec to be sure Vaudreuil does not re-issue orders. Then he travels to Montreal. Montreal is our pivot point. From there he can offer support to the west or the centre. He'll have five thousand men in reserve. That should be sufficient."

"You seem worried."

"I am. Lord Howe is no fool. We are outnumbered, our transport unsure..."

"But the defences..."

"The forts? Yes. The English can't afford to bypass them. They must at least come to us. And that is the essence of Montcalm's style."

"Indeed, I remember his fencing."

"But enough of this, my friend." Bougainville sat up suddenly. He leaned across the table. "We've become obsessed with war. You realize we've spoken of nothing else all evening? Now, pass me the flagon! All this talk has made me thirsty. It's your turn to talk. Speak of trade, of women, anything. There are other things to life!"

His eyes glimmered as he sat back again, his cup held in both hands. The two men talked long into the night.

## 33

The social season commenced in earnest. Rounds of soirées, card parties and suppers were brought on by release from winter's hard grasp. Manners were dusted and aired just as clothing and summer rooms. There was a hunger for company, for gossip and wit, for an interlude from the preoccupations of war.

Nashe had once again become a source of gossip. It had been decided around winter fires that the affair between he and the Duchesnay girl had terminated. The lady had been seen too often in public with de Vergor. Yet apparently de Vergor had been but a fanciful escapade. Now it was Nashe again. Well, the girl had every right to be fickle. She was making her choice.

In public, they were decorous, but one quick glance at their eyes was the story behind the gossip. Their differences had apparently been settled.

In a way, they had.

Their love was different now. It was filled with the ambiguities and secrets of before, but now they ignored them. They felt, mistakenly, they were protecting one another.

Often they would travel back to Anse au Foulon. They found a place at the foot of the twisting pathway down by the river where they would spread their blanket. There they would lie in the sun, conversing quietly, more often than not in each other's arms as their horses grazed placidly above.

Mostly, they were happy.

"Reine Marie...I could never picture you with another name."

"Why is that?"

"It suits you. It has a nobility to it."

"Alas, I am a simple rustic, not noble at all."

"Who has lived in Paris. Not so rural as you pretend."

"But a bit savage, yes? Unlike my sister, the epitome of civilized woman."

He felt a bitter pang.. "Let's not speak of her."

"But, Monsieur, you may be the first man I've met who did not pine for love of Madeleine."

"You have nothing to fear, Reine Marie."

"You don't like her."

"No."

"Neither do I. Oh, she is my sister and I love her, but I don't like what she has become."

"Do you mind if we don't discuss her?"

"Something is wrong."

"No."

They spent a while in silence. Below on the river a canoe glided by going downstream toward Quebec. It moved swiftly like a water bird skimming. When it had passed she spoke. "I'm leaving the city by May," she said quietly. "Father wishes to return to Beauport."

"Must you go with him?"

"It's tradition, Alan. The first day of May is a celebration. It's the day when the censitaires and habitants pay their rents to the seigneur and swear fealty to him. In all my life, I've only missed it twice, when I was in France. Madeleine has refused to go. It's my duty."

"I see," Nashe replied, his disappointment obvious.

"You are very low, Monsieur Nashe." She giggled. "These depressing fits of yours really must end. Has no one told you that women dislike melancholy in men? You really are too serious today. In fact, I feel some trepidation in asking you to accompany me. Despondence is so boring."

"You mean you want me to go with you?"

"On provision that you promise to be cheerful and pleasing at all times. Otherwise, I'll have to ask someone of a less morbid nature."

"Do so, Mademoiselle, and I will kill the man."

"Oh, posh! You are no warrior despite your show in Place Royale."

"Am I never to be allowed to forget that?"

"Never, Monsieur. It was quite fun really."

"You enjoy warlike men?"

"Indeed, Monsieur, is not the dashing officer every girl's dream?"

"Then now is a good time to tell you my news. I'm considering accompanying Bougainville to the frontier. An inspection tour of some sort. He says I'll find it intriguing."

"I was speaking in jest." She grew serious. "Don't go to the war, Alan. War would not suit you. I would rather have a living merchant than a dead hero."

"Then be assured, Mademoiselle," Nashe continued, "that your love will be as far from battle as humanly possible. After the tour, I intend some exploration of my own, in the opposite direction from the fighting. Your father has told me time and again to go to the forest, to view the fur trade first hand."

"But you'll come with me to the seigneury? Before you leave? Please, Alan, if you're to be gone all summer I couldn't stand not seeing you now."

"Your father has agreed?"

"He wants to show you his land. He's very proud of it. Please, Alan?"

"Of course I'll come. You think I'd turn this chance down?"

"Oh, I do love you, Alan. I do."

They reached for each other. They kissed, then again, growing passionate. Their bodies melded together. The muslin robe she wore slipped from her shoulders. Perfect soft shoulders. He kissed them, his lips moving down to the swell of her breast. Her breathing quickened.

Then as suddenly as it began, it ended. She sat up, her eyes filling with tears. She asked him to hold her. Just hold her. The awful tide of misgiving swelled. She would not look at him. She wept silently.

She would not look at him.

## 34

If one stood on the promontory above the shoreline of the Duchesnay seigneury one could see the entire Quebec Basin: looking east lay the flatness of Ile d'Orleans, directly south across miles of water was the outcropping of Point Levis, and to the southwest was the Cap. On a clear day one could make out the gaggle of buildings like miniatures on the great rock and the martial outline of Chateau St. Louis on the brink overlooking the narrows. The city was four miles across the basin, though considerably more by the road that wended its way along the shoreline.

The Duchesnay seigneury was huge. Situated on the Beauport Heights, the property was endowed with rich, cleared farmland and frequent stands of forest. Nashe had had no idea of Duchesnay's wealth. One hour on his estate and it became strikingly clear.

The maison itself was a great stone edifice strong enough to withstand the climate and strategic enough to serve as a fortress, as it had fifty years before in the Iroquois wars. Its grounds were planted with fruit trees: dark cherry imported from Breton, Norman apple, and pear trees from the Rhône valley.

Duchesnay's censitaires lived in outlying buildings, whitewashed cottages with Norman roofs and the healthy air of contentment. Small gardens lined the paths that led to rustic doorways, and amid the gardens, children played while their pets romped carelessly. This was a good and pleasing place.

The party had travelled by cariole, the four of them– the Duchesnays, Reine Marie and Nashe—lounging in the carriage as it left Quebec through the Palace gate and crossed the St. Charles Bridge. Then the road grew steep, its gradient making the horses sweat as they hauled up out of the valley and onto the heights of Beauport. They travelled the rim of the great basin. Nashe was astounded by the view.

"Just wait!" Reine Marie laughed. "After you've settled in, I'll take you to Montmorenci. It has the most beautiful vista."

"When the girls were small," Mme. Duchesnay agreed, "I would take them there to picnic above the falls. There is a cliff on the north side with a small cottage upon it. Second to our seigneury, that is the place I would choose to live."

"I must see this wonder," Nashe agreed.

"It is beautiful," Duchesnay interrupted, "but as to wonders...the Montmorenci is little more than a dripping tap compared to the great Niagara!"

"Near the fort, Monsieur?"

"The very place, my friend! I've seen it only once. It is one of God's miracles."

"Alan is considering a tour that will take him to Niagara," Reine Marie enjoined. "He's to go with Major Bougainville on an inspection."

"Excellent! I've told you, you must find the heart of this land. That place is as good as any to hear it beating."

"But I still hold the matter in abeyance, Monsieur. My business here may prevent the trip."

"Alan." The older man leaned forward. "Go to Niagara and beyond. This lovely girl beside you will wait. And someday you may take her with you."

"Husband!" Mme. Duchesnay laughed. "You are playing the cupid!"

"But it is near the Mai, my dear, and even an old man's fancies surface."

"And soon we shall see the reserved Monsieur Duchesnay chasing young girls round the Maypole, Monsieur Nashe. Prepare yourself for the old goats of Mai!"

"How is the land here, Monsieur." Nashe changed the subject.

"It's good, Alan, but the season is short. We grow only Norwegian wheat, a strain that matures in three months. We can raise barley, oats, and of course animals. Yet one can live from the land. We've learned a great deal from the natives of the crops natural to this climate: squash, pumpkin, and maize..."

"But what is your particular interest, Monsieur?"

"Horses!" shouted Reine Marie.

"Yes, I am proud of my horses."

"And father's are the best in the land," the girl continued. "You must convince him to show you his breed charts."

"That will take very little convincing," Mme. Juchereau enjoined.

"Indeed, horse breeding here is a luxury. I should concern myself with more domestic problems, yet I've lived with this obsession since I was a boy. It is one of my sins."

"A good horse, Monsieur, is no sin," Nashe argued.

"Agreed. And if you feel that way you will see one or two on this estate that may turn you quite religious!" Duchesnay laughed.

## 35

Their arrival was expected. In front of the main portico stood more than a dozen servants and off to one side a group of rustic habitants. On the lawn, the Maypole had been erected, a tall cedar trunk hung with streamers.

An aged servant opened the carriage door and placed a step below it. As the seigneur descended the fellow dropped to one knee saying, "Your honour, welcome home. I trust you will find it a comfort." ·

"Indeed, I will, Claude. Indeed, I will. Are the preparations underway?"

"They are, your honour. There is only the food left to be done."

"Excellent. Claude, I would like to present Monsieur Nashe." Duchesnay's voice was just loud enough to be heard by all. "He is to be treated as one of the family."

"Monsieur Nashe, should you have any needs whatsoever have me summoned. I shall deal with them personally."

"Claude here has been with us since I was a boy." Duchesnay smiled.

"An honour, Claude." Nashe smiled in turn. "From first glance, I anticipate nothing I'll need but pinches to wake me from this dream."

The old man beamed. He was very proud of his seigneury.

As Mme. Juchereau and Reine Marie entered the house, Nashe followed Duchesnay across the greensward to the waiting men. They were dressed in woollens and buckskin. Nashe noticed each of them wore a new shirt. At their head was a middle aged fellow, short, rotund, with a sparkle in his eyes. He, too, bowed as his seigneur approached.

"This has the appearance of ceremony, Antoine," Nashe observed.

"It is le Mai, the custom of spring. At this time my people make payment and the baili will give me the state of things for the season. We'll plan the crops, the fields to lie fallow, a number of details."

"Your honour." The stout little man smiled in welcome.

"Benoit! A pleasure once again. How are you, old friend?"

"Well, your honour. The wife has birthed another boy."

"Good lord, man! And how many is that?"

"Twelve, Monsieur."

"Benoit is single handedly repopulating New France. Twelve boys and..."

"One pretty daughter."

"Indeed, a most charming little girl. Benoit, I would like you to meet Monsieur Nashe."

"An honour, Monsieur. You will be at peace here."

"This is a lovely place, Benoit," Nashe returned. "Before I leave I want to explore it all."

"Then let us begin with the best of places!" Duchesnay intervened. "The stables, Benoit. I wish to see my beauties."

"They are all in good health, your honour. Each and all at peace."

"Benoit is the best horse trainer in the country," Duchesnay expounded as the round fellow led the way. "Without him this estate would be a shambles and my horses nothing more than draft beasts."

"You flatter me, your honour."

"Nonsense. I speak the truth," Duchesnay insisted. The man grinned with pride.

The stables were immaculate, the horses tall, spirited animals. Their sleek, silky hides and intelligent eyes made one want to ride them, let them have their heads and fly like the wind.

"My daughter has told me you ride well, Alan."

"Your daughter herself rides well."

"As well as any man. You know horses?"

"A little."

"What think you of that chestnut there?"

"A fine animal. He looks fast."

"That chestnut has ginger in his heels, Monsieur," Benoit joined in.

"A beautiful beast..."

"He is yours, Alan."

"What?"

"A gift. One friend to another."

"I cannot accept, Antoine. This horse must be worth a great deal."

"This horse needs a good rider. I insist."

"I must repay you..."

"Nonsense! Take him. Tomorrow, ride him, see how he flies."

"But Antoine..."

"I'll discuss the matter no further. It's getting dark and time for supper. I brook no impertinence on my land, my friend. The matter has been decided."

***

The day dawned warm. From his window, Nashe looked northwest toward the peaks of the Laurentides all grey with mist upon them. It would be a good day to welcome spring.

He went down alone and across the lawn. He strolled up the lane to the stables with birdsong about him in the air. The stables were already alive, grooms going about their business, a hayrick unloading. Nashe found Benoit in the tack room. He was devouring an eel pie.

"A very peaceful morning, Monsieur." He smiled. "A good morning to try a new horse."

"You've read my thoughts, Benoit. I was up half the night in anticipation."

"You will not be disappointed, Monsieur. Let me help you saddle."

"But your breakfast..."

"As you can see I am the victim of too many breakfasts." He patted the paunch that hung over his belt. "And by the end of today, I will have gorged myself to the full."

As they strolled across the cobbled yard, Nashe queried his companion on the state of affairs in the country. The morning ride was not his sole reason for rising.

"The estate seems healthy," Nashe observed. "I'd have thought with the rationing this winter, things would have been different."

Benoit's smile faded.

"I thank God for a wise master, Monsieur. But Intendant Bigot is increasing taxes and the war is taking the young men from us. Fortunately, we have this early spring. If we have a good summer, we may weather this. If not, well, Monsieur, next winter might be hard."

"There is reason to worry?"

"There is always reason to worry, Monsieur. But we have a lovely, warm morning for riding. That is enough for now. I suggest you take the river track. It begins over there by the pigpen. You may still hear the music of Beauport before the day heats up."

"Music?"

"Frogs. Thousands of them in the reeds by the shoreline. They will still be in voice."

"Then the river track it is. Thank you, Benoit."

"Ride in peace, Monsieur. Be sure to be back in an hour or you'll miss the celebration!"

***

By noon the hall of maison Duchesnay was festooned with the trappings of ceremony; on the long dining table lay the seigneur's sword and beside it a silver cup brimming with wine. Duchesnay, his wife, and daughter were dressed in formal attire. Nashe stood to one side intrigued by the proceedings.

A loud knock at the door announced the arrival of the baili. The family straightened themselves as Benoit removed his cap, ushered into the hall by the major domo, Claude. Benoit approached and knelt before his seigneur repeating his name three times and then reciting the foi de hommage as prescribed by tradition. In his statement of rentes and cens Benoit included the payment of each of the families on the estate. The statement was long and very complex. At the end Benoit presented a ledger containing the particulars.

Duchesnay accepted the Benoit's homage by placing in the latter's hands the cup of wine. The rotund baili drank fully then rose to his feet. Duchesnay strapped on his sword and gave orders that all citizens of the estate were to be generously entertained this first day of May, the year of our Lord seventeen hundred and fifty eight. "May God's bounty and mercy be praised."

"May they all live happily and," Benoit interjected, "at peace."

## 36

The weather was unseasonably warm. The forest regained its canopy and a carpet of spring flowers. Trilliums came and marigolds appeared in low places; dogwood, wood lily, and lady slipper grew in the new, rich depths of the woods. Spring brought the birth of calves and lambs and the shaky, leggy strutting of foals as they began life among buzzing insects that busily flitted from place to place in the quick decisions of flying things.

They would ride out daily, Reine Marie on her gentle grey and Nashe on his skittish chestnut. It was easy to forget the world. It was easy not to go back, to be with her and her people and the late suppers and serene mornings. He stayed longer than he should have. He could not help himself.

It changed in one shattering morning. It was one of those crystal days. The family was at breakfast, the sun pouring through windows as they ate dried fruit and steaming croissants. The older Duchesnays were planning a visit to the parish at Beauport. They hoped their daughter and Nashe would accompany them, but Reine Marie had other plans.

"I wish to show Alan the Montmorenci today, father. We've a perfect day and I've already ordered a picnic." She smiled at her father knowing she had carried her plan.

"I find it impossible to resist the persuasions of women, Alan." Duchesnay sighed. "It has forever been my weakness."

As he spoke, there was a commotion outside. Nashe heard a distant cheer and a young maid, no more than twelve, burst into the room.

"Your honour, I'm sorry to disturb your meal, your honour, but the ships! Your honour, come and see! The ships! We've seen them!"

"Stop stammering, girl." Duchesnay smiled. "What is all this about? Take a breath."

"The ships, your honour, the first ships! In the Basin. Rogatien saw them as he was chopping wood. They are in the Basin, your honour! They look so beautiful! Oh, come and see! Quickly!"

"Get my glass, girl, from the study."

"Glass, your honour?"

"My telescope. It sits in the window bay. The one that lets me peer into the distance..."

The girl brightened with comprehension. "Of course, your honour!"

As she skipped from the room, the family rose as one. Nashe forced himself to walk with the parents while Reine Marie flew down the path that dipped from the heights to the shore. He knew now why the Celebre had caused such a flurry. The world had finally returned, the first ships bringing long awaited contact with Europe. The family arrived on the promontory above the shore. The little maid ran up with Duchesnay's telescope.

Far across the Basin slipping from behind Ile d'Orleans, Nashe made out four ships. White clouds low in the distance, their billowing sails silhouetted against the new green of the shore. Nashe imagined the shoreline all around the Basin dotted with expectant, excited groups. It made a strange, romantic picture. Then Duchesnay handed him the telescope. The older man looked sullen.

Nashe peered through the glass and caught the lead ship, a frigate. The clear air allowed him a glimpse of men on its decks, and more. Nashe panned the glass to the next in line, and then the next. He noticed splintered yardarms and twisted gunwales; these ships were not in good shape. But it was not rough weather that had brought them to this state. It was cannon. He lowered the glass and looked at Duchesnay. The seigneur muttered quietly.

"The English blockade."

"They look as though the English found them." Mme. Juchereau lowered the glass. "How many, I wonder, were lost?"

"No telling," Nashe said flatly.

"It appears things are going to get worse." Duchesnay turned slowly. "Alan, we'll keep this from our people. Soon enough they'll find little to celebrate." He walked dejectedly back up the pathway to the house. He looked suddenly old.

Nashe remained. His eyes followed the ships as they neared the narrows at Quebec. They limped into port, exhausted. Nashe thought for a moment of Pitt's strategy. This had been an English victory. He should have been happy. But he was not. The loyalties, loves, and friendships of a year clashed now with old values. Someone would win this war, he knew, but more and more Nashe realized that whatever the outcome, he himself could not win. He too turned back toward the house. Below him on the shoreline the servants were dancing a rough, joyous jig, Reine Marie dancing with them.

\*\*\*

His study was Antoine Duchesnay's private retreat from the bustle of the house. Its wide bay windows offered a view of the Basin, its shelves lined with the volumes of his prized library. Over the fireplace a mantle held the trophies and souvenirs of a life and above on the wall a favourite fowling piece and a portrait of Louis XV. It was the chamber of a French gentleman.

Nashe found Duchesnay staring out the window. He set the telescope quietly down on the desk and began to leave, respecting the man's melancholy, when Duchesnay turned to him.

"Damn, Versailles!" The curse exploded across the room. Nashe noticed Duchesnay nursed a brimming tumbler of cognac. "They have fallen under the spell of Voltaire!"

"Monsieur?" Nashe mumbled, perplexed both by the early brandy and the curse.

"A patch of snow! That's what he calls us."

"I seem to recall hearing that," Nashe said.

"And Versailles agrees with him! If the fools would see the value of what they have..." he blustered, so angry he lost his words. He took a long drink from the tumbler. It settled him a little.

"Excuse a foul old man on a foul day." Duchesnay walked to the mantle. "Do not mistake me. I am loyal to France, as are we all. I would like to show you something, Alan, something I value beyond everything but my family."

From a shelf recessed in the mantle, Duchesnay withdrew a small, gilt box. Opening it, he handed the box to Nashe. Inside, on a cushion of blue satin lay a golden cross of eight points, enamelled in white, and edged with gold fleur de lis.

"That is the Croix de Saint Louis, the highest honour a man may attain in New France. When a man dies his cross is returned to the King; it is not passed on. That man alone earned it. No one else is allowed it. I am proud of this little bauble, Alan. I simply cannot comprehend this blindness in Versailles. They'll allow us to die, unconcerned with this 'patch of snow', thinking only of Europe and the old ways they so frantically strive to protect. Versailles does not look to the future. The future is here. Yet they will let it pass them by."

"But, Monsieur, if this has to do with the ships today...they ran the blockade, that says something."

"I have connections, Alan, as do you. We both know the English are massing. We need reinforcements and supplies to counter them. We can't hold forever. The ships today, what did you notice?"

"They were badly scarred."

"That is unimportant."

"Then what?

"They rode high in the water. Too high. And all I saw on their decks were sailors. No soldiers. France has given us nothing."

A polite tapping on the door interrupted him. Reine Marie entered. When he saw her, he smiled, concealing his worries. She returned his smile, and Nashe felt a familiar catch in his throat at the sight of her.

"Father, you did say I might take Alan to Montmorenci. The picnic is prepared and the horses saddled and waiting."

"I apologize, daughter, for keeping him too long. We will speak again, Alan, but for now my girl awaits and as we both know she is a woman of little patience. I'll go down to see you off."

A few moments later, their panniers loaded, Nashe and Reine Marie were mounted and bidding the older couple farewell. As they turned to leave, a strange, distant rumble interrupted their goodbyes. It sounded like far off thunder.

"Oh, posh!" Reine Marie grumbled. "Now the picnic will end before it even started. I don't even see a sign of a storm."

The two men exchanged alarmed looks.

"No matter, Messieurs." The girl looked perplexed. "We'll come with you, father, to the parish. Oh, there is that thunder again. But where are the thunderheads?"

"Which direction do you think?" Duchesnay addressed Nashe curtly.

"Quebec."

"Quickly, we'll go to the promontory," he shouted and was off almost running down the path.

"Whatever is the matter?" Reine Marie queried.

Nashe dismounted. "That was not thunder, Reine Marie."

"Then what was it?"

"I don't know yet. I hope to God it's not what I think."

From the promontory they could see the city perched on the Cap. Sails indicated the ships had not docked. But they were no longer interested in ships.

"You think it was at the docks?" Duchesnay queried.

"No way of telling."

"Mother of God," Reine Marie gasped, "look at that!"

From below the cliffs a black funnel rose. Reaching into the sky, then wreathed by the wind, it covered the city. Soon they could see nothing of Quebec, only black, twisting clouds.

"It's the Lower Town," Duchesnay said flatly.

"I must leave, Monsieur," Nashe said. "My warehouses. May I take the chestnut?"

"Of course. I'll follow in the calêche."

"I'll go too," the girl interjected.

"No, daughter, you will not. That is final. Remain here with your mother until I send for you. Alan, I'll have your belongings returned to the city with me."

"Thank you, Antoine. Reine Marie, I must fly."

He was gone, riding breakneck across the heights of Beauport. Occasionally through the trees, he could see the black cloud that shrouded Quebec. He knew he had been gone too long.

## 37

No menace was more terrible than fire. Disease might come and pass, winter might be harsh and freezing, but the thought of flames roaring through narrow streets set fear in every soul who lived in Quebec. And the Lower Town was the worst of all places—buildings pressed side-by-side, buildings of bark-shingled roofs dry with age.

Nashe crossed the St. Charles hell bent into the town. He rode round the Cap flying past docks and clapboard slums and down the Rue Sault au Matelot. The smoke was so thick the horse's breathing became laboured, and Nashe could barely see in front of him. He slowed the animal as people rushed past.

The fire had spread quickly. Nashe turned up Rue St. Pierre by the traders' maisons. He watched men throw buckets of water onto their buildings or rush to smother flying sparks that nestled in the dry eaves. The fire had not begun in the Cul-de-Sac; the newly arrived ships were not at fault. St. Pierre was the centre of the conflagration. But Nashe could not determine what had caused that massive explosion.

His horse shivered with fear and exhaustion. Nashe turned away from the fire, leading the animal up Ruelle du Porche and stabled him at the Perthuis maison. Perthuis' house was safely upwind, and as Nashe gave his beast to a servant with curt instructions as to its care, he met Perthuis himself returning from the fire. Between spasms of coughing, Perthuis told Nashe what had occurred.

"The fire began at Charest's. An explosion. His maison is burning." The old man paused, choked with a fit of coughing. A servant brought him water. "The fire has leaped downwind; Rivet's place is in flames; St. Amant's is upwind but so close that it too is going. There are hundreds in the bucket lines. The sailors from the ships have been pressed." Again the old merchant coughed and spat. His colour was returning. "It is hell on St. Pierre right now, Nashe."

Nashe left him and ran down Rue Notre Dame into the Place Royale. The square was a madhouse. The bells of Notre Dame des Victoires rang a constant alarm. The smoke was so thick that he could not see to the other side of the square. All around him was confusion. People were running, shouting orders, calling desperately for children, their voices ragged, their eyes streaming.

Nashe went against the tide until he could see the Rivet maison at the lower corner of the Place. He saw flames lick the air from atop the tri-storied building. He entered the narrow street of Ruelle de la Place between Rivet's and the Barbel establishment. Perthuis had not exaggerated. In the dark, writhing reek of St. Pierre hundreds of men passed buckets in a line up from the river.

Nashe turned the corner and stepped into a seething furnace. Someone handed him a wet cloth. He held the rag to his mouth. Around him soldiers passed buckets—Guyenne regiment, probably set to leave for the frontier. He followed the line to its end. Hoarse voices croaked commands; men collapsed and were carried off, replaced by more men fighting desperately to keep their strength. Buckets of water sloshed up the line, some thrown over the men to cool them, others passed to Rivet's house. Nashe passed the burning wall there and went closer to the inferno, sweating now, breathing in ragged gasps, toward maison Charest.

There the fire roared like an animal, sparks floating in air, the air itself black. A huge beam crashed down in front of him smashing to the street, its embers scattering. It crushed a man beneath it. Six others burned their hands hoisting the fiery beam, hauling the screaming man out.

In the street Nashe encountered Francois Daine, commander of the colonial police. With him was Charest. The man had been badly burned, his right side and arm swathed in bandage, the bandage brown and bloody. But Charest would not leave the scene. The noise of the conflagration, the crackling of flames, the roar of the updraft made normal speech impossible. One look at these men told Nashe the fire had won. Daine's voice was hoarse and choked.

"Have you any men available, Nashe?" he shouted. Charest had turned away to gaze in agony at what had been his home.

"If you wish, I'll go for men."

"There's no time!"

"What can I do?"

"Join the line. No. Wait. There is an aid station set up in Leber's vaults. Better if you go there and make some order out of it."

"Immediately. Have you any idea what happened?"

Charest turned slowly, his voice cracking. He looked directly at Nashe. "Arson."

"What?"

"Gunpowder," Daine interrupted. "One of Charest's men saw a voyageur running, half on fire, just after the blast. Had Charest not been in another room he would be dead now. The entire thing stinks of a plot."

"Did anyone recognize the man?"

"We know what he was wearing. We know he was burned. I have men searching. And when he is caught, I will personally hang him with my own hand!"

Then the smoke roiled up even thicker, and Daine was gone. Nashe hustled across the street to maison Leber, directed by a panicked soldier toward the harbour side of the house. Once there, he saw a stream of men helping others through the doors into Leber's vaults. The smoke was not so bad here, the wind from the river blowing westerly. Nashe prepared himself for the horrors inside and entered the doorway.

He was not prepared for Vadnais, yet the great man blocked the passage, his arms filled with bandages and ointments. He too was blackened and dirty and as astonished as Nashe at the meeting.

"By the beaver's teeth what are you doing here?" he cried. Two men down the passage looked back at him. He quickly shielded his packages from them. "I thought you were in Beauport."

"I was. I just arrived."

"Come with me."

"I've been told to help here."

"Well, I am telling you something else." He looked menacing. "It's bedlam in there." He shrugged toward the interior. "No one knows who is where in all this confusion. Now turn around and follow me out. Don't ask questions. Follow!"

Vadnais stuffed his burden into his pockets as he led Nashe along the harbour and up Ruelle du Porche. Vadnais avoided everyone. Then Nashe realized Vadnais' purpose. There had been an explosion. Charest had nearly been killed. A voyageur had been seen running, burning. Nashe cursed himself for not having understood earlier.

Sous le Cap was nearly deserted. Vadnais led Nashe into a hovel.

"How is he?" Nashe asked as they descended a rickety stair. The smell of the basement was damp from mildew. Vadnais' face was a stone.

"Bad. He came here knowing he had allies. Why these people help him, I don't understand. I suspect he pays them well. But beware, he's delirious. He could say anything."

Vadnais knocked softly at a narrow door. A small, dirty looking girl opened it. The girl was wide-eyed with fear. On a pallet lay Jeff Ledrew, a pistol in his hand. He was in agony, his eyes wide with shock. Half his beard was gone; in its place a charred and pitted half face. His shirt had been peeled off exposing more oozing flesh. The girl had been bathing him. Nashe could smell the acrid sharpness of alcohol used as disinfectant. At the foot of the pallet lay an empty bottle of rum.

"You brought it?" Ledrew croaked.

"Yes." Vadnais produced a flask of brandy. Ledrew drank greedily, still holding his pistol. He drank to kill his pain. Waiting for the liquor to dull him, he registered the presence of Nashe.

"What are you doing here?" he muttered, his eyes opaque. "Did the girl see you?" He suddenly panicked. "What if you were recognized?"

"Owl asked me to come. I see why."

He waved his pistol, shouting: "I can care for myself!"

"If you'll put down that pistol, Jeff, I'll dress your wounds. Put it down, man, or I'll think you're trying to kill me."

"Sometimes I think you need killing, Nashe!" came the vicious reply. "The way you twist people. You do it now. You will not twist me! Never!"

Before he could say more, Vadnais popped a gag in his mouth. Until the wildness in his eyes settled, the big man would not release him. Then the brandy took effect, and Ledrew mumbled himself into insensibility. Nashe took the ointment from Vadnais and applied it gently. Occasionally, the wounded man roused as the pain seeped through his unconsciousness. Vadnais helped Nashe with the bandages. The girl was sent for a lamp.

"It seems Ledrew tried to kill Charest," Vadnais said once the girl had left. "I don't know why. But something went wrong. Ledrew raved about another powder barrel. It exploded before he had time to get out. He's sure he was seen."

"He's right," Nashe answered. "There's a rough description. They're looking for him."

"Then I must get him out of the city. I know a camp of coureurs up the Chaudière—until he recovers."

"That may take a long time."

"I know. Look, he awakens."

As he came to, Ledrew's pain seemed worse. It was a good sign. The shock was wearing off.

"We've decided to move you to safety, Jeff. It's going to take you some time to recover."

"Where?"

"The Chaudière," Vadnais answered.

"No!" Ledrew panicked. He looked at Vadnais with fear in his eyes. "I can't leave here! There is too much to do."

"You have to, Jeff," Nashe murmured. "You're in no condition, and Daine has troops looking for you. It's a matter of time until you're found. I'll take things over."

"No! It's my work! With Charest dead you are safe."

"Charest is not dead."

"Liar!"

"I've seen him myself."

"Then I'll go at him again."

"Don't be foolish. There is Howe's advance. He needs intelligence. Listen to reason. You're injured. I'll go to the frontier."

"They'll suspect you!"

"I've a perfect reason to go south. Bougainville has asked me. I'll say I intend to explore the fur territories, and then I'll disappear. Just give me your agents..."

"You can't do it. You'd die in the forest."

"Not with Vadnais."

"You could jeopardize the entire operation."

"Take the time to think..."

"You must follow the plan. You must..."

He fainted, the strain of argument too much for his weakened body. Nashe turned to Vadnais.

"You'll have to get him out of the city."

"I will. He's been strange lately."

"It's the strain. He's been here a long time, Owl; too long. He needs this rest for more than his burns."

"I'll take him up the Chaudière."

"Good. And I'll go with Bougainville. Meet me at Carillon. Have you ever been to Albany?"

"The English headquarters? Hardly."

"Well, you're going there now. I need you to guide me."

"You think this necessary? Ledrew said..."

"He need not know."

"Is that safe?"

"It's past time I went to work. Howe needs intelligence. I am the man who has it for him."

"You know." Vadnais smiled. "I'm beginning to understand those stories Ledrew told me of you. By the great beaver's balls, Nashe, I'm beginning to love you!"

## 38

The circumstance of the fire brought Bigot back to Quebec and with him de Vergor and Madeleine. The fear of blackmail weighed heavily on Nashe. He would have worried less had Reine Marie too not returned from the country. Each day he expected the worst. On a Tuesday it came.

The market was held each week in the Upper City in the Basilica Square. The square itself was at the confluence of four thoroughfares commanded by the huge bulk of Notre Dame at its eastern end. But few came to worship on Tuesdays. By eight o'clock, the place was filled with morning shoppers, government inspectors, and dour men dragged in by their wives. Nashe was there to meet Reine Marie.

She was at worship, he knew. They had arranged to meet on the steps of the church. He was across the square when he saw her emerge. She greeted acquaintances above the milling crowd. Nashe felt a brief moment of joy knowing soon her smile would be for him. He stopped for a moment to buy her some flowers. And when he next looked, her smile had vanished. He followed the direction of her gaze. De Vergor was waving at her. His blonde head stood out in the crowd as he made his way toward her.

Nashe frantically pushed toward the far steps jostled by the crowds, moving too slowly. De Vergor was nearly at the steps. Nashe cried out, to no avail, his voice lost in the din of shouting peddlers. Chevalier was suddenly in front of him smiling a greeting. Nashe pushed past the astonished merchant. Then de Vergor was beside her. Nashe found his path blocked by a cart. De Vergor spoke to her. She appeared reticent, then angry. Nashe was only half way across the square. Madeleine appeared from the Basilica's interior. She joined them. She spoke. Nashe knocked down a woman with groceries. He helped her up, apologizing, his eyes glued to the three on the steps. Reine Marie's face changed to shock. Even from thirty yards he could see it. Madeleine nodded her glorious head. The younger sister burst into tears. De Vergor comforted her in his arms.

Nashe screamed at them. They looked toward the distraction. He reached the steps below them. Reine Marie retreated into the church. De Vergor stepped directly into Nashe's path as he tried to follow. He was smiling.

"Why, Monsieur Nashe, you seem out of breath."

"What is the meaning of this, de Vergor?"

"Meaning? Meaning? I merely spoke to my woman concerning her problems with a certain unfaithful lover."

"Indeed, Monsieur," Madeleine joined him, "I found it necessary to protect my naive little sister from lustful wolves."

"You told her?"

"Everything, Nashe," de Vergor grinned.

"I expected blackmail at least, from you."

"Oh, nothing so mundane as that. We have done this simply for the pleasure and, of course, to protect the name of Duchesnay."

"I will see her."

"I doubt very much she'd appreciate that. You overestimate yourself. The girl is mine, Nashe."

The force of his fist was tripled by hatred as it hammered into the Frenchman's stomach. De Vergor heaved, and then made a gurgling sound as last night's wine spewed from his mouth. He doubled over and fell headlong down the steps. Madeleine tried to go to him. Nashe grasped her arm.

"And will you strike me too, Monsieur? I have known all along you are no gentleman."

"You're not worth the time," he muttered viciously. "But your spewing friend will soon demand satisfaction, and I will give it to him. He and I have duelled once. That time I did not treat him seriously. This time, I will!"

She shook his hand loose. A crowd had gathered. She fell to her knees on the steps by de Vergor. Nashe, shaking with rage, ran into the Basilica. The great church was cold and, but for a far off chanting, silent. Nashe's heels clicked hollowly as he crossed the stone floor of the vestibule. He peered through the archway leading to the nave. She was not there. Turning left, he came to a spiral stair leading up.

An open door led to the gallery. He knew instinctively she was beyond it. Then through the door he saw her, her hands resting on a stone balustrade. She was not weeping. She simply stared out over the space below. Turning slowly, as she heard the soft click of his boots, she did not appear angry; only empty. Her eyes had lost their lustre.

He moved toward her then hesitated as she half raised her hands. Her hands were trembling.

"It's true..." she said. It was no question.

"Yes."

"My sister?"

"Oh, God, what can I say? It was while you would not see me. The sleigh trip. I was drunk most of the time, I..."

"I don't wish to hear."

"They planned it, Reine Marie. I was a fool; you must believe me."

"This is one of your secrets?"

"Yes."

"There are more?"

"Reine Marie..."

"As awful as this?"

"In honesty," he sighed, "yes."

"I must go home, Alan."

"Surely we can talk..."

"Are you prepared to divulge everything? Now? This is a place of truth."

"I can't..." The words seared his soul.

"And neither can I. It's good you are leaving."

"I will not leave!"

"I will not see you. I will go home to Beauport."

"You hate me."

"I can never hate you." Her voice echoed softly in the cavernous church.

The softness of her steps as she departed rang in his ears like cannon fire. He stood where she had, overlooking the gothic grace of the cathedral. He thought, this once, he should pray. Yet he could not bring himself to do it. He had never prayed. Even in the shadowed confines of his father's little church in the Cotswolds, seeing his father stern and loveless before him, he could not pray. In this war, the French were his enemy. Yet his father had married a French woman. The French were his enemy, yet his mother had been good and loving.

He would not pray. Not in a French church. Not to a French god. No matter the depth of his love for a French woman. No matter how French he believed himself to be.

## 39

Bougainville was so filled with his plans that he failed to notice Nashe's state. It had been given the major to arrange the western expedition. He attacked with his usual vigour the organization of the twenty barques that would carry men and supplies upriver to Lachine. It was a time consuming and meticulous task, and it was Bougainville's forté.

Nashe met his companion on the appointed morning, packed and ready for the journey. It was a warm, pleasant morning, the sun rising above the hilltops of Lauzon, the St. Laurent still as glass, as two hundred soldiers from Guyenne embarked. A fife and drums saw them off. With Nashe accompanying Bougainville and Bourlamaque and two Guyenne officers in the lead boat, they departed. Only once did Nashe steal a wistful glance back. As they passed a mile upstream of the city the little cove of Anse au Foulon, Nashe could not help himself. The bank was covered in foliage now. He could not see the steep, winding path to the top. But there in the reeds at the river's edge was a small, grassy glade. As his feelings welled, he turned from his past to gaze upriver. He had no idea then that his future would bring him back to that placid cove.

The fleet rowed its way up the St. Laurent and when the wind was right broke out its sails. There was little to do but watch the shoreline. Their pace was steady, the days warm and easy. They played cards a great deal, and talked. Inevitably the talk was of war. Captain Berthier, one of the officers, spoke of seeing the English at Louisbourg.

"We saw fifteen ships lying off the coast. Our ship's captain was worried. He found it irregular that the British navy would not give chase to French frigates."

"What did he make of it, Berthier?" Bourlamaque asked.

"He believed the English were massing for an assault on Louisbourg. Probably they have begun by now."

"And it will be weeks before we hear the outcome." Bougainville chafed. "That is the problem with this country...it's too big. Why this little jaunt of ours is equivalent to a journey across half of Europe."

"Indeed," Bourlamaque returned. "But if Louisbourg should fall our eastern flank will be open. And the St. Laurent will become an English river."

"Only as far as Quebec. That is one place they will never pass."

"This pessimism troubles me, Messieurs," Bougainville intervened. "You assume the English will take Louisbourg. I have been there, my friends. The fort is impregnable, rocky coasts lined with cannon...the English could never land. No, Messieurs, Louisbourg will halt the English in their tracks. And they cannot bypass it for fear of our forces attacking them from the rear."

"There is a problem with Louisbourg," Nashe said quietly.

"Ah, the merchant becomes general." Berthier smiled. "And what, my dear Nashe, is the problem with Louisbourg?"

"I landed there last year. I took a tour of the batteries with a gunnery officer. He mentioned that all the fort's cannon faced seaward. An attack from the land would cause them great difficulty."

"Have you any idea the problems presented in landing men from boats under fire?" Berthier was patronizing.

Nashe decided further argument would only create suspicion. He leaned back against a gunwale languidly. "Of course, Captain, this armchair generalship of mine has its faults. First, I am ignorant of military ways and second, I am, Monsieur, a confirmed coward."

"But you are with us on this tour." Bourlamaque smiled. "That hardly indicates cowardice."

"But if you look closely, Colonel, you will see the nature of my reasoning. I enter this war accompanied by two hundred of France's best troops and her most accomplished officers. Besides, I'll be turning west and hiding myself among the gentle beaver. My fight will be for comfort, Messieurs. I do not envy you yours."

They disembarked at Lachine, the great rapids preventing further progress by river, and transported troops and supplies on the arduous portage around the rock strewn waters. When they reached the southern end of the rapids, Nashe found a surprise waiting. There were no more barques to be loaded. Instead, harboured in the river at Ile Perrot, was a ship.

It was a schooner complete with cannon and swivel guns, and loaded to the scuppers with casks. There were large rolls of lead sheet for casting into shot, and sacks of dried apples, demijohns of military rum and room enough, barely, for the soldiers of Guyenne. Nashe looked to Bougainville for an explanation. The major was smiling proudly.

"An improvement on open boats, is it not? We control the lake, Alan. This beauty and her sisters hold it for us. You see now why the English hesitate to attack our centre?"

"An inland navy," Nashe murmured.

"It will not be so easy for the English to try our forts at Niagara and Frontenac. We want this land, Alan. This proves it to them."

"Indeed it does."

This was the beginning of wilderness for Alan Nashe. Albany was a long way off. He had no idea how he would get there. Nashe thought he knew a great deal of Kanata. He was about to discover how ignorant he was.

## 40

The schooner sailed upstream in a wide river dotted with thousands of islands. They made a strange and beautiful picture. And in the midst of this maze of waterways, Bourlamaque joined Nashe as the latter stood on the ship's prow. It was not something the quiet colonel often did, and Nashe prepared himself for orders. But Bourlamaque had not come to discuss war. As he spoke, the river slowly widened into the expanse of Lac Ontario.

"There are five of these, Monsieur Nashe."

"Of what, Colonel?"

"Five inland seas. Each connected to the other by narrows and straits. You can travel more than a thousand leagues on these freshwater oceans, Nashe, further and further into the land. It is breathtaking to think of it."

"And strategic as well, I understand," Nashe mentioned.

"Of that there is little doubt." Bourlamaque smiled. "These waters are our highways. They connect the forts and are passages for the fur trade. But to think of the size of these lakes, to consider the beauty of their shores, is to contemplate God's work. This may be an age of scepticism, Monsieur, an age of man's growing self-importance, yet to see this, this timelessness. There is little need for man here. Bring Hume or Voltaire to this place and ask them to quote their theories here. They would not know how to begin."

"You are beginning to sound a little like Rousseau, Monsieur Bourlamaque."

"No, Monsieur, Rousseau is beginning to sound like the new man, like men I have heard here. This is the wave of the future, Nashe. These are the wild lands we will try to tame and in the end they will change us. Unfortunately, we may lose all this."

"Colonel, do you really believe that?"

"I believe we might, Nashe. Though not," he added, "without a fight. I thank you for listening to me, Nashe. I enjoy your company."

"It's been a mutual pleasure, Colonel."

"The world is changing. I just thought I should let you know," he smiled. Nashe spent the next hour wondering about the colonel's motives.

\*\*\*

Frontenac was a rough-hewn structure, wood palisades above which flew a gallant, lonely fleur de lis. It was a typical frontier fort: uncomfortable, spartan, and cramped. It squatted on a hill overlooking the green expanse of marshland that surrounded it, but there was a channel from the lake and below the fort was a sheltered harbour safe from the weather and seaborne attack. Nashe saw three schooners at rest in that harbour, the fleet Bougainville had spoken of.

From here the supply lines fanned out to the western forts. It was a strategic place, but the swamp made life especially hard here and not just in winter. Spring brought hordes of mosquitoes. Nashe hated the place and was only too pleased to leave it behind. He hoped Niagara would not be the same. He was eaten alive by insects. Bougainville laughed at his sufferings.

"There are men who thrive on this life, Alan. In a short while, we'll meet one of them. We'll follow the coastline to the Toronto carrying place. There we will pick up Joncaire."

"What is his importance to us? And what in heaven's name is a carrying place?"

"This Toronto, as the natives call it, is a great bay where two rivers run into the lake from the north, passages to the fur grounds. It's been a meeting place for years for voyageurs and natives on their way to Montreal. There is another such place across the lake called Oswego. There was once an English fort there. It was destroyed a few years ago in the fighting. Still, both of these places are strategic. We've heard rumours the English are returning to Oswego. Joncaire will know. And he is to be our guide to Carillon. He knows this land as you know certain ladies' boudoirs."

"How far is it across the lake?"

"With a good wind a day's voyage."

"It truly is an inland sea."

"And one very important to us."

"Frontenac seems safe; a long way from the fighting."

"Our worry is Niagara. It's at the western end of this lake, at the confluence of a great river that flows from another lake called Herrie. Niagara is close to the English. Montcalm expects an attack upon it. But look there, those grey herons...this land may have its evils but even paradise had snakes."

"But no mosquitoes, I'm sure," Nashe muttered wondering where next to scratch.

They sailed for two days with the coast in view. Seagulls squealed overhead, and osprey would fish alongside the ship. The men too fished and caught copious numbers of pickerel and the largest trout Nashe had ever seen. Then on the second day, as it passed a line of sandy bluffs at the water's edge, the schooner entered a bay.

A single canoe set off from the shore. Nashe noticed four natives standing in the vessel, paddling with assured, strong strokes. At its prow a strange looking fellow stood on the gunwales. Nashe knew enough about canoes to realize the precariousness of this position. Yet the man seemed at home there. All of them did—the vessel an extension of their legs, as though they walked on water.

The man in the prow was old, judging from his weather-beaten face, at least in his fifties. His hair was tousled salt and pepper and hung as the natives wore theirs, long and greased. He was balding slightly at the temples. Yet for the age of his face, his body, clad scantily in buckskin, was muscle, the arms sinewy, the stomach taut, and his dark skin bronzed by the sun. He was the portrait of a man accustomed to hard life, toughened by it, at home in it.

It was not until they were introduced that Nashe realized how small Joncaire was; his head barely reaching Nashe's chin. He instantly took a liking to the small, aging half savage with his gat-toothed smile and sparkling eyes.

Joncaire was a fount of knowledge. He knew of the English at Oswego. Maybe fifty men. He knew of scouting sorties by Rangers around Niagara. He told them the native alliance was leaning away from the French. Even Joncaire himself was having trouble with the tribes.

"I don't understand this preoccupation with natives, Monsieur Joncaire," Nashe queried, wanting to know more of this hidden side of the war.

"It's a complex issue, Alan," Bougainville enjoined. "But simply, in forest warfare, the natives are as indispensable as cavalry in Europe."

"In what ways?"

"They know the forest, Monsieur Nashe," Joncaire broke in, his mouth stuffed with food. "The tribes fight total war...and expect the same in return. They are peaceful people most of the time, but lead them to war and they mean it. To the south of us, lay the domains of the Mohawk, Oneidas, Onondaga, Cayuga, and Seneca. They have wavered to both sides for years. Now they have joined together. They see themselves caught in the middle. So they profit by it. They belong to the side that offers more guns and kettles and rum. If these Five Nations as they are called swing toward the English, and it looks like they will, we are in for trouble. They control the land to the south, and as an alliance the other tribes fear them."

"But why? Surely other tribes can form together?"

"Because of all the tribes, these ones know war. A hundred years ago they formed an Iroquois nation and nearly wiped out the Huron. They are dangerous, Monsieur. And speaking of that, Colonel Bourlamaque, I suggest we arrive at Niagara before dawn tomorrow. We may catch some English scouts lurking."

"I'll give the orders."

"And I will to bed, messieurs," Joncaire smiled. "It has been some time since I last used a bed. I look forward to it."

***

Dawn was a cold, grey drizzle. The schooner ploughed slowly toward Niagara its decks lined with men peering through telescopes trying to pierce the fog. A cry issued from the bowsprit, then another from the yardarm. Sails were unfurled quickly and the ship took speed. Nashe lifted his glass in the direction of a pointed finger and made out a hazy motion. They came closer. He saw suddenly two whaleboats filled with men. Then the boats disappeared in a bank of fog. When he saw them again, they were off in a different direction.

"They've seen us," Joncaire muttered beside him. "They've turned for shore. If they get in close, we'll lose them." He ran to the bow, Nashe following, and grabbed a swivel gun attached to the railing. Shouting orders, the little man swiftly loaded. The ship gained on the English boats. Nashe could see faces through his telescope now. He could hear the creak of oarlocks.

The bow swivel gun opened fire, and grapeshot rattled into the water around the boats, splashing silver and grey. Some men twisted as they were hit. The ship closed. Another volley split the air. One of the boats ripped into pieces, and its men spilled into the water. They swam for their lives.

Musket fire opened up from the masts and another volley of grapeshot. The second boat was holed. The ship ploughed in among the swimmers. Joncaire was suddenly on the railing, a knife in his teeth. He dived from the boat disappearing beneath the surface, then re-appeared behind a native. His weapon raised and plunged in a spurt of blood, and then Joncaire and the man were gone, the native gone forever.

When next he surfaced, Joncaire was directly behind a Ranger. No knife. He grabbed the man's hair, keeping well away from his grappling fingers. Two sailors dived to his aid. The ship came about. In a few minutes all four were aboard, and the Ranger's hands were quickly bound. Nashe offered Joncaire a towel. The little man refused it simply shaking himself like an animal.

"Why did you spare the Ranger?" Nashe queried.

"We need information. The Mohawk would not have told us. The white man will."

127

"You are so sure?"

"I am."

"As you said, the native expects no mercy..."

"You are learning, young man. In this war the merciful quickly become the dead."

## 41

Where Frontenac had been a bare, infested outpost, Niagara was a sanctuary. Set on a triangular spit of land with the river on one side and the lake on another, fully half the fortress was protected by water. The landward side was an imposing system of earthworks, palisades, ravelins, and a moat. Entry to the fort was gained through a blockhouse inside which the engineer Pouchot had placed a drawbridge. He called this entrance, ironically, "The Gate of the Five Nations".

For a year, men had laboured to make Niagara invincible. They were regulars, troupes de terre, men who knew their business. The walls of Niagara controlled the west. And the English, all these men knew, would come. They would have to hold a long time whatever the cost. So along with their work, they drilled daily. Few complained. Not among proud men. And the proudest of all seemed to be Joncaire.

"And well he should be," Bougainville noted. "His father and a man called de Lery created this place. This is his home. He was born here."

As they crossed the drawbridge, an honour guard snapped to attention, every man in dress whites, every man sharp and disciplined. Inside the walls Nashe noted stone houses and magazines, a bakery, a parade square and across the square, its bulk backing onto the lake, a magnificent stone chateau. The building was three stories high and fifty yards in length, its upper floor a watch deck peering over the palisades or out across the lake. Five hundred miles from civilization, Nashe had not expected a castle, yet here one was, the centrepiece of an impregnable stronghold.

In the centre of the parade square, a straight-backed captain of the Béarn regiment greeted them. His name was Jeunesse. He looked every inch the professional. By the end of the greetings, the troops had formed lines in the square, on one side Guyenne, on the other, Béarn.

"I welcome you to His Majesty's fortress Niagara, Colonel Bourlamaque," Captain Jeunesse spoke stiffly. "My men and this stronghold await your inspection. After the inspection, dinner is planned in the officer's dining hall. Perhaps I might have the honour of inviting Messieurs Nashe and Joncaire to join us. With your permission, Sir."

The tour of the fortress took two hours. From the twenty-foot earthworks, their huge cannon threatening the river, to the meanest of bakeries and latrines Bourlamaque noted everything. It was an imposing place, and by the end of the tour, Nashe recognized the genius of French engineering.

"Impressed, Major Bougainville?" Joncaire, who had accompanied them through every inch of the tour, smiled proudly.

"Indeed, I am. Your father and this de Lery must have been great men."

"Thank you, Monsieur. They were."

"And you have lived here all your life?" Nashe inquired.

"Not exactly here, Monsieur. Two miles upriver is the beginning of the gorge. It has been a carrying place for years. My father built a blockhouse there long before this place. And a trading post as well. That is my true home, and that of my brother. Perhaps you might meet my brother, and after that we will go to the greatest wonder that nature has ever wrought."

"I've been told of the falls, Monsieur. I look forward to it, and the visit with your brother."

"But meanwhile, Messieurs," Jeunesse intervened, "the wonders of my kitchen await you. Through here, Messieurs. We have much to discuss."

The dinner was a paragon of fellowship. Stories were exchanged freely and a great deal of wine consumed. Joncaire, however, departed early. He said he had work to do. Nashe thought little of it. That night Nashe shared a small room in the officers' quarters with Bougainville.

As he pulled the wool blanket over himself and rolled his face to the wall, he noticed he was cold. Even in summer the stone was damp. Winter would be hellish here, he thought. But more than the cold kept him awake that night. Joncaire was at his work. The Mohawk would not talk, he had said. The Englishman would. Nashe discovered that night what he meant.

His opinion of Joncaire changed then. He had been fooled by the unassuming nature and the man's quick smile. No longer. He was reminded of something Trémais had said to him once that the forest took certain men for its own. Nashe shivered a little. The room was frigid. He listened a long time to the Ranger's screams from somewhere below him. Winter would be hell here, he thought again, but hell was where you found it.

One man had found it now.

## 42

The river's placid surface belied its current, a powerful wash that emptied into the lake. Their canoe stayed near the shoreline in easier waters. Still it took the three of them paddling hard, Joncaire, Nashe, and a silent native who was Joncaire's companion, to move upstream to the great escarpment that rose from the land like a huge sleeping beast. The mouth of the beast was the gorge, narrow and three hundred feet high, from which spewed the river. At the mouth, at the very base of the gorge, was Joncaire's blockhouse. No soldiers here, the compound was populated by coureurs and natives.

"From here, we can go no further upriver," Joncaire said as the canoe turned for shore.

"But why?" Nashe queried. "Surely we can enter the gorge?"

"The river is not so friendly from here. Just listen."

Nashe tuned his ears but heard nothing more than birdsong and the voices of men on shore.

"Listen more closely," Joncaire insisted. "You've become accustomed to the sound."

And just beneath the other sounds, there was indeed something, a subtle vibration, a distant constant sonorousness audible only when listened for. It was as if the air itself were breathing.

"You hear the sound of living water, Monsieur Nashe, the pulse of this land."

At the trade house, they discovered Joncaire's brother gone. Strangers had been seen across the river. The brother had left to investigate. The three climbed the escarpment following a portage path. Up the slope of the mountain it ran, twisting through trees and then along the lip of the gorge. The climb was difficult. The three men carried only muskets, but Nashe could imagine the strain of canoes and packs on such a climb. He did not envy the men who had to make it.

They took the edge of the gorge when they reached the summit. The forest here was light and nearly shadeless, almost magical. And always there was the sound of the river. They came to a great bend in the gorge and Nashe saw something he would never forget. In the depths of the canyon, the river's incredible force prevented it from making the turn. And so instead of turning it had gouged a great bowl half a mile wide and within the bowl a huge, hissing whirlpool. The river ran into itself, reversing its flow and then around and around in hypnotic circles until in the centre it seemed to spin faster than the eye could perceive. Nashe felt the awesome power of the thing, almost alive. He turned dumbstruck toward Joncaire. The Frenchman nodded.

"I've seen trees the size of towers come down there, and they have disappeared. One may wait and wait and still see nothing return. It must be a great depth."

They travelled again upstream; deep in the gorge the river became a seething torrent. The noise of the roiling water forced the men to shout to be heard. And yet as they continued along the gorge the roar of the torrent was slowly overborne. Nashe became aware of the other noise only in an instant of realization. A boom. An endless boom, like thunder never ending.

Through the trees he glimpsed it first; through the trees that edged the impossible pit and the preposterous immensity of one sea emptying into another. Joncaire held his arm. It was good he did so. The cacophony of rolling thunder, the fantastic horseshoe of falling silver and mist, enticed Nashe close to the edge. He could not see the bottom. Mist and a wondrous rainbow in the depths of the pit obscured it.

Joncaire drew him back into the trees. "To the natives this is a holy place. Each year a girl is chosen. She is placed in a canoe above the falls where the river is fast and wide. They tell me girls go willingly. I think you understand why. My father has seen it. I never have. It is something they allow to no strangers, something important to them."

They remained an hour. Silent. Unspeaking. They watched as the waters roared over the cliff and into the cup of the gods. And finally Joncaire shouted that it was time to return. They followed the twisting canyon again. The sound fell away. All seemed hushed. They passed once again the whirlpool.

Suddenly there was a different sound, the spit-fire of muskets from across the gorge. The three men saw running shadows amid the trees. Two natives emerged from the forest, peered quickly about, and then dived back in. More men were running further down. The fight had no order, just quick fire, reload, and fire again.

"Rangers," hissed Joncaire. "My brother has found the strangers he sought. Are you much of a shot with a musket, Nashe?"

"Across the gorge? I can't tell who is friend or foe."

"I can. Prime your piece and make ready."

As Joncaire spoke, three Rangers in green uniforms emerged. They moved cautiously down the edge of the gorge, obviously in a flanking manoeuvre.

Down from them, two other men came out of the trees and into clear view of their enemies.

"My brother," Joncaire said grimly.

"He hasn't seen the Rangers," Nashe observed.

"No, but we have. Fire at the last man in line, Nashe, when I tell you."

Joncaire's brother moved along the lip of the precipice oblivious to the Rangers. The three Englishmen deployed themselves behind cover. But their backs were in plain view of the three who watched from across the gorge. Nashe wondered why Joncaire did not give the order. The men came closer. The Rangers' weapons rose. Then Joncaire shouted. Nashe missed his man on purpose. The other two died instantly. Nashe's man gaped across the chasm toward them. Then the two Frenchmen went after him.

He ran. But a native appeared in his path. The native charged, skimming the broken ground like a deer. The Ranger pulled a pistol and fired point blank. The man spun with the force of the ball. He kept his feet, blood gushing from his neck. His momentum carried him into the Ranger and the force of the charge drove both back to the lip of the cliff. The native was dead already. The Ranger with the body draped around him scrabbled desperately for a handhold. Then they fell. It seemed as though a long time passed, the two men falling, one silent, one screaming. Down, down so far, touching no protruding edge, free fall and flailing limbs in slow motion turning over and over. It seemed they would fall forever.

Nashe could not hear the splash. The roar of the river had swallowed it just as its waters took the two men...gone, as though never existing. Joncaire was smiling. His eyes glittered with a strange light. Those eyes were not human.

An ensign from the fort met Nashe when they returned to Joncaire's compound. The ensign was in a hurry. He took Nashe quickly to a waiting boat.

"The English prisoner has given information," he said briefly. "Major Bougainville sent me to tell you the inspection has been cut short. He and Colonel Bourlamaque are leaving tonight for Carillon. The major thought you should know."

Nashe left immediately with his escort. He did not bid Joncaire goodbye. Again Nashe recalled Trémais' words. The forest indeed had taken this man and had made him its emissary. For all the crooked, gat-toothed grin and friendly manner, Nashe feared Joncaire as he feared no other.

Joncaire was an alien.

## 43

"The English have begun to move," Bougainville spoke quietly in the twilight. He stood facing Nashe on the wharf below the fort. Men were already boarding the schooner. "Apparently a large force has set out north from Fort Edward. Howe's army. It seems certain they will attack our centre. Bourlamaque and I must reach Carillon before they arrive."

"You believe the ravings of a tortured man?" Nashe interjected. "Joncaire could have made him say anything."

"He simply corroborated our suspicions. Scouts have been reporting activity for weeks. And the English have sent a force to Oswego."

"But surely that means they're considering Frontenac. Oswego is far west of Carillon."

"It is a feint. And a good one. It prevents our sending reinforcements east."

"But with Oswego occupied how do you propose to get through?"

"That's why we leave tonight. By daybreak we'll be far out into the lake, away from prying eyes. We will land tomorrow night below Oswego, then travel cross-country to Carillon. With Joncaire leading and only six men as bodyguards we should slip through easily. I simply wished to bid you goodbye before we left. It's been good having you along."

"I'm going with you."

"What?"

"I wish to accompany you. I will be no bother."

"But what of your trade inspection?"

"It can wait. This war is far more important now. If Howe's army is moving, Montcalm will need every man he can lay hands on. It's time merchants became soldiers. This is our land too."

"That, my friend, is the spirit more merchants should acquire."

"Then I may come, untrained as I am?"

"I've seen you fight, you remember. And your assessment is right. Montcalm will need every man. But see, here are the colonel and Joncaire. Pack your things quickly. Now you become a soldier for France!"

\*\*\*

In the dark chill before dawn, a whaleboat wafted in the choppy waves of the lake. Ten men skimmed down ropes into the waiting boat. They travelled light, each man bearing only a small pack: rations for twelve days, flint and steel, ammunition, a spare pair of boots. They took their positions quietly pushing away from the schooner's shadow and with muffled oars began the task of rowing to shore. They rowed quickly, one man at the tiller, six at the oars, the other three peering into the gloom their muskets cocked and ready.

In a matter of minutes they arrived at the beach. It was still dark but the men could glimpse a subtle lightening on the horizon. Two men stripped off their clothing and hauled the boat back into deeper waters. Once there, one of the swimmers slipped into the boat prying loose a cork plug wedged in the bottom. Soft gurgling mingled with the sounds of the waves. The two men rested on the gunwales keeping the vessel steady as it slowly filled and sank.

They swam to shore, dried themselves, and dressed. In ten minutes the beach was swept with branches and its environs swallowed by the forest. As dawn's grey harbinger rose there was no trace of the visitors. Birds began their morning chorus. They too had not been disturbed.

\*\*\*

For days the ten men toiled through rolling mountains. The mountain chains ran north-south so the journey east was arduous. It was a realm of ancient forest, old as the earth was old, filled with leaves dappled by sunlight and the quiet of a primeval world. And the mountains, their dark green flanks flecked with morning mists, their distant summits seen through trees almost purple against the blue sky. It was a place so wild and trackless that it was a tomb to the inexperienced. But Joncaire was at home in it. He moved through this world as easily as Nashe navigated the byways of London. Always in the lead, always sure of his direction, he would often turn to smile at the men behind him trudging uncertainly through the tangle.

And always there were the clouds of mosquitoes and layers of sunflower oil and mud pasted on each day as an antidote. The insects never seemed to bother Joncaire. He would chuckle quietly at his companions' misery then turn to the lead again.

Occasionally, on a summit Joncaire would find a high tree and climb it, peering through its foliage at the verdant carpet that spread interminably around him. He scouted for signs—wood smoke, a flutter of birds, anything that might betray another presence. Until they neared Carillon, there was always nothing.

But as they closed on their destination, Joncaire became more careful. He saw smoke one morning ahead. He said it was soldiers; no woodsman would give himself away so easily. Joncaire was often gone for hours as he scouted ahead. They went slowly, carefully picking their way. They came upon more signs. Once it was a canteen, English regular issue, other times they found shreds of clothing torn by thorns and held there.

Then one afternoon, Joncaire appeared suddenly ahead of them. Without a sound he signalled them off the path. They hid in the underbrush and soon heard the sounds of men, the tinkling of metal on metal, the crunch of boots, and the shock of English voices. A large party passed by, led by Rangers. The troop was dressed in scarlet; Nashe could not see their facings. It dawned on him suddenly that all he need do was make a sound and the English would have two of Montcalm's senior officers. But Joncaire was near him. And Joncaire would kill him quick as light. This was not his moment. Somehow he sensed there was more for him yet.

The party passed, thirty men rumbling through the forest oblivious to watching eyes. The English still had much to learn, Nashe decided. And the ten men quickened their pace putting distance between themselves and the English patrol. They were a little more hurried now, a little less careful. Even Joncaire appeared to relax. It was, of course, a mistake.

They arrived at a fast flowing stream. Joncaire informed them it was the last before Carillon. Their anticipation betrayed them then. Rather than scout the opposite bank, Joncaire encouraged a quick crossing. Nashe was one of the first to cross following a soldier through the fast flow. The rushing stream obscured all other sounds.

The first arrow pierced the soldier in front of him. The man died clutching the shaft that transfixed his neck. The second arrow drove through his chest just as he melted into the water. Nashe was in midstream. The next arrow would be for him.

He tried to run in the waist deep water but succeeded only in floundering. Musket fire opened up to his rear spurring him on. He tripped on a submerged rock and just as he did an arrow sang by his ear stabbing the shoreline in front of him. He wheeled around, desperately searching the treetops. The first shot had been a lucky miss. The next would be his death.

**44**

Bougainville and Bourlamaque plunged into the stream with one of the guards. The brave soldier waded backward facing the skirmish, his eyes searching out snipers. Joncaire and the four other guards stood their ground on the bank firing madly into the undergrowth.

Nashe saw the arrow shoot from the leaves of an overhanging beech. He fired. A native fell in a crackling, smashing drop from the tree. He was dead before he hit the ground. But Nashe's shot had come too late and Bourlamaque spun around, the arrow deep in his shoulder. He wavered, saw Nashe and stretched his hands out to him, then fell into deeper water the current hauling him quickly downstream. His bodyguard dived after immediately; then Bougainville after both. There was nothing else to do, swim or die like a duck in midstream. Nashe pushed off the shallows and into deep water his arm holding musket and powder away from the wet.

Shots from the forest splashed around them like raindrops. The soldier now holding Bourlamaque was hit but kept swimming. They reached a bend where the current washed them ashore to the bank opposite the ambush. Only a hundred yards downstream the landfall afforded them the chance to regroup. The firing from above was heavy now. It was obvious the attack was in force. Joncaire and the guards stood little chance.

"Where in the name of the Virgin did they come from?" Bougainville gasped.

"By their numbers it seems they're the party we hid from," Nashe answered.

"But there were no natives in that party!"

"We should have known better."

"Joncaire should have known."

"He is paying for that now, Antoine," Nashe said as they heard the litany of fire upstream.

"They need help, Nashe. Are you wounded?"

"Just a graze; nothing."

"We must help those men somehow."

"No Sir," Bourlamaque's guard spoke. He was bleeding from the side of his head. The miniball had torn away part of his ear. "Our aim is to get you and the colonel to Carillon. The men back there know that, Sir. They're fighting so we can escape. They expect no help, Sir."

"How is the colonel?"

"Poorly, Major. The arrow has pierced his shoulder through to the bone. He's fainted."

"And you?"

"Good enough, Sir. I can carry the colonel."

"Then we'd better move quickly."

"But where, Antoine?" Nashe exclaimed. "We'll be lost in an hour. We have no idea where the fort is..."

"East," Bougainville countered. "The trail seemed well trod. It must lead to Carillon."

"The trail is the first place they'll seek us."

"We need the trail for speed."

"I think the major's right, Monsieur Nashe," the soldier intervened. "I can't carry Colonel Bourlamaque through thick brush. We must use the path. We must go now. When that shooting ends, they'll come after us."

"Then I'll take the rear," Nashe stated. "My powder and piece are dry. We may need them to cover the retreat."

"Agreed," said Bougainville. "I'll take the lead. I'm afraid you must carry the colonel, Corporal, by yourself. When you tire, I'll take him."

"Load your piece with shot, Monsieur Nashe," the corporal instructed. "Miniballs kill only one man. Shot will stop a few."

They pushed their way through the tangled verdure finding the path quickly. It seemed to curve to follow the stream. It was a well-travelled way, hard packed and easy this side of the stream—a man made path, not the spoor of animals. The corporal was a strapping fellow who had little trouble with his burden. Nashe, in the rear, kept listening to the firing of guns.

They ran on for some time. Then the corporal stumbled where he should not have. The man staggered a few yards then sank to his knees. His head and ear were bleeding profusely. It was clear he could carry his colonel no further.

"We'll rest two minutes," Bougainville ordered, "then I'll take the colonel. After all," he smiled weakly, "I am an officer's aide. Now is the time I prove my worth."

"Listen," Nashe summoned them to silence. The shooting had stopped.

"The end of Joncaire," Bougainville murmured. "We must move now. Help me with the colonel, Nashe. Corporal, take the lead. Up the path as far as we can then into the forest. We'll hide."

"From natives, Major? They'll track us as easy as follow a river."

"That can't be helped. Go. Fast. If you see a place, turn off and wait for me. Alan, I'm afraid I must ask you to take the rear again."

They ran hard, as fast as Bougainville could carry the colonel. In fifteen minutes, they covered some distance. The path was good. It helped their speed. And then they entered a valley so deep in the forest bowels, so surrounded by verdure that Nashe thought of it as some cloistered way. Its pillars were the trunks of trees, its arches of leaves. It was a beautiful, mystic place, long and straight so that he could see from one end to the other. A forest cathedral two hundred yards long. It was a good place to surrender.

His work could end now. The truth would come out. He would be a hero: Bougainville and Bourlamaque in one swoop. He would never again see Reine Marie. He would go back to England and try to forget.

The path began its uphill climb out of the valley. Nashe stopped at the foot of the incline. He could see the full length of the leafy corridor, a suitable place for betrayal. But up the path, he saw Bougainville stop. Looking back at him, the young major simply nodded and set his burden down.

Six natives appeared at the opposite end, their faces painted black and red. They ran silently, moccasins skimming the earth. Bougainville stepped to Nashe's side. He primed his pistol. Behind the natives came redcoats and then the green of Rangers. Thirty men at least filled the long passage. And then Bougainville did a most surprising thing. He stepped into the path, smiling grimly. He was not preparing to surrender. His pistol rose as he aimed at the leaders. Nashe could hardly believe what he saw. He raised his own arm to strike down the major's weapon.

Then the valley exploded; from both rims through the trees, volleys of musketry blasted down on the English. There was chaos; men screaming and smoke filled the air. Another volley let loose. From both sides, French soldiers streamed into the valley. Those pitiful few English remaining raised their hands in surrender. The smoke cleared slowly, wafting upward into the leafy canopy. Men lay moaning on the ground, others kneeling beside them trying to help. One youth wandered aimlessly blood streaming from his mouth. The ambush took less than five minutes.

"At your service, Major Bougainville. I see you have convinced my friend Nashe to become a coureur du bois," a cheerful voice rang out behind them. Charles de Longeuil stood ten feet up the path looking happily at the carnage. He strolled casually down the gradient as if he were out for a morning walk.

"De Longeuil! I must say I've not seen so welcome a sight since I left the embrace of my dear Naudière." Bougainville tried to be light, but the shock remained in his trembling voice. "How in heaven's name did you find us?"

"Quite simple, really. Routine patrol in force. I have forty men with me. We heard the firing near the stream. No idea it was you, of course, but this is the only path from that ford. We assumed an English patrol had met one of ours. It was just a question of waiting, though I must say when I saw you two scurrying down the valley, I nearly gave it away. A very brave thing, you two: stopping there to fight them. Splendid, Messieurs. You should be recommended for decoration. Nashe, my dear fellow, you seem at a loss for words."

"I am overwhelmed. Thank you, Charles. I feel somewhat weak. I am no soldier."

"But of course you are, Monsieur! I've seen few soldiers stop and stand to the odds you faced. Magnificent! The general will be ecstatic!"

"Still and all, I could do with a drink."

"And that you shall have! We are barely two leagues from the fort. You gentlemen deserve a celebratory bottle. That will be my gift of welcome!"

"Your gift, Charles, has already been given." Bougainville smiled. "I thank you for my life."

"Nonsense, Major. You'd probably have killed them all with your bare hands."

In a few moments, the French gathered their prisoners. In a column, they led them past the three men discoursing on the path. As the line of men passed, de Longeuil studied them, then again turned to his friends.

"Have you noticed the English uniforms?" He pointed to the passing redcoats. "They are cut to the waist. Fit for forest war. See, the coats are so short they will not catch in brambles. The English learn their lessons quickly."

"That will be Howe's doing. Obviously his reputation is deserved."

"Indeed, Major. They've learned to fight in the woods. They were careless this time, but this is the first. The summer will not be an easy one."

"We have been careless too, Charles. Six of our party are dead in a rearguard action at the stream. Would you detach a patrol to search for them?"

"Of course, Antoine."

"If any men deserve medals, it is those."

As they turned to go and the last of the prisoners passed, Nashe noticed a young Ranger looking directly at him. The man seemed to recognize him. And he too thought he'd seen the fellow before. But the column passed and the blonde youth turned away, and Nashe thought little more of it.

## 45

Carillon was an armed camp. The wooden fort sat at the end of a spit of land jutting between Lac Champlain and the Richilieu River. This was the so-called highway of death, the waterway that ran north-south from Montreal to the British forward command at Fort Edward. Control of the Richilieu meant control of the centre and Carillon, perfectly positioned, was the key to that control.

With July came the shimmering heat that turned the forest stifling; men and animals suffered the torments of that heat. And all to defend a flat, dusty isthmus from which there could be no retreat. Frontenac had been a dreadful place, Nashe reflected, but this oven of weather and war was far worse.

Yet Carillon was an example of Montcalm's genius. The palisades were built to house a garrison of two hundred, not a battle array of four thousand. And so the general was faced with the problem of protecting his men. He solved it in his usual style: the fort became a supply depot while Montcalm turned the entire isthmus itself into a masssive fortress. He ordered construction of earthworks covered by an abatis of sharp stakes and brambles to run the entire half-mile from shore to shore. In front of it his men cleared the forest leaving a rough, dangerous terrain, an open range for two hundred yards.

It was a deceptively simple plan that took advantage of position and offered maximum protection. Not many men would have thought of it. Not many would have ordered their troops to build such an unprecedented construction and seen them work willingly. All the men worked: officers, drummers, even the wounded...even Alan Nashe.

Nashe was toiling at the centre of the earthwork when Bougainville arrived to see him. The day was humid. Nashe welcomed the water that Bougainville brought. But Bougainville offered more.

"I intend to impress you once again, my friend," he said, himself quaffing from a cup. "Your work will wait. You have a meeting to attend."

"The last time I attended one of these meetings I lost one sixth of my trading fleet." Nashe grinned.

"Always the devious merchant." The major laughed in return.

# The Betrayal Path

The gathering occurred in the parade square of the fort. The day's stifling humidity was somewhat alleviated by the cold tea served beneath the awnings of Montcalm's marquee. The tent's sides were rolled up to catch the least suggestion of breeze. There was none. Battle flags and awnings hung limp.

Groups of officers chatted around map boards and benches placed in the tent. Montcalm himself had not yet arrived. It fell to Bougainville to seat the officers according to rank. Nashe wished silently for a glass of wine but the thought was stillborn. Montcalm had given orders that no alcohol be served during the heat of the day. The wine would have to wait for supper.

The officers sweated in full dress, mandatory for staff meetings, and no one deigned to loosen so much as a collar. Montcalm's discipline saw to that. Nashe began to feel under-dressed as he found a stool in the rear of the gathering. The officers stood to attention at the arrival of their general.

"Be seated, Messieurs." Montcalm looked fresh, seeming unaffected by the weather. He took a chair on a raised dais beside the map boards. Bougainville stood behind him, notebook in hand. The general waited for his men to settle, then motioned de Longeuil to the platform.

"Messieurs," de Longeuil began, "reports indicate the enemy is advancing up Lac George by a flotilla of whaleboats and rafts. We estimate upward of... twenty five thousand men." He paused then, awaiting the uproar he'd caused to subside. "Howe's Fifty-fifth regiment is in the van along with a battalion of Rangers. My scouts report regiments of the Royal Americans, Twenty seventh, Forty fourth, Forty sixth and Eightieth foot, the Forty second Highlanders, provincials, and some elements of artillery. Howe is in command with Abercromby as his second. It appears, Messieurs, the English mean business."

"Questions, Messieurs?" Montcalm stood. His reply was a discouraged silence. De Longeuil had confirmed the worst. The English numbered seven or eight to one of the French. Each man kept his thoughts to himself.

"Well, at least we know what we face," Montcalm said calmly. "Pontlery, would you favour us with the state of our defences?"

A stubby major approached the dais replacing de Longeuil. Pontlery was an engineer. His evaluation of the defence of Carillon was so exact and detailed that Nashe found himself an enrapt student of the man by the time he had finished.

The next man up was Bourlamaque, his arm in a sling and a little weak. He'd been given the job of analyzing English alternatives.

"They have several options. First and most obvious, flanking attacks. But on both sides we are protected by water. Their other choices require time, bringing their cannon forward and pounding the abatis to shreds, or going round us and cutting our supply lines. Either way we are speaking of weeks, if not months, of siege. I don't know that they can afford it. They must know we have reinforcements in Montreal. The problem is this Howe fellow. We don't know him. I simply cannot say what the man might do."

"You have forgotten, Colonel, one other alternative," Montcalm interrupted.

"Sir?"

"A frontal assault. A direct attack using waves of men to overcome our defences."

"I discounted that, General. Even with their numbers it would be suicide..."

"And that is precisely why I will to coerce them into it."

"Sir, with all respect, I believe in this case we are on the defensive. There is no way they could be culled into..."

"There is one way, Colonel."

"Sir?"

"Panic."

Bourlamaque was doing his best not to shake his head. "I'm not sure I understand you, General."

"There are one or two details the British have not considered. One is the forest. The forest is so thick in this vicinity that any march through it would split their army. You have all been in it, Messieurs. It is impossible for any but small parties. That fact, coupled with our raiding parties, should successfully prevent a quarter of the enemy from ever reaching Carillon. Half of them, I expect, will become so lost in the labyrinth they may never come out again." He smiled. "And as for artillery, I think that eventuality may be discounted, unless they decide to spend a year building roads."

"That still leaves them the option of skirting us."

"If they pass us, they run the risk of cutting their own supply lines. No self respecting commander would risk that."

"We do not have the men, Sir."

"But do they know that, Bourlamaque? This camp has been sealed off since I arrived. In actual fact, Colonel, we have six thousand troops within this enclave, and another six thousand on the way from Montreal!"

"Sir, I believe you're exaggerating..."

"Of course I am! But what will the English believe? They must consider the worst or be unpleasantly surprised."

By then, even Bourlamaque began to smile.

"And so, General, they capture some prisoners, an officer perhaps. And each one confirms the same story..."

"Now you've got it! I have a number of volunteers: brave, loyal men willing to sacrifice their freedom for France. They fall behind their patrols, they are mutinous soldiers, they are taken in a skirmish...and all of them swear to six thousand here, six thousand there..."

"And so the English panic. Rough terrain, reports of our strength…"

"And they are forced to attack quickly, a frontal assault."

"But surely, General," a colonel of the La Reine spoke up, "surely this is a risk. If they discover the deception..."

"Colonel Rambien, war is always a risk. What other choice have we? Major Bougainville will give you your orders for a defence against frontal assault."

Bougainville stepped smartly forward and referring to his notes rattled off in quick succession the posting of troops.

"La Sarre and Languedoc regiments will take positions on the left subject to Colonel Bourlamaque. The Berry and Royal Rousillon to the centre under General Montcalm. The right will be held by La Reine, Béarn and Guyenne, commanded by Colonel Rambien until the arrival of Brigadier de Levis with reinforcements. Commanders of the troupes de la marine and our native allies should report to Captain de Longeuil for their orders. They will take skirmishing positions at the extremes of each flank. Grenadiers from all regiments will form a reserve commanded by myself. Questions, Messieurs?"

There were none.

"Thank you, Major," Montcalm again spoke. "Now, Messieurs, there is a great deal to be done. Our defences are not complete. Major Bougainville has the orders for night shift construction. That is all, Messieurs. Thank you for your attention."

As he passed through his officers, Montcalm caught sight of Nashe. His sharp eyes lit in a smile, and the general made his way toward Nashe's place in the rear. He shook hands warmly.

"Monsieur Nashe, I regret my neglect of you since your heroic arrival from Niagara. I have heard of your actions, Monsieur, and I'm very pleased. Walk with me, Nashe, to my quarters. It is pleasant to see you again."

"Your strategy is much like your fencing, General."

"Monsieur?"

"The study, the feint, the parry, then the thrust." Nashe smiled.

"You like my plan?"

"I think it brilliant. Of course, I'm a simple merchant."

"If it works, Monsieur. If it works. I appear more confident than I feel. I do not know this Howe. There is no judging what he might do. But there are other problems." The general's face turned sour. "Vaudreuil is countermanding my request for de Levis and his reinforcements. Levis has three thousand men in reserve, and they sit useless in Montreal. Vaudreuil wants to use them for an offensive. An offensive in God's name! And there are twenty five thousand English troops on our doorstep."

"Is there anything you can do, Sir?"

"Wait. I wait for Levis, wait for the English. And," he smiled, "I wait for my trap to spring. The English, you see, have lost sight of a very important factor."

"As I learned from the meeting."

"Oh, nothing like terrain or tactics. This is more abstract, something of such import that it makes men worth ten times their number."

"I don't understand, Sir."

"We will hold this dreadful little spit of land, or we will die in the attempt. This little spit is France, Nashe. The English fight on our soil now. They will soon regret it."

## 46

News came that the English had landed. Preparations intensified. Montcalm sent out his skirmishers and with them his seeds of panic. French raiders took their toll, as did the forest. A day's grace as the English lost entire battalions in the undergrowth. Another day as they tried to re-organize. And still de Levis and his men did not come.

Then the French pickets were driven in. The English were near, gathering strength. There was some argument for a sortie to prevent the English organization. Montcalm refused to consider it. Thus far his plan had worked. The army waited.

Nashe entered the fort itself that night to join the officers in the central hall. There was none of the boisterous talk or gambling of evenings past. This night the room was quiet with men just off duty, silently quaffing mugs of thick spruce beer.

Montcalm was among them. All that could be done had been; now he could only wait with his men and think of other things. As Nashe joined them Montcalm was speaking.

"A soldier thinks too often of war, Messieurs. I reflect tonight on my home in Candiac. I miss it. The day would end warm, not humid as here, but with breezes through the orchards. I think sometimes the south of France is an Eden to tempt me away from my duties. In my old age it will become my cradle."

"But you are not old, my General!" Bougainville interrupted. "And your cradle has always been your occupation."

"Ah, but that was not my dream. Once I was determined to be a scholar of history. Now, despite myself it seems, I am in the midst of it. It is exciting, Messieurs, to be in a place where history is made, but soldiering is for young men, and it was much simpler before. It is difficult to believe I defend Candiac when I fight my battles half a world away."

"Still, this is French soil, General," Bougainville rejoined. "This is New France."

"My good Antoine, I miss my land, and my hearth and children. And so you gentlemen must fight like the very devil for me so I may have my retirement and make way for you. And you must fight for France tomorrow and so become the heroes I know you already are!"

The discussion continued but Nashe did not join. Montcalm's reflections led him to his own past. He thought of his home, of the rolling Cotswolds and the sheep grazing its hills, of the market towns and their eccentric names, of his father's house set back from the road amid ivy and daffodils and the gnarled trees so easily climbed. Even as a boy he had been the adventurer. His father was a magistrate, a stern man filled with the moral code of his Anglican background. His mother had been his father's single step beyond convention, a French woman, a woman often gossiped over not because she deserved the rumours, but because she was French and so often smiling.

He recalled visits to Paris; his father never came with them, to see his mother's family and the wonders of that magnificent city. And even then, glimpsing the scope of the world outside the rural Cotswolds, he had yearned for it.

There were the village girls and his first awareness of them. He remembered the gentle love for a girl so fresh with her freckled smile and red hair—innocent love, passionate explorations. And then the disgrace. He was blamed. It was laid on the French blood in him. A furious father sent his son to military school to beat the French wildness out of him.

He'd hated the school and had, at first, fought back. But the masters had simply beaten him until he'd learned Latin, Greek, mathematics, history...deception. There had been pranks and secret runs to London with its narrow streets and its women and gin houses. Then came one prank too many, and a duel, even then he had learned the sword well, and another disgrace. Then escape to France, disinherited by his father, by his school, by England.

He'd spent a penniless year in Paris afraid to go to his mother's people. And that year had taught him many lessons amid the cheap wine shops of the Seine side. His mother sent men to find him. When they did, she still smiled even through her tears, and sent him to the Sorbonne. Then life was the art of Watteau and the music of Scarlatti. There were readings of Voltaire and Molière's satires and the plays of Corneille.

When his father died he did not attended the funeral. But his inheritance, restored to him by his mother, brought him back to England. It bought him a commission in the English Marines; it might as easily have been the French. He reflected on that for a moment: the irony that Montcalm might have been his leader; that these men with whom he shared the table might be his comrades.

A sudden rumble of drums brought him to his feet. The others were quickly on theirs as well, spilling their tankards, grabbing for swords as they ran from the hall on the heels of Montcalm.

"Stand to! Stand to! Boats on the lake!" a sentry bawled. Men ran everywhere. Nashe caught a glimpse of trepidation in Montcalm's face. His plan had failed. The English had outflanked him. Montcalm rushed up the narrow steps to the wall's top shouting instructions. He reached the sentry.

"The boats, man, where? Where are the boats?"

"There, Sir, to the north, off that spit where the pines grow!"

"Give me your glass!"

"There. To your left a bit. They're coming fast."

Montcalm struggled to see through the dark, quartering the horizon. When he lowered the instrument, he was smiling. Below him the drums still rumbled and men rushed about in confusion. Montcalm spoke to his bewildered sentry: "Ensign, I am pleased to note your vigilance. I wish only that all men of this army were the same. But do you not find it peculiar that a flanking English flotilla would be running with torches in their bows?"

"Give the order to stand down, Ensign," Montcalm rested his arm on the fellow's shoulder.. You've discovered not the enemy but your own reinforcements. I suggest, Messieurs, that we go to the shore to meet our tardy comrades."

His mirth subsided when the first boat landed. Its commander stepped on shore and from his look it was obvious there would be nothing further to smile about. He marched immediately to Montcalm and presented himself with a stiff salute.

"Captain Doucet reporting, Sir. Brigadier de Levis sends his regards. He will arrive tomorrow with the remainder of the auxiliary troops."

"Very good, Captain. The voyage seems to have been taxing."

"The voyage, Sir, was easy. However, I'm afraid my arrival will be met with disappointment. I've only three hundred men with me, Sir. Brigadier de Levis has two hundred."

"What?" Montcalm blanched.

"Governor Vaudreuil would not release the men, Sir. Brigadier de Levis pleaded to no avail. And then Monsieur Cadet demanded payment for use of the transport. We were lucky enough to have even this complement."

"You see what the fools do to me!" Montcalm exploded, his temper flaring. "You see how they throw their land away for pettiness and greed! I swear someone will pay for this. You see this, Nashe? Nashe? Where has the fellow gone?"

"There, Sir," a soldier pointed, "by the shore."

"Who is that great bear of a man he is talking to?"

"No idea, Sir. He volunteered to come with the boats. Shall I retrieve Monsieur Nashe?"

"No. The less said in public of this the better." Montcalm settled himself with an effort. "At least we have five hundred good men. Captain Doucet, come with me to my quarters. I should like a full report."

\*\*\*

"Ledrew is gone," Vadnais muttered.

"What?"

"Disappeared from the camp where I left him. If Bigot's men found him, he's dead by now, or worse, he might have talked. The whole thing is a shambles."

"We must get to Albany immediately."

"We can't leave here now; too obvious. We'll have to wait until this is finished."

"We remain here then until we can slip away."

"Yes. We'll have to. Anyway, if the reports I've heard are true, we may find the easy way to Albany."

"How do you mean?"

"As prisoners. Now, can you get me a place to sleep?"

The night's melancholy had been swept away by the drums and Montcalm's temper. The arrivals set men on edge. In the night the camp prepared for battle.

## 47

Drums rolled up and down the line as soldiers in battle grey moved purposefully to their places bringing with them the things they would need for the long day of waiting. The day dawned warm and the men resigned themselves to another baking sun on the flat spit of Carillon.

Nashe, having volunteered to serve as a messenger for Montcalm, stood with the general on an earthen platform at the centre of the lines. He peered across the jagged field to the trees two hundred yards beyond. Already flies buzzed in the heat. All was silent but for the flies and the occasional sharp command from a sergeant.

Through the morning hours the silence became ominous. Men shifted uncomfortably in their places. By ten o'clock they had removed their coats. Even Montcalm discarded his as the sun beat down mercilessly. Montcalm ordered rations: each man refilled his canteen and received his bread and salt pork. The extraordinary quiet continued.

By noon they heard sporadic shooting from within the trees. French and native scouts filtered back to their lines, the last of the forward posts driven in.

Though they tried not to show it they appeared frightened. A young lieutenant just returned spoke quietly with Montcalm. No one but the general heard his words, but everyone noticed Montcalm's grim smile. The officer had looked terrified, yet Montcalm had smiled.

By one o'clock the day was scorching. Men sweated, grew thirsty, the waiting was rancorous. And then in the shimmering heat they began to see mirages at the tree line: fluid wraiths dressed in green and brown. A few sputtering shots broke the silence and puffs of white in the distance brought splinters of woodchips flying and the sound of ricochets. It was too hot for anyone to care. Nothing across the clearing seemed real.

"Rangers," Montcalm muttered quietly. "It shan't be long now. Major! Get those men up! They look half asleep. Make them get up, I say!"

To the shouted commands of their officers the soldiers shook off their lethargy. Ten minutes later there was no need for orders. Every man was watching; agape at the sight that formed in the distance.

Scarlet. Columns of scarlet, great long lines that emerged from the trees like rivers of blood, from one end of the isthmus to the other. Thousands. And men knew that behind them were more, hidden now in the forest, ready to follow their comrades to the attack. The French army looked on astounded at the display of power birthing before it. And suddenly to a distant command thousands of bayonets flashed from their scabbards and they looked like flames in the hands of men as they were locked onto weapons. Steel on steel, the harsh challenge of war had been given.

"My God," Bougainville whispered, "look at them."

Then from behind those lines, from deep in the forest, came a strange skirling wail. Men who had earlier been stupefied by the heat now looked at each other aghast. It seemed the English had brought with them the martial music of hell.

"What is that?" Montcalm muttered calmly.

"Bagpipes, General," Nashe answered. "Highlanders. That will signal their attack."

"I'd best get to my post," Bougainville said flatly, departing.

"That sound is enough to frighten the souls of heaven," Montcalm again spoke softly. He turned to his line commander: "Have the men stand to."

"How many do you think, Sir?" the officer asked the question riding in everyone's mind.

"They look formidable," Montcalm returned, "but they've fallen for the ruse. I find this Howe surprising. I did not believe he would panic so quickly. This kind of tactic is Abercromby's."

"But sir," the captain murmured, "surely their numbers will overwhelm us."

"They look strong now, Captain. But they have to cross that field. They will fight in the open. We are entrenched. No, I think not even those thousands will carry this day. Their lives will be wasted."

With the skirl of the bagpipes the red mass advanced, but the stumps and limbs that littered the field broke their lines. Men stumbled and fell, companies ran into each other as they swerved to avoid impassable obstacles. This was not the flat terrain of Flanders where their tactic would overwhelm the opponent's lines. This was another war. As the French observed the columns break up, their tension lifted. Down the line a young ensign stood on a parapet in full view of the enemy. Sword held high he cried: "Vive le Roi! Vive notre General!" and somehow over the pipes his voice carried. A great cheer drowned his final words. And then three thousand guns opened up in a thundering salvo. The first line of the British toppled like toys in the hands of a mischievous child. The second line trod over them and into the next French volley. Then so much smoke and dust filled the air that it smothered the battle. Nashe caught only glimpses of waving flags and rushes of scarlet as the bedlam of war took the field.

The British came on, firing now, men screaming encouragement to one another. Grapeshot riddled their ranks. Miniballs buzzed through the air as thick as the flies had been. Still the intrepid redcoats advanced. Their third wave actually reached the abatis. It was stopped in its tracks, the zigzag of entrenchments placing the English in a murderous crossfire. Scores of them died. Nashe nearly wept at the sight. The French fought cheerfully at first, then grimly, destroying their foes like machines. The day became sweltering: musket barrels burned hands, cannon cracked from over use, the water ration was long gone.

And finally the British were driven back. They limped and crawled but not one soldier ran. They retreated like an army. A carpet of scarlet was left in their wake. And to the cheering of the French they melted back into the forest.

Rest. Blessed rest. Men fell to the ground completely spent. Others searched for water and shared what little was left. Montcalm busily continued his orders. Controlled, composed, he seemed almost serene.

"Now they will try the flanks. Have runners go to Levis and Bourlamaque. Tell them to watch for attacks. Nashe, go back to Bougainville and have him stand ready for manoeuvres, then return here."

Nashe signified his understanding and turned to leave. He was stopped by Vadnais' big hand on his shoulder. Looking up he saw the man's face fill with wonder.

"Sweet Jesus, they come again."

The red host again appeared. There was firing from the left flank. But the flanking attack had been mistimed. Too late the British commanders ordered their men to rush forward trying to counter the error. Their men broke into a run shouting as they charged. They died before they reached the entrenchments.

"It seems this Howe has no regard for the lives of his men," Montcalm said softly. "This will not be an easy day, Nashe. Now go to Bougainville, tell him to be ready."

Six times the British charged their lines. Once or twice they nearly broke through. Montcalm was everywhere up and down the line, anywhere trouble threatened. Word came that Bourlamaque was again wounded. By five o'clock both sides were exhausted, yet the battle raged on. Men had become automatons, killing machines, lost in the heat and bloodlust. A messenger came running hard from de Levis' positions.

"General," the soldier gasped, "the Highlanders have broken our line! They will overwhelm us!"

"Nashe, get Bougainville immediately. Tell him to follow my flag. The grenadiers move now!"

"Sir, you can't go there," an officer shouted, "the Scots have broken through!"

"Then that is where I should be."

\*\*\*

They arrived at the breach with Bougainville's grenadiers just behind. The fighting was savage. Fanatic Scots had forsaken their muskets for the deadly claymores they knew so well. They offered no quarter. The French line was disintegrating.

Montcalm stood slightly back of the action, his rapier drawn as he signalled Bougainville's troops to attack. The grenadiers stormed the wall firing point blank into the Scots then charging with bayonets. They were big men. They were fresh and eager for battle. The fight for the breach became a battle of giants. And slowly the disciplined grenadiers drove the heroic Scots back.

From the masses of men a Highlander appeared and charged directly toward Montcalm. He screamed wildly and swung his sword in huge arcs. Montcalm saw the man and prepared for him, but Bougainville stepped into his path. He fired his pistol but the man did not fall. Dying, the Scot swung his sword in a vicious cut that Bougainville tried to parry. The force of the blow drove the Frenchman's own sword back into his ribs. Bougainville fell wounded with his dead assailant on top of him. Nashe tried to run to his friend but found himself stopped. Vadnais held him by his collar.

"Damn you, Vadnais, let go!"

"To help an enemy?"

"That man is my friend!"

"That man is a French officer."

"He's wounded!"

"And you are confused. This is not the side you fight for."

The grenadiers swept the enemy back through the breach. Once the Scots were outside the breastwork the Frenchmen began lobbing short fused bombs over the parapet down among the helpless belligerents. Nashe could not see the men below, but he could hear their screams. When the butchery had diminished Montcalm detached two soldiers to carry Bougainville from the field. Nashe went with them; Vadnais following close behind.

Nashe had never been so bewildered. At that moment he hated Vadnais, and yet the big man had been right. Bougainville was indeed the enemy. But Bougainville was his friend. Friend or foe seemed suddenly not to matter, and right and wrong relative. As they arrived at the hospital Nashe could smell the stench of suffering. English or French, it made no difference; the only enemy here was death.

And in that moment with the moans of the wounded and the smell of blood and his friend unconscious beside him, the seeds of something unfamiliar began to germinate within him. It was not something tangible. He did not recognize it yet. There was too much happening around him and too little as yet inside. The seed of humanity is not a thing that spurts somehow instantly into view.

Alan Nashe had lost his youth.

\*\*\*

By seven o'clock the British had lost the field. They had taken their wounded and left their dead and were gone. Montcalm, having viewed the carnage, came into the hospital to look to his beloved soldiers. There were tears in his eyes.

"General," an officer intervened, "we have them on the run. We should sortie out and finish them."

"Go and look at your men, Monsieur," Montcalm muttered bitterly. "They are exhausted, filled to the brim with killing. The English are finished here. We may fight tomorrow but for now these men deserve their supper. See to it, sir!"

With that he went to his colonel. Bourlamaque was unconscious. Montcalm stayed with him a while. He prayed. Then he approached the newly revived Bougainville.

"Antoine, thank God you're alive. You have saved my life today. I shall never forget."

"And you, my General, have saved New France today. That, no one will forget."

"We have won, Antoine, but it is not my victory. I will plant a cross on the ridge of the breastworks. I have never seen men give so much as today," Montcalm said. "I hope we have men of the same mettle at Louisbourg. Now, I'm afraid I must leave. I need sleep, Antoine. So do you."

They watched him leave, his back bent with exhaustion.

"What did he mean about Louisbourg, Antoine?"

"I suppose it won't hurt to tell you now. This morning when de Levis arrived he brought a message from Quebec. The general did not want it known until the end of this day. The English succeeded somehow in landing at Louisbourg. They've besieged the fort."

In the cool of the evening the flies returned to the field between forest and fort. Where there had been morning green was now blackened soot and blood. The ground was littered with scarlet. And the flies feasted upon it.

## 48

The English defeat had become a rout. A brief visit to their landing place told the story: a shambles... all the earmarks of panic. Nashe found it hard to conceive of Lord Howe in panic. He had not seemed that kind of man in

Bath. French soldiers rejoiced picking over the remains of the English goods. They found a good many guns discarded in flight: the famed "Brown Bess" so much heavier and more dependable than their long, fragile fusils. They took the guns as their own.

Bougainville and Bourlamaque had been returned to Montreal with the wounded. Bougainville had protested, stating flatly that he was much better and needed only a few days rest. But the cut had been deep and the major was weak. Bourlamaque was much worse. He slipped in and out of consciousness until Montcalm feared for his life. The general sent his personal physician along with the beloved officer, hoping the doctor's skills would keep his man alive.

Montcalm himself had decided to remain at Carillon. It seemed even he could not believe the extent of his victory. The British had lost hundreds in their futile attack but they still remained a force Montcalm knew would have to be reckoned with.

So Nashe and Vadnais, politely refusing Montcalm's offer of a bodyguard, decided to leave. They announced they would travel on foot to the west. They took with them light packs, their muskets, and Vadnais brought along a hunting bow. Shots could be heard for miles in the wilderness and neither man desired undue attention. This journey would be a quiet one, taken in easy stages through the forest's hidden depths; the more hidden, the better.

And once again Nashe found himself in a realm of dappled wilderness. Occasionally they would find the remains of deserted settlements. The cabins were low browed log huts with moss stuffed in the chinks, their roofs of bark, and their chimneys clay. The two would sleep in these abandoned shelters when they came across them. Eventually they grew careless of them, assuming all were deserted. It was not something they should have assumed.

In the forest silence the musket shot boomed. They heard the ball tear through the leaves beside them. They dived to the ground. The shot had come from a half burnt shell in which they'd intended to take shelter. A single puff of white smoke curled from a narrow window.

"One man," whispered Nashe, "or there would have been a volley."

"And not a very good shot at that," Vadnais replied. "I'll draw his fire; you get around him from the back."

"On the contrary, I will draw fire. You are much more adept at quiet."

"If you're killed the journey is over. Our plans ended."

"You said yourself he's a poor shot."

"He might be lucky. That's better than good shooting."

Another shot tore through the branches above them. They flattened.

"He wastes his lead too."

"I'm protected here, Owl. Go. The quicker you get behind him the less chance he has of luck."

Vadnais shrugged and crawled into the underbrush. Nashe knew the art of drawing fire: a flash of a hat, a wriggling bush... he had done it before. He kept to the ground. Most men expected a man to run, they shot high. This one was no different.

The sporadic shooting continued. Nashe let off one or two shots to keep the fellow in his fortress. And twenty minutes later Vadnais called to him. But the big man's voice sounded strange. Nashe wondered if he had run into trouble: perhaps there had been more than one. Nashe crossed down a depression. The ditch brought him close to the house, ninety degrees from the window. The man had not fired in a long time. Nashe picked his way to the blind side of the hut; he heard a scuffle inside and then a shout of pain from Vadnais. He leaped from his concealment running hard around the house to the door. It was already in pieces, kicked in. Pistol in one hand, knife in the other he leaped through the doorway and was stopped in his tracks.

There was indeed a scuffle, but not what Nashe had expected. The cabin was only one room, its roof half burnt away. A table stood upended in its centre, against one wall was a broken, rough bed, crockery lay smashed on the floor and by the window Vadnais was locked in combat with a woman. She was unarmed but her nails had raked the side of his face and her teeth were tearing at one of the meaty hands that held her. She kicked, scratched, gouged everywhere there was an opening. Vadnais struggled, yelping in pain. He grabbed her hair, pulling it back, and Nashe realized the woman was terrified. As the big man pinned her by the shoulders she burst into spasms of sobbing.

She had wispy blonde hair, filthy now. She was very thin, her body all angles. Once she must have been pretty, yet now as Nashe gently took hold of her and looked into her depthless grey eyes, he saw she had been robbed of her beauty and youth by privation and pain.

"We are your friends, Madame," he spoke French, then switched to English. "We will not harm you."

She calmed a little. She did not speak. Nashe explained that they were going south to Albany, that they had thought her home deserted, that they would make a supper and would sleep outside, away from her. Her fear subsided. She strayed to a corner and folded herself into it, looking out at them with her vacant eyes.

Nashe tried to straighten the cabin while Vadnais retrieved their packs. The place was a shambles, unliveable anymore. He told her so. She did not answer.

At dusk Vadnais started a cook fire; in the half-light no one would see its smoke but he was careful to use dry hardwood. He cooked venison. Nashe took some meat on an old piece of plate and set it before her. She picked at the meat, eating little. Then after supper Vadnais lit his pipe. The men settled themselves and decided what was to be done with her.

"We could mend the roof," Vadnais suggested, the smoke of his pipe curling up through the rafters. "And we can leave food until we send help."

"Surely you can see the state she's in. She must go with us."

"She would hold us up."

"Nevertheless, she comes."

"You forget, Alan, this is the frontier. Her man may be off hunting, he might return anytime. It's not uncommon to be left alone here. If he should return and she is gone?"

"We'll leave a letter explaining. She can't stay here. What of roving natives, of the war?"

"The natives will not harm me, Sir," she spoke softly from her corner. "I am mad, you see, and they fear me. I am untouchable."

Her voice was astonishingly childlike. This woman, Nashe thought, was deceptively young... the voice and the face at odds with each other. The voice held a trace of Dutch lilt in its English.

"Then you wish to remain? Your husband will return?"

"My husband is dead, my child dead," she spoke as though in a trance. "Some time ago, I know not how long, men came out of the forest. They demanded food. We gave it. They stayed. When they demanded me my husband tried to fight. They took him and stripped him and tied him to trees and they peeled his skin away with their knives. He lived for two days. Screaming. My child cried for him. They took my child and smashed his skull on a rock.

Then they kept me here, lashed by ropes to my husband's bed. They came to me when they wanted me. They did unspeakable things. When they went away they left me tied. They set the house ablaze. It rained. The fire stopped. I would have welcomed the fire, but God has seen fit to punish me.

I chewed my ropes away. I have buried my man and my child. You must say words over them, sir. God hates me. If you say words they will be accepted. God will not listen to me. Please say words for my man and child... a few words..."

The poor woman swooned in the shock of remembrance. They nursed her and washed her and lay her on skins on the floor. Nashe took the bed outside and destroyed it. Through the night they watched her. At times she would twist and writhe on the floor, at times half awaken moaning. Nashe cursed the men who had caused this agony.

"Outlaws," Vadnais told him. "I've killed a few in my time."

"You agree then, she must come with us. She must be cared for."

"Yes. But I think she is past needing care."

In the morning when she awakened it was as if she were returning to hell. The lines that had succumbed to sleep reappeared on her face. She was once again old. She ate a little breakfast... a dried apple she did not finish. Then she showed Nashe the shallow graves of her family. Something had been digging at them. Vadnais covered them with stones. Nashe said some words. When they were done she returned to her burnt out house, going inside without a sound.

As they prepared to leave she came out. In her hand she carried a locket. It did not take much to realize what was inside. Nashe choked back his emotions as she spoke to him.

"I will go with you now. I am going home."

Throughout the journey she never once spoke again.

## 49

They found the Hudson River and followed it downstream. It was easier going then, the forest became huge sycamores, elms, and chestnut trees and these great beings shaded the forest floor so only ferns and moss grew. The ground was soft and springy.

This far south the English patrols were frequent but they were noisy and careless. The small party easily avoided them. And as they closed on Albany the forest thinned and cleared land demarked the beginnings of civilization. Farm buildings dotted the fields, rustic abodes with long well sweeps and vast kitchen chimneys, and around them the fields of pumpkin and corn matured as cattle grazed contentedly. Stone fences or cedar rails divided the fields. The land had been domesticated, cleared from what had once been wilderness. Now it was cluttered with tools and roads and buildings. Vadnais did not like it.

"Everything smells of manure and sawmills. If this is what the English bring I will go west if they win, my friend. There is no room here."

* * *

Albany. If Fort Edward was the last bastion of English strength before the no man's land of the wilderness, Albany, fifty miles south, was its centre. The town served as a supply base, a headquarters and staging point for fresh troops. In the half-light of dusk folk meandered a broad main street that descended from the hilltop fort to the river. At the bottom of the street was a Common, populated by roving cattle, their bells tinkling in the evening air. Nearby was the English camp, thousands of tents and the dull murmur of an army.

The trio kept off the main street as they made their way to the fort. But the woman stopped them. For the first time since their meeting Nashe saw she was smiling. Even in the dark Nashe could make it out. It warmed him.

"I will thank you now, Mr. Nashe," she spoke softly, "for your trouble and kindness. I am nearly home now. I know what to do."

"But surely we may escort you to your destination. It's no trouble, Madam, I assure you."

"No. Thank you. Where I go you would not be welcomed. Goodbye, Mr. Nashe. Keep well."

With that she was gone, a frail wraith into the shadows. Nashe caught one final glimpse of her eyes. Despite the smile, her eyes had not changed. Then Vadnais gave Nashe a tug on the arm and the two men continued up to the fort.

The gates were closed. Four guards stood outside in the light of torches.

"Halt! Who goes?"

"I cannot give my name, Sergeant. We have come to see your commanding officer."

"One step further, Sir, and it will be your last."

"Sergeant, my friend and I have travelled a great many miles to arrive here. May I speak to your duty officer?"

"He is behind you, Sir," a voice replied from the dark. "There are only the two of them, Sergeant."

Six more soldiers appeared from the rear, weapons trained.

"Now, Sir, you look a bit bedraggled to be paying a visit to an officer. And your friend here looks more like a forest bear. Who might you be, big man?"

"He speaks no English, Captain. He is French."

"I see. And you Sir, your name?"

"He refused to give it, Sir," the Sergeant intervened.

"To me he will."

"I'm afraid not, Captain. I must see your commanding officer."

"Where do you come from?"

"I can't divulge that information either."

"A mysterious circumstance, Sir. I'm afraid you and your companion are under arrest. Sergeant, take these men to the stockade."

"Captain, if we were French agents would we have come here? Think, man!"

"You could be assassins. That fellow has the look of it."

"He can't help the way he looks. I have information. At least tell your commander..."

"Tell him what? Two vagabonds at the gate are demanding an audience?"

"Just tell him," Nashe muttered, his frustration boiling.

"What is his name?" the Captain asked.

"Whose?"

"The man you wish to see."

"I have no idea, Captain. I've never been here before."

"That settles it then. Sergeant, have these two placed in a cell. Take them off, Sergeant!"

"Tell him my name is Ledrew!" Nashe shouted desperately. "Damn you, Sir, you're a fool if you don't."

"Hold there!" the Captain's look changed. "You said Ledrew?"

"I did."

"Bring them inside. Hold them at the gates."

The officer strode through the gates as they opened, the guards hustling the two men behind him. Five minutes passed before they were summoned. They were escorted across the parade square to a low browed building, heavily guarded. The two were searched carefully, their belongings confiscated. In the office a single man sat at a desk. The walls behind him were covered in maps, the desk littered with paperwork.

"General Amherst!"

"Do you know me, Sir? You are certainly not Captain Ledrew," the general scowled.

"I'm afraid I haven't shaved in weeks, General. When last I saw you at Howe's estate..."

"Nashe? Captain Nashe?" the general peered at him. "Good God it is! But you are dead!"

"Only half, Sir. It was a long journey," Nashe smiled.

"We had a message from Quebec. We were told you'd been killed."

"As you see, I have not. And I think I can explain the message."

"But how on earth did you get here?"

"Permit me to introduce Mr. Owl Vadnais. Unfortunately, he speaks no English, but he is an invaluable guide and protector." Nashe took a seat.

"I can see his worth as protection. Rather a rough character is he not?"

"Protocol is not his forté, Sir."

"If I recall correctly neither was it yours. But where did you come from?"

"Carillon."

"You were there?"

"I was. I wonder that Brigadier Howe could waste men like that. Even the French were in tears..."

"Howe is dead. He died in a skirmish two days before the assault. It was Abercromby who ordered the attack. It was also Abercromby who panicked and bolted. He claims he faced twelve thousand troops."

"Four thousand, Sir. Montcalm fooled him."

"He will have that chance no longer. Abercromby has been relieved. Lieutenant Colonel Bradstreet has assumed his command. The loss of Howe was a bitter herb, Nashe."

"I heard at Carillon we've besieged Louisbourg. The French are worried."

"I've just arrived from there, not two days ago," the general smiled.

"Is the fortress taken?"

"Not yet. Drucour, the French commander, has put up stiff resistance. But we've gained their landward side; they are surrounded. It's only a matter of time. I only wish events had not called me here though in any case it would not truly have been my victory."

"Sir?"

"A young brigadier by the name of Wolfe: against heavy odds he landed his troops by boat in Gabarus Bay. We thought it impossible. Apparently he did not. He personally led an assault on the French guns. You'll hear more of this fellow, I reckon. Now I suggest you take a bath, Nashe. A uniform will be provided in the morning. And I think we should keep your friend out of sight. He is a trifle obvious, and there are eyes..."

"I agree, Sir. If I may, I have a favour to beg."

Nashe explained the woman's story to Amherst. He requested the general send someone to see to her care. Amherst replied he would do so in the morning.

"Meanwhile, Captain, you should spend your night writing reports, especially your witness of Carillon. As you are not dead, I intend to use you. Our intelligence is a shambles."

"Yes, Sir."

"Good. And by the way, Nashe, I am not accustomed to having my junior officers sit in my presence until they are asked. Do I make myself clear?"

"Yes, Sir."

"It seems you've been too long among the French."

On the way out Vadnais muttered something. The general did not hear it. Nashe hustled his companion through the door. It would not do to be imprisoned for insulting the lineage of a general officer, even if Vadnais did not, apparently, understand English.

## 50

Two men over a small breakfast table, the remains of their meal now nothing more than fish bones. Brigadier Offingham was as shocked as Amherst that Nashe was alive. Yet through the breakfast he'd noted changes in Alan Nashe. This was not the flippant rake he recalled. Offingham was a sound judge of character. He'd known someday Nashe would evolve; he'd had no idea how much.

"Then we're back to Ledrew," Offingham muttered abjectly.

"We've been over that, Sir. What could be his motive?"

"I don't suggest him as a suspect. But whoever it is, he's good at his work."

"So whom haven't we considered?"

"What of this Vadnais, Nashe? He seems a likely candidate."

"I used to think that. But he brought me here. He's had more than one opportunity to assure rumours of my death would come true. I trust that man with my life now."

"Well, we have no one else. Ledrew's contacts are mostly woodsmen, not party to our plans. This Charest was never in our employ nor was he ever, as far as I can tell, out of France before he came to Quebec. The only others Ledrew deals with are Rangers..."

"Rogers' men?"

"Yes. You know Rogers?"

"We've met," Nashe stated flatly. "But I thought he'd been killed last winter."

"A few escaped. Rogers was one. That man has the lives of a cat. He seems able to move with impunity through French lines and back again."

"Perhaps there's a reason for that. I gather Rogers knows our plans?"

"This is all conjecture, Alan. After all, it's his duty to infiltrate French territory."

"I wonder. Who brought the message of my death?"

"I don't know. Let me think... If I remember, the report was relayed through... Yes! It came through the Rangers! I think you've hit on something, Nashe. But why would he?"

"Gain of some sort: money, power... he's ambitious. He is also completely without a conscience."

"I'll speak to the officers he's worked with. We'll watch him. He's to attend this morning's meeting. And now we must be off. The meeting begins in five minutes and Amherst is not a man to be kept waiting."

As they took their seats Offingham murmured softly the names of those present to Nashe. On one side of the room sat Amherst and with him the intense presence of Bradstreet. Beside them was a rather stout brigadier named Monckton.

Across the room sat Governor Pownall and behind him his colonial officers. Rogers stared at Nashe as he sat through the meeting. Their mutual dislike was obvious. Nashe had been told that Rogers was bitter over the massacre of his men. Veiled references had suggested that Nashe and Ledrew having left just a week before the ambush was far too much a coincidence.

But there was another man whom Nashe noticed: a giant of a man, nearly as tall as Vadnais. His face was craggy and pockmarked and when he had smiled a greeting at Nashe, his teeth, broken and brown gave the man an ugly appearance. He eschewed a wig, preferring to wear his hair tied. Nashe discovered, to his surprise, that the man was Colonel Washington. Before they could speak the meeting was called to order.

"The campaign as it stands now, gentlemen," Amherst spoke sharply, "is behind schedule. Louisbourg continues to hold. Of course Carillon has been an unmitigated disaster. I believe you have seen Captain Nashe's rather brief reports. It seems Montcalm is remaining at Carillon. We must discuss alternatives. We must catch Frenchie where he does not expect us. Brigadier Forbes is on his way to Duquesne. I estimate his arrival in the west by early September. The mountains are hard going, but I have every confidence in him."

"His supply lines are stretched to the limit, General," Monckton intervened. "How are the French supplied?"

"Very well. They use the lake system."

"Then how will Forbes compete, his own supplies being so tenuous?"

"I see the point."

Bradstreet rose from his chair: "I have ten thousand men, Sir, to support Forbes."

"You mean to cut the French supply line?"

"I do. I propose to advance to Oswego and from there, stage an offensive either upon Niagara or Frontenac. If one of these is taken Duquesne would be cut off."

"I concur. But which of the two?"

"I believe Niagara to be the more strategic, sir. At the very strait through which traffic must pass. I would say Niagara, pending further investigation."

"Niagara is the wrong choice, General," Nashe stood uncertainly.

"Indeed," Amherst muttered, put off by the interruption. "You have something to add, Captain Nashe?"

"I've been there, Sir. My report, I know, has been sketchy. I think an addendum necessary. The outcome of Lieutenant Colonel Bradstreet's plan hinges upon it, Sir."

"Go ahead, Captain. I do hope this is important."

"Niagara has been fortified. They have heavy guns, a garrison that is fit and disciplined and they have control of the lake. A siege is doomed to failure. They know that fort's importance, Sir, at least a much as we."

"I see. Then you suggest…"

"Frontenac. The French believe we would more naturally move against Niagara. If you want surprise, General, Frontenac is where you'll achieve it."

"But the fortifications, Nashe, and the troop strength?"

"The fort is a wood palisade, indefensible against cannon. And it does offer a bonus. The harbour there has become a depot, the staging area for the lake fleet. If you time your attack using scouts, you might have a chance of finding the fleet in dock, along with their winter supplies."

"Interesting, Nashe," Amherst almost smiled. "I believe I am changing my mind about you. Offingham, I commend you on your intuition."

"Thank you, Sir," Offingham responded.

"Bradstreet, your thoughts?"

"I think our young captain here knows a great deal. I concur. Offingham, can you spare me your man for a day or two?"

"Of course," the old brigadier was smiling.

"Good then," Amherst announced. "We shall begin work on this course of action immediately."

"I say, Amherst," Governor Pownall interrupted, "this is all quite fine but what of protection from French raiders? Colonel Washington has had the devil's own time defending our border. And now Nashe reports a force poised in Montreal. We need more intelligence."

"Sir," Rogers interrupted, "my men can be in and out of French territory before they know it. I will supply Colonel Washington the details he needs."

"Perhaps some intelligence in that area would be useful," Amherst agreed.

Nashe glanced toward Offingham. The older man was already writing a note. He handed it to Amherst while Rogers continued expounding his plan. Amherst looked up quickly. Only Nashe and Offingham observed the surprise in his face. He interrupted Rogers.

"It seems you would be of more value here, Captain Rogers. Security reasons I believe. Offingham has informed me of French spies infiltrating south. He thinks he has discovered their route. Your men have the expertise to stop them."

Amherst was a convincing liar. Rogers, taken aback, sat down.

By luncheon they were all tired. Amherst dismissed them. As the meeting ended a messenger appeared for Washington. The colonel was given a note. There was a brief, whispered conversation; then Washington approached Nashe.

"Captain Nashe, you requested the whereabouts of a woman you rescued from the forest?"

"Indeed, Colonel, I did."

"Then this is for you, Sir. My men have located the woman."

Nashe took the note from Washington, perplexed by the man's discomfiture, and read it.

'I wish to thank you, Mr. Nashe, for your kindness. You have helped me find my way home.'

The note was unsigned.

"What is the matter, Colonel? Where is she?"

"I'm afraid she has hanged herself, Captain. My men found her this morning, this letter pinned to her dress. I'm sorry."

Just then Nashe realized he did not even know the woman's name. As it turned out, no one did.

## 51

"She was one of so many, another mark on the ledger no one keeps. She will be buried tomorrow, a simple funeral with no one there to remember her," George Washington muttered as he ate. Washington had asked Nashe and Offingham to supper. The meal was simple fare: vegetables, fruit, some cheese.

"I have set a bad example, Sir. The British staff does not like me. It is my fault they don't see the worth of colonial troops. But it is we who have held the French at bay for so many years. It is we who understand this land's worth. This war will determine our future," he waved away Nashe's attempted interjection. "Mr. Nashe, this is the war of the New World. The entire armies of both sides here would be lost in a corner of Europe's battlefields. But Europe is old and set in her ways, this just another of her many wars. It is the ends of wars, what comes after, that make history. And history, gentlemen, will be made here. As Montesquieu would say, we are caught up in history."

Returning from Washington's rooms, Nashe and Offingham discussed the man's view.

"I like his feeling of a sense of history, of being caught in it. I like that very much," Nashe intoned. "We are all of us little men and history will take us where it goes."

"But Montesquieu has missed something, Nashe. There are also men who take history and lead it down its path. That man back there could be one of them, I think."

"Agreed."

"He is young yet but the seeds of his future are planted. For now he is our ally. But a man with his thoughts could never conform. You mark this, Nashe. He will someday be the enemy. And he will hang for it."

In the soft light of Offingham's room that night, Nashe was given his orders.

"You'll be with Bradstreet for the next few days. I'll be gone tomorrow, north, to our forward lines. Rogers must be investigated. You are to return to Quebec, to continue as you have but for one small matter: Ledrew is to be relieved. Use what parts of his network you deem necessary, but be careful. You must get Ledrew out, to me."

"But I've told you, Sir, I have no idea whether he's dead or alive, imprisoned or free..."

"Find out, man. That's your job. Find him, and send him out. And whatever happens, don't be seen here in Albany. Get out as soon as possible. When the offensive comes you'll be in Quebec, likely cut off from us. Ledrew will be needed."

"You seem so sure we will reach Quebec."

"Not this year. But certain people I have in Versailles tell me the war is tiring the French. They are worried over their homeland, not over distant holdings. They'll send few men here. Montcalm is very good, but in a year's time his army will be worn out. And we must be prepared for that. Not this year, perhaps not next, but we will arrive."

"Brigadier, is it absolutely necessary for me to return to Quebec? Is there no one else?"

"Whatever do you mean?"

"A great many things have happened there... some unpleasant things. Perhaps someone else would be more suitable. I've left considerable confusion in my wake..."

"Don't be ridiculous, Captain," Offingham's voice hardened. "Who else has your contacts? You have work to do, Nashe. I expect you to perform your duties no matter what other affairs stand in the way. Remember, you are not your own man. Someday you will be, but not now. For now, you are mine, and England's."

## 52

They left Albany as they had come, in the night. But now they paddled northwest, travelling by the moon, gliding along the stillness of rivers. At Oswego they did not turn north as Nashe had expected. Instead, Vadnais steered them around the lakeshore to Toronto. To Nashe's questions he answered simply: "You have seen only two sides of this war. I'm taking you to the pays en haut, to the high country where white men are scarce as sea birds. A brief detour; and you said you wanted to see the fur country."

So they continued west, their travel quick and easy. As they made their way upriver they began to travel by day. There was no fear of patrols here. They would meet no one now, enwrapped in solitude as though men did not exist.

They spoke little as they paddled, listening and watching instead the subtle world around them. The tremble of streams as they passed them, clouds scudding across wide lakes their shadows drifting on the waters, the quickness of deer raising their heads, sometimes an osprey diving into grey waters then surfacing with a fish... it was a world so wonderful that Nashe found himself less troubled with his private problems.

Each night they would camp and share a brief meal of pemmican and barley cakes. They would speak of what they had seen that day, Nashe always full of questions, Vadnais patiently answering. And then they would fall quiet again, close to the small fire, each man with his thoughts, alone with himself and the night wind.

One night Vadnais told him more of what lay to the west.

"From here the forest goes on and on, the land becomes rocky and there are lakes like oceans. They lead eventually to the grasslands. I am told a thousand miles of land without trees. I have been to the fleuve Rouge and the lac Winnipeg. There are fur posts there. And I've seen the bison. They look like great cattle with the hides of bears. They run in herds stretching to the horizon and the ground trembles when they pass. And further west stand mountains as high as the sky they say. What is beyond them I do not know. I would like to find out. I have a mind to do that someday."

One day they rested. With Vadnais asleep beneath the canoe Nashe decided to walk alone. He found himself in a clearing where once lightning had struck and burned the trees away. Now there was grass and a few scrubby bushes as the forest reclaimed its own from the sky. At the edge of the glade Nashe heard a soft bawling. Intrigued, he crossed to a fall of trees. Inside a shaded depression, he saw two bright eyes staring out at him. A frightened bear cub was caught in the tangle. As he reached inside and pulled the cub out it whimpered and did not struggle. In the sunlight it blinked, putting its paws to its eyes and rolling over clumsily. Nashe laughed aloud at this thing so young and helpless. He petted it and it rubbed its flanks against him rolling over again.

Suddenly from behind him he heard an animal's roar and turned to see a great black she-bear thundering down on him from across the clearing. And then the bear was on him savage and gaping jaws and its claws ripped open his back and the jaws closed on his forearm. He saw the inch long teeth sink in and tear and there was an awful pain as he was thrown into the air.

## 53

There were walls on either side of him, close, holding him fast. There was the sound of flowing water and where he lay it was cool. He was in a canoe, the canoe was moving. His wounds were bound so tightly he could not move. He saw Vadnais in the stern, paddling. There was sweat on the big man's brow. He was paddling hard, his face a mask of concern. Nashe wanted to speak to him. Then the pain welled again and he fell into darkness.

When next he came around he felt he was in a dream. All about him were brown men and he was being hoisted up. As they turned him he saw vistas of blue water disappearing into sky and a long curving beach where dark-haired women in deerskins and naked children came running toward him. He was carried on shoulders into a compound crowded with a chattering mob of natives.

The pain returned but with it came clarity. He was in a village of big bark-covered houses and there were dust and smoke and yelping dogs. He was taken to a small wigwam and laid on a platform of reeds and leaves. The bed was cool. Smoke burned his eyes. There were strange odours. He slept.

He was awakened by a sweet smell he did not recognize. He noticed Vadnais squatting by the low wall of the hut. Beside his bed two shamans were chanting. One rattled shells as the other applied a viscous substance and then moss to Nashe's wounds. The man's hands were gentle. His face was old and lined and brown. His head was shaved but for a top notch filled with beads and feathers. His breath was sweet, his voice deep and hypnotic.

He bound the poultice tightly around Nashe's chest and arm tying it with bark and hemp. It made an effective cast. He gave Nashe a bowl of hot liquid that tasted strangely of peppermint and earth and then his chanting lulled Nashe to sleep again.

For two weeks he lay on his reed platform too feeble to move. Women fed him and the shaman changed the poultice daily. Slowly the pain dulled, then became merely a discomfort. He found after a time he could sit up. At first it made him dizzy and he worried over that, but eventually the light-headedness went away. When he was not sleeping he would lie listening to the village sounds: the dogs, the children giggling and running, the clank of cooking pots and the strange language of these people. And every day Vadnais would come to sit with him. The day Nashe first sat up relieved his friend's concern. Vadnais broke into a broad, infectious grin.

"I thought I had lost my Captain," he pronounced, "who so foolishly walked in places he should not. You came between a cub and its mother, my friend. You have much to learn before you try walking the forest alone."

"How long has it been?"

"Since the she-bear? Eighteen days. You lost much blood; your ribs were broken. We feared you had internal wounds we could not heal. It's good you do not. You may be the luckiest man I have ever met. Whatever it is you have over you, it is powerful medicine."

"Where are we?"

"This was our destination when we set out. When you were injured I brought you here quickly. Here I knew you would be safe."

"But what is this village?"

"A Ouendat village. A small place now compared to what it once was."

"Ouendat?"

"The French call them Huron. The scalp locks of the warriors reminded the French of boar bristles, thus the name. It is not an honourable name. These people do not use it."

"Are the Ouendat a large tribe?"

"No longer. Once they were a great race, but not warlike. The Iroquois came. The Iroquois slaughtered them. There are a few scattered villages left now. This village no longer goes to war."

"This is your village. This is where you came from."

"This is the village of my mother. I am tolerated."

"Then I look forward to meeting your friends, and your mother."

"I have no friends here," Vadnais murmured. He rose from the earthen floor. At the doorway he turned slowly. "And you will not meet my mother. To her, I am a dead man."

He was gone before Nashe could question him further. And after that he told Nashe not to speak of the matter. Nashe accepted his wishes. It was little enough to do for the man who had saved his life.

*⁂*

As his strength returned the shaman no longer came to change the dressings. Instead young women, girls really, appeared each day to do the job. They giggled quietly behind their hands as they replaced the poultice. Nashe was perplexed at their behaviour. Vadnais told him he had become something of a celebrity. Everyone wanted a close look at him. And the girls were awaiting his sign.

"A sign? What type of sign? I can't speak the language! How can I give them a sign?"

"Simple, my friend," Vadnais chuckled. "When you give the sign they will know. And so, I might add, will you."

In the days that followed he sat in the warm sun outside, observing the ways of the Ouendat, recovering his health. He noticed that families shared the long houses he had seen when he first arrived. Several families lived in each house communally. The houses were huge, sometimes nearly a hundred feet long. The tribe itself seemed to be one great family.

Maize was the staple diet. He watched the women prepare his food. They baked unleavened bread under hot campfire ashes and added dried fruits and venison for taste. The food was plain, but it was good food and filling. For flavouring they used a sprinkle of ashes on their food, they had no salt, and delicious syrup taken from the maple tree of which Nashe became quite fond. He ate heartily, his appetite returning with his strength.

Other than hunting for fish or game, it seemed women were responsible for all the work: they farmed, prepared meals, made clothing from deerskin and baskets from reeds. The men contented themselves with making clay pipes. They competed for the best pipe, creating bowls that took the shapes of animal heads or strange symbols that Nashe could not comprehend. They would spend a great deal of time grooming themselves: their scalp locks greased with

170

oils, their feathers chosen carefully. They reminded Nashe of the men of Bath, or Versailles. Men's nature is immutable, no matter where they might be.

The women wore little more than the men: skirts of deerskin, moccasins, often they went bare breasted in the heat of the day. Nashe was attracted to their fluid grace. He watched them return from their daily swim, fresh, glistening, inviting.

After the swim his dressings would be changed. He no longer felt the need but the girls continued to arrive daily and insisted he submit. It was not an unpleasant experience. One particular day a lovely young girl took him inside the hut for his dressing change. He found himself overwhelmed by her gentleness, by her strange dark beauty, the joy of her smile. It was as if all the girls who had helped him were embodied within this one. He took from his neck the gold cross he wore, a part of his masquerade, and gave it to her as a gift of thanks. For a moment her eyes went wide, and then a slow lovely smile crossed her lips. She stood, and before he could prevent it, slipped out of her skirt and stood naked before him.

She knelt by him and began to caress him. He kissed her. She looked surprised, then blank, but then she giggled and pouted her lips for another kiss. He responded. She lay beside him. The arousal began just as Vadnais strode through the door.

The big man grinned as Nashe tried to cover the girl's nudity. She continued smiling.

"I see you've recovered, my friend. That is good."

As Vadnais turned to go Nashe panicked.

"But what are the ramifications of this? For God's sake, Owl, I don't know these people! What am I in for?"

"A great deal of pleasure I should say. You have given the sign. A good thing too, the women were beginning to worry over your health." He grinned.

"For heaven's sake, man, what if she's married?"

"Has that ever stopped you before?"

"This is different!"

"She is not married. She will be honoured among her peers. If you refuse her she will be shamed. The women here choose whom they wish if they are not married. There are no repercussions. On with it, my friend! Restore your health!"

He departed, pulling down the hide coverlet that served as a door. And Nashe was left with the girl.

It did wonders for his health.

**54**

Time drifted through warm dusty days in the village, summer slowly departing as nights grew cooler and the tribe busied itself with harvest and winter storage. In the evenings he sat with them around their fires eating sagamite and venison and drinking spruce beer.

He had enjoyed this hibernation among the Ouendat, far from the cares of the world he belonged to, but still, he belonged to that world. He was not yet finished there. One night he decided to seek out Vadnais and ask to return.

He could not find him. Eventually he searched away from the fires, behind the long houses in a dark quarter of the camp where he had never been before. The place seemed forgotten by the tribe: grassy and untrodden. In its centre was a little tumbledown wigwam and before this discarded hut, squatting rigid and trance-like in the dark, was the silhouette of Vadnais.

Nashe spent a while studying his friend, deciding whether or not to disturb his vigil. And just as he made up his mind a warrior appeared from the dark. He murmured in French: "Do not disturb the Owl, Monsieur. This is the night he keeps his watch."

"Is this a custom?"

"Only for him. He is trying to make his peace."

"I don't understand."

"If he wishes he will tell you. Come back to the fires, you are not welcome here. Speak not of this. It would be very bad manners."

Nashe did not argue. He had no understanding of native ways and in that moment he realized how little he knew of his friend. At the fireside he was silent, pondering what he had seen. And some time later Vadnais appeared, solemnly touching his shoulder.

"There is someone who wishes to see you, Alan. Come with me, it isn't far."

Nashe had anticipated the walk back to that darkened quarter, but that was not the way Vadnais led him. Instead, he took Nashe away from the village and up the shoreline of the bay.

"Where are we going, my friend?"

"To the sachem, the village chief."

"Outside the walls?"

"He likes to spend his nights alone with the water."

"I'd thought we'd be going to the hut in back of the village."

Vadnais whirled on him as he spoke.

"You were there? You saw?"

"I came upon you by accident."

"You will not speak of that place, Alan. If you value my friendship you will not speak of it."

"I understand." He did not, but the man was so agitated Nashe thought better of pursuing the matter.

"No, my friend, you do not," Vadnais softened slightly. "Later I will tell you of this. But now we have a meeting. You are going meet an unusual man. A very old and wise man."

The two clambered out into the lake over boulders shoved there in a line by storms. As they neared the end of the point Nashe observed a figure. And just then moonlight touched the granite where the figure sat and, as it turned, Nashe saw silver hair and a face that was a thousand lines, as old as stone but living. The face slowly smiled and as it did its lines transformed into another face, yet still the same. It was a wondrous, fascinating face, its character like water: never the same, never constant, like waves. Sitting there in the moonlight with the phosphorescence of the lake around them the old man spoke, his voice surprisingly clear. He spoke in halting French.

"The Owl tells me you are English. I want you to explain the English to me. I want to know the wave when it comes to wash over me."

"What do you mean?"

"I am facing the end of something. The French have come; they will not leave. The English have come; they too will not leave. At first we did not accept white men. Yet the white man conquers in subtle ways. He trades for furs with iron pots and guns, with liquor. Now we cannot live without these things. And now it is the end of something. We will smoke, and the smoke will go to our brains and enlighten us. And then you will tell me of the English."

The pipe smoke made Nashe dizzy. When it was finished the old man set the pipe carefully between them.

"I have been to Montreal," he murmured. "I have seen people living in stone. The French do not much change the land. I hear the English do. I hear they divide the land and declare all beasts and all men and all waters within their walls to be theirs. This I do not understand. How can one own a stream?"

Nashe tried to explain European culture to a man as old as the stones. He told how Europe was divided into countries and duchies, farms and gardens. He told how men would pass ownership on to their descendants... and how some men would never own anything. As he spoke he observed the old sachem's face: a frank, worried face trying to comprehend. And Nashe knew then that the man was right, that something irreplaceable was going to be lost. The old man interrupted him.

"You say these men come here to begin again. Yet they have changed nothing."

"They know no other way."

"And you now, you think one life better than the other?"

"I don't know. Both have good and bad. They are too different to ever meet."

"You will return to your people soon?"

"Yes."

"We will share this land with you, young man, and your people. That is the way things will go. Tell your friends when you return. You are welcome here, but do not try to own a stream."

He spoke no further, simply turning toward the lake sitting motionless, his back to them. And after a while Nashe ceased to feel the hardness of stone beneath him. He watched the moon pass across the sky and, when the moon was gone, watched the passage of stars. He had never before taken time to watch stars pass. A little breeze played about his face and the waves whispered beneath him among the rocks. When the stars had faded and light began to crest the horizon the old man turned to them again, his voice barely audible.

"I feel in you a stream battling against its own rocks. You have made obstacles in your life. You should return to your people. That is your life. But remember obstacles are to be passed, not dwelled upon."

Then he spoke to Vadnais: "Did you see the witch last night?"

"No," Vadnais answered him.

"But you kept the vigil?"

"Yes. She will not make peace."

"It is enough that you try."

"She will never make peace. She is lost in her spells."

"Does this man have knowledge of what has passed?"

"No," Vadnais murmured.

"You have told me he is your friend."

174

"This is a private thing."

"The entire village knows of it. Perhaps, young man," he turned to Nashe, "you have something to ask the Owl?"

"Who is the witch?" Nashe asked the old man.

"She is my daughter."

"She is my mother," Vadnais choked on the words.

***

In the half-light of early morning the village had come to life. Vadnais and Nashe sat outside sharing a breakfast of berries and bread. Vadnais spoke in low tones.

"My father was a trader. Trade was good then. Bigot had not come to power. When he did he hired Cadet, Varin, Penniseault... men known for their greed. Soon they controlled everything. Traders either worked for them or slid into debt and were sent to prisons. Some men did what my father did, became coureurs du bois. They took to the forest ignoring the taxes and licenses. That is how my father came to this place. He was accepted here. He married.

When I became old enough my father took me with him to trade. As a youth I was swayed to the ways of the French. Even when my father returned here I remained in Quebec. My mother blamed my father. He went back for me.

My father was called an outlaw. He should not have returned. They struck at the trade fair in Montreal. Men burst in on my father and me. Five of them stabbed my father to death. I was sixteen then. I tried to stop them. This scar on my face is the result.

Later I killed one of the murderers. Choked him to death. Two fled to France. I wanted to kill Bigot but I could do nothing. He is protected. I swore then to end his corruption. That is the beast of this country. That is why I work for Ledrew.

A year later I returned here. My mother would not stop grieving for my father. She had spent that year alone in the forest. People feared her. They said she was a witch. They said she could talk to stones. When I found her she was mad. She did talk to stones, but they did not answer.

What could I do? She was my mother. I brought her back to the village. I took her to our old hut. She closed the door skins on me then. She has not

175

opened them since. She considers me French. She will not make peace with the French. She will not make peace with me.

Everyone abandoned that part of the village. My grandfather causes food to be left there and in the mornings it is gone. That is how we know she still lives. Each year I return to keep the vigil.

Now you know.

And now it is time to leave here. You must begin your work again. You must help me bring down Bigot."

## 55

In the first days of autumn they returned to Montreal. They arrived with a group of returning voyageurs. It was in Montreal that they saw the first bodies: charred remains hanging at crossroads.

"This is how they execute traitors," Vadnais told Nashe soberly. "There must have been some sort of rebellion. You'd best be careful, my friend, this has the look of panic."

Nashe left his friend to care for whatever business his own voyageurs might have brought, hired a horse and set out north on Chemin Royale for Quebec. All along the route, usually a peaceful and pleasant journey, were more bodies. In the taverns and parish squares men spoke of the bad harvest. The summer had been too hot and dry; too many young men were away at war...not enough labour, not enough rain, a hard winter coming.

Nashe found himself one of the few who possessed any money. A meal that once cost three sols was now ten times that. A new form of currency had been issued. Bigot had created his own money. The ordonnances, promissory notes signed by Bigot, were created from playing cards. Nashe thought grimly of the irony: Bigot, the gambler, had issued cards as currency.

The war's effects were being felt. In the noon sun outside a tavern in the village of Champlain, Nashe discovered the extent. He shared a meal with a wizened old fellow.

"When I left Carillon I left victory. The English were scattered, in ruins."

"Perhaps, your honour," the old habitant answered him, "but this is not the field of battle and someone must pay for these victories. Here our women and children go hungry. Still the taxes increase. Tell me, your honour, does the army go hungry?"

"I've been gone a long time," Nashe replied. "Have things changed so much?"

The old man peered carefully at Nashe. Before he began he looked carefully around.

"I do not know you, Monsieur. I am an old man. I have little left to lose. So I will tell you what has happened, and if you are the police then that is my luck. The Intendancy requisitions our food for the army. There is little food left, your honour. And now the Intendancy billets soldiers among us. They're supposed to work the farms where they stay. Few do. Still, we are forced to keep them. The ordonnances of Intendant Bigot are a joke. Everyone knows they won't be repaid. And Bigot himself lives very well, I hear. They tell me it's worse in the cities. They say refugees flow in from the east. We are told the war goes well. But it does not seem so, your honour."

Nashe bought the old man a flask of wine for his trouble and continued his journey. When he reached Quebec he found it too had changed. In the markets long lines formed at a few near empty stalls, fights broke out over even a slice of fish. And in the streets were Daine's police. People stepped fearfully out of their paths. The Esplanade, once a beautiful park, was a muddy quagmire choked with refugees' tents. Hungry children mixed with ragged columns of troops on Rue St. Louis and Nashe noticed few carriages in the streets. The rich had hidden themselves away.

He had left a city ready for victory. And there had been a victory. Yet this city had the look of defeat.

The only cheerful event of his day was his arrival at his apartments. Mme. Courvier had dusted his rooms and placed a bouquet of autumn flowers on his table. He'd forgotten the comfort of his rooms. But when he ordered a steaming bath and a bottle of claret he was apologetically informed that the claret was gone. He settled for the last of an old flask of cognac. Then he restored himself in the bath.

On his bureau he found a note from Bougainville. The note was brief:

> 'If you return you will find this waiting. I thank God that
> you are alive. By now you will have seen the situation. I
> have a great deal to tell you. I can only hope you will return
> and if you have, tonight we will share the last of my Gascon
> wine. It is a pity.
> I remain your friend and servant, Bougainville'

Soon the cold north winds would whistle down the St. Laurent bringing the first harsh signals of winter. And with the snow the war would ebb. But the sharp northern gales would no longer subdue those subtle winds from the south. The winds of war fly low to the ground. For Alan Nashe war was just beginning.

## 56

He found Bougainville at the Jesuit college. The interior was a cobbled square enclosed by three storied whitewashed buildings. It was choked with hundreds of wounded men nursed by the black robed brothers. Nashe passed through long hollow halls. He came to a central foyer. Its desks were choked with papers; its clerks harried men running about trying to organize the hundreds who crowded its doorways. And then Bougainville, recovered from his wounds, came from an interior office and greeted Nashe like a lost brother, his eyes filled with emotion. "This is as good a place to meet as any these days," Bougainville murmured. "I've been assigned to this, this chaos." He led Nashe to a small office shutting the door against the confusion outside.

I left a victory, Antoine. What is all this?"

"I take it you've been through the city..."

"And the countryside: the crossroads are not a pretty sight."

"There are few pretty sights these days," Bougainville muttered wearily.

"What has happened?"

"Happened? Happened?" Bougainville paced the room as the words spilled from him. "Have you no eyes, man? The blockade, the English offensive, and more than that the enemy within! Have you seen this?" He produced two playing cards each with Bigot's signature.

"Yes. The country people think little of them."

"And they are right! Playing cards! Have you any idea how demoralizing this is? And Cadet is either an idiot or the worst of criminals! He charges the army for provisions, he attaches duty to transport, he commandeers civilian goods and the goods disappear in the bottomless pit of his wastage. Meanwhile he and Bigot flounce about fat as hogs, using soldiers to suppress the resentment they cause! And Vaudreuil is worse. He is greedy for power. After Carillon, when he would not send us troops, he claimed the victory and disparaged Montcalm for not annihilating the English in retreat! And now there are rumours he has sent to Versailles demanding the general be replaced!"

The tirade ended with Bougainville falling into a chair. He massaged his temples. Nashe waited for him to recover then asked about Montcalm.

"The general?" Bougainville sighed. "Frustrated, tired, furious. He constantly speaks of resignation. He's in Montreal now with de Levis. He has ordered me to France. Hopefully with my contacts at court I might sort this mess out!"

"You? To France! Why that's wonderful, Antoine. When?"

"A month perhaps. Just when the man is needed most he is called into question. But it is not just internal problems, Alan. The English too have offered surprises."

"After Carillon?" Nashe feigned surprise. "That looked to be the end of them."

"Well it was not," Bougainville returned sharply. "Louisbourg is lost. You've seen the refugees from the east? They pour into the city daily."

"What else?"

"Frontenac. Less than a month ago. That's why Montcalm is in Montreal. The English surprised the fort in late August. They caught us sleeping, Alan. Cadet had placed all supplies there for Duquesne and Niagara. The lake fleet was burned. Now our centre is cut. We have intelligence that an English force is nearing Duquesne, but we can do nothing about it. Carillon may be our only triumph. And that is my second reason for visiting France. I must convince Count D'Argenson, even Pompadour herself, to give us more aid."

"So you think we'll lose?"

"No, my friend, not for a moment! Morale is low now, but these men are a long way from beaten. This will be a long war. The English will lose a great many men at Niagara and Montreal. And all men know Quebec's power. The city is impregnable. And as Quebec stands, so stands this land!"

Nashe inquired about Bourlamaque.

"Not good," Bougainville replied. "His wounds are infected."

Bougainville paused then, as though considering something.

"But I've indulged myself too long in this jabber of war," he said. "Other things have occurred in your absence, Alan. Monsieur Duchesnay has instructed me that he wishes to see you as soon as you returned to the city. He'll be at home now, on the Place d'Armes."

"What can it be? Is Reine Marie ill?"

"No, not that."

"What then? Tell me, Antoine…"

"Better he tell you. I have another message as well. A month ago I met your friend, Tremais. He came seeking you at our apartments. There is something wrong with him, Alan. He refused to talk with me. He left this sealed letter, directing me to keep it for you."

Nashe took the note and opened it. Scrawled across the page was one line: 'Each Tuesday. Canoterie docks. The old eel pier at dusk.'

He folded the note into his pocket. It meant nothing to him and he had other things now on his mind. He left the office quickly, bidding his friend goodbye, fearing his meeting with Duchesnay. She had decided, he knew. Suddenly all the machinations of war seemed to pale.

She had decided.

## 57

The house on Place d'Armes appeared silent, but there was light in an upper window. Nashe pounded on the door and after a moment was greeted by a frightened servant. Recognizing Nashe, the fellow took him upstairs to a small drawing room. A single candle illuminated the room.

On two straight wooden chairs facing each other Antoine Duchesnay and his wife sat drinking cocoa. They looked older, their faces drawn. Nevertheless he was offered brandy and the usual greetings. Nashe wondered if they knew what had separated him and Reine Marie. If they did, they did not let on.

"Major Bougainville has told us you went to the pays en haut, Alan," Duchesnay began politely. "I'm glad you did so. I hope you've learned more of the country."

Nashe chafed under the vagaries of manners. He told them parts of his journey. But that was not what he had come for. In the end he shifted the topic in his own direction.

"I've discovered something else." Nashe took a deep breath and braced himself. "I have discovered how much I love your daughter. I'm here to ask your permission for her hand."

The old man stiffened. He looked at his wife then back to Nashe with a face like a frozen mask.

Mme. Juchereau finally spoke, her voice the personification of sympathy.

"Reine Marie has entered the Ursuline."

"What?"

"Sit down, Alan. Listen carefully. Whatever passed between you two is not known to us. We do not wish to know. She would have told us had she found it necessary. After your departure she changed. We tried to talk with her, but she would not respond. Then one day a message arrived saying she was in the Convent. There is some problem with her becoming a novice; nevertheless, she has told us she intends to remain there. She cares for the prisoners in St. Louis."

"We never see her, Alan," the old man choked. "She cannot take the vows yet, but she insists on a life of devotion. I know not whether to feel joy or despair. I do not know…"

"Well, I know!" Nashe roared. "She is the woman I love and I'll not have her throw herself into a half-life."

"Alan," Mme. Juchereau interrupted, "it is the Ursuline you blaspheme."

"To hell with the Ursuline, Madame! They have no right…"

"It is her decision."

"But I know why she made it! She believed I didn't love her. I must explain to her!"

"You cannot see her."

"Then I will batter down their doors!"

"It is not a bad thing to serve God, Alan."

"It is if it is done by mistake. She has at least the right to have the record straight."

"She left instructions that you should not see her."

"Damn the instructions!"

"This is blasphemy…" Mme. Juchereau said after him. He did not hear her. He had bounded down the stairs and into the night.

***

He pounded the studded door, then pulled his dagger from its scabbard and hammered with the butt. A barred wicket opened, a little window with the face of a frightened portiere. She wore a black veil that fell on each side of a snowy fillet that covered her forehead.

"What seek you, Monsieur? Where are your manners that you wake the house?"

"I seek an interview with Mlle. Duchesnay. I must see her tonight."

"Mlle. Duchesnay is indisposed. Perhaps you should return tomorrow."

181

"I must see her tonight!"

"I'm afraid that is out of the question, Monsieur. If you leave your name I shall..."

"My name is Nashe. I beg you, Sister; at least have her come to the door."

"I will see Mere Superieur. Wait here, and please be quiet."

He paced the alcove's stone flags impatiently. When the portiere did not return quickly enough, he again hammered on the door. After a time the wicket opened. The face that filled it was stern. Mere Superieur was furious.

"Monsieur Nashe, you are to leave my gate immediately. The police have been summoned, Monsieur. If you wish less trouble than you have created I suggest you depart."

"Reine Marie!" he screamed through the wicket into her face.

"She will not see you. You have caused the girl enough pain. If you love her, leave her in peace. Goodnight, Monsieur."

As she slammed the wicket, Nashe howled a curse and sank his dagger into the door. Again and again the knife stabbed into the wood. Then Nashe, exhausted, slipped to the stone flags of the alcove. He heard boots pounding on the cobbles. The soldiers sent to arrest him. One of them used a gun butt, striking Nashe on the temple. The blow stunned him. Arms held him. The cursing soldiers beat him. And then a clear voice, one he well remembered, put a stop to it. There was no arguing with that voice. Nashe was released.

"Mme. Beaubassin!" an officer exclaimed.

"I know this man, Captain. He is a friend. If you wish to retain your rank you'll refrain from further brutality. Look what you've done to him!"

"He was resisting arrest."

"Nonsense, Captain. Monsieur Nashe, are you badly hurt?"

"No, Madame." Nashe wiped the blood from his eyes. "I caused the disturbance. I apologize."

"More nonsense! Whatever is the trouble?"

"Reine Marie. They won't let me see her."

"Say no more. Captain, this gentleman will come with me. I shall assume responsibility."

"I'm afraid that's not possible, Madame. He is under arrest."

"He is a gentleman, Captain. I am quite sure you do not arrest everyone for disturbing the peace. If you did, half the Lower Town would be in prison. Now, let me have him."

"I cannot, Madame. I have orders to take him to Colonel Daine."

"You will inform Monsieur Daine that I shall be at his headquarters presently demanding a reason for this effrontery. Monsieur Nashe is a personal friend of General Montcalm. The general will want an explanation."

"That is not my affair, Madame. I must carry out my orders."

"Alan," she came to his side, "don't resist them. I'll have you free in no time."

"I am in your debt, Madame."

\*\*\*

Nashe was beginning to feel his bruises as he sat across from Francois Daine. The office was a plain room littered with official papers and on one wall a detailed map of the city. It was the office of a policeman.

"Now, Monsieur Nashe, it appears you've not been on your best behaviour tonight. Perhaps I might ask of you a few questions."

The matter is personal."

"Of course. Still, I must inquire."

"Yes."

"Fine. Where have you been for the past two months?"

"I don't see how that has anything..."

"Answer the question, Monsieur!" the sharp-faced officer shouted.

"I was in the west inspecting the fur grounds."

"In the midst of a war?"

"I trade, Monsieur Daine. War or no war, commerce continues."

"You ride a high horse, Monsieur. Be careful it does not throw you. The city is under martial law. Creating a disturbance such as you did tonight may carry a heavy penalty."

"No court will imprison me for that."

"Agreed. But trials can take time to arrange. You might spend a long time waiting in a cell, Nashe. I suggest you co-operate."

The questioning was intense. Nashe lied well. Trained in the subtleties of interrogation, the examination was no problem. What bothered Nashe was its motivation. Had they known he was a spy Daine would not have been alone.

The questioning brought back Nashe's self control. He realized he'd acted foolishly. Soon the entire city would hear of it. He had been away too long, had forgotten why he was here. He concentrated on Daine's questions. Finally, Daine came to the crux of his interrogation.

"Tell me the whereabouts of Claude Querdisien Trémais."

"What has that to do with me?"

"That is none of your affair. We heard he visited your apartments last month."

"As you know, I was not there."

"You have no idea of his location?"

"Surely you have more important matters than finding one minor bureaucrat."

"Listen well, Nashe! I have had enough of your arrogance. A night or two in the cells will straighten you around. Perhaps you'll be in a better frame of mind after the dungeon of St. Louis!"

As Daine uttered the threat, his door flew open and a hostile and very determined Beaubassin pushed her way past a secretary and marched, her great cloak flying, directly to Daine's desk.

"I demand an explanation, Monsieur! This gentleman is my acquaintance. I was at the scene of the unfortunate altercation and other than a little shouting he has done nothing illegal. Don't doddle, man. Answer me!"

Daine stood dumbfounded before the onslaught of the formidable Beaubassin. Were it not so serious a matter, Nashe would have risked a smile. Daine tried weakly to counter.

"The Ursuline sisters laid a complaint, Madame," he sputtered.

"This is a gentleman, Monsieur! Unfortunately he had a little too much to drink while visiting my salon. One does not incarcerate a gentleman for a misdemeanour. If you were a gentleman, Monsieur, you would understand my meaning."

"Are you saying, Madame, that Monsieur Nashe was present in your house this evening?"

"You doubt my word, Daine? This case will be taken up with Monsieur Bigot. As your superior, in every way I might add, he will see to this shameful breach of justice."

"Monsieur Bigot will not see you, Madame."

"There is where you are wrong, Monsieur. A note has already been sent. He will see me. It is only his lackeys he has no time for. I now understand why."

Daine went pale.

"I have finished with the prisoner, Madame. He is to be let off with a warning."

"Let me remind you, Monsieur Daine, that Monsieur Nashe is not a prisoner. He is a merchant in good standing. You are the prisoner, Monsieur, of your own lack of manners. Good night to you. Monsieur Nashe, if you would take my arm and lead me from this den of peasants I would be much obliged."

Nashe did so. Beaubassin had rescued him. She smiled knowingly at her own display of power. Yet despite her smile Nashe felt a tinge of foreboding. He had made an enemy this night.

And Reine Marie had made the wrong decision.

## 58

Two weeks after the Ursuline incident, the scandal had diminished. Beaubassin had seen to the local gossips. She had also promised to intercede with Reine Marie. The attempt had been useless. The girl remained adamant. But Nashe noticed he was being followed. He resolved to be very careful, especially careful now on the Canoterie docks.

Canoterie was not a place Nashe had expected Trémais to frequent: a beleaguered slum, dangerous with footpads and drunken sailors, the wharves old and all but abandoned. Only fishermen used Canoterie now, and no one with any sense went near the place at night. The place was deserted but for Nashe who awaited contact by the eel pier.

In the mist, Nashe discerned the shadow of a man. As the figure materialized, Nashe's hand rested on his sword hilt. The man came carefully, he too with a hand at his side. One was never imprudent in Canoterie. Life was too fragile there.

"You are Nashe?" he whispered hoarsely.

"I am."

"Step into this doorway." He directed Nashe to an alcove. The two men stood close. The fellow lit a piece of tallow holding it up to Nashe's face, the glow illuminating his own. What Nashe saw he did not like: a ferret's face, sly and shifting, the eyes never still. The man's breath stank of garlic and eels and cheap wine.

"If you're satisfied, I suggest you put out the candle; the light will draw attention and Daine's patrols are heavy tonight."

"What ship did you arrive on?" The ferret face breathed out the light.

"Celebre."

"And what happened on the voyage over?"

"It was a rough voyage."

Without a word he turned away. Nashe grasped his arm, holding him. The man glared.

"I must be sure, Nashe. Trémais told me to be sure."

"I killed a man."

"Come with me and be quiet."

They made their way through a maze of alleys. They encountered no patrols, only the fires of drunkards trying to stay warm. And by the river, they came to a hovel built half on land, half on piles above the river. It was a decrepit, filthy place. As they entered, Nashe nearly did not recognize the emaciated form awaiting him, what remained of Trémais.

He appeared sallow, the once round face angular and dark. He had not shaved in several days. His clothing was torn and filthy. As the two men met, the ferret face left the room. Trémais quickly locked the door behind him.

"Nashe. Thank God you've returned. You cannot know how relieved I am." The voice was as tired as the face.

"What has happened, Claude? This place, you..."

"Since I last saw you, on the road to Montreal was it not? Since I last saw you, there have been three attempts on my life. Once they nearly had me. I have a miniball in my leg. In the damp it hurts..."

"Let me see it."

"No. The flesh is healed over. I couldn't take the chance of seeing a surgeon. I'm waiting to smuggle myself aboard a ship to France. I must get out of here. The patrols are searching for me. That is why I live in this sty and why I have Lefebre."

"The man who brought me here?"

"Yes. The bastard extorts money for protection. This is his house. I'm at his mercy and he knows it. My funds are depleted. I haven't paid him in a week. I can't get more money. I can't even venture outside. I live in terrible fear, Nashe. You still have the packet I gave you?"

"Of course."

"I didn't know then the depth of this snake pit. Dissolute men have their claws in this country."

"Cadet. I know. Everyone knows, Trémais."

"But I have proof! And it isn't simply Cadet. It's the entire Grande Societé: Varin, the Intendant's deputy in Montreal; Martel, the King's storekeeper; Le Mercier, chief of munitions; Rigaud, the governor's brother; your friend de Vergor; Penniseault, Péan, Corpon... the list is endless!"

"You say you have proof?"

"Sworn affidavits from the scoundrels who worked for them, secret records I've laid hands on. I even have some of their contracts."

"How? What contracts?"

"In '56 they sold materials worth eleven million livres to the King, for twenty three million! They work through a company in Bordeaux called Gradis and Sons. They get stores there then ship them here and sell them again. Supplies requisitioned by the military are halved and the records falsified. The forts' clerks receive bribes to keep them quiet. Remember that little sleighing excursion to Montreal? That cost a quarter million!"

"Then Bigot is in on this."

"In it? He directs it! He is the one who signs all the papers. But he is a fox. I've no proof on him. He's covered himself so well there is no way to unmask him. He keeps two houses: the Intendancy itself and a mansion outside Quebec near Charlebourg. He calls it the Hermitage. Two secretaries are kept in each residence: one for the day, one for night. The secretaries never meet. Their identities are kept secret even from each other."

"Then nothing can be done?"

"Possibly. Each year a shipment of gold is sent from Versailles, enough to cover projected costs. Yet now we have these ordonnances when there should be gold. Where is the gold?"

"In the Hermitage?"

"Not well enough guarded. I've been there. But what place, other than Chateau St. Louis, has more guards than anywhere else in New France?"

"The Intendancy!"

"More specifically the Intendancy vaults. They are massive, the entire basement of the palace. And no one without Bigot's expressed clearance is allowed inside them. I would dearly love a look at those vaults. Still this is all conjecture..."

"But you have evidence of everything else?"

"Absolutely."

"Look, Claude, you recall the Celebre, when I searched your cabin?"

"Yes?"

"I found papers that would allow you to march into chateau St. Louis and assume control of the Intendancy. Why not go to Vaudreuil and tell him? Or is he in it as well?"

"I don't think so. He's too much the fool."

"Then why not do it?"

"Because Rigaud, his brother, is involved, and Bigot. They are his most trusted advisors. Do you think that arrogant popinjay would believe a thing I said? Anyway, I'd never get near him. I'd be murdered before I set foot a mile from his presence. The patrols have been searching for me for months. My only hope is to get to France."

"What do you want me to do?"

"I have a second packet of documents. If I'm killed, get to France. It tells the story."

"Major Bougainville is leaving for France. He's a friend. He'll protect you."

"A miracle! Can you manage it?"

"Easily. Come with me now. We'll go straight to his rooms."

There was a sudden hammering on the door.

## 59

"**O**pen up, Trémais!" The voice was de Vergor's. They heard the shuffling feet of more men. Trémais stared wide-eyed at Nashe. "You were followed!"

"Impossible. I made sure."

"Then Lefebre has turned on me."

"Open the door or we break it down!"

"Quickly, help me," Trémais ran to a pallet pulling it sideways. A shoulder rammed against the door. Nashe drew his pistol.

"Don't be a fool," Trémais rasped. "They're assassins; they'll be ready. Here, take these planks. I've prepared for this."

He ripped four boards from the floor. They had been pre-cut. Below was the night. The stench of the riverbank wafted up into the room. Again the door shuddered.

"Mud below. Jump quickly. I have a canoe under the wharf."

Nashe dropped into the muck. Trémais followed. They heard the crack of a musket. The men above tried to blow the door in. Another shot. Trémais cleared away branches concealing a canoe. The door above gave way. Footsteps pounded into the room.

"I moved the bed back," Trémais whispered. "It gives us a few more seconds. In this fog, we'll be safe."

They hauled the vessel into the water. Trémais took the stern. There was shouting behind. They heaved at their paddles. Shots rang out above them. Then the fog closed around, the ghosts of the river their friends. Sweating with fear, they glided out into the current.

"Go east," Nashe murmured, "across the St. Charles. I know a place we can hide."

"I've another place at the south end of the Cap. We can be there in minutes."

"Trémais, I feel water..."

Trémais leaned forward to investigate. He discovered two jagged slits just at the water line below the gunwale.

"Children," he muttered. "The children of Canoterie run wild, damn them! Nashe, do you still have the packet?"

"No."

"Where is it, man? You didn't leave it in the room?"

"Don't panic, my friend. I hid it in a crack between the wharf and its pilings. It won't be found."

"Listen, I hear horses on shore."

"Likely patrols responding to the shots. Is this place we're going safe?"

"You mean from Lefebre? Yes. See that torch there? That's Batterie Royale. A little further down is our landing place at the foot of Rue des Carrieres."

"You have a propensity for slums, my friend."

"I have little money and the people in slums tend not to co-operate with the police."

Their vessel went slowly, gradually filling with water. In the fog Trémais had trouble getting his bearings. They were forced to land, the canoe sinking beneath them. They stayed on the shoreline away from the hovels of Rue des Carrieres. Trémais peered into the grey for some landmark. They moved as slowly as they had done on water, their eyes to the ground so as not to trip.

"I remember this grove," Trémais remarked. "Nearby is the place we seek."

"Not nearby, Messieurs, right here will do." De Vergor's voice came out of the fog. He stepped from the trees. "Don't try to run. You're surrounded. It was a hard ride to get here, but at least we knew where to go."

"How..." Trémais was dumbstruck.

"You are a man of habits, Trémais. Lefebre has followed you everywhere. I could have had you long since. I just wanted to wait a while and see who your friends were. This friend, Monsieur, is a poor choice. But I'm pleased to meet him here. How do you do, Nashe? Discouraged, no doubt."

Others came out of the fog. Each held a pistol. Nashe offered nothing in reply.

"I'll take my money now, your honour," the face of Lefebre appeared in the gloom.

"Indeed," de Vergor answered. "I have a reward for you much greater than promised."

"I wish only what I asked," his face turned to a suspicious scowl.

"But you shall have more; all the treasures of heaven if you were a good man. If you were not, you deserve nothing anyway."

A knife drove into Lefebre's back. It made a sucking noise as the assailant pulled it out again. Lefebre collapsed at de Vergor's feet. De Vergor smiled.

"An untrustworthy soul. You should have done that long ago, Trémais. You are a stupid man. And now you'll pay for your ignorance."

Two men in front of Trémais drew their rapiers. Trémais' mouth opened but no sound came out. He raised his hands in front of himself in a vain attempt to stay the thrusts. Three men behind him hauled swords from their scabbards. Trémais half turned. All five men thrust simultaneously. Nashe heard the blades rasp together inside Trémais' body. Trémais gurgled once, blood spurting from his mouth. His eyebrow went up quizzically, just once. The swords pulled away but for one that had stuck in bone. Its owner held Trémais standing, placed his foot on the man's stomach and wrenched the sword out. Trémais was dead before he hit the ground.

Nashe was nauseated. He screamed for help. Again and again he shouted. The circle of men laughed. De Vergor stepped quickly up to him and kicked. Nashe fell to the beach, his breath gone.

"No one will come, Nashe. I'm surprised you were fool enough to think it. You are below contempt, an idiot drowning where he thought he could swim. You have bothered me long enough." He aimed his pistol at Nashe's head. Nashe closed his eyes and with his last gasp cursed the murderer.

"Unfortunately, this will have to be quick. I would have preferred another way," de Vergor spat.

Francois Daine's voice interrupted the murder.

"Vergor! You know the orders. It's bad enough you didn't tell me of Trémais; this one is not to be killed."

"Damn the orders!" de Vergor muttered. "He's mine now and I shall have him."

A pistol fired. Nashe opened his eyes to see de Vergor's face twist in pain, his wrist bloodied.

"This one has done nothing but help a friend," Daine said, a pistol smoking in his hand. "Our work is done. We're leaving."

As he turned, de Vergor aimed one frustrated boot at Nashe's skull. The night for Nashe went to bursting brightness. Then nothing.

*** 

He came to the next morning in the mud and morass of the riverbank. His head felt like a split melon. When he tried to stand, he fell to his knees and vomited. He stank of rum. They had poured rum over him. Two fishermen had come to his aid. They joked together about young gentlemen feeling their oats. There was no sign of Trémais' body.

Still, Nashe knew the author of the past night. Bigot. Yet the cunning Intendant had finally made a mistake. He had not finished the business. Nashe resolved to destroy de Vergor, then Bigot. Vengeance played in his mind like a snatch of song that will not go unheard.

## 60

The fur harvest was late coming to Quebec. There was not much fur. A raw November morning, Nashe arrived at the Cul-de-Sac to meet Vadnais and his own shipment. The docks were busy. Even in the cold, men sweated as they heaved the huge ballots onto tumbrels to be carried to their masters' magazins. The furs would be stored until a ship could take them to France.

There was little hope. There were too few ships. The blockade had had its effect.

The remainder of the fur, the quart tax, was transported around the Cap and offloaded at the Friponne, the government warehouses, and taken into the Intendancy vaults. It was that final destination Nashe considered now. He wanted his best furs in the Intendancy.

Nashe stood with Chevalier on a tumbrel, the two men surveying the bustle when he first caught sight of Vadnais. The big man came from a ship's hold, one of the few schooners spared to bring furs from Montreal. Chevalier saw him too. Vadnais was a hard man to miss.

"Good day, my friend." Nashe smiled. "You know Monsieur Chevalier. Chevalier, if you will excuse us the Owl and I have some conferring to do...far from the ears of our competition."

The two men laughed good-naturedly as Nashe climbed down from the wagon. But Nashe moved quickly away from prying ears. He spoke softly to Vadnais.

"Don't unload the best furs, Owl. I want them left for the quart. A great deal has happened since we parted ways."

"More than you think," Vadnais growled. "Follow me now."

"But this plan I have..."

"Will wait. Ledrew is back."

"What?"

"You'll not like what you see. Prepare yourself."

Without another word Vadnais led Nashe up the ship's gangplank to the deck. Past bustling dockworkers and through the piled ballots they travelled to the ship's hold. They came to the stern of the ship, below the waterline. At a doorway, hands folded across barrel chests, were two husky voyageurs. Nashe noticed each man bore a brace of pistols. Vadnais led him between them to the interior of the strong room.

The room was stygian, but suddenly a light flared and Nashe saw Ledrew sitting on a bed of pelts. Leaner now, his face hollow, his eyes were like stone. He reminded Nashe too much of Trémais. This was a hunted animal.

"Why did you disobey my orders and travel to Albany?"

"Are you alright, Jeff?"

"Never mind my health. I asked you a question."

"With your disappearance," Nashe replied calmly, "I felt it best to establish a line of communication. We thought you were dead. Where in heaven's name have you been, man?"

"If it's any of your affair, Nashe, I was betrayed by some coureurs. I escaped. I lived in Trois Rivières with a contact I have there. By the time I was ready to work you had already gone."

"I was concerned for you, my friend."

"Friends do not disobey orders! Friends do not endanger friends by jeopardizing their work and their lives! What if you were seen in Albany?"

"We were careful."

"How can you know? Remember that double agent you've been so concerned with?"

"I'm sorry."

"I remind you that this is my operation."

"Listen, Jeff...Offingham has placed me in charge. He wants you to leave, join him in Albany."

"Now see here, Nashe, I've risked my life for this. I won't go! Offingham knows nothing of it!"

"I don't want to argue. We can do as we always have, work together. In Marseilles there was no need of a leader. Leave it the way we work best."

"Marseilles was different."

"Not to me."

"But to me it is! I'll communicate with Offingham. You've set up a system?"

"I intended to. I was injured this summer, out of touch."

For the first time Ledrew betrayed a hint of a smile: "Then we are still on mine."

"In Albany, Offingham and I discussed the double. We decided it was Rogers."

"Or Charest."

"Not according to Offingham."

"Offingham again! That damned old fool has no right to meddle."

"He has every right."

"How would he know?"

"Charest, then," Nashe agreed doubtfully. "And you won't go south?"

"Not now." Ledrew shifted topic, "We'll have to deal with Charest."

"I have some business to take care of first."

"Of what nature?"

"I intend on killing Duchambon de Vergor."

"Over the girl? Ridiculous."

"It's beyond the girl. De Vergor is dangerous. He suspects something. And there are other scores to settle," Nashe muttered. He did not explain further.

"Wonderful. Our pivotal agent in New France calls a man out in a duel. What has happened to you, Nashe? Bigot protects De Vergor. You of all people should know what that means. He's a favourite son. A duel will finish you here."

"There are other ways to dispatch a man."

"Murder? Bigot would turn the city upside down looking for the killer! The patrols are already heavy enough. There is a war on, Alan." His voice softened to the old friendliness. "Don't throw off everything we've done for a woman and an old French bureaucrat. You're right; we must work together. I'm sorry for the way I behaved. This fugitive life has taken its toll."

"I think that best," Nashe said, his words carefully chosen. He had just learned he had not been careful enough. "We work as we've done before. Now I must go."

By the time they reached the deck, Nashe told Vadnais of his plan for the Intendancy and made him swear not to tell Ledrew. Nashe knew the big man and he were alike. Both lived for revenge. Bigot was the common target.

And Ledrew was no longer a friend.

## 61

Nashe contemplated the invitation in his hand. It was the usual style: scented, gold embossed, effusive in its flattery welcoming Nashe's return. It complained of the summer's emptiness without his enjoyable presence. It prayed Nashe would once again partake of the fruits of civilization at a soirée in celebration of the recent arrival of fur. It indicated the affair had another purpose as well: to bid adieu to the noble personage of Major Louis Antoine de Bougainville who would be departing for France. The party would be a small affair, only fifty or so for supper and cards. The ladies awaited; the cards were warm with anticipation; for the party to be a success, it implored, Nashe must, absolutely must, attend. It was signed simply: 'Bigot'.

Nashe peered at it coldly. No one was better suited for what he was about to do. He presented himself to the guards, his character changing like a chameleon: the perfect guest... with vengeance in him.

The Intendancy was a jarring antonym to the city. The city remained rationed. Bigot's residence was sumptuous: filled with finery and warm fires belaying the cold of autumn. There was one accession to the times: whereas normally the visitors' gallery was opened to the public to gaze down upon the great ones at their leisure, it was now empty. No one entered the palace without invitation. The gates were closely guarded.

Bougainville attended the affair not for pleasure, but in a professional mien. He was the guest of honour and considering the state of affairs between the military and government, he was there as a diplomat...another chameleon.

The tables were laden with salmon, beef and fowl, the best of clarets and brandies, Gascon wines, Norman ciders and Portugese madeiras; with delicate salted cucumber for desert and fine milled bread, choice fruits from the Antilles, dishes of Parmesan cheese, caviar; the list was as endless as it was ironic.

Bigot himself received his guests beside the ravishing presence of his mistress, Mme. Péan. He wore a suit of red satin trimmed in blue with just a delicate touch of gold lace. His brocade vest was gold inlay, a white silk blouse and fall of lace completed the ostentatious costume. He greeted Nashe with a warm embrace. Nashe returned it smiling. There was the usual challenge to cards then Nashe moved on.

After dinner and euphuistic toasts to Bougainville, flasks of burgundy and cognac were transported to the card room. The guests followed.

It was a spacious apartment, lit by a chandelier dangling delicately from a frescoed ceiling. The tapestried walls were rich in Italian scenes, the tapestries from the looms of the Gobelins. A black marble fireplace warmed the company. And it was in this room, among the comforts of the baroque and rococo, amid the luxuries the Intendant loved so well, that Nashe's plot against Bigot would begin.

There was an hour of friendly gaming, the ladies and gentlemen meandering from table to table losing some, winning some, drinking a great deal. Bigot drank copious amounts, as was his custom. Nashe did not drink. At the end of the hour, he approached his host.

"Monsieur Bigot, I do not believe we have had the pleasure yet to sit together at cards."

"Of course, my dear fellow! Martel, please relinquish your seat so that Monsieur Nashe may partake of the table's pleasures."

"I was thinking more, Monsieur, of just you and me. My furs are in, my travels completed, I feel lucky tonight. Perhaps a private game of Piquet?"

Bigot's eyes narrowed, but then the squat Intendant relaxed, not a little disdain in his look.

"I should remind you, Monsieur Nashe, that when I play Piquet there are no limits on the stakes."

"My feelings exactly. I have waited a long time for this opportunity, Monsieur. Your name, as I have said before, is known in many places."

The double entendre did not escape Bigot. Bloodshot, pig like eyes answered Nashe with an overt glare. Bigot had risen to the challenge. Nashe sat opposite him. A small group gathered.

The two packs of thirty-two were divided, each man accepting one. Bigot dealt: twelve cards each, the stock on the table...five cards, and three. They drew and discarded, Nashe first. The betting began as Bigot preferred it, with the scoring of sequences, sets and points. Then came the declarations. Bigot won with the higher cards and a tierce. Then the play began. Nashe took most of the twelve tricks. They counted, paid, and began again.

The play continued through game after game. First Bigot would win, then Nashe. The stakes went ever higher, both men played well. Bigot, as usual, bantered across the table. Nashe encouraged it with his own asides.

Then Nashe began to lose. He lost badly, a run of poor play and thoughtless bidding. The stakes piled higher against him. By midnight, he was nearly fifty thousand livres down. His eyes were hollow; he had begun to drink carelessly. The whiff of scandal spread quickly through the room. The young trader was in above his head, using credit now. It was possible he could not pay. Bigot was a master player. It would be the end of Nashe in Quebec should he be ruined and it became increasingly apparent that he would be.

Bougainville went to his friend. He spoke with him in low tones. Nashe appeared drunk. He kept shaking his head to the entreaties of the major. It was remembered through whispers in the room that this was the man who had lost the Duchesnay girl. Obviously, he was bent on self-destruction. And he had always seemed so cool.

He tottered up from the table, helped by Bougainville, bowling over his chair as he rose.

"But, Monsieur Nashe," Bigot sat quietly, his manicured hands folded on his lap, "the round is not yet finished. I am prepared to be merciful, Monsieur, but a gentleman never breaks off in the midst of a game. There are two hands remaining."

More whispering drifted the rounds of the spectators. What was Bigot doing? Surely he could see the man was finished. Of course, it was poor form not to complete the game, but it was worse to end in ruin. Nashe stumbled around the table, his hands grasping the edges where Bigot sat. He breathed into the Intendant's face.

"Monsieur, I am more than ready to finish these, these, er, hands! You accuse me of bad manners?"

"Indeed no, dear fellow. I simply stated the rules."

"Then I shall play, Monsieur. In these last two hands we will follow strict rules of the game." He belched. "Rules of the game...agreed?"

"Of course. Your deal."

"Good!" Nashe sat unsteadily back in his chair. He dealt the cards wildly and as he dealt he barked loudly, "I propose odds of double or nothing, Monsieur! I propose to let loose all stops. Total points is the winner!"

Before Bougainville could stop it, Bigot shouted, "Done!" with immeasurable glee. Rumour spread that there was more at stake here than simple money or reputation. Everyone knew of the connection between de Vergor and Bigot, and of de Vergor and Nashe. Yet until now Nashe too had appeared a favourite of the Intendant. The room was mystified. The hand began with Bigot's opening declarations, Nashe countering with his.

"Four."

"How much?"

"Thirty seven." Bigot smiled and turned to Martel. "It should have been forty, eh?"

"Not good. I have thirty nine."

And then I have a sequence of three, tierce," Bigot muttered.

"How high?"

"Ace!"

"Good," Nashe stumbled over the word.

"And another tierce. I score six. I have three kings."

"Not good. Tens. I start with eighteen."

"I start with six." Bigot grinned knowingly at Martel.

"Are you sure?" Nashe countered.

"Of course!"

"Fine. The play..."

It was close. Very close. The Intendant won on total points. The whispers became a rumbling. Nashe was finished. He continued to sit blankly at the table. Nashe had just lost a fortune. He could never pay but continued to sit there. He waited until the noise had subsided.

"I had thought we were playing rules of the game, Monsieur?" He looked coldly at Bigot.

"Yes?"

"You have made a false declaration. You distinctly said you began with six. Correct?"

"Yes."

"But before that you said to your friend here that rather than thirty seven on the four it should have been forty."

"I was jesting."

"But the rules, as everyone knows, permit no conjecture during the declarations. You have lost, Monsieur."

Bigot's face went livid. "This is ridiculous! You are drunk, Monsieur, you misunderstood."

"As you misunderstood my earlier attempt to leave the table? I'm afraid we are even, Monsieur. I have my fifty thousand, plus yours."

"He is correct, Monsieur Bigot," Chevalier intervened. "In the rules of the game you have made a false declaration. Strictly speaking, of course, yet true."

"So this is how you win at cards, Nashe," Bigot growled. "By niggling, ungentlemanly rules. Well, there is still one hand left. And I am the dealer. I propose the same game: double or nothing, total points!"

The room erupted in an astonished gasp...two hundred thousand livres! Even in this extravagant crowd two hundred thousand was a king's ransom. Bigot might, just might have the money. Nashe would never have it. Nashe swiftly agreed to the terms. The room lapsed into silence.

Bigot fumed and muttered as he dealt the cards. He was furious. The cards flew from his hands like weapons. Sharp, slapping, they leaped from his jewelled fingers onto the green velvet. When the cards were placed, there was another gasp. Only seven cards sat in the stock. There should have been eight. Bigot had dealt the wrong number of cards.

"I see a misdeal here, Monsieur Bigot. According to the rules I have the option of declaring a new deal. I do not choose to do so. As well, I shall take five cards from the stock. There. Unfortunately, Monsieur, you will not have enough cards to take the final trick. Shall we play on, or do you concede?"

"Play!" Bigot shrieked, his face nearly purple. He looked ill. His play was poor, angry, frustrated actions that doomed him before he began. In the end, Nashe claimed a repique adding sixty points to his score. The result was obvious. Bigot sat stunned, his face twitching involuntarily. He looked very, very old.

Amazingly, Nashe no longer seemed drunk. As he rose, he stood steadily. His eyes were clear. Bougainville smiled. Bigot stood with Nashe. Looking down at his feet, he bent with difficulty and picked up the missing card from the floor.

"Is it possible, Monsieur, when you accepted my challenge," Bigot spoke evenly, like an automaton, "that as you leaned on the table you may have accidentally brushed this card off, and played your own deal without it?"

"I have no recollection of it, Monsieur. According to the rules you should have had good count of your cards before dealing. If, as you say, I too dealt short, you should have noticed."

"Naturally, I do not have such a sum at this moment. Perhaps this will do." He took pen and ink from the sideboard behind him, his hands shaking slightly, and signed the sum of one hundred and fifty thousand livres on the card that had been missing. It was an ace of diamonds. He handed the card to Nashe slowly, his pig eyes burning.

Nashe studied the card a moment. He turned it over as though evaluating a precious jewel, and then returned the card to Bigot. His point was not lost on the spectators.

"I prefer my payment in gold, Monsieur. These ordonnances have an air of transience."

The crowd fell hushed. Bigot froze, the card between his fingers slowly crushed into a ball. Then his veneer shattered.

"Damn you, Nashe!"

He quickly recovered, pulling what remained of his dignity together.

"I shall have the necessary louis delivered to your residence in the morning."

"Afternoon, please." Nashe took some snuff.

"To be sure," came the flat, ugly reply.

"Now if you will excuse me, Monsieur, I shall take the night air. You should take yourself to bed, Monsieur, you have a pallid look about you."

"I shall soon, Monsieur Nashe. And you should be careful on your walk. Lately my captains have told me of murder in the streets, especially near the river. I don't suppose your walk would take you through Rue des Carrieres, but one must be careful."

The insinuation was not lost on Nashe. He turned before his own temper bested him. Instead, he walked arrogantly through the exit. Behind him the room burst into a cacophony of gossip.

## 62

As the doors of the card room closed behind him, Nashe veered left to the private wing of the palace. He knew where he was going having studied Tremais' sketch. Skirting the kitchens, Nashe arrived at a lower door in the rear of the building. It took him out under gabled roofs to the garden. The garden was an expanse of narrow walks and evergreen mazes trimmed in geometric designs, its shadows and winding ways perfect for concealment.

He moved cautiously down the path that led to the St. Charles shore. The glow of torchlight was his beacon as he passed through a grove of elms and came upon what he'd expected. In the sparse light fifty men offloaded furs; the quart was being delivered. Cadet stood on the boat's gangplank inspecting the furs, sorting the best for personal consideration. And there too was Vadnais, in charge of delivering Nashe's tax. All night he had been slow to unload his cargo. Cadet more than once had told him to get moving. Vadnais had ignored him, continuing his procrastination until he caught sight of a flash of tinder and steel from Nashe's hiding place. No one else saw it. They were cold and tired from their labour.

Nashe replaced his tinder in a pocket and awaited Vadnais' act to begin. Almost immediately Vadnais approached Cadet loudly complaining his furs were of such high quality that Cadet should take only half of them. Cadet naturally refused. An argument ensued, loud and very vocal, and suddenly Vadnais grasped the unsuspecting Cadet by his collars. Cadet was no small man but Vadnais lifted him easily into the air and held him dangling over the waters of the St. Charles. Cadet's eyes bulged. He screamed for his guards. The guards came running from the vault's entrance. Before they had gone twenty paces, Nashe was behind them and in.

Meanwhile, Vadnais had replaced a shaken Cadet on the gangplank and mollified his anger by giving up the argument and offering the greedy assistant a ballot of perfect ermine skins. The incident passed with Vadnais receiving a warning. The guards returned to their posts.

Inside, lanterns illuminated the low stone arches of the vault. Nashe climbed to the roof of the vault and burrowed his way into the stacked bales. He breathed slowly, calming his racing heart.

After an hour, the storage was completed. All that was left was a narrow passage that led from the outer door straight through the room to another equally thick inner door. Through that portal lay the mysteries Nashe dearly wished to explore. Cadet came through the outer door with his guards. He personally pulled the great oaken bar into the centre of the door, locking it in place. Then without a word, the group passed below Nashe and through the inner entrance. They did not bother to lock it. The outer door would withstand anything short of cannon fire. Nashe was left in pitch black.

He waited another hour. Then he lit a small tallow candle and drawing a stiletto from his boot he clambered down the bales and approached the inner door. He listened a long time. Satisfied, he pushed the door open careful the hinges would not squeal. He found himself in a long, low passage that ran, he assumed, the length of the Intendancy. He could see only a few feet ahead in the dim flicker of his candle.

It was cool and dry in the passage, and as he made his way down the stone flags, he investigated doors on each side. None were locked. In each room, he found stores: ammunition, hoarded meats, dried fruits and grain, rooms choked with supplies. Still, he did not find what he had come for.

Then he came to a low, recessed portico at the end of its own side passage. Unlike the others, this door was locked. Quietly he set the slow burning candle by the door and produced from a pocket a small set of wires and keys. It took two minutes to pick the lock. Not an easy lock, Nashe observed. He had come to the right place.

Even expecting the sight, he gasped involuntarily at what the candlelight reflected. The room nearly lit itself in the dull richness of gold louis. Nashe observed wryly Bigot would have no trouble paying his debt, from the King's store. Here was the reason for the ordonnances and the country's financial problems. Here was the country's gold. Nashe shut the door behind him, amazed at Bigot's audacity. Then his reverie was ended by footsteps outside the strong room. Nashe was trapped.

As the door handle turned, Nashe dived behind a chest in the rear of the room, smacking out his candle with his palm. The hand began to sear yet Nashe held it to the wick smothering the smoke. He lay perfectly still.

He heard Cadet's voice, then Bigot's, and there was another, one he knew well. Nashe held his breath. The third man was Charest.

"I've told you, Cadet, this door is to remain locked."

"I was sure I had…"

"You can't be too careful."

"You speak of careful?" Cadet muttered.

"Enough!" Bigot's voice rasped.

"What in heaven's name ever possessed you to bid so high?" Charest was complaining. "You've made him rich through your folly."

"Enough, I said!" Bigot thundered. "He trapped me. I thought he was drunk."

"You underestimated him."

"I admit it. Yet he too has underestimated. He is an arrogant fool."

"Why not just kill him?" Cadet blurted.

"If he were to die now, where would the blame rest? On me, fool! No, our trickster has made himself safe for now. We must bide our time. This small interference is nothing."

"One hundred and fifty thousand is nothing? It's enough to buy two ships to transport this wealth back home. I have only the one waiting at Bordeaux," Charest intoned. Nashe knew then why the man had been included.

"Kill the man, François. You have the power. When we skin our eels we don't begin at the tail."

"Spare me, Cadet. I'm in no mood tonight. We will get the gold back but we must be cautious, await the moment."

"I've followed you since you appointed me, François. You've never been wrong."

"Good. Now count out from this stack the monies for Nashe. And don't try to cheat him!"

Nashe heard the clinking of coins as Cadet busied himself with the gold. Charest and Bigot drew closer to his hiding place. One hand went softly to the hilt of the knife, but they were engrossed in their conversation. They stopped short of him.

"What of the winter garrisons?" Charest spoke. "If we don't release more supplies, Montcalm will march in here with his entire army."

"Let me take care of that. At any rate, we have more supplies now to dole out, one less fort to provision. We lost Duquesne. The English have it now."

"When?"

"I heard tonight. Things do not bode well, Charest. Take some advice and prepare your escape in advance. Make sure that ship of yours is here by next spring. It may be our final chance to get out."

"At least we have Trémais out of the way."

"Too bad he could not have been turned to our side."

"Too honest a man."

"His honesty is what killed him. Cadet! Are you finished?"

"Just one moment. Yes."

"Good. Post more guards in the morning. And have more of the gold moved to the Hermitage. It's too open here should someone come across it."

"I'll have de Vergor see to it."

"No. I'm sending him to France with Bougainville. His particular talents will be needed in Versailles. A government run by mistresses, my friends, and Duchambon shall be the wolf let loose amongst them. He should have little trouble obstructing the honourable Bougainville's attempts to discredit us. And it's better he leave Quebec a while. Nashe has sworn to kill him. I want de Vergor safe."

"Agreed."

"Let us to bed, Messieurs. Tomorrow's payment will be difficult. Yet be assured, we will get good return from it."

Bigot rattled the bag of gold as he spoke. The men left, locking the door behind them. Nashe was again in the dark. But not so much as others thought him to be.

## 63

The outer door would not open. Its locking bar had jammed in its socket and all of Nashe's power could not budge it. Nashe felt a tinge of desperation as he tried again to move the oak bar. Nothing. He considered taking a hammer and pounding it free then quickly discarded the thought as foolish. He calmed himself, putting his mind to the problem.

When it came to him the answer was obvious, dangerous, but perfectly clear. It would still be dark; in the cold hours before dawn, the sentries would be far from vigilant. The river was fifty yards away, an easy run. He could only assume Vadnais still awaited him in the midst of the St. Charles. There was nothing else he could do now.

Quickly, he returned to the inner vaults. When he came back along the passage, he carried a small wooden cask. Setting the cask on the floor, he split its top with his knife, being careful to make a small aperture. Then he inverted the barrel making a powder trail along the corridor. He curved the black line around the inner door. Returning to the outer door, he checked the amount of powder remaining in the cask and, satisfied there was plenty, made a depression at the door by prying up a loose flagstone. He wedged the cask into the depression then retreated to the inner room. He gathered another of the small barrels under his arm, took a last deep breath, and then struck his frisson on steel.

The black powder erupted into a crackling fuse. The flame followed the line he had made down the passage. Nashe saw it near the outer door and backed in behind his barrier. At the last moment he opened his mouth, plugged his ears, and curled into a ball.

The boom buffeted Nashe with shock waves behind his protective barrier. He leaped up and sped down the smoking corridor. The door had a gaping hole in its middle. Pieces of stone and ripped planking littered the exit. Nashe climbed through, out, into the night and away from the smoke. Even through the ringing in his ears, he heard alarms.

Raising the small cask above his head and smashing it on a rock, Nashe covered his actions then ran for the river. He heard shots behind him. He came to the river's edge diving deep. He swam beneath the surface as hard and long as he could. He surfaced far out into the river. A paddle splashed nearby. He saw a silhouette just darker than the water. Vadnais' strong arms pulled him into the canoe. He lay where he had been thrown, exhausted, feeling the canoe shoot forward almost out of the water with the force of Vadnais' strokes.

"Not exactly subtle, my friend." Vadnais did not let up his pace.

"No time." Nashe caught his breath. "Are the horses ready at Beauport?"

"We are not crossing the river, Captain. I have a better plan."

"But I told you…"

"Yes, but for once you did not think. On horseback coming into the city we will be stopped by patrols. And what will your alibi be? They will look for you at home. You must be there. You would never make it in time from Beauport. I have friends waiting to get you home quickly, without interference from the patrols."

"How? With the alarms half the city will be awake."

"Even soldiers must live. And they are paid so little. Did you find what you went for?"

"Yes. And more, I now know the double. I'm sure of it."

The canoe turned into shore by the dark piers of Canoterie. Two coureurs met it and led Nashe silently up the mountain through the Canoterie gate. Inside the guardhouse, soldiers were playing cards. The single man at the gate was nowhere to be seen. Even soldiers must live.

\*\*\*

Colonel Daine arrived at Nashe's apartments just after dawn. He seemed surprised to find Nashe in bed. Mme. Courvier was in an uproar, demanding an explanation for the intrusion. Bougainville entered, smiling, and he too questioned Daine.

"There has been a disturbance at the Intendancy," the officer tried to explain. "Someone, it seems, has tried to blow open the doors to the vaults."

"And what has that to do with me, Monsieur?" Nashe complained. "Are you suggesting I tried to take my winnings in advance? Monsieur Bigot is an honourable man. I expect him to pay me without the necessity of turning to theft."

"That is not it at all, Monsieur Nashe," Daine replied weakly. "The Intendant simply wished you to come to the Palace and take inventory of your fur tax. He wishes to know if anything is missing."

"Does Cadet not keep records? Colonel, I've had a strenuous evening, I'm sure you're aware. If I am a suspect, imprison me! If not, I suggest you go your way and harass me no further. I have paid the price for my indiscretions at the Ursuline. Good day to you, Monsieur. Your business is finished here."

As Daine left, Bougainville broke in. "I'm afraid, my friend, you must come to expect this kind of thing from now on. Our blessed Intendant was in something of a rage when you departed last night. You absolutely destroyed my going-away party." He grinned. "But you have given the city something to talk of all winter. I salute your courage, Alan, though I can't say the same for your wisdom. You've made yourself a potent enemy."

"I know, an unfortunate habit of mine."

"Look, Alan, I'm not sure I understand why you did what you did last night. It's not the Duchesnay affair, is it?"

"No."

"Forgive my probing, Alan. I only wish to help."

"Mme. Courvier, is it too much trouble to bring some coffee? Antoine, I have something to tell you. I hate to burden you now, but I see no other way."

As the landlady bustled out protesting that coffee was no trouble, Nashe led Bougainville to a divan. He withdrew Trémais' packets from a desk.

"This has nothing to do with Reine Marie, Antoine. This is about Trémais."

"You've seen him? Where is he?"

"Murdered by de Vergor. On orders, I believe, from Bigot."

"What? How can you possibly know that?"

"I was there. For some reason they didn't kill me. Daine prevented it."

"Daine! Involved in murder? Good God, man, do you know what you're saying?"

"Trémais was sent here by the ministere de la marine to investigate corruption. Versailles has apparently long had suspicions. He was sent undercover. For some reason, he took me into his confidence. He found more than he'd bargained for, Antoine. These letters are his report. He died trying to get them out. They are encoded. Only the people at this address can translate the code. All I know is that he has unearthed corruption involving the Grande Societé."

"You say Bigot as well?"

"I myself have irrefutable proof of that, but it's not written down, and I could not give it in court. Suffice it to say it is more than rumour. All but Bigot is made clear in these letters."

"They may help the campaign against Cadet and Vaudreuil."

"Beware de Vergor too. I've heard he's being sent to discredit your proposals."

"I am not without friends at court, Alan. This de Vergor is in for a lesson in politics." He smiled softly. "We'll see what comes of him. But you astound me, man! I commend you."

"Still I have no proof of Bigot. My word against his would be useless."

"I suggest you hibernate for the winter, my friend. Stay out of harm's way and await my return in the spring. Bigot can be a hard man."

Nashe did not argue Bougainville's point.

***

Bougainville's ship left three days later. De Vergor was also a passenger. It began to snow as the ship left its berth. Nashe stood at the dockside watching its sails disappear around Ile d'Orleans. The snowfall did not stop. It continued for two days turning the land to winter. Alan Nashe turned from the river half closing his eyes to the newborn sleet.

## THE ABRAHAM SECRET, 1759

### 64

It was a fierce winter, the worst anyone could remember. Even the grizzled men smoking their pipes in the corners of taverns shook their heads in wonder. The snow piled upon itself until cabins were hidden and landmarks buried beneath the smothering white. There were no sleigh trips that season. There was rationing and endless days of bouillon, pea soup, and frozen eel.

Nashe did little that winter. Bougainville was in France, Montcalm and his officers had chosen to winter in Montreal away from the tribulations brought on by Vaudreuil, and Nashe was isolated now from Bigot and his nest of spoilers.

He had considered some courses of action, the most promising, his idea to foment rebellion. He thought to write a manifesto exposing Bigot and his cronies and distribute copies discreetly in the refugee camps. Once people discovered the hoarding in their midst, revolution would naturally follow. Nashe would have his revenge on Bigot and quite possibly hasten an end of the war.

He had even begun the writing when, for the first time, Owl Vadnais turned against him. On hearing the plan, Vadnais took the papers, tore them to shreds and threw the scraps into the fire.

"My friend, you chafe at the winter and nothing to do, so you make stupid plans and think nothing of consequences."

"I've considered this carefully. The city is ripe for revolt."

"And you think Vaudreuil and Bigot don't know that as well? The winter has frozen your brain, Alan. Of course there is dissatisfaction, it comes of suffering and there's no lack of that this season. So why stick your neck out with this hare-brained scheme when winter does it for you?"

"People don't know the extent of it. If they knew what Bigot holds in those vaults..."

"Beaver dung! Haven't you noticed the punishment blocks, the patrols? The least sign of mutiny and there would be worse than that. Bigot has protected himself with martial law. Even a whiff of rebellion and he would find those responsible, of that you can be sure. In his gambling, he may be reckless, but not when it comes to survival, he is a very different man then."

"You wax politic, my friend." Nashe smiled.

"Do not laugh at my ignorance. You've become obsessed with Bigot."

"I think about it, of course."

"You think too much sometimes."

So Nashe spent his winter in front of his fire, and his thoughts were bitter when he recalled Tremais and de Vergor, and his thoughts, against his will, strayed too often to Reine Marie. He chafed at his enforced stagnation. He wanted to get on with it all, get it over, and make an end. Outside, the wind bellowed into February. There were not even wolves left to howl at the winter moon.

## 65

March howled by like its winter brothers. Nashe took to reading. From Duchesnay's library, he borrowed authors he'd only glimpsed before. He read Diderot and marvelled that the man was not in the Bastille. He read Montesquieu's 'L'Esprit des Lois'. He attempted Bougainville's work on calculus and found an immense respect for his friend's intellect. And each time Nashe would return a book, he spent time over warm wine in the study of Antoine Duchesnay. They spoke little of war or winter, keeping their topics to the intellectual. Duchesnay no longer discussed Madeleine. He called her a parasite and would not broach the subject again. Neither man brought up Reine Marie. For both, it was too painful.

But those pleasant hours were infrequent. Duchesnay was busy aiding the city's unfortunates. And Nashe purposely limited his time there. It would not be good for the old man when the truth became known about Nashe, as it would some day, to have been seen too often with him.

But April brought a surprise to Nashe from a corner he had not expected. Winter was losing its grip by then, yet still the nights were raw and cold and the days oppressively bleak. It was very late one evening; Nashe had finished a volume of English poetry by a man named Gray and was preparing for bed when a soft knock came at his door. He was not accustomed to receiving visitors, and the late hour put him on his guard. Bigot would not have forgotten him. His hand found a bread knife and slipped the weapon under his robe. He pulled the door open and faced his night visitor.

Ledrew brushed past him, bundled to the eyes.

"What are you doing here?" Nashe questioned.

"Setting you straight," Ledrew answered harshly, removing his cloak and scarf.

"Don't you think you're taking a risk?"

"Not compared to your folly! Writing about Bigot. Idiotic."

"So Vadnais told you."

"Of course he did! What did you expect? So tell me, have you any other plans you haven't informed me of?"

"I'm tired of these accusations," Nashe returned shortly. "Perhaps had you yourself been less secretive this situation might not have occurred. For God's sake, man, I wasn't even told where you wintered!"

"You had Vadnais."

"And what if he'd been killed?"

"Then I would have heard. I spent the winter in conditions far less comfortable than yours, Nashe. You should be pleased with your lot."

"But I'm not! Just what sort of game are you playing here, Jeff? This isn't how we worked in Marseilles."

"Back to that again. This is not Marseilles." Ledrew scowled "And you're a fool to think it. Surely Trémais' death has told you that much!"

"Yes, tell me about that, will you? How do you know of Trémais? I've said nothing to you. Daine covered it up."

"I...Trémais...I was told by Vadnais!" The other man reddened. "At least someone keeps me informed."

"And just how did he know?"

"You think my network so useless. Of course you do. But be aware, Nashe, I have men in many places. One of them was there that night."

"What?"

"Why do you think you weren't killed?"

"Then why didn't you tell me? If you recall, we're to work together."

"Why aren't you in Montreal? Montcalm is there. It seems you've chosen to sit."

"I can't do anything without Bougainville. He's my card of admission. Until he returns from France I have no contact with Montcalm."

"And you've ruined your other contacts with that stupid insult to Bigot! You make mistakes like that and then expect me to trust you? You are entirely too cavalier about this."

"You may think what you like!"

Ledrew's answer was to turn away. He said nothing, donning his cloak and leaving without a word. Nashe was left that night in a rage. He felt in his heart the man he'd once known no longer existed.

## 66

The morning of May tenth dawned crisp and shining: a spring day, a first fair weather day when the hard memories of winter are warmed away by a bright, new sun and there is an earthy, sweet smell. And hope crested in the sparkling Basin that day; hope in the proud forms of twenty-three ships, their flags snapping haughtily in the breeze, their prows triumphantly slicing the waves between the Traverse and Cap aux Diamantes. Here was the answer to so many prayers: ships packed with supplies, crammed with soldiers. The long wait had ended; support had come from Versailles.

The flagship docked in the Cul-de-Sac; others made for berths all along the wharves of the Cap, and still more landed their cargoes by boat while awaiting a place in line. They'd been inspected the night before to save time this day and allow the celebration its head.

From the flagship stepped the glittering, martial figure of Louis Antoine de Bougainville. He smiled and waved at the waiting crowd, and as one, the multitude broke into cheers. Someone passed him a crock of wine. He drank of it fully, smashing the bottle to the ground, a symbol that there would be much more to come and the days of want were ended.

Vaudreuil greeted him. Bougainville waved again, enjoying his brief role as saviour. He had gained weight, Nashe observed. Versailles had been good to him. He looked resplendent in his uniform. He looked, Nashe mused, very happy. His winter had not been so hard.

But another scene caught Nashe's eye. Down the line of ships, a different arrival was taking place. A small group of men in civilian clothes was coming ashore surreptitiously from a nondescript frigate. They bore the displeased, tepid looks of bureaucrats sent on an unpleasant errand. Not at all interested in the spectacle surrounding Bougainville, they filed from the frigate and attempted to enter the dockside offices of the Intendancy. They were not quick enough. Joseph Cadet intercepted them with open arms and a smile as big as his distended belly. The group divided and from their midst stepped a pinched, efficient little man. A few words passed, and Cadet's beaming face suddenly turned to confusion and then plain, blank shock. The crestfallen henchman sullenly joined the bevy of clerks as their little general led them inside.

Nashe smiled grimly. Trémais had not died in vain.

Meanwhile, Bougainville stepped into a waiting barouche. Nashe joined the crowd as it followed the train of carriages and marching soldiers up the Cote de la Montagne. In the Place d'Armes, he saw his friend enter Chateau St. Louis surrounded by a flock of officials. He knew he would not see him again until the day's business was done. He went home. Once there he withdrew from a bureau the final ounce of a hoarded bottle of cognac. As the last drops splashed into their crystal receptacle, Nashe raised his glass to drink a silent toast to Bougainville, and to Claude Querdisien-Trémais. His friends. And his enemies.

***

It was a far different man Nashe observed departing the confines of Chateau St. Louis that evening. Bougainville looked weary, natural enough after his hectic day, but Nashe noticed more subtle signs. And just before the Frenchman recognized him, Nashe read volumes in the man's eyes. Bougainville had about him an air of resign, antithetical to that bright, beaming hero strutting the docks a few hours before. Nashe stepped into the major's path. At first Bougainville seemed startled. As he recognized Nashe, his face lightened.

"Alan!" he shouted, embracing Nashe heartily.

"Easy, my good man," laughed Nashe, "or people will talk!"

Bougainville stood back grinning.

"I thank God for this gift of an honest face. At last I am rid of those sneering political jackals. Sweet Mother, it's good to see you."

"I was hoping you wouldn't dine with the governor tonight."

"It was good to see de Levis again," he muttered as they walked. "As for the rest, well...I've had my fill of mouth honour and smiling lies. Tonight, my friend, we will drink!"

"There's nothing left in the city. Winter and Bigot have taken it all."

"But that is where you are wrong, my friend. Did my baggage arrive?"

"Indeed. And by the extent of it, I should think you plan on beginning another colony. How in God's name did you get permission to bring such a load?"

"A few simple comforts," he sniffed, "from the civilized world. And a few friends at court make permission a trifle..."

"These friendly courtiers...have they given other things?"

"If you mean advancement for myself, if you mean good wine and old cognac, if you mean a life of ease...then my sojourn was the finest possible. But if you hope for Quebec, forget hope. Quebec is finished."

"What do you mean?"

Bougainville lowered his voice. "Montcalm requested ten thousand troops. He is receiving seven hundred. His requests for munitions, for guns, have all been answered with tokens. Twenty-three ships, Alan. I hope you enjoyed the sight today. It is the last you will see."

"But how can that be?"

"Montcalm sent me to France with a plan. I couldn't tell you before. Now it doesn't matter. His strategy was for a diversion, an attack on English Carolina. The operation would have been simple: a few thousand troops, a little fighting, and the English would have been forced to pull half their battalions south to a second front. Then our men there would simply have left, leaving the English with an army a thousand miles from here with no one to fight. It would have given Quebec an entire year to reorganize."

"The plan was refused?"

"Refused? A brilliant concept with little risk and the bombastic fools mocked it!"

"I see."

"No, you do not." Bougainville's mood turned sour. "That isn't the worst, Alan, not by far."

"What else?"

"Both Montcalm and Vaudreuil sent letters to the King requesting that one or the other be recalled. Montcalm even offered his resignation. I explained the confusion here, the bad feelings. Vaudreuil has been ordered to defer to Montcalm in all things military. I have just given him the order. He flew into a rage. He will do as he must, but in all else Montcalm might as well ask the English for help. Still, I did accomplish certain other business."

"Yes. I saw them disembark. You sent Trémais' letters to his people."

"Indeed." Bougainville smiled grimly. "In all else, Versailles is careless, but when it comes to losing revenue, then the rapacious fools act. I have never seen wheels turn so quickly."

"So our friends at the Intendancy are in for some well deserved nemesis."

"I think more than that, Alan. Heads will roll in the next few months. This Trémais was no simple inspector, my friend. The address to which I delivered his letters was none less than the personal offices of Mme. Pompadour herself. I must say those letters served as a better introduction than all the references I took with me."

"You saw her?"

"I have a great deal more, better told in private."

"Major Bougainville, you are a wonder." Nashe laughed.

"Pardon me, Monsieur, but you now address Colonel Bougainville."

"My congratulations."

"I say it with little pride. Montcalm himself has been promoted; de Levis, Bourlamaque...all with official increases in pay."

"All are well deserved."

"And all are cosmetic. My friend, France has become a nation of cosmetics: on men, on women, on government. Powder and rouge is a wonderful thing: in the right amounts and with just enough subtlety they make us all very pretty. Too much of them and we become whores. As I said, I have much to tell you. Much you will not enjoy."

## 67

Bougainville picked up his bottle of cognac from the table by Nashe's window. He poured generously into two crystal tumblers. The two touched glasses and drank. Sharp, lustrous fumes from the old liquor wafted through Nashe's nostrils, the taste a delicate burning, the best France had to offer. Nashe saluted his friend with his glass.

Bougainville paced the floor as was his custom when he wished to deliver his thoughts. Occasionally, while speaking, he would notice Nashe's glass had emptied. Without asking he would return to fill it. Nashe sat back in a comfortable slouch, more than ready to listen.

"The war in Europe is going badly. Prussian Frederick has gained a reputation as Europe's finest general, Nashe. Rossbach, Leuthen, Prague...this 'philosopher-warrior' as Voltaire calls him has destroyed armies twice his strength. And these armies are huge, my friend, a hundred thousand men battling in the fields of Europe. So we continue to lose, the treasury empties as more men are mustered, and no one has the sense to seek peace!

We have lost India. An unknown Englishman named Clive with three thousand men defeated fifty thousand Hindu and French at some obscure battlefield called Plassey. And the English annihilate us at sea; just last month one of our fleets was nearly destroyed off Portugal. My twenty-three ships now form the rump of our Atlantic fleet. Louisbourg is gone; the blockade is regaining strength. I was told, by a man who knows these things, that the English had loosed a massive armada about the time I left France.

"And how does Paris take these developments?"

"Paris? The salons are the centres of society. If you hanker for influence you attend a man's mistress. She will attain it for you even when the man himself cannot. The men have become Pompadour's puppets, dancing on strings of perfume. She is making a shambles of the war; she sends her puppies into the field as generals. At court she rules absolutely. The king is a listless libertine. It is rumoured he never beds Mme. Fish anymore. Her real name by the way is Jeanne Poisson. But in this case the commoner Fish has taken both bait and fisherman and now rules the pond."

"You said you'd met her," Nashe murmured, a little awestruck. The queen of the civilized world seldom deigned to greet minor aristocrats. But Bougainville sloughed the matter off with a shrug and a further drink of cognac.

"My interview was unimportant. She had already decided to send her investigators to Quebec. I'll never know why she chose to see me, even for those five minutes. She asked about my book and my entry into the British Royal Society. She seemed quite pleased at that..."

"Paris sounds the perfect place for the likes of de Vergor. You must have had trouble with him," Nashe interceded, swaying to more significant themes.

"Duchambon de Vergor," Bougainville smiled, "is a dull witted lout who contented himself with the wives of minor bureaucrats. He was as lost in the corridors of Versailles as King Louis would be in the forests of New France.

And it seems that Monsieur Bigot has a rather inflated opinion of himself. He has been away from France too long to recall why he was sent here. In France he's considered an upstart, assigned to the colonies, removed is a better word, so as not to be in anyone's hair. Needless to say, de Vergor's letters of introduction got him nowhere."

"But you fared well."

"Indeed. Montcalm was the only French general to win a victory last year. His reputation made me welcome. I saw D'Argenson first, not knowing he was slipping from power. Still, he supported me. I met with d'Arnouville, the ministere de la marine, and then the Marechal Bellisle, Pompadour's new war minister. It was he who sent the letter to Vaudreuil. And finally the sultana herself...for a five minute discourse on the state of the sciences...you see my brilliant results," he muttered bitterly and poured the last of the bottle. "But enough of this prattle, my dear Alan." His tone changed to a lighter vein. "I have brought you a gift!"

He produced a small package wrapped in oiled silk, tied with a gold embossed ribbon. He presented it with a bow. Nashe opened the packet. Inside was a Dresden china box: delicate, intricate, of wondrous workmanship. Nashe looked at his friend, overwhelmed.

"I thought you might like it," Bougainville said humbly.

"My dearest friend," Nashe murmured uneasily, "I can only hope you will understand me in future as you do now. I cherish the gift of your friendship even more than this, Antoine. I only wish I had something in return."

"You grow maudlin, my friend." Bougainville smiled, touched by the other man's sincerity if a little mystified by his words. "The cognac has done that...a good bottle. It has made me too a little sad. Paris remains the light of the world. I have seen it flicker from lack of fuel. Still it is not extinguished. And perhaps it is time for the light of New France to flare. The English are in for some unpleasant surprises should they arrive here. And they will, make no mistake, arrive. But we have good men and by the Holy Virgin, Nashe, we have Montcalm!"

"And each other," Nashe added.

"And each other."

Each of them finished his cognac.

## 68

Montcalm returned from Montreal. Nashe observed a grim, tired man enclosed in a bevy of officers, as he entered Chateau St. Louis. For two days the leaders of New France closeted themselves in the governor's palace. They had their council and made their decisions. Nashe would have given a year's pay to attend that meeting.

After the meeting, Quebec remained strangely quiet. Not even Bougainville could be persuaded to speak. When questioned by Nashe, he merely smiled, placed a finger to his lips and said knowingly, "Wait a short while, my friend. Soon you will witness Montcalm's genius. Remember Carillon!"

It began with the riders, messengers coming and going by horseback, messengers every hour. Then travellers from downriver began reporting beacon fires built at each benchmark along the river. Miles apart, they said, the beacons were manned day and night and stretched as far north as the Isle of Bic. Then the ships that had rested in harbour were moved, some to the Intendancy wharves and later, low in the water, departing for somewhere upstream. There were so many rumours that Nashe had the devil's own time finding truth in them. He met with Ledrew, still accompanied by his two bodyguards. Ledrew knew nothing. Vadnais was still away so there was no information from that quarter. The only clue Nashe reported was Bougainville's forecast. Neither Nashe nor Ledrew could make heads or tails of the enigma. Their only recourse was to wait, as everyone else. They did not have long to be impatient.

Two days later, Nashe arrived at his wharves to find an officer awaiting him. He was presented with a letter signed by Vaudreuil; his and all other merchants' fur boats had been requisitioned. It was an act of martial law with no promise of reimbursement. Even as he read the letter, his boats were being removed.

Then the ships began returning from upriver crammed with battalions of soldiers. First came the regular regiments: Languedoc, La Sarre, Guyenne, Bearn, Artois, Royal Rousillon...disembarking, marching out to camps all along the Beauport Heights, the camps clamped shut by a wall of security. Each day more troops arrived, the regulars mixed now with colonial soldiers whose job thus far had been minimal. Thousands of men converged on Quebec.

Ledrew, in another of their acrimonious meetings, simply shook his head in wonder.

"I have men who work in the dockyards," he told Nashe. "Do you know where your boats have gone? Look along the St. Charles shore. There are five hundred men building floating batteries, placing cannon on rafts! And they've taken some ships and are filling them with pitch and gunpowder. Take a walk tomorrow along Canoterie; you'll see the log jam being built right across the St. Charles! They've already sunk two frigates in the channel. Nothing can get up that river."

"What do you think it all means?"

"I don't know. I can't get into the country; the patrols are thick as flies. Something is going on out there. I estimate in the past two weeks more than ten thousand soldiers have arrived. They're all out there, along the shore and you can't get closer than half a league. But they are building, all along the cliff I saw the beginnings of something..."

"Just a minute." Nashe sat upright. "You say they are building?"

"I'm sure of it. I took a canoe down midstream."

"It can't be possible."

"What? Nashe, what in heaven's name do you mean?"

"What Bougainville told me."

"I'm afraid you have me completely lost."

"Carillon! He said to remember Carillon. I'd never have thought he would be so literal."

"What are you getting at?" the exasperated Ledrew muttered.

"You won't believe it. I hardly do myself."

"I'll try," Ledrew said impatiently.

"At Carillon, faced with greater numbers and no possibility of retreat, Montcalm fortified the entire peninsula."

"What of it?"

"Jeff, you weren't there. Montcalm built a wall, a huge abatis the width of the spit. And he kept the procedure secret from the English, had his men working day and night to complete the thing."

"You think he's doing the same thing here? The entire Beauport shore? That's six miles of walls. Impossible!"

"Impossibility is not a concept Montcalm recognizes. You said you saw men building."

"Yes, but in spots, not the entire cliff line!"

217

"Montcalm's abatis was done in stages, begun at strong points, then extended."

"But it will take months!"

"At Carillon a half mile took less than five days. Jeff. I think he's repeating himself."

In the following week everyone knew. The two days at Chateau St. Louis had wrought an incredible change in French policy. Montcalm had obviously had his way, and his way was typical of the man: creative, efficient, gargantuan defence. The Beauport line began to stretch along the cliff tops from the St. Charles a full six miles to the Montmorenci. A bastion of impossible dimension, a fortress protected on each flank by rushing rivers and lined with guns. It was to be a stand, the gauntlet thrown in the face of the English. There would be no retreat.

And as it came clearer to those in the city what was occurring on the Beauport Heights, as the bastions and trenches began to take form, morale that had been at its ebb began to flourish. The call went out for all men, sixteen to sixty, to join their militias. From far upriver they came, from shops and taverns and huts in the woods: traders, craftsmen, voyageurs and even coureurs. They crammed the Place d'Armes daily, jostling for places in line, making a spirit and pride that became almost visible.

Nashe met Antoine Duchesnay amid the hearty crowds on the Place. The old man was in uniform, his Croix de St. Louis displayed boldly on his sash. Near them, boys were signing the roles, their grandfathers beside them doing the same. Duchesnay looked at Nashe and said simply, "This is as I told you. We depend on each other. Look at them, my friend! This is their land, their fathers passed it down to them and they intend doing the same."

In those two weeks the hard memories of winter were forgotten. The Beauport defences were made tangible. And behind them camps, hospitals, supply depots, redoubts, and batteries began to take form. In two weeks a nation mobilized.

At the end of that time, Bougainville called upon Nashe. There was still a great deal to be done, and the colonel had little time for social discourse. But he had come for another reason. He offered Nashe a post as his secretary. Nashe accepted.

And even as Alan Nashe answered his friend, shouting in the streets interrupted him. All men's faces were turned toward the flaring signal beacon on the peak of the Cap. It flamed now like a bright, close star in the clear May evening, illuminating the upturned faces, imprinting its enigmatic message on excited, shining eyes. Nashe turned to Bougainville. The colonel's face was grim.

"They do not know it yet," he said, "but that fire is one of hundreds along the river. They are our Mercuries, faster than the fleetest horse."

"But what do they mean?"

"The Isle of Bic has sighted the English fleet. The English are coming upriver. Within a fortnight they will be here. And then, my friend, the English will find us ready."

## 69

Quebec had become an armed camp. Its women took to hand the rolling of bandages, preparing the rations, serving the lines of hungry soldiers all along the Beauport front. Tradesmen sweated with sailors readying gunboats and fire ships, coureurs scouted the rivers for advancing enemy parties, and a fire department was organized under Chevalier. Everyone had his work and each toiled with the pride and knowledge that he, or she, was indispensable.

Nashe's new position as Bougainville's secretary developed into an arduous occupation. Yet nothing suited him better. In the course of his work, Nashe came across information he could never have known about Montcalm's plan and, as he gradually comprehended the subtleties of that strategy, his esteem for the general found new bounds.

In one particular instance, he came upon a letter indicating supplies had been shipped fifty miles upstream to Batiscan. The letter was marked secret and well it should have been. It plainly stated that should the defence of Quebec fail the army would retreat south, and its precious stores would not be captured with the city. The army could move to fight another day, the Cap aux Diamantes could not.

Montcalm knew too of the English advance up the Richelieu. He sent de Levis to counter the thrust, along with three thousand men. The orders were simple: fight a holding action, retreating in stages burning everything in his wake and hold finally, at all costs, at Montreal. The outlying forts were left to their own defences. Native allies were brought to Quebec. By June, there were ten thousand men in the capitol.

The general himself should have been exhausted. Instead, he seemed a man in his element, and Bougainville was never far behind. Nashe, to his complete amazement, was consistently included. No one doubted him. When he recalled his first day on the wharves of the Cul-de-Sac, the evolution seemed surreal. Yet he knew it was inevitable that there would be an end. He could only hope, when it came, that he would be ready.

Reports of skirmishes came from downriver. The English fleet was moving upstream picked at by small shoreline batteries. The reports became alarmed. The English ships kept coming and coming, all kinds and sizes in numbers unheard of.

There was still the hope that the English could not navigate the river. River pilots, to a man, swore the enemy could never pass the shoals and undulant currents of the Traverse. The river pilots knew their domain. They were listened to.

And so nothing sufficiently prepared Quebec for the sight that appeared one overcast day in late June; not the pilots' reports, nor the signal fires, nor the spirit that had infused them all. The sky that day threatened storm, the Basin gave them one.

It began innocently enough: first the tiny white sail of a sloop as it rounded southeast of Ile d'Orleans. It could have been a seagull, low flying and glimmering argent on the calm grey expanse. But it moved with painstaking slowness. And then its sister appeared behind it, a much larger sister bristling with guns and billowing sail. At first only a few lone sentries noticed, but as the sea birds multiplied and manoeuvred far out, more and more watchers came to the shore. There were no drums, no frivolities, no challenges or cheers, only grim silence. The English had passed the Traverse. The English had made it look easy, made of the dangerous narrows a highway. And now their warships were gathering in the sacred place. The sky behind them lowered so that even the land seemed to vanish and only the cloud and the grey of the river were left, become one, and somewhere between sea and sky the white wings of sailing eagles.

Bougainville, as usual, put it best. "If I ever decide to travel the world, I will take with me a British pilot."

On the river, the silent ships danced their minuet; on shore the silent populace watched. It seemed that nothing could disturb that frozen peace. But one man was neither awestruck nor frightened; one man had known what to expect. Montcalm.

He appeared, thundering down the incline of Place d'Armes followed by a squadron of horsemen, himself on a magnificent charger, the gift of Antoine

Duchesnay. Seeing Bougainville and Nashe among the watchers he reined in beside them.

"So, Messieurs, you too are mesmerized by this English water play. It seems they are adept sailors. They have us peering at them as though they were visions. They are no visions, Messieurs. Had you thought to bring your telescopes you could have looked closer.."

"As it is, it is enough to see, General," Bougainville mumbled.

"Not quite, Colonel, not at all. I've observed them since their arrival. This is not a simple show of force. One of their frigates has anchored off Ile d'Orleans. It appears they are going to land a party. I intend to be at Montmorenci in half an hour to view them more closely. If you gentlemen are not too paralyzed to move, I suggest you get to your horses and follow me."

With the blunt command, he was off, the horses clattering down the narrow streets and out of sight at the corner of Rue Buade. Nashe and Bougainville wasted little time. In ten minutes they were saddled and on the road to Beauport.

And on the ride toward Montmorenci, Nashe found time to collect his thoughts. The moment had arrived. Through the trees, he caught glimpses of the fleet. He should have been filled with joy. Yet he felt a strange catharsis. As his chestnut raced the Beauport road, the man who was his friend rode beside him. It would be only a matter of time now until Nashe was forced to join his rightful allies, a matter of time before this man would become his enemy. And he knew when the time came he would do as he must, but in the doing would be such regrets.

They arrived on the Montmorenci promontory to find Montcalm's officers clustered around a battery of telescopes. Nashe joined them, immediately focusing his own on the shores of Ile d'Orleans; from their flat bottomed boats fifty grenadiers landed, muskets ready, fanning out in a protective perimeter around the next group coming in. Rangers in forest green stepped onto the beach and disappeared into the underbrush. Nothing, Nashe knew, would come upon that beach unawares.

Then more boats came loaded with officers, each one with maps and telescopes. And after them, their general arrived surrounded by guards. He was hatless, a tall, thin character whose flaming red hair stood out among his men.

"James Wolfe," Montcalm murmured.

"He looks quite a gangly type from here," Bougainville quipped.

"Nevertheless," Montcalm's voice rose, "that is the man who took Louisbourg. I gather this is his first command above brigade strength, a reward, no doubt, for his victory."

"He wastes little time," de Levis said. "His ships have barely arrived and already he's reconnoitring."

"A man in a hurry," an officer snarled.

"With the glory of Louisbourg behind him, he'll be looking for a fight."

"And here he shall find it!"

The group cheered the boast, but Montcalm did not join it. He spent the time peering through his telescope, studying his alter ego in the distance.

"No, Messieurs," he muttered after a moment. "He will not get his battle here. I have seen British regulars at Carillon. They are not to be trifled with. This Englishman comes expecting battle. But he is new to his craft. He's a thousand miles from his supplies; a line that long becomes a formidable problem. I shall wear him down with patience. They must come to us. If they do not, if they cannot, then they are the ones who must leave. Prepare yourselves for a siege, Messieurs, until winter. And if this impetuous leader of theirs chooses to attack he will find the cliffs in his way and after that hard men waiting!"

He raised his voice to a shout. Men heard him and cheered, their fears washed away by the tide of his voice. The rallying cry carried up and down the line. "We await them!" And amid that clamour and the dull rumble of Montmorenci falls, Montcalm turned and signalled his officers to the rear.

They gathered inside a woodsman's cabin. Yet before they had a chance to be seated Montcalm's temper turned. Orders spewed from his mouth like a rattle of drums. The valiant trumpeter of hope was now furious.

"Alright, Messieurs! We have given the army something to cheer. Now it is time we attended our business. We are in trouble. With that many ships, and it appears the Traverse is no obstacle to them, they will surely attempt to pass Quebec. We have underestimated them and have left ourselves a gaping weakness. Point Levis, across the river from the city, is completely unguarded. We must fortify Levis before the English discover it and, judging from Wolfe's actions already that will not be long. If they take it before us, they will set their cannon at its peak and have clear fire upon the city."

"But General," Bougainville countered meekly, "we too have guns, enough to pulverize them should they attempt to set batteries. The cost to them would be too high."

"Do you forget Carillon, Colonel? They used men as cannon fodder there. You think they've changed so much in a year?"

"But what good would it do them, Sir?" an artillery officer questioned. "Their guns can only reach the Lower Town; they would still have to climb the Cap to get at us."

"But they would be perceived as having gained an advantage. Think of morale. And has it occurred to you, Major, that our most effective batteries against a run past the city are the Royale and the Dauphine? They are in the Lower Town. We will need those guns when the time comes."

"But, General, there still remains Bougainville's point. We can smash any attempt they make."

"You're not thinking, Major. I lied to those men out there. The English will be constantly supplied. You think their navy so helpless? We, on the other hand, have limited resources. We must conserve what we have. The English will expect us to hit Levis, drain us of our firepower. Then they will make their move upstream. We must have men on Point Levis!"

"Then we are lost, Marquis," Rigaud, the governor's brother interrupted. "What you speak of will take days to organize."

"It will take the English more days."

"But you are forgetting, Monsieur, that such an action comes under direct defence of the city. That is the Governor's realm. This matter must be discussed with him."

"Then discuss it, Monsieur!" Montcalm turned to Rigaud. "But tell him this: we are not simply defending the city; we are defending all of New France!"

"I believe he knows that, General," Rigaud sniffed pompously.

"I do not care whose jurisdiction it is," Moncalm shouted. "I do not care what it takes to organize. Do it! Or face the consequences."

Rigaud stormed out in a huff, De Levis after him. Montcalm busied himself with further orders, his self-control returning too late.

A wind came up that night, a great howling storm from the west. Rain beat down in a solid wall and there were savage thunder cracks and brilliant forks of lightning. For a time it seemed God had seen fit to destroy the English invaders. The church of Notre Dame des Victoires was full that night, its priests praying for deliverance, urging on the gale. Its parishioners hoped for one more miracle. The miracle did not happen. Next morning the tempest passed. Below the Cap the English fleet remained. That morning Chevalier, Bougainville, and Nashe looked down upon the English vessels.

"It seems," Chevalier murmured, "that God has underestimated English sailors."

"Be not so hard on God, Monsieur," Bougainville sighed. "He is not the first to do so."

Three days later, with lightning speed, the English took Point Levis. Vaudreuil had slowed the French preparations. There were arguments and delays. And meanwhile the red-haired enigma, Wolfe, had acted. Obviously he answered to no one. English cannon appeared on the Point. As Montcalm had promised, they received a mere sputtering of fire from Quebec.

## 70

High above the Basin, outside Montcalm's headquarters on the Beauport, Nashe peered through the night at silhouettes ghosting on luminescent waters toward the tight-packed British fleet. Slowly the silent flotsam glided toward its target. With him were Bougainville and Owl Vadnais. Vadnais, since his return, had stayed close to Nashe. Any moment might bring about the necessity for escape. Vadnais was to provide the route. Nashe passed the big man off as a loyal retainer and unofficial bodyguard. No one questioned the ruse.

Each night, Nashe recorded the information he had gleaned that day. Each night, he gave the encoded papers to Vadnais who would disappear into the dark to meet in some shadowed alcove with Ledrew. Nashe included every detail in his reports: troop movements, fortifications, the locations of supplies, and even the various tribes of natives who had come to Quebec. He'd wanted at first to deliver these materials directly, but Ledrew refused saying Nashe's position made it too risky. Thus Vadnais became the go between.

But Alan Nashe modified the plan. In addition to the letters to Ledrew, he kept copies in a secret folder carefully concealed in the false bottom of a drawer. It was a dangerous thing to do. If he were found out, the evidence to put him to death would likely be discovered. It was something he had never done before, something that went against his grain. But he followed the drift of his suspicions now.

Nashe's ruminations were disturbed by Bougainville's voice. The colonel made no attempt to mask his excitement. "They are less than half a mile away! It had better work. That agglomeration out there has cost half a million livres."

"I know," Nashe answered glumly. "You forget, Antoine, part of that is mine. My boats, expropriated."

"Alas, the pain." Bougainville smiled. "An expensive tactic but if it works the English fleet will soon be burning. And together, when this is over, we will build you new boats. That, my friend, is a promise."

"Good."

"You seem little pleased with this, Alan."

"It's a fierce manoeuvre, Antoine. If it fails, the English will return it in kind."

"This single night could destroy the English hopes. If they lose their ships they are finished."

"There are always more English ships."

"But not for this year. They will have to leave, Alan."

Suddenly an orange flicker touched the shimmering dark. A torch had been lit. Even so far away, they could see it, like a guttering, sub aqueous star, and then there was another, then another. Nashe could hear Bougainville's intake of breath. And then there was a flare so bright it extinguished the smaller glimmers. It grew quickly, becoming a wall of flame, a floating bonfire that moved on the water. Bougainville cursed.

"The cowards have lit it too soon! Look there, men leaving the raft. It's too soon! The English will have too much time!"

Across the Basin, they heard the alarms of the English. The floating furnace drew near, yet not quickly enough. Beneath the crackle of flames, they discerned shouted orders. The fire was a great sun now. It grew, fed by its oily cargo and sometimes the blast of powder kegs set to stir it on.

The outriders of the fleet were first to meet it. Ships a hundred yards from the main body tried to veer from the path of the hypocaust as it rolled into them. In ten minutes, two ships were burning. There was panic among the English. Through his telescope, Nashe could see men on fire. Ships lumbered about, crunching into one another in the wild flight to escape the inferno. One of the ships opened up a ragged broadside hoping to shatter the chains that held the monster together. It did not work. That ship too was enveloped in flame.

Small boats appeared rowed by gangs of sailors. At first, Nashe thought they were abandoning their comrades. But they turned as one toward the raging inferno and using poles and oars tried to slow the flotsam down. Nashe had rarely seen such courage. Men died. A great many men...screaming in burning agony heard even above the raging blaze.

The English ships weighed anchor and order gradually appeared. Other boatmen hauled frigates and transports and even the huge men-of-war out of the current away from the threat. Then with no warning the great conflagration exploded in a thunderous blast. The force hurled huge beams in the air, rising in spitting arcs slowly, as if loath to leave their fiery mother. By this time even the men on shore could feel the heat of the fire.

"That was the central magazine," Bougainville muttered. "Had the fools lit the fire when they were instructed that would have happened amid the main fleet! I will find the coward who commanded this fiasco, and I'll have his head!" He turned to leave, shouting back at them: "It could have ended this, and now it is only beginning!"

"The English will not take this lightly," Vadnais murmured.

"Before this is through, Owl," Nashe answered, "I think we'll see worse."

Below, in the distance, the fire continued. An hour or two of hell played out before them. Men continued to row into the furnace. Another ship, late in preparing, was caught by devouring flames. The raft drifted toward the Traverse. By then it was a glowing penumbra. The fleet closed again in its wake. Battered, burned, yet still there. But lessons had been learned in that furnace. The French had gambled and lost. It would come back on them. Lessons were learned.

*** 

Montcalm's headquarters was stifling. Leaving Vadnais outside—the coureur was not allowed among gentlemen—Nashe overheard the last of an angry dispute on the fire ship fiasco. He took his seat with the other aides, the only man present not in uniform.

"The English are constructing batteries on Point Levis," de Levis reported. "The townspeople can see them from their windows, General. They are angry with us for not having done something about it."

"I've explained to Vaudreuil my strategy," Montcalm answered. "I will not be drawn into a skirmish. The English are beginning to probe. They intend to lure us into action. They will escalate that action before we know it, and we'll be forced into a pitched battle."

"Still, General, there is fear in the city, especially after tonight."

"Let them talk, de Levis!" Montcalm shouted. "I will play Fabius to this English Hannibal. As we stand, we are inviolate. An army that finds itself going nowhere soon loses its morale. And that will become Wolfe's problem."

"Sir," de Levis interrupted, "there is more to this business. Vaudreuil is organizing civilians, volunteers under Dumas, all panicked over the English guns and ready to take them by force."

"That is not Vaudreuil's mandate," Montcalm grumbled. "I have charge of military operations. Send a counter order, Colonel Bougainville, reversing this idiotic scheme."

"General," de Levis continued, "Governor Vaudreuil commands the city's defences. You placed him in that position yourself..."

"To keep the fool out of the way!"

"Nevertheless, Sir, he considers the English guns a threat to the city. He feels he has the strength to attack. Vaudreuil will ignore your order, Sir, and legally, he will be in the right."

"God take that man!" Montcalm raged. "The operation is doomed from the start. Green troops crossing the river; I assume the fools plan to attack in the night!"

"They do."

"Cross a river at night then organize an attack? Is Vaudreuil mad? Is this Dumas so sure of himself he believes the thing will work? Let them do as they wish, Monsieur, but go back there and tell them not one French regular will cross the St. Laurent. Not one man under my command shall move without my orders. And my orders are to stand!

Bougainville, I want messages sent to each company, each squadron if necessary! Make it very clear to them, Antoine. No one, no matter what happens on Point Levis, is to move. Is that understood?"

"Perfectly, General."

"Good. De Levis?"

"I shall make the point clearly to the governor, Sir. And if I might add an opinion, I am in complete agreement with your assessment. Vaudreuil undermines your authority. The guns are a threat, General, but your strategy is solid."

## 71

The Dumas sortie was disastrous. Lost in the dark on their crossing, frightened men fired on their native scouts. The natives, mistaking them for English, fired back. Twenty men died before Dumas recognized the confusion and ordered retreat. The motley collection of would-be heroes made an ignominious return across the river. The batteries on Point Levis remained untouched. The only question was when they would open fire.

The answer came the following night at nine o'clock.

The city had watched in trepidation the gathering of English guns just a thousand yards across the river. It was a slow process: soldiers stripped to the waist in the sweltering heat hauling cannon up the precipice, placing them in prepared positions. Nashe saw six thirty two pounders and a number of thirteen inch mortars on the Point, the dull iron of their barrels glinting ugly in the sun. Attendants scampered and crawled upon them like bees on a honeycomb. Through his telescope, those insects became men with hard, efficient faces, marked sometimes by anxiety as they stared across the chasm toward Quebec, expecting anytime the salvo that would blow them off their hard-gained entrenchment. It did not come. Montcalm stayed to his word. No shot would be wasted until the moment of crisis, until the British should try to pass upriver.

And so on the evening of July twelfth, a hot, sultry twilight ominously peaceful, they decided on Point Levis that they were ready. The first missiles boomed from the big guns shattering the evening solitude, and landed short, shooting up great silver geysers in the river. The booming brought hundreds out into the dusk to gather at the edge of Cap overlooking the Lower Town.

Through his glass, Nashe observed cannoneers adjusting their elevations. The range was fixed, the ritual of loading took place, each step efficient and calm and done quickly. Then the gunnery chief's flag descended and a second salvo split the air and suddenly the Cul-de-Sac exploded in smoke and flying debris and the awful cracking of smashed houses. Nashe heard a gasp from the crowd. Five minutes passed. Then another booming volley and again the wharves blew apart.

More guns opened up. But these were more precise. They fired on the Batterie Royale and further down, the Dauphine. The English commenced a walking destruction, raining their shells in slow moving lines ever further into the Lower Town. First one row of streets would disintegrate, then another.

On the Cap, standing in safety, hundreds lined the edge while below them a moving terror advanced ever closer toward the base of the cliff.

There was a great, moaning wail as Notre Dame des Victoires was hit. The church, the symbol of so much hope, became a burning symbol of some other meaning. Drums rolled below, and men could be seen running toward the fires: Chevalier's fire brigade. Nashe admired the courage of those men working amid the carnage, but the walking barrage passed them. It moved on through the town and fires ignited everywhere. As darkness fell, the salvoes continued. And then the unthinkable happened.

Pontlery had calculated long before that cannon could not reach the Upper City. He was correct. But from the trees in back of the English batteries another kind of fire opened up. Howitzers. Pontlery had not counted on howitzers. The mortar shells arced up from the belching mouths of their grey mothers, and whistled down upon the Cap. Concussion and fire exploded hell on the crowds. In an instant, the cliff's edge became pandemonium. Nashe knew this atrocity was planned. Wolfe left the mortars until the end and then gave death and terror in one awful cannonade. The English had remembered the fire ships. The English had answered in kind.

There were no more volleys. With the mortars opening up, the English gunners were given free rein. They commenced a tremendous rate of fire all through the night. And they would continue so for weeks, replacing cracked cannon when they wore down, changing their range to strike unawares any place, raining bombs on the city until little remained but its shell. There were fires each night, and sometimes infernos that gutted whole streets. The Basilica was hit time and again, a high easy target for the gunners. Homes were destroyed, hospitals smashed, streets churned into swamps of stone and timber. All calculated. All bent on the destruction of the people's spirit, part of Wolfe's plan to force Montcalm out.

But the worst of all nights was the first, when the quiet of summer became a maelstrom.

In the midst of it, Nashe came close to panic. That first sudden mortar projectile awakened in him thoughts that lay just beneath his surface. Reine Marie was in danger. He ran with singular purpose across the Place d'Armes amid the alarm of the mob. Up Rue St. Louis he raced. On Rue du Parloir, as he turned and up the narrow lane, the wall of the Ursuline burst into dust and jagged stone. The concussion threw him to the ground. Then he was up and running again, close to the edge of the street for protection. Windows blew out above his head. Debris crashed heavily down upon him. He heard shouting. Others had seen the convent hit. They came running to help the beloved sisters. Two of them hauled Nashe to his feet. There was blood in his eyes.

Together they pushed through the Ursuline gate. In the convent, they came upon three sisters. One was bleeding badly. A wall had collapsed. There were women trapped inside.

In the dark, in the dust, they scrabbled at blasted stone, hauling the women from the debris. Someone brought torches. In the flickering light, Nashe looked for the girl. She was not there. A sister mumbled she had seen Reine Marie in the kitchen. She took him there, and the kitchen was in flames; together they rescued a woman trapped by the fire. She had not seen Reine Marie.

In that unholy night, Nashe searched wildly through the grounds of the Ursuline, not finding her. He heard the French guns on the Cap finally return fire in the vain hope of destroying the English batteries. Their fire was slow, never wasted, so much the reverse of the massive assault of the English.

In the midst of this, Nashe met François Daine. The officer was directing his men in search of survivors. Enemy or not, Nashe knew Daine was his best chance of finding the girl.

"Monsieur Daine!"

"Who is that?"

"Nashe."

"What are you doing here?"

"Searching..."

"For Mlle. Duchesnay," he said grimly. "I should have known."

"Have you seen her?"

"I have. She is safe."

"Where?"

"I've been told she does not wish to see you."

"That was before this."

"Yes," the colonel agreed. "This changes everything. She is in a cellar past that grove of fruit trees. They need someone there. I have no men to spare. It might as well be you."

"I thank you, Monsieur, with all my heart."

"I've heard you work for Bougainville now."

"I am his aide."

"Then you and I fight the same war. Can you forget the past?"

"I can."

"Then so shall I. My hand on it, Nashe. Now go to your woman."

The subterranean vault was calm, its grey walls splashed by the smoky glow of candles. Several sisters were there and some children, one or two whimpering softly. As he entered, she saw him. She crossed the floor, stepping past sleeping children. In the candlelight, in her plain grogram dress, she was more beautiful than he remembered. A smudge of dirt on her cheekbone made her all the more lovely. As she came to him, unspeaking, they embraced. And even in the midst of bombardment, by the door of a dim, musty cellar, those delicate arms encircled him, and he forgot for a moment the rest of the world. Her lips as she kissed him extinguished it completely. And then she brought him back again.

"I must get to my parents, Alan. I must find my mother. Take me there," she pleaded.

"It's too dangerous."

"I know they're at home. I must see if they need me."

They made their way through the city, he holding her hand and leading her past the fires and the sudden explosions. They ran from place to place in the startling calms that occurred when at times the English guns expelled their fury and paused to reload. They reached the house on Place d'Armes to find it damaged, but not burning.

Then it was her turn to lead. She took him downstairs to the vaults where they found the servants and her mother. For a moment her eyes leaped from Nashe to the girl then back again. If she was surprised, she said nothing. She said she was awaiting her husband. And below the thunder and fire the little group ate cheese for breakfast, and prayed for the safety of Antoine Duchesnay.

The old man arrived shortly after. There were tears in his eyes. When he saw his daughter, he halted in his tracks, the tears replaced by a slow growing smile. And the father went to his daughter and held her a very long time. He stroked her hair with his blackened hands. Then he noticed Nashe.

"You brought her here, Alan?"

"She chose to come, Antoine."

"I heard they've hit the Ursuline badly."

"They did. I've been there all night."

"There are soldiers searching for you. It seems Colonel Bougainville needs you. He's planning an evacuation, the women and children to go upriver."

231

"When?"

"As soon as can be arranged, unless the English stop."

"They will not stop."

"I know."

"Where is Bougainville?"

"In the dungeons of Chateau St. Louis. It seems the only men safe tonight are English prisoners. I'll go with you."

"Stay here, Antoine. Your family needs you. Even in the worst of times," he glanced toward Reine Marie, "We can find some good."

He left them then, but part way up the stairs, he was halted by her voice just behind him. They kissed long and lovingly as though there had never been the months between them.

"I've been wrong, Alan," she whispered. "I've been a coward when I should have known the better course."

"It's past now."

"When I saw you in that cellar, I knew I'd been a fool. I love you. I know I love you. There is nothing more to say. Whatever your secrets, I'll live with them. I shall wait. And one day God may grant us the grace to share."

"I must go, Reine Marie."

"I know."

"It seems there is never time when we need it."

"There will be time."

"I love you."

"Be careful, Alan. Be careful for me."

He departed then into livid daybreak. The bombing continued, the fires burned on, and Alan Nashe was seen that day strangely smiling through it all.

## 72

There was no attack on the city. English motives were clear. The bombardment continued sporadically, sometimes a few lobbed shots, other times intense cannonades. On the fourth night, shot poured into Quebec until the conflagration it created burned out of control. The next day the centre of the Upper Town was in ashes. And in the Lower Town, Notre Dame des Victoires lay reduced to a pile of smouldering stone. The streets became impassable. A man could be walking, food in his hand, drink in his belly, and suddenly be blown to pieces.

Nashe spent those days surrounded by men organizing the evacuation. Bougainville determined the village of Point aux Trembles, a few miles upriver, as the refugees' haven. And so a chain of tumbrels, wagons, coaches and hundreds of stumbling, tired feet made their way out the Porte St. Louis and onto the King's Highway. A stream of people left the city, looking back sadly to the blasted ruin that once had been their homes.

Nashe's post was at that gate overseeing the flow of the crowds, and it was there he saw her once again. Upright and proud, beautiful, disdaining a carriage, she walked with a gaggle of children. As she saw him, she handed her charges to an Ursuline sister and went to him, unsmiling, her eyes dark and serious.

"Alan, I must speak with you alone."

"Is something wrong?"

"Is there a place we can go?"

He led her to a magazin deep inside the walls. It was cool there and quiet. The only light came from narrow slits cut through the thick walls to aerate the chamber. One of the bars of light crossed her face as she spoke.

"I shall never forget your bravery the other night. The sisters told me you helped them. They are very grateful."

"I was looking for you."

"And you found me."

"At last."

"And I have found myself."

"I don't understand."

"Since that night, I've thought of nothing but you, of the two of us and our future. I realized the moment I saw you the mistake I'd made. I cannot be a nun. My heart is too impure. And...I have done things that make me unworthy, that make me unworthy of you as well."

"Nonsense."

"So I've resolved to tell you my secret, the thing that's prevented you knowing me, that has caused so much pain. The thing that has kept us strangers."

She paused then, a sigh escaping as she gathered her strength for what was to come. She moved a little and the shaft of light touched her mouth.

"You shall decide, Alan, if I am to be forgiven."

"You're forgiven now, whatever it is." He smiled.

"What I have to tell you is horrid, horrid even for me to say." He waited, not understanding her passion. But when the words came they flowed from those perfect lips like bile.

"When I returned from France with Madeleine, I had become a spoiled child. Madeleine persuaded me to join her in living as she did. I thought at the time it would make me more worldly. I wanted so badly to be a sophisticate, as I thought Madeleine to be. I was an ignorant girl, not knowing a sister could become a whore.

I took up with Duchambon de Vergor. We were childhood sweethearts before I left and then, when I came back, he'd become a handsome man, a man such as those I'd longed for in Paris, whom my sister so easily ensnared. I thought de Vergor noble. I misjudged his flesh for his soul.

We were often together, Madeleine and her various beaux with us. My father despaired. I did not listen. I drank too much wine and attended gambling parties, always with Duchambon. One night after a party there were only myself and he and my sister and two other men remaining. We were all very drunk." She paused, her breath coming in ragged gasps.

"You need say no more," Nashe entreated.

"But I must. I have to tell you. You must listen as you never have before, to all of it."

"I will...if you wish."

"I do not wish," she cried, "but it must be so. After a while my sister disappeared with the two men. Duchambon talked to me in a manner different from any other time. He told me strange and obscene jokes. Then he began to paw at me. I resisted, telling him ladies had standards to uphold. He laughed at me. I shall always remember that laugh. It was pitiless.

He asked me if I considered my sister a lady. I told him I did. Then he said he would show me how ladies behaved. He took me to a room, to see my sister. I saw her as he opened the door. She was naked. Drunken and naked. The two men were naked. They were...they...she was like an animal. I tried to leave. Duchambon held me, held my face. I could not close my eyes. I wanted to, but I couldn't. They were grunting and moaning and when they finished they laughed at me.

I was crying. De Vergor put his hands on me and when I resisted he tore my clothing, then the other three came to his aid. They stripped me and pushed me onto the bed. They laughed while they did it, laughed about ladies and gentlemen. Then, with my sister holding my arms, de Vergor...raped me.

234

When it was over I wanted to kill myself. Madeleine stayed with me and told me de Vergor was in love with me. I wanted to believe her. Anything she said. So the shame would die.

He never touched me again. He was the perfect gentleman. And so I convinced myself of my own love for him.

And then you appeared. And I knew I loved you. But if I did then was I not a whore? Like Madeleine? When Duchambon returned I went to him. I told him my feelings. He threatened to tell you everything. So I stayed with him.

Now I am spoiled. Dirty. And that is all there is to say."

"I am no paragon of virtue, Reine Marie," Nashe replied.

"With my sister? What I feared was that you had become like her, like the rest of them. I thought it was my doing somehow, for having been with Duchambon. I thought you had joined them to be with me. And then I ran like a frightened child, not to my father who could not understand, but to a greater power. One who forgives. Can you do the same?"

In answer he took her and held her and his mouth placed kisses softly on those lips that so entranced him. At first she was unsure, thinking he did what he did out of pity. Then slowly she answered, her lips responding, her hands in his hair, and then they were one. In the dusk of the cellar, among the thin shafts of light they found beauty and tenderness, and they established their love.

When they returned to the sunlit crowds, he felt whole, complete, as never before. She bid him goodbye, smiling, and they were careful to be respectable. She begged him to take care of himself. And when she was gone it dawned on him that she had been the only one to tell secrets. She had asked nothing of him.

Still the English guns fired on Quebec. Until the night it rained. In the rain their powder became damp, and they did not bother to shoot. With damp powder, they could not reach the range across the river. So then, when the firing stopped, the English did the impossible.

## 73

It was a warm rain, a misty, grey rain that soaked the land through to its bones and brought peace to the city. A welcome rain, soft and easy, dampening powder and making the guns fall silent. That evening, Nashe and Bougainville were at early supper. The evacuation complete, they had found time for food, a little wine and conversation that took them away from the war. Amid the remains of pork and cheeses, over coffee and brandy, Bougainville waxed optimistic regarding Reine Marie.

"The more I consider it, the more I believe no two are better matched. You are lucky. She is everything any man could want."

"But she is in Point aux Trembles and I'm here. It seems just when things begin to work, there is something to keep us apart."

"You are together in spirit," Bougainville comforted," though the distance divides you. Which is more than most men can even wish for."

"We should speak of something else, Antoine."

"Then we shall! This is no time for sadness, Monsieur. The English guns are silenced at last, you are in love, my general is finally getting some rest...what could be more favourable?"

"You worry over Montcalm?"

"I was in Beauport yesterday." Bougainville grew grim. "He's on the edge of exhaustion. He worries over an English attack. I've never seen him so preoccupied."

"But we're safe as you said, behind our defences."

"For now. Reports have come from the south. The English are advancing toward Carillon. He worries over de Levis's chances."

"But he's said himself if de Levis makes a careful retreat he can slow the English advance."

"Indeed, the maxim rings true especially now. In the forest, the defender has the advantage, so long as he can hit and run, so long as he's not forced to protect any one place. De Levis will do that. The English will get no favours from him. But some time he will be backed against the St. Laurent. Some time he must defend Montreal. And so the General worries. But that is what makes him successful."

"You see we're talking of war again." Nashe smiled. "Love or war—two polarities."

"See the trees; the wind is coming down from the north."

"Another topic!" Nashe laughed. "In New France, there is always the weather to keep people occupied. If love and war do not rule our lives, then surely the weather will!"

"Because it is so changeable."

"Like love and war."

"Indeed."

As they spoke, the muffled sound of an explosion seeped through their window. Mystified, the two men rose, and Bougainville opened the casement. Rain drifted in along with another louder report.

"Cannon," Nashe murmured. "Are the English fools? With damp powder surely their shot can't reach the city."

Bougainville did not answer. He stood poised at the open window, awaiting the next report. When it came, the colonel slammed shut the dormers and strode across the room grabbing coat and sword as he went.

"Those aren't English guns. They're ours."

"But why?"

"The wind is from the north." Drums rolled then, a hundred drums beating the alarm. Then bells began clanging: the signal for men to ready for battle.

"Antoine, what is happening?"

"It's raining, Alan, the wind is in their favour...don't you see?"

"You mean the English..."

"Are going to pass us."

"Upriver?"

"Where else? We'll go to the Bishop's bastion. We'll see it from there."

By the time they had run the distance to the lip of the Cap, the French army had mobilized. A hundred guns began to belch fire in wild, desperate salvoes. The Bishop's bastion was alive with heaving activity: men rolling up iron shot, others filling the huge guns with powder, the noise so tremendous one had to shout to be heard.

Nashe had his telescope. Leaning on a parapet, he peered into the dark just ahead of the thickening smoke that began to envelope the guns' positions. It took time for his eyes to adjust to the night. Then, barely visible, like sylphs in the thin, dark rain, he distinguished the paleness of English sail running off Point Levis; the ships seemed almost touching the shore that showed black behind them. They were as far from French guns as they could get.

"You see them?" Bougainville shouted.

"Yes. I think three..."

"This Wolfe must be the devil himself!"

"They're so close to shore they'll run aground!"

"These are the men who passed the Traverse! Is our shot having any effect?"

"It's short. I can see geysers in the river."

"Captain!" Bougainville screamed to the gunnery officer. "Raise your elevation!"

"Sir, we're already at the maximum! The powder's damp. We can't reach the range!"

"Then double charge the guns! Twice the powder, man! Hurry!"

"Colonel." The captain strode forward. "You realize the guns will crack. They might explode."

"If those ships pass, our entire defence will crack! This is your moment, Captain!"

The man saluted solemnly. In moments, the guns were double charged.

The guns fired hard, smoke filling the air mixing with rain, streaking the faces of their masters. A twenty-four pounder, double charged, exploded in its gunners' faces killing them all. Bougainville snatched Nashe's telescope. He peered into the void cursing; the range was still short. Down the line across the Cote de la Montagne, a cannon at the chateau battery blew apart. Everyone was double charging, the cliff side guns speaking again and again. Nashe saw one ship hit, its forward mast cracking, sails imploding. But it did not sink, and all kept up their slow progress along the shoreline in the face of a hundred guns. Reckless courage on both sides of the river.

"This is hopeless," Bougainville muttered. "Even with our height we can't reach them. Come on. We're going down to the Lower Town. The Royale battery is two hundred yards closer than this!"

"The Royale is a shambles, Antoine. The British have pummelled it for days!"

"It still has guns, and our best gunners man that bastion!"

They sprinted down the steep mountain road, slipping in the wet, falling, then rolling into a run again. Bougainville was like a man possessed by the time they reached the shattered remains of Royale. The battery had four guns left, its men sweating and cursing, still managing to fire. The cannon barrels steamed with heat, dangerously close to cracking. Still the gunners worked over them. Still their shot fell short.

"Ferney! Where is Captain Ferney?" Bougainville grabbed a sergeant.

"Dead, Sir! One of the guns blew up. It took the subaltern too. I'm in command now."

"You're firing short!"

"We don't have the height. The powder is damp!"

"Have you double charged?"

"Since the first shot. A pox on the English swine! They knew just the right moment to pass!"

"If we can sink even one of them," Bougainville shouted. "They must be following a narrow channel. It would block the rest. Then we'll have them!"

"Colonel, my guns can't reach them in the rain!"

"Triple charge, Sergeant!"

"Sir, I cannot!"

"What did you say?"

"I must refuse the order, Sir. The guns are hot already. Every man in the battery will die."

"You will be the first, Sergeant, if you don't do as you're told!"

"Better that, Sir, than cut to ribbons by flying iron. The guns will never take the charge!"

"Load them! Aim them! Then get out of here. I'll light the fuses myself!"

"You'll light only one, Colonel. And then you'll be gone."

"Do as I say!" Bougainville screamed like a man possessed.

"Antoine!" Nashe ran to his friend's side, grabbed his arms, and hauled him away from the terrified sergeant. "Listen! This man knows his business. The guns won't take the charge. What is the sense in killing yourself?"

"There's a chance!"

"There is no chance! The guns will explode and you will be dead. You can fight the English another day!"

Then suddenly the booming voice of Owl Vadnais raised itself above the fracas. "You are a fool, Colonel Bougainville! By the great beaver, open your eyes! They tell you the truth. You are an officer! Act like one."

"Be careful how you speak, Vadnais," Bougainville rounded on the big man. "You address a French officer."

"As I said, Colonel, what you propose is madness!"

Bougainville quivered in Nashe's arms. With a visible effort, he calmed himself, rage ebbing as his reason returned. He faced Nashe then, close to him, and there were tears on his blackened cheeks. He looked almost childlike. Nashe pulled him close, embracing him.

"You are the best of men, Antoine. There is too much value in you to throw it away in a gesture. I love you for the thought, my friend. All these men do. But none of us will allow you to die."

Then Bougainville went to the sergeant.

"My behaviour was inexcusable, Monsieur. I apologize. You and your men have done everything possible. I was the one who lost my head. Can you forgive me, Sergeant?"

The man stood dumbstruck before his superior. Never in his life had a noble asked of him absolution. Vadnais interrupted before the fellow could find words to speak.

"Montcalm has entered the city, Colonel. He sent me to find you, to tell you to join him. I think he was heading for Chateau St. Louis."

"Yes," Bougainville had recovered. "Alan, you'll be needed."

"Colonel," Vadnais interrupted, "I've come to fetch Monsieur Nashe also, but for a different purpose."

"What is it, Owl?" Nashe queried.

"A friend of yours has been injured. He has asked for you."

"But I must go with Colonel Bougainville."

"Not if you have a friend who needs you, Alan," the noble colonel intervened. "You have aided one tonight. I thank you for it. But go with Vadnais. My business will keep till later."

"Is it Monsieur Duchesnay?" Nashe asked.

Vadnais led Nashe outside the bastion. Behind them, the cannoneers had resumed their futile work, hoping against hope that something would come of it. With the hammering of the guns, Vadnais had to shout into Nashe's ear. "Ledrew has been arrested!"

"What?"

"Bigot had him arrested. He was taken outside the city to Bigot's Hermitage."

"What can we do?"

"Get him out. It's time for you both to get out. Ledrew will be interrogated, likely tortured."

"You're sure of this?"

"I have a man there. He said he saw Ledrew himself."

"What of Bigot's guards?"

"He hasn't many. Nearly every soldier in Quebec is positioned at the defences. We've got to do this quickly, Alan. Ledrew will talk. They'll make him talk. It's finished."

"Owl, I have to tell you, I have suspicions about Ledrew. I think he might be a double agent."

"If that were true, don't you think I'd know it?"

"He's told me things he shouldn't have known."

"Alan," Vadnais said, "I've been with him almost two years. He's not what you think. You'll just have to believe me. And he's in trouble now."

"Give me a moment."

"Quickly."

Nashe returned to Bougainville. He would not leave before saying goodbye. Bougainville was puzzled by the intensity of his friend's parting. They embraced as brothers. The guns continued. In their flashing, eerie light, Nashe looked back to see once again the face of his friend. Bougainville waved. The guns thundered on. The English were passing.

That final wave, that good, gentle face in the hellish light of fuses and fire, in the wild cacophony of battle, was the last Alan Nashe glimpsed of his friend...of his enemy...Louis Antoine de Bougainville...of the man he'd come to love and respect above all others.

He would never see him again.

# 74

In the rain, in the dark, their horses pounded out onto the Charlebourg road. Passing the city gates was a simple matter; Nashe's papers signed by Bougainville saw to that. They crossed the St. Charles riding hard and veered northwest toward the mountains.

They rode for an hour until in thick forest, the road narrowed to a winding cart track. Vadnais reined in and stopped, Nashe following suit, the only sound that of the horses' quick breathing and the spatter of millions of droplets on leaves. This far inland the wind had abated.

"A half mile up this track is the Hermitage."

"I don't like the feel of this, Owl," Nashe muttered. "Why would Ledrew be here?"

"Bigot's special prisoners are brought here. If you're worried, let me go in, look around first. You stay with the horses. If anything goes wrong, if I'm not back in a quarter hour, you get out of here faster than osprey going for fish."

"No. It's time I earned my pay. If I don't return, find your way through to the English and tell them what's happened."

"I should go with you."

"Not this time, Owl. I'll find out what I can. Remember, Bigot knows nothing of me. I'll simply tell him I'm here to inform him what's happened in Quebec, say Bougainville sent me. That's plausible."

"Be careful, Alan. Ledrew might have talked already."

"I doubt it. If he's not a double…"

"He's not."

"I believe you. He's a tough individual, a trained agent. He won't have given them anything. You forget, Owl, I've worked with him too. Now, I'm wasting time."

Nashe took to the forest, his senses brought to their height in single-minded concentration. Not until he had come to the edge of the manor's clearing did he pause, concealing himself in a thicket. The massive stone lodge was set at the foot of a rising slope that in moments became Mont Charlebourg. Lanterns illuminated the entrance and guards huddled in an alcove protected from the rain. With a shrug of his shoulders, Nashe decided his course of action. He stood and walked toward the entrance. The time had come to gamble.

A grim faced colonial captain stopped him at the doorway.

"My name is Alan Nashe," he answered the captain's growl. "I've been sent by Colonel Bougainville to see the Intendant. My horse went lame two miles back. In my walk here, I lost the road. I've been wandering in the forest. Thank God I saw your lights."

The captain peered at him suspiciously, and then nodded his head.

"Your papers, Monsieur?"

"Here. You will find them in order."

"You are Colonel Bougainville's aide, I see. But before you enter you must be searched. The Intendant permits no weapons inside. I apologize, Monsieur, but it is required of me."

Nashe was expertly removed of sword and pistol, and the knife concealed in his boot, and escorted into the foyer of Bigot's private lodge. The hall was magnificent, covered in trophies: huge heads of moose on the wall, bearskins lying thick on stone flags, friezes of hunting scenes carved into the oaken walls. It had all the appearances of a well kept, much frequented hunting lodge, and Nashe wondered about this side of Bigot, a facet he'd never dreamed the man possessed. He was about to discover more about the Intendant, a great deal more.

# The Betrayal Path

The captain tapped softly on a double door off the foyer. He waited. In a moment, Bigot's muffled voice responded. As Nashe entered, the portal swung shut behind him. None of his guards entered with him. Obviously, the Intendant demanded solitude in his private haven.

The room was apparently a library, but it was less a place of study than a gallery for objets d'art. The central hall was rustic; this room was its antonym. It was lined with Gobelins and Beauvais tapestries. The floor was awash in Persian carpets. One wall displayed the paintings of Boucher and Falconet. Faience platters lined the mantel of a marble hearth. Scattered about amid intimate settings, rococo furniture sat placid in the softness of the library's mood.

A second level, a gallery running round the room's circumference, displayed shelves of leather bound books. Every few feet, large silver candlesticks illuminated the balcony. A magnificent chandelier hung from the domed ceiling. It was suspended from a silk rope two inches thick that passed from the ceiling down to a wall bracket above a massive table.

And behind that ornate table, its mahogany finished to mirror proportions, sat the sumptuous, ugly figure of François Bigot. He wore a heavy brocade dressing gown, and his fingers were bejewelled with rings. He was smiling, a dreadful grin that made Nashe's nape hairs stand on end. His face glowed with powder and rouge. He wore a feminine patch on one cheekbone. It was black and in the shape of a heart.

He was completely alone.

"Ah, Nashe." His voice dripped irony. "Come in, come in. Take a chair. You are impressed with my little domain? I have always reckoned on your good taste, dear fellow."

"I had no idea you'd be so pleased to see me, Monsieur Bigot. When we last parted, it was not on the best of terms."

"Of course, Monsieur, but that is all in the past, is it not? A touch of cognac, perhaps? The night is chill."

Nashe accepted the glass. He chose a chair to the right of Bigot's desk.

"I do enjoy my little retreat far from the hubbub of responsibility. What brings you here?"

"I have news from Quebec."

"Of course you do. And I'm sure you've come to seek news as well."

"I beg your pardon?"

"Oh, I think you know what I mean."

243

"And I think this charade has gone long enough," Nashe answered roughly. "I find it beneath us both."

"I see." Bigot's smile swept away. "It seems, Monsieur, even in defeat you diminish the other man's pleasure."

"I'm afraid I don't take your meaning."

"Oh, surely you cannot be so naïve. But perhaps I have once again overestimated you. Very well, to business; it's time to collect the stakes, Nashe, to reel in the fish if you will."

"There seems little point in trading insults, Monsieur. I find the experience unpleasant. With your permission, I'll return to the city."

"Sit down!" Bigot's rasping voice filled the air. Nashe paused a moment, remembered the guards, and took his seat. Bigot no longer pretended to humour.

"You've been given the freedom to run for quite some time now, Nashe. But with your friends just a short swim away you've become a trifle dangerous. Surprised, Monsieur? My, my...you are an innocent.

I have known your identity since the day you set foot in this land. Trémais, ironically enough, reported you. He had a good nose for things like that; that is why the nose was removed. Still, even his news was old. You, Monsieur, have been a marked man since you so hurriedly left Marseilles.

Ah, now that does surprise you, doesn't it! I will admit, Monsieur, you do have your points. Your disappearance from the sleigh trip and the time you spent with the Rangers concerned me, and your little jaunt to Albany made me almost think we'd lost you. Still, true to form, you returned. Why even after Trémais was killed, you stayed. Yes, Monsieur Nashe, you truly are naïve."

The shock of Bigot's words rolled over Nashe. In those few seconds, he recognized his own incredible incompetence. He had seen the signs, seen them often, but had not considered them. Desperately he mumbled something about loyally serving Bougainville.

"Ah yes," Bigot sighed, "the military. But the military knows nothing of you, Monsieur. They are so...rude in their ways. Had they known they would likely have had you shot! No, my dear fellow, there are certain things better kept to oneself. My spies far outdo those of the military. But then I have more to protect."

"Then might I inquire why you yourself did not have me murdered long ago? You certainly had opportunity."

"What? And end the game I so surely was winning? Poor simple Nashe, can you be such a boy? If there is one diversion we French enjoy, it is intrigue. The halls of Versailles are its very fountain. You have entered a match far beyond your meagre talents. Simply put, Monsieur, you have underestimated the other player."

"And you haven't answered my question," Nashe interrupted.

"As to that, better the devil we know than allow the English another who might slip through. We had you. What else could we want?"

Nashe's fingers shifted imperceptibly to the edge of the chair's arms; his feet moved slowly beneath the chair as Bigot spoke, resting on their toes. To all intents he appeared relaxed. He was not.

"But you've neglected to mention one thing. Your game, as you call it, would have been nothing without the co-operation of a traitor."

"At last, Monsieur, you become perceptive. Yet it was my doing that swayed the man to me. Would you care to hazard a guess as to his identity?"

"What you know of my movements could only have come from one source—Ledrew."

"Correct!" The Intendant laughed aloud. "You are quite right, dear fellow. And there is the heart of the difference between us."

"How so, Monsieur?"

"He told me you suspected him. Had I suspected I would have made sure of two things: first, I would not have been foolish enough to gamble my life coming here and secondly, the man would have been long dead. You think too much, Nashe. You merely react...where I act!"

"Agreed, Monsieur. I must learn to act."

Nashe was up and across the table in an instant, his hands grasping the man's fleshy throat throttling the choked scream. Bigot's fingers clawed bloody gashes along Nashe's face. Nashe held on. His left hand released its hold and shifted like lightning to Bigot's face, twisting the head. In seconds of turning the neck would snap. Nashe pushed harder. Bigot squealed, his eyes bulging in terror.

"That will be enough, Alan. Release him or die. It's your choice."

Ledrew stood by the tapestried wall a pistol pointing directly at Nashe.

## 75

Nashe sat once again in the chair, Ledrew's pistol aimed at his heart. Ledrew remained poised and ready; he knew Nashe too well to consider relaxing. Bigot, after a fit of coughing and a hefty tumbler of cognac, had nearly recovered. He was pale and the look on his face murderous. Nashe did not address the Intendant, however. He spoke directly to his former friend.

"It seems you've turned traitor, Ledrew. Tell me, was it you who gave the operation away at Marseilles?"

"Would you believe me if I gave you an answer?"

"I'm not in the habit of placing my confidence in turncoats."

"Really, Alan? It seems to me that's exactly what you do. Turning innocent people to your means, subverting them, using them up until they are useless..."

"And you don't? I assume your absences of the past two years were for a reason."

"I would go south..."

"With lies for reports..."

"Suffice to say I returned with more information than I gave."

"That was why Offingham was concerned. He sent me to help you."

"On the contrary, Alan, I told you when we first met I'd requested you. Who better? I knew you trusted me; I knew your methods."

"You used me from the beginning."

"Even to the fight in Place Royale," Bigot interrupted. "I must say I consider my thespian talents second to none following that."

"The man who followed me the first days I was here." Nashe levelled on Ledrew. "Did you send him?"

"He was Charest's man. Charest wanted you killed. He suspected you from the beginning."

"You see, dear fellow," Bigot grinned, "Charest was sent from Versailles along with Trémais. His job was counter-espionage. A good man, but he got in our way. We tried to get rid of him, that little error of the fire, but he was lucky. In the end, we decided it better to bribe him. I must say the man is unscrupulous. He's a full part of our circle now."

"You and he are alike, Monsieur," Nashe retorted acidly. "I assume your orders prevented my death the night de Vergor murdered Trémais."

"Trémais was a fool, much like you," Bigot countered sharply. "He suspected too long, waited rather than act. You saw the price of procrastination."

"Yes," Nashe murmured, turning from Bigot. "So tell me, Jeff...why?"

"I was caught. Monsieur Bigot offered me a choice: torture, death and the death of friends I'd made here, or this. The Intendant promised me a pension, a new life in France with a new name."

"That simple? I thought you were a man."

"And if the Duchesnays were threatened that way, your lovely girl, what would you do? I'm not like you, Alan. I tried to tell you on the way to Batiscan last winter."

"You betrayed Rogers."

"Can you think of a better man to betray? I hated my life, a shadow life. Marseilles was the final straw. We took people there and twisted them to our own wretched aims. We ruined them. Why? They were not our enemies, Alan. They were simply caught in our web. They were not our enemies until we made them so."

"You could have retired."

"I'd never have been allowed. And if I had, I'd have been condemned to a life of dishonour and poverty. England is a hard mother, Alan."

"Yet you still live the life you hate. You've simply changed masters."

"It's the price I pay for release. I was a dead man. This is to be my reincarnation. When this is finished, I'll choose a rural village, marry a good, simple woman, make ordinary plans with ordinary people. You've had a taste of it, haven't you, with Reine Marie? Do you like it? Do you think for a moment she'll accept you, knowing who and what you are?"

"Do you really think this life you have planned will be so easy? You're a traitor, Ledrew. The French won't forget that. You think you'll be left alone?"

"A brilliant dissertation," Bigot intervened, "but nonetheless wasted. You are typical of the English, Nashe: you wallow in sentimentality. This is the age of reason, dear fellow. I quote Helvetius, a most eminent philosopher: the key to survival is self. Even vice is good if it serves the purpose of self-fulfilment. We all have choices to make. Ledrew here has learned rationality. He sees the way of the world. I'll make sure his life is a good one. Were you not such a romantic, much the same could have been your fate."

"I think I prefer honour to reason."

"Alan, I..."

"Be silent, Ledrew! Monsieur Nashe, I see, tires of our company. Just as well. There is business to be dealt with, certain information which must be uncovered. The little matter of the burglary of my vaults, for instance. I would like to know what you told Trémais' inspectors. They ask difficult questions. They've already ruined Cadet. I do not intend to meet them unprepared."

"You'll not find me so easy as Ledrew, Monsieur," Nashe muttered.

"Alas, I feared as much. Well, I was prepared for this."

He pulled a bell rope behind him. In a moment a tapestry parted and Nashe blanched at the sight of the man who entered. He knew then his fate. His end would be a horror, a screaming, reeling blackness of pain. He knew he would give Bigot what he wanted, wail it out in agony from mutilated lips and a twisted soul.

"I see you recognize my guest, Monsieur Nashe. Monsieur Ledrew has not had the privilege. Ledrew, I would like you to meet Monsieur Joncaire, a man of varied talents."

The little man smiled his gat-toothed smile. In his belt were a hatchet and pistol.

"You are not happy to see me, Monsieur?"

"I thought you dead at Carillon," Nashe managed the words.

"It was a close thing, but it will take more than a few clumsy English to catch Joncaire in the forest."

"You left the others to die."

"As did you, Monsieur. We all have our ways of staying alive."

"By now," Bigot turned to Nashe, "you'll have deduced what's in store for you. You will die anyway. I offer you options; you may reveal the information I request and we'll discuss it in a civilized manner, or Joncaire will strip each inch of flesh from your body until you co-operate. It's your decision, Monsieur, dignity or humiliation."

"You promised!" Ledrew blanched. "You said he'd only be imprisoned."

"Don't be a fool. The man knows too much."

"You can't…"

"Hand me your pistol. Now!"

Bigot's hard voice filled the room. Ledrew, broken, simply stepped forward and gave him the gun. Bigot set it on the desk.

**76**

At that moment, the door burst open and guards rushed in. "What is it, Captain?" Bigot, for once, looked alarmed.

"I apologize for disturbing your honour..."

"Is there a problem?"

"We've received word by courier, your honour, the English have moved upriver of Quebec."

"What?" The Intendant's face blanched. "When?"

"Three ships passed two hours ago; when the courier left, more were trying."

"How, in God's name? The shore is lined with cannon!"

"Monsieur Bigot," Nashe intervened, "have you ventured outdoors this evening?"

"Of course not, it's raining."

"Precisely."

"You knew..." Bigot returned flatly.

"Things have changed a little this night, Monsieur."

"But not for you, my friend, not for you."

"Your honour," the captain interrupted, "the courier also brought a request from Governor Vaudreuil that you join him at Chateau St. Louis. I had your caleche and a squadron of horsemen brought round to the door."

"I'll come immediately," Bigot responded.

"Yes, Sir." The captain turned on his heel and departed, the door closing behind him and his men.

Bigot turned to Ledrew and, incredibly, returned the man's gun to his shaking fingers, patting him on the shoulder as he would a favoured pet. Nashe noticed Joncaire's knife slide softly from his boot to his hand.

But Ledrew was half a man now. Bigot scolded him gently then forgave him his moment of English sentiment. Ledrew accepted the remonstrance, his spirit annihilated. Joncaire's knife hand relaxed.

"Now, Joncaire," Bigot turned his back on Ledrew, "you'll take Nashe to the vaults. You know where to put him. And you, Monsieur." He turned to Nashe. "You will have time to think. Think well. I am sure you'll choose wisely."

With that he was gone. Joncaire grinned and directed Nashe to the tapestried wall behind Bigot's desk. Pulling aside the heavy curtain, Nashe discovered a door. Joncaire nudged him through the opening almost inviting Nashe to try something. Nashe knew that against this man he would have little chance. Not unarmed. He passed through the door.

A narrow flight of steps led Nashe down a dimly lit passage. He had no alternative. To run would mean a knife in the back, to turn and fight, the same end. He would not face torture, he decided. It was better to end it now than screaming in some barren room. Heart throbbing, Nashe turned to face his captor. The man was three paces behind, smiling.

"I thought you would try this, Nashe. But I won't kill you. Bigot reserves that right for himself."

"You'll have to kill me, Joncaire. I'll leave you no choice."

"As you wish."

The pistol shot exploded like a cannon in the narrow passage. Nashe stood frozen to his spot. His opponent turned, clawing at a wall to stay his collapse, then fell. His back was a mass of blood.

Ledrew appeared from the shadowed stairway his pistol still smoking. He kicked Joncaire's head making sure the man was dead. Then he took the pistol from Joncaire's belt and pointed it at Nashe.

"That shot will bring guards. Go back to the library. The balcony leads onto the roof. Smash a window. I can help you no more than this."

"Since when does a traitor reverse himself?"

"Just get out of here, will you! Take Joncaire's hatchet. Go back up the stairs, quickly."

Nashe brushed past him. Ledrew still held the pistol. They peered at each other warily. Then Nashe ran up the stairs. Part way he stopped, looking back at Ledrew. Ledrew said nothing. He turned the gun on himself.

"You take the coward's way even in this," Nashe muttered.

"Not exactly, Alan. They'll think you wounded me in the escape."

He fired. The miniball ripped into his arm. Blood spurted, the arm twitched wildly then dangled uselessly at his side. He dropped the gun.

"Now get out of here. Get out of Quebec. It's over for you!"

Nashe bounded up the stairway into the library, shoving home the bolt that locked the door to the passage. The library was silent. Beyond the door he heard men approaching. The alarm had been given outside.

A guard appeared on the landing above, then the doors burst open and four more rushed into the room. Nashe leaped onto Bigot's desk, his boots scoring the wood and, one hand on the chandelier's rope, he swung the hatchet at the wooden stay. The guards' guns levelled but the rope was free. The chandelier dropped like a stone whipping Nashe up toward the roof in a wide, fast arc. He released his hold as he passed the balcony's edge, the force of his ascent carrying him over the balustrade and into a shelf of books.

As it hit the floor, the chandelier crushed two soldiers. Nashe bounced off the shelf and ran pell-mell for the window between himself and the guard on the landing. The man fired wildly. He missed.

Nashe pitched the hatchet through the glass, covered his face and dived headlong through the jagged remains. He hit hard on the roof's cedar shingles, rolled, and then scrambled for a hold. He was on the back half of the house. The captain had ordered horses brought to the front. They would be awaiting Bigot.

Nashe crossed the roof's peak. He peered over the edge. Six feet below the saddled back of a horse greeted him, the animal's handler standing beside it. Nashe leaped, landing square on the saddle his boots lashing the horse's flanks. The animal shot forward its reins ripped from the hand of the groom. The landing had knocked the wind out of Nashe. Nausea wracked him as he grasped desperately the saddle's pommel. Shots fired behind him. The horse ran in a panic. He shouted to warn Vadnais to run, then held on as the horse pounded down the track. When he reached the main road, Nashe was able to draw the beast around to the west.

He did not try to return to the city; instead, he took roads leading south, far inland. Confidently, he showed his papers as he passed roving patrols. It was too soon yet for the alarm to have caught up to him. But he kept a steady pace, trotting the exhausted horse, relentlessly pushing on.

When he'd gone far enough south to skirt Quebec, he took a trail leading to the river. It took him through a little hamlet called Jeunne-Lorette. As he passed through the gaggle of cottages, the rain let up and the grey half-light that signalled dawn slowly came.

He heard the rumble of guns to the north. Quebec had increased its thunder. No more English would pass this day. He rode inland of the Samos battery and finally reined in his haggard beast in the soft groves that shaded the cliff above Anse au Foulon. Here, between the guns of Samos and the lines of Quebec, he chose to make his escape. He descended that path so well known to him and Reine Marie.

And in the river, so narrow now, less than three hundred yards wide, a ship cruised slowly against the current. It was a man-of-war, bristling with guns, its foresails hoisted. It flew the Union Jack.

As he reached the secluded beach where so long ago he had loved a woman, his heart was a mixture of furies. The old compulsion returned. He almost climbed back up the cliff, his mind filled with half formed plans to return to Point aux Trembles, to her, to try to explain and bring her with him.

She would soon know the truth. Soon, too, would Bougainville and Antoine Duchesnay, Chevalier, Montcalm, Mme. Courvier, a hundred people he had played at knowing. And of all of them he owed only one an explanation. He knew she would not accept it.

He turned again to the river and entered, soon swimming in the slow current. Ledrew had been right; his time had come, unexpected as always. It was finished.

An English longboat, outrider to the big ship, saw him. It glided closer, wary; its young soldiers' hands white as bones as they gripped their guns and aimed at him. For them it was all just beginning.

And for Alan Nashe, nothing had ended at all.

## 77

It was four days before Captain Rous of His Majesty's ship, Sutherland, could be persuaded that Nashe was not simply a French deserter. To Nashe's repeated requests, then demands, for his release the captain was politely evasive. Nashe's insistence that he meet with General Wolfe brought a dignified, ironclad reply: security was very tight in this hostile land, there had been many such requests, and Captain Rous for one did not intend having his commander in chief assassinated by some fanatic French patriot posing as an English spy. Even if Nashe's English proved impeccable, the scenario was a little too circumstantial for Rous.

Nashe remained in the ship's brig.

But on the fifth day events altered. Nashe was awakened to a morning meal and a change of clothes, a crisp, new uniform. Rous saw him off the ship, profuse in his apologies. The marines who escorted Nashe downstream to Montmorenci proved equally deferential, a little in awe of this stranger of such sudden importance.

Apparently Offingham had finally heard, through the bureaucratic channels of the army, of Nashe's situation on the Sutherland. The usually quiet, methodical brigadier had flown into a rage at his underlings, upbraiding them for their inefficiency and promising demotions was not Nashe immediately produced at headquarters. And so Nashe by that afternoon found himself below the Montmorenci promontory. In the morning he had been a common prisoner; now he awaited an interview with the leader of thirty thousand men.

Wolfe's command post was a pretty cottage perched near the lip of the Montmorenci chasm. Here, on the north-west corner of the Basin one could view the panorama of war. Just beside the cottage, the river tumbled a hundred feet into the Basin. Then looking across the mouth of the falls, the tidal flats and the sudden inhibiting rise of the Beauport Heights loomed, the dugouts and revetments of the French on its brink, a quarter mile away. The line of cliffs was lost as it dipped westerly into the great bay that ran to the St. Charles but then, so far distant yet so implacably clear, one could view the narrows of the river and the Cap aux Diamantes, its now shattered towers and blasted walls the result of tiny flashes from guns across the river on Point Levis.

It was a strategic point, the Montmorenci, the best possible for a general to view firsthand his tactics in action. Nashe remembered Mme. Juchereau having told him of this place, this quaint cottage high on the cliff. He recalled the time wistfully. It had been a good day. He and Reine Marie were to have picnicked here. Just across the Montmorenci was the Duchesnay seigneury. It might as well have been the moon. Once, a short walk would have taken him there. Now a gauntlet of guns and hard soldiers barred the way.

For the first time in two long years, Alan Nashe could finally relax his vigilance. The little cottage and its gardens were surrounded by the hum of an army encamped. His army. Yet still he recalled Reine Marie. As he stood safe amid the bustle, he began to feel alone. Alone as never before.

At that moment, Offingham appeared. He beamed as he pumped Nashe's hand in welcome.

"I say, Nashe, it's good to see you alive! But where is Ledrew?"

"I'm afraid that's complicated, Sir. The double agent…"

"Was him?"

"Yes."

"Then I'll have him! When this is up he'll be hanged for a traitor."

"He's also the reason I'm here. He helped me escape."

"What? It doesn't make sense."

"As I said, it's complicated."

"This entire campaign is becoming senseless. I hope you can shed some light on the French."

"Why does Wolfe destroy the city?"

"That? He believes it will draw Montcalm out."

"You disagree?" Nashe returned, hearing dissent in Offingham's voice.

"It's inhuman. I must tell you, Nashe, Wolfe has me concerned. He's a good enough man, I suppose, but he's ill and the stress of command, well, the effects have made him irritable and sometimes dangerous. He refuses to listen to his brigadiers. He's had four different plans of attack since he got here. He's now obsessed with the Beauport Heights. This single-mindedness leads him to any lengths, including this mad bombardment of the city."

"How do his officers react?"

"The rank and file love him. But the senior officers...well, look at this."

He handed Nashe a rough drawing. It was a vicious caricature of Wolfe: his nose elongated, his limbs narrow and foolish. Nashe was shaken by the artist's malice.

"That...sketch was done by Brigadier Townshend. There are divisions among the staff."

"Still, his tactic to get those ships upriver was next to brilliant..."

"If you lay credit to him."

"He didn't plan it?"

"That was Admiral Saunders' doing. As I said, Wolfe is obsessed with the Basin. All else is lost on him. Two nights ago, upriver at Point aux Trembles, Commander Carleton probed to check French defences. There were none! Carleton returned with a bevy of women."

"They were evacuated there from the city."

"Wolfe was furious. The probe was made without his approval. He upbraided Carleton publicly for bringing the women. Carleton thought it necessary for security. The whole thing is a shambles. Morale is beginning to falter."

"Sir, about Ledrew..."

"We'll discuss him later. I'm afraid we have a briefing to attend. The general wishes to see you."

## 78

The cottage's interior had become a command post filled with officers and aides, and a hint of trepidation. Offingham offered Nashe a seat near the back of the single room. The proffered chair was beside a youthful naval captain. Nashe at first thought the man a mere adjutant; there was no other reason for such a near boy to be present. His rank surprised Nashe, who put it down to connections, or money. But Nashe discovered quickly, upon introduction, the reason for the man's presence. His name was James Cook. He was the navigator who had led the British fleet through the dangers of the Traverse. A nautical prodigy, and Offingham, by his behaviour toward young Cook, knew it.

"My compliments, Captain." Nashe shook the man's hand. Despite his youth, Cook's rugged complexion bespoke his life on the sea. "You may assume the French have been amazed by your prowess. Until now, they prided themselves on being the only men who knew the Traverse."

"I fail to understand their problem, Sir." Cook's reply was tinged with humour. "There are places on the Thames that give this Traverse of theirs the air of a bathing pond. I merely had the privilege of being first in the line."

It became apparent they were awaiting something. As time passed, the men grew restless, Brigadier General Townshend especially.

"Bloody typical of the man," he addressed no one in particular. "I say, we have things to do, gentlemen, other than be at his beck and call."

"Settle yourself, Sir," Admiral Saunders muttered. "You may be a peer and he may not, but he is your superior officer as, I might add, am I. I will brook no scatter mongering in my presence!"

"He's inspecting the forward posts." Brigadier Murray glanced up from his charts. "Point Levis today."

"He's not yet used to commanding an army," Townshend countered. "The man must learn that a Major General does not mingle among his troops. Bad for discipline, I say. He becomes too familiar."

"The troops respect him, Townshend," Brigadier Monckton answered. "They expect to see him. Still, this infernal waiting wears on the nerves."

Coffee was served. Conversation grew quiet. Outside, Nashe heard the clatter of arms coming to salute. The door opened and in a moment Nashe understood the meaning of Townshend's caricature. Major General James Wolfe wore a plain scarlet tunic, eschewing the trappings of rank. The man looked less like a general than anyone Nashe could think of. He looked, in fact, more schoolmaster than soldier. He was rail thin, his slender body accentuating his six-foot height. His complexion was pasty and the sharp boned face ended in an upturned nose. Wolfe's walk was ramrod straight. As the officers stood to greet him, he waved them to their seats. Nashe could not help but notice he seemed in a great deal of pain.

"Gentlemen," Wolfe was not in good humour, "I have just returned from a tour of inspection and what I have seen appalls me. I see disorganization. I see sloth. Townshend, you were to have a plan for disbursement around the Basin. Where is it?"

"I am working on it, Sir."

"You've been working on it for a week! When, Brigadier, will this plan be completed?"

"General Wolfe," Townshend's voice was equally harsh, "you must be aware this division of forces will weaken our strength. The French might attack anywhere in force."

"I have more than once stated my policy in this, Brigadier." Wolfe's voice raised half an octave. "Montcalm is entrenched. We have no way of getting at him. With this division of troops, he might be enticed into battle. I have enough faith in the English soldier to believe our battalions will hold, even outnumbered, until help arrives. But at present we've no idea when and where the French might strike. Intelligence is a mishmash of rumour. Offingham, you said you had a man among the French. Where in God's name is he?"

"Sir," Offingham stammered, "I present Captain Alan Nashe. The man I spoke of. The man in Quebec…"

"So, you are Offingham's spy. You should feel well at home in this group, Captain." Wolfe's petulance peppered his words. "Have you a report? Offingham?"

"Sir, he's just arrived. I had no idea of his escape until last night."

"Typical. Well, I hope Captain Nashe, there is more to you than our usual failures. Offingham tells me you've infiltrated the highest French ranks. My congratulations, Sir, it is reassuring to know some men prefer to serve their country rather than themselves. Tell me, what do you know of French strength on the Beauport Heights?"

"Quite a lot, Sir," Nashe answered stiffly. "I was assigned under Colonel Bougainville to record the positions of the battalions around Quebec."

"Better and better, young man."

"But with your ships having moved upriver, General, there will have been alterations."

"What do you know of troop strength above the city?" Brigadier Murray queried.

"That will be enough, Murray," Wolfe snapped. "Allow me to conclude my interview before you begin to cloud the issues. Now, Nashe, I want everything you have about Beauport. And I wish to know something of this Montcalm. Offingham says you were friendly with him."

"We were only slightly acquainted, General," Nashe hedged. He'd begun to feel uncomfortable in the presence of Wolfe and his officers. It was clear neither side was willing to listen with open minds.

"Begin with the troop placement as you recall it. For once, Mr. Nashe, I anticipate an honest tale."

For two hours Nashe poured forth each bit of information he'd gleaned. Seldom was he interrupted. Once or twice the general broke in, needing more detail, arguing a point, often congratulating Nashe on his astounding success. Still, it was clear he refused to believe Montcalm would not commit to battle. Often his pain appeared with a twitch in his face. He was obviously weak. Yet he sat straight in his chair, disdaining comfort. Nashe wondered what kind of man lay beneath that ascetic exterior.

"Gentlemen," Wolfe announced as the interview ended, "I am pleased with Captain Nashe's report. I hope you have all listened well for this is the type of thing I require to end this damned siege. Captain, I am attaching you to permanent service with headquarters staff. I admire your adroitness, young man, and I'll surely need your expertise further. You are to be promoted, Nashe, and well deserved too! Orderly! Find this man a major's trappings and have him fitted for a dress uniform.

Major Nashe, your work begins this evening. You will be my aide tonight, and my source of information. You have precisely three hours to be barbered and tailored. And have those scratches on your face looked after. We go to the Stirling Castle, Sir, for a dinner you will not soon forget!"

Amid the mouthed congratulations and outraged faces of the staff, Nashe departed the cottage. He had not gone far when Offingham joined him.

"I don't believe I've been drawn and quartered so many times by so many eyes in my life," Nashe mused as they strolled through the camp.

"The brigadiers are jealous," Offingham explained, "and worried he's replacing them with a shadow cabinet of junior officers. You can hardly blame them. This promotion of yours, deserved mind you, but now he'll use you as an aide. Still, some good might come of it."

"How so?" Nashe was puzzled.

"You may become privy to his thoughts. He's refused to communicate with his staff. You will do so for him."

"Spy on our own general, Sir?"

"You'll report to me each day. I will relay your information to the staff."

"You don't trust him," Nashe said.

"He's given us little reason to," Offingham replied. "It's a sorry state, but it is as it is. I'm sorry I can't give you leave, Alan. God knows you deserve it, but it appears you've become involved whether you like it or not. It seems a habit of yours," he smiled sympathetically.

## 79

It was warm that night, the barest hint of a breeze fluttering birdlike through the Basin. The river glittered darkly. The men in the longboat were silent, the only sounds the soft dipping of oars and the faint rustle of night wind. The boat veered into a little bay at Ile d'Orleans, safe anchorage far from the threat of attack. The longboat bumped, wood on wood, against the bulwark of a great man-of-war. A ladder descended. As the men from the boat climbed the ladder, new sounds disturbed Nashe's meditation. In the distance, the guns on Point Levis opened up once again on the helpless city making harsh flashes on the horizon. As he reached the deck, Alan Nashe turned to glimpse the distant orange billows. He shrugged his shoulders, lowered his eyes, and turned back to face the Stirling Castle.

She was massive. Eighty-four guns was her complement and scores of sailors serviced her. Saunders' flagship, but this night she was transformed— no longer the beast of war, she had become a domesticated thing, her decks littered with coloured paper lanterns whose light mellowed the dire engines of her work. Tonight she was civilized, her primitive nature rouged over in papered light. And the men aboard her shared in her masque, each resplendent in scarlet and braid, wearing powdered perukes and white gloves.

"All the perfumes of Arabia..." Nashe mused, smiling grimly at the bard's knowledge of men.

The pomp intrigued Nashe. He'd been told of Wolfe's disdain for the trappings of ceremony. He wondered why the same man would order up such a sham. He looked to Offingham for an answer and received only a smile. Below, the gun deck had been festooned with finery; summer bouquets rested on fine linens that concealed rough plank tables. A harpsichord played somewhere amid the crowd. Goblets of wine were served from doily-covered powder boxes. Streamers camouflaged the oaken beams of the ceiling. Nashe felt as if he'd been transported back in time, back to Quebec, to the elegant soirées of summer with men in glittering uniform, servants wending here and there among the smiling faces, the buckled shoes, the gowns.

Gowns!

For a moment, Nashe could not believe his eyes. Suddenly the dream became nightmare. Carleton's captives from Point aux Trembles were here. He began to recognize faces. Instantly, he wanted to run, to escape what would soon be astonished, accusing stares. He tried to step back into the doorway but the crush of descending officers prevented him. Helplessly, he was pulled forward with the current of eager men.

The women were prisoners, yet they were not treated as such. Wolfe had decided they would be returned to their city in the morning. Those same gentlemen who even now rained death upon their men afforded them every kindness. Yet their behaviour was equally genteel. If there was hatred, it was not shown; if fear beat in their hearts, their smiles concealed it. English officers were astounded to find such refined urbanity in this far and untamed place. Nashe, of course, felt no surprise. His only feeling was fear. In five seconds that fear met its maker.

Again, as they had always done, they saw each other simultaneously. At first her face lighted with joy and then instantly, as revelation burned into her, the look changed. She came toward him then, unsteady, leaving the other women behind, ignorant of the approving glances of men all around her. Two colonels attempted an introduction. She passed them in a trance, her eyes fixed on Nashe. As she neared him, an aide introduced General Wolfe; she ignored the man, continuing her awful advance. She heard nothing, saw nothing but him...her eyes riveted to his.

A hush fell on those gathered near. Other women had recognized Nashe. The men stood awkwardly by, sensing something was wrong. All eyes levelled on them as she neared. She stopped so close to him he could distinguish the aroma of her perfume. Sandalwood. Her eyes left his. They shifted to his uniform travelling up and down the scarlet as though it were hallucination. And again the deep, dark eyes fluttered upward, meeting his. For a second, he glimpsed her incredible beauty, then her eyes, soft jewels, turned to stone.

Her face became a mask, a veneer so decorous, so civilized, he felt as though he had been crushed. His hope, his life, in a second was obliterated.

"Major Nashe." Wolfe appeared behind her. "It seems you are honoured to have the acquaintance of this most radiant beauty. I beg you as a man for an introduction." He smiled. "And I order you as your superior to make me known to this lovely lady. Never, Mademoiselle, have I glimpsed so perfect a beauty. You are like a summer evening."

"Like the moon..." Nashe murmured.

"Good Lord, Major, have you lost your manners? My name is James Wolfe, Mademoiselle. And you are?"

"I have the honour..." Nashe forced the words out, "to present to you, General, Mademoiselle Reine Marie Duchesnay. Mademoiselle, Major General James Wolfe...my superior."

"General, a pleasure..." she answered, but her eyes never left Nashe.

James Wolfe was not a stupid man. Sensing himself in the midst of something, he departed, his last look at Nashe one of pity. He took the attention of the crowd onto himself, presenting himself gallantly to a nearby group. The hush became lively chatter. The two were left alone.

When she spoke, her voice was a winter. "This is your mystery, the secret you couldn't tell me."

"Reine Marie..." he choked on her name.

"We have both been betrayed then. I hope God will forgive me for not returning the forgiveness you have accorded me. Yet even that must have been a lie."

"Try to understand. I had no choice."

"This is not the man I loved. You are my father's enemy, my country's enemy, worst of all enemies...the liar."

"I love you," Nashe uttered softly.

"I am your prisoner, Monsieur. All of the ladies here are your prisoners."

"All of us, everyone, is a prisoner," Nashe returned.

"Then that is the only bond we share. Now if you will permit, I will go to my own."

She turned on her heel and walked away joining her mother and Mme. Chevalier. She never looked at him again.

He could not follow. His legs would not carry him. He could not again face that awful contempt. Later, as he sat at the table and watched her not watching him, he ate nothing. The dead require no sustenance.

The party was false after that, each of the revellers uncomfortable, their talk and laughter subdued. They had seen two lovers part; by then everyone knew why. In the end Wolfe curtailed the evening with a toast.

"Ladies, I hope you will pardon my rough handling of your lovely language; alas, I am merely a simple soldier. But let me say that even the unschooled would revel in the delights I have witnessed this evening. You are, each of you, paragons of your sex and your country.

Tomorrow you will leave us. The bombardment will end. We will refrain for two days so you might again reach refuge outside the city. But ladies, be aware you take with you the respect of those you leave behind. I, for one, feel the loss of your departure already. Even a soldier has a heart, even if that soldier be a general." He smiled and took his seat.

Mme. Juchereau handled the response.

"We thank you, Monsieur Wolfe, for your kindness and generosity to us. In another time, we might have been friends. However, your bombs devastate our city; our men die beneath your guns, and you are unwelcome guests in our land. I drink to you as a man, Monsieur Wolfe, and to these others as men. I may not drink your health as soldiers."

"Such are the fortunes of war, Madame." Wolfe smiled stiffly, taken aback by the woman's frankness.

"Why must you cannonade our city?"

"As I have said, Madame," Wolfe was beginning to redden. "The fortunes of war dictate I must. General Montcalm will not meet me in battle. He does not fight like a gentleman."

"Monsieur Wolfe," Mme. Juchereau returned smoothly, "a gentleman need not follow rules when his business is to protect his country. You have an example beside you, it seems. Alan Nashe. We have known him, Monsieur, and he is no gentleman either."

"Nashe has his duty, Madame," Wolfe countered.

"As does Montcalm."

"As do I."

The party dispersed soon after.

## 80

"We've been far too long, gentlemen." Wolfe's eyes glittered beneath his pale brow. "A month since our first landing and we are at an impasse."

The little cottage at Montmorenci was again packed with officers; Monckton, Murray and Townshend were there, each in various stages of discomfort. They had just been reprimanded and none had enjoyed it. Carleton appeared angry. Saunders stood stiff as brass nearby. The room was littered with the residue of a long meeting. Nothing of consequence had been decided.

A bevy of junior officers, Nashe included, stood by making notes for their superiors. Each of them would far rather have been somewhere else. Nashe spent his time staring through a window. He could see Montmorenci Falls and the shore beyond it. His mind would not relinquish the thoughts of that far shore.

"The season is passing, gentlemen," Wolfe continued, his face sheened with sweat. "Montcalm must be forced from his roost!"

"But that's the point, General...what is to be done?" Townshend eased forward in his chair. "Montcalm is entrenched, his flanks protected by natural barriers. Murray has been up the Montmorenci, nothing but ravines and impenetrable bush."

"It's true, Sir," Murray agreed. "I probed for two days; advance was impossible. To cross the river, we must descend the ravine then climb back up in thick forest. The men who tried were cut to pieces."

"The other flank, above the city, is less difficult, Sir," Carleton enjoined. "Six miles upstream is a beach, the cliffs disappear."

"We are all aware of your valorous attack on Point aux Trembles, Carleton." Wolfe's eyes pierced his former friend. "Against my orders. Perhaps you've not read the latest intelligence. Captain Rous of the Sutherland reports a thousand French waiting on shore. Your little escapade has done nothing more than forewarn them."

"Sir," Monckton interrupted, "Carleton's point is valid. If we could get enough men upriver at least we might cut the supply line to Batiscan."

"The French would slaughter us on the beach."

The meeting dissolved into silence. Wolfe called for maps and had them spread on a table before him. He lowered his head to regain his flagging strength. When he spoke again his voice was tremulous.

"I have observed a French redoubt part way down the bluffs here, across the river where Montmorenci becomes the Beauport Heights."

There was an almost audible groan as Wolfe reiterated his plans, his obsession with Beauport well known by now. He looked up as a schoolmaster does, peering at his errant audience, then continued.

"The place is far below the main French entrenchments. I propose we attack up the Heights at low tide. We will force a French retreat and our men will then hold and fortify the bastion. It may just be the thing that forces Montcalm to respond."

"General," Townshend snorted, "in the first place our men will have to charge up a steep grade in full view of the French lines. And secondly, once we have the place if, by God's will any men actually get there, it remains exposed to French fire. How could we reinforce it?"

"You have an alternative, Townshend?" Wolfe's voice was hard edged.

"If we must make a frontal attack, the Lower City itself is open to us. Our cannon have nearly destroyed it. The Point Levis guns can shoot higher than those from our ships. An attack there would mean at least decent artillery over the infantry."

"And what happens once we have captured the place?"

"We sweep forward up the Cap, forcing whatever obstacles in the way."

"If I may, General?" Nashe stood, shaking off his reverie.

"What is it, Major?" Wolfe queried.

"Brigadier Townshend," Nashe said, "the French have anticipated that move. There are three roads leading from the shore to the Upper City. Each of them has been fortified. No one could breach them, Sir. And beside that, they are backed by artillery. Their fire thus far has been minimal. They fear wasting powder. But if we should actually threaten the city..."

"I believe I've sat silent long enough, gentlemen." Admiral Saunders' voice boomed from the rear. "I agree with Nashe concerning the city; those guns would make mincemeat of landing craft. The upper reaches of the river are also impossible. A mobile brigade of French regulars follows Rous' ships up and down with the tide. Little will get past them. Yet, as General Wolfe asserts, the men are becoming apathetic. The only choice now is the general's plan to force the Beauport redoubt. Captain Cook here has been reconnoitring. He tells me our flat-bottomed craft can reach shore at high tide just below the French position. My frigates' guns could provide covering fire to that height, though they will not reach the crest of the ridge. I realize the thing sounds risky, but it far exceeds this self defeating siege."

"I thank you, Sir," Wolfe responded. "Now gentlemen, I propose to use the grenadiers supported by a company of Royal Americans. I intend to make the attack on July thirty with the...high tide. I myself will oversee the action from one of Captain Cook's transports."

"But, General," Murray objected, "you'd be in the thick of fire. It's too dangerous."

"I have made my intention clear, Brigadier. Monckton will lead the assault, but for the good of the men my presence is necessary. They've come to expect I be with them. I will not be a braid-covered doll to be seen only in the moment of victory. Those are my principles, Murray, and you know as well as I that I'm far more use in a fight than in a staff room."

He dismissed the meeting. It was then, as the officers filed from the cottage, that Nashe approached Wolfe.

"Sir, I request to be allowed to accompany you in the attack. I find this present inaction unbearable; my mind is on...other things."

Wolfe searched long into his eyes.

"No girl is worth dying for, Nashe, if that is your intent."

"You do me an injustice. I simply wish to fight. I beg you, Sir, grant me this."

"Done! I'm more than pleased to have a good man beside me. But you must promise me to be careful. I still need you, Major."

"I understand, Sir. I'll remain beside you."

"Good. Now I must detail the plans. Fetch Saunders back, and Cook. If it works, this assault will be a short affair. The business will be to keep what we gain."

## 81

Nashe stood beside Wolfe in the transport just off Montmorenci. The French battalions far above were firing hard. The boats were stuck and lead rained down on them like a hailstorm.

The action had begun well. The dawn saw landing craft off the Heights. The navy had commenced its bombardment. Then things changed. Cook's calculations were, for once, tragically wrong. The transports had grounded offshore amid hidden sandbanks. They had waited for hours until the boats could be organized. And as the afternoon wore on, Wolfe fumed at the delay. He was finding, to his frustration, that an army moved more slowly than a brigade.

It was five o'clock by the time landing boats crammed with grenadiers reached the shoreline. The sky lowered as ranks of heavy thunderheads wheeled in above the flotilla. Monckton arrived in his command boat.

"Sir," he shouted gallantly, "the grenadiers are ready!"

Wolfe smiled. His sword slid from its scabbard. He held it high for all to see. The men in the landing boats cheered. The blade descended slowly, levelling at a sandy point directly below the redoubt.

"There, Monckton! There is the place!"

So into the rain of fire Monckton led his barges. The French redoubled their efforts above. Broadsides answered them from Saunders' frigates. The little redoubt was blown to pieces as volley after volley slammed into it. But for all its fury, the bombardment was useless against the main French forces. They remained untouched far above.

"Well, Major Nashe, I think it time I joined my men."

"In the landing, Sir? Would that be safe?"

"Indeed not, Sir. You are the last man I expected to hear that from. Have you lost your nerve?"

"I welcome the chance. It's time I did some honest fighting."

A thousand men heaved through the shallows onto the beach. French fire was withering. The advance soon became a shambles. The grenadiers were shouting and falling as they lunged toward their enemies. In moments their ranks were broken.

Wolfe shouted at the top of his lungs for his men to regroup. It was useless, his voice a mere whisper amid the boom of battle. His barge landed. In the open stretch of beach there was no shelter. Men scrambled in the loamy sand frantically building cover. They died before their trenches were dug. Others shuffled about, their sergeants dead, their weapons gone, blood pouring from dreadful wounds. Through it all, Wolfe paced the beach, upright, sword in hand, his red shock of hair an enticing target. He refused all offers of shelter. He urged on his men, in his element, seeming to know no fear.

But the tide rolled out and with it the boats. His men could no longer retreat. Around him, they fought like snared animals, desperate, ferocious, their bullets useless against the French cover. They died by the score.

As he stood beside his general, Nashe felt the hit like a hammer, felling him to the beach. He found himself looking up at the black, ugly sky. Then Wolfe's face hovered above him. There was no pain; it was too soon for that, only the disbelief that it could happen so easily. In the hellish noise, the general's lips moved. Nashe did not hear.

Then above the noise, a tremendous shattering boom blotted all else out. No gun could reach that metaphysical level. Thunder. Great claps of thunder began repeating and repeating and the awful sky opened up shedding sheets of rain. In moments, he was drenched. Lightning bolts ripped across the heavens.

"Lay still, Nashe," Wolfe shouted. "We are saved! The powder's wet. There will be no more shooting this day, thank God."

In the downpour, the brave grenadiers tried one last time to reach their enemies. They charged up the escarpment and went nowhere. The rain made the incline slippery. Wolfe called an end to the futile attack.

With low tide a relief force of Highlanders forded the Montmorenci and came to their aid. From their sanctuary they saw the hell their brothers had lived through. Two hundred men left the beach wounded, another two hundred never left.

Nashe was carried across the river on a stretcher. Every movement made him feel as though his flesh were tearing. Wolfe, who never left his side, issued orders to a Highlander captain.

"Have this man taken to my quarters. My surgeon is to care for him."

"Sir?"

"This man took the fire meant for me. I owe him my life."

"As you command, General. But where are you going?"

"Away for a while...to think."

"But it's raining, Sir."

"I worship this rain, Colonel. Were it not for this rain we would, both of us, be dead now. This rain is God's tears, Colonel...for brave men and a foolish commander."

## 82

It was grapeshot that felled Nashe on the Beauport beach, iron shards embedded into his back and upper legs. He was lucky. One piece had lodged an inch from his spine. Wolfe's personal surgeon probed, removing all he could find. He was pleased with his work. Nashe would own some horrible scars and would limp for the rest of his life; but he was alive and not paralyzed, and so the good doctor was happy.

Nashe was still many days passing in and out of consciousness. At times the agony seemed unendurable. He was given laudanum to quell the pain. And each day, Wolfe was at his bedside, the general convinced Nashe had spared his life, though Nashe himself had no recollection. Nevertheless, Wolfe's gratitude allowed Nashe a comfortable bed in the cottage loft and the constant attention of a doctor. In the cleanliness of that sick room, he slowly recovered; something he might not have done had he been consigned to the crowd and stench of a hospital ship.

But Wolfe too was not well. Each day, he seemed to grow paler and increasingly irritable. The Montmorenci was a disaster. Montcalm's defence had proved indomitable. August was wearing; the short northern summer would draw to its end. Winter would come, and the end.

The French, on the other hand, found new hope from Montmorenci. With August came French raids, scalping and mutilation so savage that soldiers would wound themselves rather than be ordered out on patrol. English morale was at its ebb, undercut by Montcalm's strategy and the increased apoplexy of its own commanders.

They blamed Wolfe for the failure at Montmorenci. He had gambled and lost. Their meetings grew stormy. More than once, Nashe, listening from the loft above, heard them shouting. Eventually all three brigadiers sent underlings in their places. They used the excuse that constant French forays left them little time for meetings. And so Wolfe became introspective. Often his orders were cloudy or poorly considered.

It was the times then, and these things, that led him to his terrible decision.

\*\*\*

The meeting became difficult, the officers surly. Nashe, who had been carried down for a much-needed change of scene, watched from a cot as Wolfe grew furious. By the end, the various aides gathered up their materials even as the general was speaking. Then Wolfe brought in Isaac Gorsham. It took Nashe a moment to recognize the burly Ranger. He was dressed in buckskin and possessed a great flowing beard. When he entered, the colonels ended their packing, their eyes levelled on the strange apparition.

"Hello Isaac," Nashe greeted the man from his corner.

"You know this man, Nashe?" Wolfe seemed surprised.

"When I met him he slaughtered my horse at a roadside for food."

"You!" The Ranger exclaimed in recognition. "T'gentleman goin' to Montreal; so you're one of us after all."

"You have a good memory, friend. I see you escaped de Longeuil's ambush."

"Aye. And I pray nightly to meet the man who betrayed us."

"The man was with you, Sir, in your camp. You recall Ledrew?"

"He's a dead man should I set eyes on him. My brother was killed in that fight."

"If you two would continue this conversation later," Wolfe interrupted irritably, "we'll finish our business." Wolfe turned to his officers. "You will recall, gentlemen, when we arrived here, I issued a proclamation of clemency to all French civilians who chose to remain neutral. Obviously with these raids and the lack of co-operation shown by the local populace, they have chosen to ignore my edict. The time has come for them to pay. I have issued Captain Gorsham a mission to march with his Rangers down river to St. Joachim, and then march back along the other shore. On the way they are to burn every house and barn and lay waste every field. The French have turned to a tactic of terror. I intend to show them the meaning of the word!"

After a short, shocked silence one of the colonels attempted to argue.

"Have you considered the impact on the French?"

"I have."

"They will be enraged, Sir."

"Colonel, as I've been advised so often in the past, this is not a European war. So I will fight this new kind of war. And I'll better them for teaching it to me. Gorsham, do you foresee any problems?"

"None, Sir. There be debts come due in this. The Frenchies done the same to our land for years. We know what to do, Gen'ral. We've seen it oft' enough."

"Gentlemen, you may inform your brigadiers of my decision. Time grows thin. Whatever it may take, I intend to end this siege. Gorsham, you have your orders."

After the men departed, Nashe watched his ailing commander sink to his chair, head in hands, as though he had just condemned himself to infamy.

"General," he uttered softly, "it's not too late to call Gorsham back."

"You think I'm wrong too."

"What you've decided is an awful thing."

"I never thought my career would bring me to this. I suffer it more than anyone. But it must be done. If the rape of this land will end this conflict, then I have no qualms. I have never been defeated, Nashe, not until I came here. I find I do not like the taste. It is not my duty to lose. I will do my duty, and I shall win."

"At any cost?"

"We all have our destinies, Nashe. I find mine bitter."

"As do I, Sir."

Two days later Wolfe fell sick. There were times when he raved in delirium, bereft of his army, of his principles, owning only torment. His command passed to Saunders. Through those days Nashe remained with Wolfe, repaying the bond he owed. But Nashe could see what Wolfe could not: a day did not pass when the sky was not ribboned with distant smoke; Gorsham's work up and down the river. The French would not soon forget this rape. The war became a terror. It would go worse for all men.

## 83

James Wolfe was bedridden nearly all of August. His hours on the beach at Montmorenci and the fording of the river had inflamed his chronic rheumatism and aggravated his kidney stones. Nothing could be done. All that was left to him was bed rest and the hope he would recover.

And in that time too, Nashe recovered. He walked short distances, his limp painful and pronounced; nevertheless, it was good to be mobile again. He began a regimen of exercise, slowly regaining his strength and conditioning, increasing his powers a day at a time. And as the general regained too what was left of his health, Nashe found himself reading correspondence to the weakened man, writing his letters, becoming a confidante.

Wolfe was a strange character. Thirty-three years of age then, he was not a great deal older than Nashe. Yet he had arrived at his present, exalted position through an irascible ambition. He was a man of insecurities and that awful will that comes to dreamers who must attain their dreams. He was arrogant and petulant, the one brought on by his fear of failure, the other by nagging illness. Nashe learned from him what agony it was to seek greatness. He did not envy Wolfe.

"You know, Nashe, I've never understood what it is to be a civilian," Wolfe murmured quietly in the light of the oil lamp, as he finished the soup Nashe had brought him. "My family have all been soldiers. As a child, I grew up with soldiers around me. Even as a boy I played the little soldier for my father. He was a lieutenant general, a strict man, a good soldier. He died this year, not six months past while I was preparing this offensive in England. I was with him at the end. He was proud of me then. I can only pray his ghost does not look down on me now."

"This isn't over yet, General," Nashe comforted.

"I was a good regimental commander, Nashe. I love soldiers as no man alive. At Louisbourg I had good men, trained men of my own making; the amphibious assault I knew well; I've made a study of that kind of fight. Still, Louisbourg was an accident, you know. My men and I came ashore at a rocky cove; the French fire was murderous. I signalled a retreat with my cane, my drummer was killed so I couldn't make my messages heard. My men thought I was giving the attack. They stormed the French and overwhelmed them. I was a victor, all through the mistaken wave of a cane.

When I returned to England, I was famous. It's as if God himself had taken a hand in my life. Pitt called me to his offices. He told me I was the only man who could take Quebec for him. He passed all others in line of command.

So my officers are envious. Oh, I'm not naive. I've seen Townshend's drawings. I know what he thinks of me, and he affects the rest. I've given them reason. I made a mockery of English arms at Montmorenci. I've seen my limitations, Nashe. That is a hard thing for any man. Impetuousness is my weakness. The things that made me a good colonel make me a bad general.

Tell me what you know of Montcalm. Has he any doubts? Give me the truth of the man, Nashe. I'll listen. Sometimes I think he is more than a mere man. He frightens me."

Nashe looked at the frail general lying on his sickbed, a frightened man in the throes of self-doubt. Nashe answered him honestly.

"Montcalm is a strategist, General; one of the best I've seen. But he too has weaknesses. For instance, his strategy is always defensive. I've never seen him plan for attack. I think there's a reason for this, and that's his second weakness. One he well knows. He has a mercurial temper. He holds it mostly in check but more than once I've seen it flare. The results are devastating. He loses all sense of reason. Once, I saw him publicly insult Governor Vaudreuil's wife. He had reason but nevertheless, the situation could have been handled more delicately. I think if he's faced with a crisis he'll react irrationally.

In a sense, Sir, he has troubles like yours. His command is a shambles. You're actually facing two armies up there, divided. You at least retain the respect of your soldiers; half Montcalm's troops, the colonials in particular, just might not follow him. If you can force a battle the French could fall apart."

"But that's exactly what I wish! In pitched battle my soldiers are the best in the world. It's this insufferable siege that brings them down!"

"Montcalm won't fight unless he's given no choice."

"So he must be forced! The question is how?"

"Sir, the Beauport will never be taken. It's far too strong. But there is a breach in his defence."

"Above Quebec."

"You realize that?"

"Of course."

"Then why..."

"Politics. Perhaps this sickness has been a blessing. It's forced me to look at myself. My rise was too fast. I became too stubborn about my power. I feared losing it, particularly to the men who have plotted to replace me. You told me before Montcalm's supplies are upriver..."

"He shipped his supplies south to Batiscan in case Quebec fell. He intends to retreat there if all else fails."

"If I could land a strong force and cut that line above Quebec, he would be obliged to fight...on my terms."

"And as I said, Sir, a surprise might throw his reason awry. He's a strategist, not a tactician."

"Unable to improvise!"

"As far as I know."

"If I do this, I give in and admit my limitations publicly."

"General, winter is coming and winter here is a far greater enemy than the French."

For a moment, Wolfe lay back on his pillows, lost in thought, his eyes closed. In the dim lamplight, he looked nearly like a corpse. When he raised himself again, he handed Nashe a delicate silver locket. Nashe opened the object carefully. Inside was the picture of a woman, young, not beautiful, but the artist had captured a delicate soul.

"My betrothed, Miss Catherine Lowther."

"She is lovely, General."

"That beauty on the Stirling Castle; you've said nothing of her since that night, yet she is still with you I sense."

"I'll never see her again."

"Then we are much the same, Alan. I too shall never see my Catherine again."

"This will end, General. You'll go home."

"I don't think so. I am going to die. Do you believe in God, Alan? I believe He has set my fate. I believe it was He who caused that wave of the cane, He who caused me to be here. I'm not afraid of death, but I'd far rather die on the field than waste away in a sickbed. Those seem my only remaining choices."

"I can't believe we have no choice. Our lives are our own making."

"Then you must see that girl again. You must make your life, as I must make mine. I do not intend on allowing God to let me lose this battle. Look there, the sun is up."

He raised himself from the bed for the first time in weeks. Standing shakily, he cupped his hand around the lamp and blew it out. He would never again be the invalid.

## 84

By August's end, the frail general once again took command of his army. His illness still afflicted him but he himself had changed— his will strong, his orders concise, his demeanour no longer petulant. Nashe watched the transformation amazed. In his absence, the English had become an army of grumbling men. There was little order, no pride, and a single overriding concern: September had come and with it the knowledge that winter was on its heels, and with winter would come sure defeat.

Within two weeks, James Wolfe changed all that. He began by touring the camps. He spoke to his soldiers in confident tones. He was hard on them, pushing them back into discipline. His leadership soon became inspiration.

And his manner toward his brigadiers became uncharacteristically mild. He admitted his errors openly. He requested council. He listened and acted. Shifting the army's main strength to Point Levis, in two days the 15$^{th}$ Foot, the 43$^{rd}$, his old regiment the 67$^{th}$ and his beloved 78$^{th}$ Highlanders were marched six miles south opposite Cap Rouge, above Quebec.

Nashe rarely saw him in those days so it was unusual to receive a summons. Nashe crossed the Basin by sloop to Wolfe's new encampment behind the guns at Point Levis.

The camp was a bustle of activity. He was led through a phalanx of guards directly to Wolfe's bivouac. The tent was within a copse of birch, the trees serving to give it some privacy and deaden the constant boom of artillery fire from the Point. In another time, the little grove would have been beautiful, now it served a utilitarian purpose, nothing more. Soldiers have little time for beauty.

Wolfe met him on the path leading into the grove. He was busy with MacKellar, his chief engineer, studying maps on a camp table set up in the sunlight. His greeting was cordial but far less familiar than it had been a fortnight previous.

"Major Nashe," Wolfe spoke formally, "I intend once again make use of your services. If you will follow me, we have a prisoner to interrogate."

With that, he led Nashe down a narrow trail. In a shallow valley, closely guarded by Rangers, he made his way to a small group of tents. Offingham was there to greet them.

"Which tent, Brigadier?" Wolfe queried bluntly.

"The centre, Sir."

"No one knows of his presence here?"

"Only the men he surrendered to. They've become his guards."

"I compliment your security, Offingham. Major Nashe, will you enter the tent?"

"Sir?"

"All will be clear in a moment, Major." Wolfe permitted himself a wry smile. He lifted the tent flap and Nashe peered inside.

"Vadnais!"

The gargantuan form rose from a stool. The great black beard divided in a gleaming smile. He nearly filled the tent with his bulk. Then he rolled forward, arms outstretched, and embraced Nashe in such a mountain of flesh that the smaller man all but disappeared.

"Owl Vadnais." Nashe smiled up at the broad rough face. "Thank God you're safe."

"Of course, I am safe. Tell me, my friend, when is the Owl not safe? The winds are my messengers, the forest my house! Vadnais will not die until he chooses!"

"You got to safety the night of the Hermitage."

"You went by me like a fiend from hell. I saw soldiers follow you. I followed them. But you didn't go to Quebec. They lost you."

"It would have been senseless. I was finished, Owl, before I'd even begun. Ledrew is a traitor."

Vadnais' demeanour changed then, his smile fading.

"That brings me to my point, General," he spoke French slowly so Wolfe would understand. "You have done as I requested. Nashe is here. Now I'll keep my part of the bargain, but only with you and Nashe, no one else."

"Brigadier Offingham is Nashe's superior," Wolfe responded.

"As you wish," Vadnais turned to Nashe. "Ledrew wants to see you."

"The traitor?" Wolfe started.

"Ridiculous!" Offingham shouted. "That man was nearly the death of Nashe. Tell him to come here if he wants to see him!"

"He's afraid. He won't come."

"Then the discussion is pointless."

"Brigadier," Nashe interrupted, "Ledrew may have placed me in danger, but he's also the man who helped me escape." He faced Vadnais. "Why does he want a meeting?"

"He's had a change of heart. I believe him."

"How can you?" Offingham reddened. "The man's word is worthless."

"I've not been arrested," Vadnais countered.

"You're sure of him?" Nashe questioned. "This could be another trap."

"He says he has information that might end this."

"Why not give it to you?"

"You were his friend. He believes you understand what happened to him. He hopes you'll help him regain his honour."

"Then it's settled," Nashe murmured.

"General," Vadnais turned to Wolfe, "the Point Levis guns are to cease fire for one hour the day you select for the meeting. That night Nashe and I go to the city. Ledrew knows where to meet us."

"Alan," Wolfe turned to Nashe, "I will not order this. I know what you've been through..."

"He was my friend, General. And if this is true it could lead to something."

"I hope so. Tomorrow morning the guns will fall silent. But tomorrow night when you go in, gentlemen, the French will have their heads down. They will suffer such a barrage as they've never seen before. I guarantee you'll not be seen on the way in. Once there...well, that is up to you."

## 85

Point Levis pounded mercilessly upon the city. Wolfe was as good as his word. No head would rise this night in Quebec. Two men floating in on a bushy log would never be seen.

Nashe had decided to kill Ledrew. Men do not change so quickly. Ledrew's death would at least save Vadnais. And Vadnais would, in the end, find Bigot. If any man were capable, it was the huge coureur. Bigot would pay. And with that forfeiture, a good many scores would be settled. But by then Nashe would be out of it. He'd settled that in his mind as well.

They landed below Canoterie when the barrage, as planned, travelled through the Lower Town and up onto the Cap. It was a black night, clouds concealing the moon. The only light came from gun flashes across the river and the flames of buildings again on fire. The Lower Town was little more than rubble. A few skeletal buildings still stood, half smashed, leaning crazily. The streets were morasses of shattered stone and timber and sometimes the stink of rotting flesh. Nashe recalled the days when those streets were sunlit and filled with children.

Vadnais led Nashe to the shattered remains of a warehouse. It was once a prosperous maison owned by a man named Dubril. They descended a stairway to the vaults. In the dark, they went carefully. Still cold and aching from the water, Nashe limped badly. They came to a doorway. The weak light of a candle flickered through the open space. Nashe touched his dagger with his fingertips.

In the room—the room stale smelling—Ledrew sat quietly on a stool, his arm in a sling. A rough table, the kind used for tanning furs, concealed his lower body. The candle flickered on the table. Ledrew did not smile.

"Hello, Alan. I half expected someone else." He hauled two pistols from below the table, setting them carefully in front of him. Their embossed butts gleamed with the sweat from his hands.

"I understand you want to bargain," Nashe uttered coldly.

"In a sense, yes."

"I am in no mood to quibble, Ledrew. Say what you have to but make it quick. This place has the smell of a trap."

"You've always had a nose for that sort of thing, Alan. Unfortunately, your sense of smell was delayed this time."

"Then you are a dead man, Ledrew. If you shoot me, Vadnais will kill you before you can get a second shot."

"Unfortunately for you, I am the jaws of the trap." The words were in impeccable English. They came from behind Nashe, from the deep throat of Owl Vadnais.

Suddenly nothing was clear anymore. There was no time to think. On the edge of desperation, Nashe swung his fist in a backhand roundhouse into the face where the voice had been. He connected. Vadnais grunted heavily but the big man was immovable. His left hand grabbed Nashe's wrist like a vice. Nashe swung himself around his foot smashing into the giant's knee. Vadnais howled and let go the wrist. Nashe drew his knife. Vadnais stepped back, his hands outstretched. He looked indomitable, a mountain of man.

"You may limp but you are ever dangerous, little man," he smiled thinly.

"Let me pass, Vadnais, or I'll kill you," Nashe threatened emptily, half expecting hot lead in his back. But Ledrew did not fire.

"You think you can kill the Owl?" Vadnais sneered. "I've told you more than once, the Owl dies in his own time."

Nashe thrust for his belly but Vadnais moved equally fast. His right hand crunched down on Nashe's forearm. The knife skittered across the room. Nashe's arm went numb. His right foot flew up for a kick to the groin but then his body deserted him. His lame leg crumpled under the sudden weight. Vadnais was on him. Nashe clawed, pounded, writhed in the gargantuan grip. In moments he was exhausted.

Then Vadnais hauled him up over his head. Nashe's shoulder crushed into the ceiling beams. Vadnais turned to face the wall. And Nashe remembered with horror the death of another man smashed against stone in a street long ago.

"Would you waste that mind, Vadnais?" Ledrew shouted suddenly. "Set him down, man! What good is it if he dies ignorant of your powers?"

For a moment, Nashe lingered in the air. Then the big Frenchman dropped him. He landed on pile of boards. The boards saved him from a broken spine. His wind was gone. Gasping for breath, he was helpless as Vadnais trussed his hands to a beam leaving him dangling a foot from the ground. He could not even find breath to curse. Vadnais sneered into his face.

"I've kept you alive two years, little man. I have saved your life more than once. Now it is my right to take it. But I am not called the Owl for nothing. Before you die you will learn, fool, how powerless you have been."

He stepped back laughing. Nashe turned his head toward Ledrew. Ledrew's face was rigid.

"You see, Alan," his voice was emotionless, "Owl Vadnais is chief of Bigot's counter espionage. He is the one who captured me."

Nashe's brain reeled. He felt weak, used up, there were no reserves left.

"You wonder about the Ouendat village?" Vadnais' sneer had not left his face. "My grandfather is an old man, Nashe. He believes anything. I killed my father myself, for Bigot. My father was useless. And that is why my mother is crazy: She saw me kill him. So she is a wizened witch woman who never speaks. I keep appearances and the tribe's alliance with my annual performance. The Ouendat love performances, Nashe. It's all they have left to live on."

"When I was burned at Charest's," Ledrew added, "Vadnais took me to Bigot to recover. There was never any coureur camp. I recovered at the Intendancy."

"But why did you save my life?" Nashe looked again to Vadnais. "The ambush in Sous le Cap, the bear...you could have left me to die."

"Bigot's orders," Vadnais said scornfully. "And where would I find a more innocent dupe? No, little man, keeping you alive meant you would trust me, and there would be no other spies to root out. Even our jaunt to Albany had its purpose. Ledrew, in a fit of stupidity, had word passed that you'd been killed. I had to take you there to make sure the English would see you alive and not send a replacement."

"Why bring me here? It doesn't make sense."

"You seem to think you were finished when you crossed the river. I'm not so sure. You have a quick brain in some ways, and there are chinks in our defence. And you are to serve another purpose. Ledrew is going to return in your place. He will mourn your drowning, as will I. Your leg is weak, the river's current strong. Your body will be found on an English shore. Then Ledrew will give certain information to Wolfe. That information will be correct. There will be an attack on Montmorenci. Wolfe will know through Ledrew in advance. He will win. Ledrew will again be established. There will be more leads, some true, others, more important to us, complete fabrications. Winter will come. The English will leave.

You see, little man, the subtlety. We thought we'd lost you at the Hermitage. Yet you returned. Bigot is right; you English are too sentimental."

"The point is," Ledrew added, "that Bigot has an escape plan. That plan can't come to fruition until spring and the arrival of Charest's ship. Quebec cannot fall this year, Alan, for any of us. And you could be the fly in the ointment.

You see, Alan, I know the world. I join with the strongest possible ally. Bigot has taught me well, and Vadnais. They think you dangerous, so you are to be eliminated. I will tell you how one kills a dangerous man. One shot through the eye right into the brain."

Ledrew raised the gun, its barrel directed at Nashe.

"Don't be a fool!" Vadnais cried. "If you shoot him, the English will know he didn't drown!"

"Yes, but it's time to pay my debts, Owl. The dangerous man is at my mercy. The power has shifted. Are you so blind, you great bear? Have you forgotten our English sentimentality? Have you forgotten what you've done to me?"

Too late Vadnais recognized his error. The shot barked sharply in the room. Owl Vadnais stood for a moment, his left eye gone...a hole now, spewing gore. His face was a stupefied mask of astonishment. He had not chosen his time to die.

As he fell, the dust from the cellar smoked around his great weight when it crashed to the floor. In death, his face retained its amazement.

Nashe looked up from the supine body. Ledrew had picked up the other gun.

## 86

Ledrew rose and walked around the table, the pistol held limply in his bandaged hand. In his good hand he held a knife. He reached up to cut Nashe down. Nashe collapsed heavily to the floor. Ledrew gave him the gun. The guttering candle weaved weird shadows on the room's walls. Ledrew's face was calm.

"I know you've come here to kill me, Alan. What man could be persuaded to believe me now? All I ask is that you listen. If you shoot me after what I tell you then so be it. But first you must listen. You can give me that much, surely."

"Why did you kill him?" Nashe murmured.

"The slave has the right to kill those who enslave him. He was a brutal master."

"I understand nothing of this..."

"Three months after I arrived I was captured. You were not the only one fooled, Alan. I too trusted Vadnais and so fell into his snare. He was about to finish me when Bigot intervened. The Intendant offered me an alternative. I knew I would be of no use dead, so I agreed. It was not cowardice, Alan, but a ploy until I could get free. How could I know then the chains they would devise? I had no idea such evil existed as these two men.

For months I did nothing. Vadnais had me watched. Escape was impossible. So I tried subterfuge. I told them another agent would be sent, one I wouldn't know, to work independently of me. That worried them. I told them I might persuade Offingham to send someone at my request. They agreed. I asked for you. I hoped you would be Vadnais' match. I hoped you would see the change in me and so sort everything out. You did, but by then it was too late."

"But why didn't you simply tell me? You had plenty of chance."

"Don't you see I couldn't?" Ledrew's voice cracked. "They told me that given the least suspicion they would kill me... but not just me, Alan. They said they'd kill you and every English hostage in Quebec! Mass murder. I could not have that on my conscience, Alan.

And then I began to realize I wasn't so different from them. I hated myself. I tried to tell you at Batiscan. And when you didn't understand me... I was so twisted then... I began to hate you, Alan. I thought you no different from them. I felt helpless, entangled in a web. It was then, after Batiscan, that I went to pieces.

I resolved to play havoc with both sides. It was a foolish, stupid idea. I betrayed the Rangers. And then to make the score even, I tried to kill Charest. Now I know it was all misplaced frenzy fuelled by Bigot, yet against Bigot, yet somehow controlled by him. Bigot is a man of limitless evil. He used my insanity, Alan. Bigot took me in when I was burned. He nursed me and gave me kindness when I most needed it. I came to depend upon him. He was father to me, and friend... you must understand there was no one else; I was so alone... he convinced me. He told me there were no sides to war, that the only good is to protect one's self. I believed him. He had taken my mind and wrung it dry and then filled it full of his. I became Bigot's dog. I did anything he wished, some things I cannot even now bear to think.

The change came when you were captured. I'd been told you would be imprisoned, nothing more. I had no idea Bigot was planning to kill you. For once he underestimated. He trusted me, thinking I was completely profligate. I was, until Joncaire entered. I had heard of Joncaire. And I saw in him the same rabid animal I had become. I reacted then, you remember? I tried to stop it, but I wasn't ready to challenge Bigot. Only when he was gone could I summon what remained of myself. Killing Joncaire was my release, but it opened new doors.

I knew then to be free I must kill both Vadnais and Bigot. It's half done now. When I've killed Bigot my humiliation will end, and I will be a man again.

If you shoot me now I die half a man. If you choose not to, then I'll continue. And when it's over I intend to surrender and face the consequences of what I've done. It's in your hands now, Alan."

He stepped back then opening his arms, accepting his fate. But though his eyes glowed with a feverish light his face had become itself again. Nashe lowered the pistol.

"It seems so typical of us to meet in a cellar," Nashe muttered, "as we've always done. You're right, Jeff, we've wasted ourselves. I too have debts to pay. This won't be over until I can leave it, and I can't leave until I've made things right."

"Reine Marie?"

"Once it was all so simple."

He handed the gun to Ledrew. His friend took it, half smiling. He raised the gun to his head. The muzzle touched his temple. Nashe could do nothing but look on in shock as his friend pulled the trigger.

The gun clicked. It was empty.

"You couldn't be sure of me when you came here, Alan. I too couldn't be sure. You're right, things aren't so simple now."

"How will either of us become normal?"

"We won't, my friend, until this work is finished. And it's time to finish it quickly."

"Agreed."

"Before you go, I have something to tell you; and a plan to go with it."

They lit another candle, a new one, from the dying flames of the old. Fire is resilient.

## 87

A heavy rain drummed its tattoo on the roof of Wolfe's tent. Inside, in the yellow light seeping through canvas, Alan Nashe sat at a table with Offingham and the general. On the table lay a map. As he spoke Nashe drew markings on the chart: circles, arrows and small crosses. Each of the men was immersed in his demonstration.

"The French have re-deployed," Nashe said. "Ledrew has it from informed sources that fifteen hundred men are upriver of the city. They are under command of Colonel Antoine de Bougainville. That explains their efficiency in tracking our ships. I know Bougainville: he's an intelligent man, but not an accomplished soldier. He'll do as he's been ordered: march his men up and down the shore staying with our ships to prevent a landing. He'll not embark on other initiatives without specific orders... and those orders must come some distance: Vaudreuil still commands the city and Montcalm, thanks to you General, remains at Beauport. Ledrew says the French expect another assault there. So Montcalm is ten miles from Bougainville."

"They are spread thin," Wolfe interjected. "You said this Ledrew has a plan?"

"His plan hinges on the disbursement of French troops. And we can control it, Sir. If we send our ships south to Cap Rouge, Bougainville will follow. If we manoeuvre more ships off the Beauport, Montcalm will be forced to stay with them. If we hammer the city with one final barrage Vaudreuil will have no choice but to believe we might attack there."

"But what is the point, Major?" Wolfe was growing impatient.

"With the French concentrating their forces at those three points, spread too far apart for quick communication, we can surprise them. In the night we move a striking force by boat across the river and land here."

Nashe's finger pointed to a small inlet just upriver of the city. He circled it carefully with his pen.

"Anse au Foulon!" he murmured.

"Major Nashe," Wolfe muttered, "I myself have observed that sector by telescope. It's a two hundred foot cliff! And worse, it's less than a mile from Quebec and a quarter mile from the Samos battery. Do you expect serious consideration of this?"

"I do, Sir," Nashe replied strongly. "What you've seen through your glass is trees. But beneath their foliage is a path. I've used it myself many times. It winds up the cliff, a good path, steep, but easily climbed. The landing would be at night and this inlet is recessed enough that neither the city nor the Samos guards can observe it."

"Surely the French know this path," Offingham intervened. "They must have troops posted."

"That's the point, Sir. Through his connections, Ledrew has learned a small squadron is stationed there, commanded by Duchambon de Vergor. This man, too, I know. He's corrupt. Apparently he's given leave to most of his men to have them harvest his fields. Ledrew estimates less than twenty men there now, all inexperienced soldiers."

"But none of this intelligence is corroborated, Nashe. Can we truly trust Ledrew?"

"I've told you his story. He was never truly a traitor, and twice he's saved my life."

"Have you considered the problem of moving our battalions up the shoreline? French patrols are along the river. How can we pass them and make our way to the landing?" Wolfe's voice betrayed his growing interest.

"Ledrew is still close to Bigot. Bigot remains in charge of supplies. He's ordered a shipment to come down river some time this week. Ledrew will ascertain the specific night and the passwords. He's arranged to get across the river to us when he does. If we can move our force in ahead of the French supply boats, the guards won't know the difference in the dark. Your men, Sir, will climb Anse au Foulon and establish positions between Bougainville and Quebec. You'll have cut Montcalm's escape route, and you'll be above the cliffs."

"We've forgotten in all this, gentlemen," Wolfe grumbled, "that I've already committed the army to an assault on Cap Rouge. My officers are prepared for it. I think only God can stop that attack now."

"God seems to be doing so, General," Offingham said. "If this rain continues it will cost another day. We can't attack in the rain, sir."

"You like the plan, Offingham?"

"I do, Sir."

"Then, Major Nashe, you will take me in a small boat this evening out onto the river. We'll wear civilian clothes. I want a closer look at this cove."

\*\*\*

An hour later in the evening rain a small rowboat coasted downstream between the frowning cliffs of the St. Laurent. Little was thought of it. The rain prohibited snipers from taking their toll and few found sense anyway in shooting two silly adventurers out in search of thrills.

It passed all the way down to Point Levis, landing there. And when it did the two men who disembarked were quickly escorted up the cliff to the English camp. They went directly to Offingham's little valley. In a tent there, where Vadnais had once been, Ledrew now awaited them.

"The provisions order has been cancelled," he told them. "The French got wind of an attack on Cap Rouge. Bougainville's men are remaining there."

"How could they know?" Wolfe stuttered.

"I've no idea, Sir. Bigot has many spies. He cancelled the order only a few hours ago. The shipment was for tomorrow night."

"Well, that ends that then."

"No, Sir, not quite. I eliminated the messenger. As far as anyone knows the supply boats are still coming. The codeword is "La Reine". That name will get your boats past the shore patrols and into Anse au Foulon. I agree it's a risk but the reward, Sir, is the Plains of Abraham. When Montcalm sees you've blocked his path he'll have no alternative but to fight."

"I hope you gentlemen are right in this. If you're not I'll be the biggest fool in British history."

"Does this mean you accept the plan, General?"

"It does. If I can get enough strength above the cliff, well...I know my men. Nothing will push them off again. It's up to you to get me there, Nashe. And if you do, gentlemen, then you'll both be given your rightful place in history. I shall see to it personally. But until then you must maintain secrecy. That way I'll have no further French discoveries of my plans. No one is to know of this until they must. And now, gentlemen, I have a great deal to do. My army must learn to change tactics like a brigade."

"I must return to Quebec, Sir," Ledrew said. "If anything goes wrong I'll be in place to gather more information."

"I'm sorry, Captain. You must know you're still somewhat suspect. If this is a trap, Sir, you will pay with your life. That is the way things must be."

"But General, I have things left to settle in the city."

"I regret to say..."

"General," Nashe spoke up, "Captain Ledrew risked his life coming here. He and I have made other plans for the city. They're important to us, Sir."

"This business of yours...is not military?"

"No, Sir. I beg you, Sir, give us permission."

"This is highly irregular, Nashe."

"I know that, General, but just as victory is your goal, so is this business of ours to us."

Wolfe paused a moment, reflecting on the two standing before him. When he spoke again he extended his hand and took Nashe's own in a warm, firm grip.

"I accept your word on this, Nashe. I'll trust your judgement. But you must accompany my boats. I need a man who knows that cove."

"I've always intended that, Sir. Ledrew will return to the city alone."

"I see. I'll not ask your plans. You've done a great deal for this army, Nashe, and for me. Consider this a repayment of debt. Please send for my surgeon, Major. I feel somewhat tired, but I must prepare."

Nashe did so and when the surgeon entered both Nashe and Ledrew departed. But as the tent flaps closed behind him, Nashe overheard a rasping, tortured voice quite unlike that of a moment before. Wolfe was pleading with his doctor.

"I know very well you cannot cure me, but pray make me up so I'll be without pain for a few days and able to do my duty; that is all I want."

The rain ended that morning, the morning of September twelfth.

## 88

Two o'clock in the morning, a fine, cool darkness with the moon in its last quarter, the river like frosted glass, the trees far above in jagged relief against the sky. The scene dwarfed the line of boats bumping softly together in the slow current, each of them crammed with English soldiers, eighteen hundred silent men waiting, immersed in their thoughts.

Wolfe's penchant for improvisation had turned his army about in twelve hours. The Light Infantry and 78th Highlanders had the lead boats. They would be the first flight down river, the most dangerous, drifting in dark through the gauntlet of sentries along the far shore. After them, if they made it, more landing craft and armed sloops—the Lowestoft, Squirrel and Seahorse— would follow. The third flight waited above Point Levis in the shadowy shore opposite Foulon. Meanwhile, the big Sutherland remained as a decoy at Cap Rouge. In the Basin, Saunders manoeuvred his fleet off the Beauport Heights. The Point Levis guns still fired incessantly.

Alan Nashe sat in the first boat under the charge of Captain Delaune. The men were volunteers, their uniforms covered now in dark coats. Nashe, however, wore French livery, the white and deep blue of the Royal Rousillon, concealed by a cloak.

No one spoke.

Wolfe had placed himself in the fourth boat of the flight; it bumped now against the gunwales of Delaune's vessel, close enough to keep him at the fore, far enough behind to escape should the first boat be fired upon. He had done all he could. Now he was like any other soldier; he waited.

He held a dog-eared volume of poetry. He read by moonlight, bringing his face down close to the book, then closed the volume clasping it tight in his long, thin fingers. He murmured to Nashe in the boat beside him.

"Major Nashe, have you ever felt the thoughts of another could match your own? Strange, how, after reading him time and again, it should be this night the poet touches me."

"In what way, Sir?"

"Listen." Wolfe again opened the book. He spoke in whispered tones:

> The boast of heraldry, the pomp and pow'r,
> And all that beauty, all that wealth e'er gave,
> Awaits alike th' inevitable hour.
> The paths of glory lead but to the grave.

He sat back a moment, then said simply, "Gentlemen, I would rather have written those lines than take Quebec."

"It seems poets know the world, General," Delaune, having overheard, responded.

"Yes." Wolfe paused. "But my destiny is Quebec. And I will make a poem of this battle."

He put the book aside and studied his watch.

"It's time, Captain Delaune. Go with God, Sir, and go stealthily. From this point all depends on you. You are the first stroke of my pen. Lead me on to the rest of my verses."

In minutes, they cast off and were drifting down river with the tide, the boats each fifty yards apart. They steered toward the French shore passing beneath the high, brooding cliffs where their enemies lay. The moon had set. They received no challenge from shore. They went slowly until they reached the jutting hump of Samos, its cannon unseen far above on the promontory.

Then from the shore a muffled challenge stayed their progress.

"Qui vive!"

Each man stiffened. Fingers went silently to triggers. In the midst of the men, Alan Nashe removed his cloak and stood. In the dark, in the water's luminescence, the pale uniform was barely visible. But it was enough.

"'France!'" he whispered.

"'A quel régiment?'"

"'De la Reine.'"

A young Scot, his face creased with tension, began to raise his musket. Nashe placed a hand firmly on the man's shoulder. The soldier quivered, then relaxed. They heard faint whispers from shore, then a voice.

"Passé."

The boats floated on.

They travelled round the Samos promontory. No further challenges came from the shore. Then quietly they entered a bay and from that bay an inlet. They had come to Anse au Foulon.

As the boat shoved gently on the pebbled beach, Nashe leaped from it searching the shadows for signs of the path. He could not find it. He tried to recall landmarks, a stone jutting into the water, a stand of cedar; desperately he scoured the shoreline to no avail. He returned just as Wolfe himself stepped on shore.

"Sir, I think we've landed too far down. I can find no trace of the way."

Wolfe took the news calmly, in his element now.

"There's no time to find it, Major. The rest of the boats are due in. If we bottleneck here on the beach we are lost. Can you think of another alternative?"

"I can, Sir," a rough Scottish voice interrupted. Captain Fraser, commander of the Highlanders, presented himself. "This wee precipice y' see here presents litt'l problem. It be treed t' th' top, Sir. My men'l just hae t' climb."

"But there's hardly a foothold," Nashe argued. "The bank is soft shale. It will take hours."

"I dinna think so, laddie," the Scot smiled. "I hae men here who know wha t'is tae climb."

"Could you find the path more quickly from the top?" Wolfe whispered.

"From the top, yes, Sir," Nashe answered. "Easily."

"Then we have little choice. Choose twenty men, Fraser, and take Nashe with you. Should you meet French sentries, dispose of them quietly."

"Aye, Sir, if y'll gie me a minute..."

So began the incredible climb from Wolfe's secret cove. In the night, sweating, straining men struggled upward. It was hard and dangerous work, the ground soft and breakable, never giving a moment's respite. They hauled themselves up by tree roots grasping ever higher. Then the ground would suddenly crumble and the men would slide down grappling at bushes and other men's arms, the panic of building speed and the awful slide and knowing if they kept on they would end at the bottom with a splintered spine. There were abrasions and one or two men suffered broken limbs, but they continued the ascent. In the end, they leapfrogged over one another in a human chain hugging the cliff, their bodies the handholds of others. They finally made the summit.

Nashe, his leg by this time causing him agony, was hauled to the top to join Fraser. The two men peered warily through the long grass marking the edge and saw nothing, no movement, no shifting of branches, no patrols, nothing. Ledrew was right. De Vergor had deserted his post.

"Can y' find th' path, Mister Nashe?" Fraser whispered softly.

"Beyond those birch trees, less than fifty yards. But where are the French?"

"You find th' path, laddie, an' leave th' Frenchies tae me."

"I'll need two men. My leg's given out."

"Take three. Send one doon th' path tae Wolfe. Then wait at th' top for me."

Three brawny Scots helped Nashe limp past the birch grove. In moments, they came to the head of the trail. One of the soldiers descended, stringing ropes from tree to tree as he followed the tortuous way to its base. As more of the Highlanders appeared from their reconnaissance, they too descended with ropes to continue the work. The handholds of an army were quickly set in place.

And then, finally, a challenge rang out of the dark.

## 89

The youthful voice was choked and frightened. At the head of the path, the Highlanders crouched in concealment. Nashe stepped out of the underbrush approaching the terrified guard. As he closed, he could see the musket trained on his chest. The guard was a mere boy, not yet fourteen by the look of him, and skittish in the dark. Nashe began to speak softly. Slowly the gun lowered.

"Where are your companions, soldier?"

The boy having seen Nashe's epaulets snapped to attention.

"I can't say, Sir. Orders."

"My name is Major Duflor, young man. I'm inspecting guard posts in this sector. Where are the others? Where is your commander?"

"Sir, Captain de Vergor is in camp. There are no other guards but me. The Captain didn't think them necessary."

"You will escort me to this de Vergor. Show me his tent."

"But the captain is asleep. Sir, are those others there of your party?"

"They are." Nashe smiled. "Come with me, I'll introduce you."

"Yes, Sir." The lad seemed relieved. "It gets lonely this late, Sir. I'd be glad of some company."

The two returned to the thicket at the cliff's edge. Immediately six Scots, their claymores drawn, surrounded them. Too late, the boy realized what had happened.

"Now, boy." Nashe turned to him. "You can see for yourself who we are. You will take me and these men to your camp. You will direct me to de Vergor's quarters. Do you understand?"

"I will not, Monsieur." The boy's face quivered with fear. "You're a spy. These men..."

"These men are Highlanders," Nashe's voice went hard, "and they are desperate men. You've heard of the Scots, I assume. They are savage men, boy."

For a moment Nashe thought he'd gone too far. The boy blanched in terror; he nearly fainted. Nashe slapped his cheeks. Their colour returned. The boy's eyes darted fearfully from one hefty Scot to another.

"You will do as I ask?"

"I...I will."

He would be no more trouble, Nashe knew.

"Captain Fraser..."

"I heard, Monsieur Nashe." The captain grinned, responding in French, then returned to English. "You forget, Sir, tha' Scotland and France once had a guid deal in common. We're used tae bein' called savage. 'Tis guid for our reputations."

"I apologize, Captain." Nashe smiled.

"Ach, there's no need, Major. Th' men are assembled at th' head o' th' path here. Some others hae gone off tae Samos Battery. I suggest we gae noo, Sir, before these Frenchies hear that fight begin."

"Captain, I'd like the boy to lead me to the officer's tent myself."

"I assume y' hae a reason."

"Let's say I have old debts to pay."

"I see. Well, guid luck t' ye then."

"And to you. Let's hope we can do this quietly."

There was little need for concern. The Highlanders filtered like wraiths among the grey outlines of tents. There were no guards. The French were ensconced in their shelters huddled against the chill of morning in the hour of deepest sleep. Each tent was silently invaded. The French awoke to Scots' blades in their faces. Not one had the chance to resist.

Beside a tent set away from the camp, Nashe handed the boy to a Scottish corporal and entered. At the rear of the tent, he distinguished a sleeping form on a cot. Taking a seat in a camp chair, he found tinder and steel and lit a candle. The unconscious man did not move.

"It's time to greet the new day, Duchambon," Nashe spoke aloud.

De Vergor rolled over, drowsy and half asleep. It took him a second to recognize his visitor. When he did, his eyes widened and his hand reached out for a pistol.

"That would be more than stupid, Captain." Nashe's own pistol clicked as he drew back the hammer. "Your death will come soon enough. Why hasten it?"

"Guards!" de Vergor screamed. Nothing happened. Then two burly Scots entered the tent. De Vergor sat up.

"These are your new guards, Captain. It seems you encourage your men to sleep or steal away to work. These men will not, I assure you, be sleeping. I have two questions, Duchambon. You will answer. If you do not, or if I believe you are lying, I'll shoot off your kneecaps. I mean what I say, Captain, and believe me, I would do it with pleasure."

"What could you possibly want from me?" de Vergor muttered.

"Where is Bigot, precisely?"

"In the city. How would I know? I've been posted to this beaver-licked place for two weeks!"

"And Reine Marie...in Point aux Trembles or in the city?"

"She's in Quebec now. But if you hope for reconciliation, Nashe, then you're a bigger fool than I thought." His lips formed a satisfied smile.

"I think I'll find out for myself."

"She despises you!"

The sudden rattle of musketry punctuated his epithet. Shouted commands invaded the tent. One of the Scots guards ran outside; Nashe stayed the other.

"Remain here, corporal! Guard this man carefully. Be sure of him, he's devious."

"But, Sir, there be fightin'."

"You'll see enough later today. Now look to this man. And de Vergor," he rounded again on the Frenchman, "I will be back. We have a score to settle."

"A duel, Nashe? I look forward to it!"

"You're beneath the bother of that, Monsieur. I think prison for you and a trial for the murder of Trémais. Your duel will be with the hangman's rope, de Vergor."

The shooting stopped. The darkness was giving way to a rose-grey dawn. In the half-light, Nashe left the tent and hobbled toward the camp's centre. There he found Delaune and Fraser. Neither man seemed alarmed.

"Some French from the Samos," Delaune reported. "Fraser's men have them surrounded now. They're surrendering."

"Aye, it be too late f'r them noo," Fraser added. "Our men are landin' in strength. We hae a foothold, Nashe. We'll no soon relinquish it."

Then there was another shot: a sharp report in the distance.

"De Vergor!" Nashe shouted. "It came from his tent!"

He ran, the two officers following. They caught up to him in seconds, his leg again giving out.

By the time they reached the distant tent, they could hear a horse tearing through the underbrush. They found the unfortunate corporal, shot in the back.

## 90

Since the landing, men had been pouring up the steep path guided by the Highlanders' ropes. Dawn's harbinger found five hundred men at the top of Anse au Foulon. It was there, in the midst of his men, that Nashe found James Wolfe studying a rough map.

"Major Nashe." He motioned impatiently. "For God's sake help me! This chart is incomplete. What lies beyond these trees?"

"Sir, I have news."

"Later. Right now I must know the terrain. You've been here before."

"Beyond the trees there's a ridge, just here, about a half mile from where we are now. It runs nearly the width of the Plains. It's low, but it gives some advantage."

"Then the ridge it will be. Gentlemen." He wheeled on his officers. "I propose to form ranks and await the French. On our right by the cliff's edge I want the 35th Foot to deal with French skirmishers, next to them the Grenadiers, then across the plain the 28th, 43rd, 47th, 78th Highlanders and the 58th Foot on our left flank. The 48th will be held in reserve, the Light Infantry will protect our rear should this Bougainville fellow arrive to harass us. I will take the centre. Monckton, you have the right, Murray the left. As the men arrive here form them up and lead them to their positions."

"General, you must listen to me!"

"What is it, Nashe?"

"A French officer escaped by horseback. No doubt he's on his way to the city."

"So the French will be warned."

"He has no idea of our strength. He may believe we're a raiding party."

"Doubtful. Well, gentlemen, we shall have to work quickly. How many cannon has Carleton brought up?"

"Two, Sir. Six pounders. It's all the men can do to hoist them up here."

"Then we have two guns. Forget the rest. We need men up here now. If we have time, if the French move slowly and I doubt they will, we'll bring more up later. As for now, have the men hurry. Tell them I have need of them, Murray."

"Sir," Murray interrupted, "the Plains are too wide for a regular line. I suggest we encircle here, protect this point and await more men."

"I've considered that, Brigadier," Wolfe replied, "but we have the element of surprise now. We'll adjust the line; rather than three deep, the men will be placed in two ranks...one man behind the other."

"That will weaken their firepower, Sir. Two volleys instead of three. An advancing force would overwhelm them."

"Would you rather be flanked, Brigadier? The thin line will have to suffice. The volleys must be controlled. Pass the word that no man, not one, is to fire before my command!"

"Sir, this runs against established tactics!"

"So does this cliff, so does this war, so for that matter do I! There is no time for argument, Murray. Form the men as I've directed."

As morning came, more troops ascended. They marched, sweating and tired onto the Abraham Plain, then onto the ridge that dissected the rolling expanse. They could not see the city. It was obscured by higher hills and copses of trees beyond. But neither could the city see them.

Four thousand scarlet clad men formed by eight o'clock that morning in a long, thin line that stretched across the Plains, the first thin red line in British history.

James Wolfe had once again improvised.

## 91

Duchambon de Vergor thrashed his horse to the animal's limits, fighting his own rising panic. But he did not ride to Quebec; rather, he veered northeast across the St. Charles and on to the Beauport Heights. His fear had not stopped his thinking and he knew now there was but one solution to the events he had witnessed. Old alliances were no longer important; the petty struggle for power was finished. De Vergor rode to Montcalm.

He found the general surveying the ships manoeuvring in the Basin. Montcalm turned to face the wild rider who leaped from his mount. Even in his haste, de Vergor noted the stoop in the general's stance. The strain of the siege had taken its toll. Montcalm was exhausted.

"The English have landed at Anse au Foulon!" de Vergor shouted hoarsely.

Montcalm blanched. For a moment he looked white as death.

"How?" he uttered.

"They somehow passed the Samos pickets and climbed the cliff surprising my men!"

"Your men were not on the shoreline?" The words came cold and abruptly.

"General," de Vergor changed the topic, "I myself was captured. I managed to escape."

"Of course."

"I think it must be another probe, Sir. There were few men there from what I could see."

"But enough to take yours."

"Sir, I'm convinced it's a raid."

"How long did you observe? What kinds of troops were they?"

"Scots, sir, and the English spy, Nashe."

"Nashe? You mean to say you saw Nashe with them?"

"Yes, Sir."

"You're sure?"

"I spoke with him before I escaped. But why..."

"That settles it."

"Perhaps they were simply putting Nashe ashore again."

"Captain, you are not only corrupt, you are a fool! Of what use would he be? No, if Nashe is coming so is Wolfe's army. This naval action is a feint. They have committed themselves. They've fooled me."

His last words were harsh, almost a curse. He paused a moment turning away, looking out over the Basin. Whatever his thoughts, they were kept to himself. His officers questioned de Vergor. Their uproar drew Montcalm from his reverie. The general seemed to grow a little, to straighten, and when he turned again to his men, there was iron in his look.

"Messieurs, it seems the English threaten our supply lines. We have no choice but remove them. Bourlamaque, order the call to arms. We march within the hour. Captain de Vergor you must ride again to Quebec. Tell Governor Vaudreuil what has happened. Inform him I'm marching in strength to the Abraham Plain. Tell him there are no alternatives now; he must support me with men from the city. Be clear, de Vergor; be exact. Tell him there will be a battle, and I need his troops to win it."

Drums rolled along the miles of the Beauport calling the thousands to arms. The sun rose brilliant and warm taking the chill from the air. In an hour, each man learned of the threat on the Plains. They moved south gathering regiment after regiment as they went. They marched with urgency. No longer tired, siege weary men, they transformed themselves on that desperate march into warriors. Pennants and colours broke from their masts. The white and gold of Bourbon flags snapped brilliant above them. They knew that today was their test, and each was resolved to meet it. By half past nine they reached the Plains of Abraham and formed their lines just behind the summit of Buttes à Neveu.

And as they reached the top of the ridge, they saw before them the waiting English. The long, thin line stood to attention, its colours snapping in the breeze, the sun glinting dully off brass and steel and the scarlet tunics so hot against the land's green.

## 92

The weather was damp that morning on the fields of Abraham Martin. It frosted the breath of exhausted men as they trudged with their regiments into position. Half light, too early yet for dawn, but enough to see the glinting blades of their officers pointing directions with muttered commands. They knew the stakes of this desperate action. They had climbed the cliff at Anse au Foulon, a hard, treacherous struggle up through shale in the dark, grasping for holds, following the tenuous rope strung by the Highlanders who had ascended first, pushing upward to this place where they had come... unexpected.

A shamble of soldiers now trying to find some order, some kind of defence for what they knew was coming. The French would respond. The French had no choice now. Their defences were breached, and they would have to fight. Months of siege were ended this morning with the perilous ploy of General Wolfe.

And that General chivvied them, each troop as it passed, to move quickly, move surely, to get to their hastily chosen positions before they were discovered. They were a pittance of an army. James Wolfe knew this as he studied them, secretly wondering if this could be done, if he would live in infamy once it was over; if he would live at all.

Sunrise, with storm clouds gathering in the west and from the west too, the distant rumble of French drums. They were marching. But the British could see nothing, their searching stares obscured by trees and the rolling hills of the plain. They took comfort in that, for it meant the French could neither see them, see the thin red line, a delicate ribbon that straggled across the low ridge they would try to hold.

Morning opened, the sun ever higher, and with it the brightness of day. Now they could only await the arrival of the French thousands. Some Rangers, dressed in green, reeled back over the hills driven in by the advancing enemy. One look at their faces told the tale.

The two six pounder cannons were wrestled into position. Little help from them. This would be Brown Bess at work, the volley fire of four thousand muskets against overwhelming odds. Now the high, sharp commands of the sergeants major ran the soldiers through the trained ritual of loading. Like automata, concealing their fears, they obeyed, the rattle of ramrods pushing lead balls down the throats of steel barrels, the jangle of metal as men presented then shouldered their arms.

Only a few were distracted, only those close enough to catch a glimpse of a single French uniform in their company, its whiteness glimmering in the new sun, so contrary to the ranks of red. The man wearing it stood beside their general in the centre of the field. No one knew who he was; only that somehow he'd brought them here.

***

Montcalm, with Bourlamaque, studied the British formation when de Vergor once again rode up to them. The captain led a battalion of militia. The ragtag force was ready to fight, but there were not enough of them.

"This is a meagre advance guard, Captain," Montcalm commented. "When does the governor bring up the rest?"

"General," de Vergor muttered shamefully, "there will be no further reinforcements. Governor Vaudreuil has sent to inform you he feels the city must be protected. He is in readiness within the walls."

"And what in the name of God does he think we're doing out here?" Montcalm shouted. "The city is useless without supplies. Did you not tell him, man? The English are established!"

"I am here, General," de Vergor answered quietly. "I could have remained in the city."

"Yes. I apologize, Captain." Montcalm too grew quiet. "And I regret my remarks of before. You will lead the Quebec militia?"

"They have their own leaders. I'd like to stay with you."

"You realize I intend to lead the charge."

"That is what I supposed."

"General Montcalm," Bourlamaque interrupted, "surely you can't mean to advance? We can wait, Sir, for Bougainville. He must know by now what's happened. He has fifteen hundred men to their rear."

"Do you not see the British are strengthening?" Montcalm's fury burgeoned just below the surface. Vaudreuil's decision had affected him. "If we procrastinate, they'll gain enough force to make them invincible. Right now we outnumber them. We must advance and break them now!"

"In the centre, General?"

"Along the entire line! There will be a weakness somewhere. Alert your subordinates to the advance. This must be done and done quickly!"

"General, take time to think! We have no reserve, nothing to force a weak point should we find one. And half these men are militia, not trained for regular battle."

"Damn it, Bourlamaque! If we wait any longer that red ribbon will soon be a wall. Now is the time to thrust. Form your men and have them prepare."

The Quebec militia, what there was of it, and their native companions, were sent to the right flank to harass the English from the trees at the northern edge of the Plains. It was what they did best. Next to them on the open field was the La Sarre regiment and following to their left the Languedoc, Béarn, Guyenne and Royal Rousillon. On the left flank, Montcalm placed the militias of Trois Rivières and Montreal, and then by the brink of the cliff a cloud of snipers and more natives. He placed himself finally at the head of the Rousillon. Though he did not know it, he was directly opposite Wolfe who stood between his beloved grenadiers and the hardened veterans of the 28th

Foot. This would be the touch point, the leading edge of battle. The French aligned themselves for the charge.

They were a gallant corps, six thousand strong in their lines of white and grey. There was little time for second thoughts as Montcalm, pacing his horse up and down their lines, gave them courage and inspiration. At last they would prove themselves warriors. No man would run. No man thought of it.

De Vergor remained beside Montcalm. His land was threatened; the men and women he'd known all his life were suddenly under the clouds of calamity. De Vergor was a poor, corrupt spirit, but this day he put aside those things. He would fight. And he, too, with Montcalm, had set himself opposite his opponent, a white speck in the midst of scarlet.

*\*\*\**

Alan Nashe, clad in French uniform, watched the English preparations with a practiced eye, troubled that he was somehow wrong to do this, to be part of it, to betray those he had come to admire and love.

"You see them here, Nashe." Wolfe turned to him. "How splendid they are, my soldiers. The best soldiers in the world."

"I do, Sir," Nashe responded, "but I wonder will they be enough."

"I can only hope your thoughts on Montcalm are right. If so, I think the day will be ours."

"He has fooled us before."

"Yes," Wolfe sighed, "if he waits us out, allows Bougainville to come up to our rear…"

"Bougainville is six miles away. By the time he arrives you'll have half your army up here."

"That's what I count on."

"Sir, as I said, I ask again your permission to get to the city."

"Not before our advance. If you moved before that, you'd likely be shot by one of us first."

"And if there is no advance?"

"Then we'll have failed and nothing will matter."

Still they waited, the thump of the drums beating ever closer. Captains paced in front of their ranks, sharing brief conversations together, glancing too often westward trying to see what would meet them here in this farmer's field.

Shots from their right flank stirred them. Natives or French irregulars probing, moving along the edge of the cliff in the trees, meeting English Rangers in the kind of war both knew so well—stealth, concealment, and ambush. The men in the ranks did not envy them. It was not the kind of fight they excelled in. Then from the left, more action as the French sought a way to outflank them, the scarlet ranks skittish with anticipation, their subalterns calming them, dressing their lines, forcing them to the business at hand, too occupied now to dwell upon what they could not control.

Suddenly they were there, the French, their greys, blues, gleaming officers' whites across a half mile on the rise beyond, filling it, battle flags unfurling, stretching across the field as one column arrived then another then more, until they smothered the ground they claimed. The drums stopped. Distant cries of officers, in that fluid language so different to Nashe's ear from the gutturals of English, brought them into formation. The commands echoed in the morning air.

So many. English muscles tensed, the jokes became stiffer, and officers' telescopes appeared, each one sweeping the massed French lines. The answering glitters of glass from across the field told the same tale from the French. Now they would see the red ribbon. Now they would know with a single charge they might sweep away the invaders, despoilers of their land.

"There, in the centre, by that Rousillon flag, is that not Montcalm?" Wolfe turned to Nashe offering his glass. Nashe took it, found his bearings and saw clearly, as though standing next to him, the Marquis de Montcalm leading, as usual, from the front.

"It is, Sir", he muttered; the sight of the man recalled to him better times past, when he was one of them over there, when he was trusted, encouraged, befriended. Only to find himself here, opposite; the despised enemy unable to go back in time no matter how much he wished it.

Brigadier Townshend joined them. "They form in columns, General."

"Yes," Wolfe breathed, "he's not going to wait. Best get to your position, this has the look of a full on attack."

"We need more men to contain it."

"We have no more, Townshend, and no time."

"He's decided, General," Nashe offered. "You've decided it for him."

"Finally," Wolfe said, "we'll see what they're made of with no walls to protect them." His voice rose. "To your places immediately, gentlemen! We must take what comes!"

The bevy of officers departed quickly, each to his place along the line, some nearby, some a brisk walk behind the thin ribbon, the wait nearly over, the time upon them to prove their mettle.

Nashe gazed across the shallow valley as the French crested the Buttes. On his side the redcoats stood solid and ready. And it came to him then how small they all were. Two little armies, minuscule entities that would be swallowed whole in the battlefields of Europe, tips of waves in the sweeping tides, yet here they presented themselves as proudly as a hundred thousand. And today, he recognized, these little armies would fight to decide a continent's future.

Wolfe removed his cloak. He was wearing not his usual unadorned coat, but a glittering uniform. He carried with him his trusty cane, disdaining a weapon, and strolled calmly among his soldiers.

"You look magnificent, General," Nashe said.

"I look the part I am to play this day. I've had a uniform brought up for you as well. Those French togs displease me. I'd like you to change."

"Sir, this uniform will allow me to fight my own battle. I've done all I can for you, General. Now I do the things left to myself."

"As you wish. You're an unusual man, Nashe. Whatever your battle, I wish you luck with it. But you realize if things become thick here you run the risk of being shot by your own men? You make a target of yourself, sir."

"I stand beside another who has done the same." Nashe smiled.

"I bow to your character, Major," Wolfe smiled in return, "as I concede to my own. Now if you don't mind, Nashe, I feel just a little nervous yet. Perhaps we might walk a bit."

A hoarse, heavy cheer from across the valley interrupted him. Then the roll of drums up and down the French line signalled Montcalm's call to advance. Lines of men and fluttering flags smothered the hillside with measured tread. The French had organized. They would not wait.

## 93

The scarlet lines stood shoulder to shoulder their subalterns pacing nervously. Another rumble of drums brought the French columns advancing in quick time toward them. Still there was shooting from the flanks; Nashe noticed men falling, fired upon as they waited, struck before they had a chance to strike. Wolfe observed as well this waste of his few.

"Order the men to lie down. No point in making targets," he ordered, and English drums gave the signal up and down the line.

Each regiment found welcome earth beneath the line of fire. Wolfe himself went to one knee. It was then he was struck the first time, a spin and a fall. He did not cry out. Instead, he held his wrist as blood gushed from between his fingers. Nashe kneeled beside him as the general struggled up, the wrist shattered by a musket ball. Surgeons appeared, binding the wound.

Then Nashe caught a glimpse again of Montcalm amid his advancing soldiers. He trembled a moment at the irony of the two commanders face to face in a little battle that would answer so much.

"At eighty yards the men are to stand," Wolfe gasped through his pain. "No one will fire until my command. Pass the word."

"Sir," an aide shouted, "they are coming fast. You must move behind the line!"

Nashe helped Wolfe through the ranks to a small hill in the rear, a slight rise in the ridge but enough to see the field beyond. From here the general would direct his desperate battle.

At two hundred yards, the emboldened French began to charge. The troupes de la marine, unaccustomed to European methods, bolted forward too quickly. The charge flew out of control.

Still they came. One hundred yards distant. The scarlet lines remained prone and impassive. Closer the French advanced, irregulars madly shooting as they approached. There would be no ordered volleys to rupture English ranks. At eighty yards, Wolfe ordered his troops to stand. The drums again relayed the message and four thousand men rose as one. The French were a matter of yards away now, bayonets bristling, their mouths open in that bellowing that would take them into the madness of their charge and run them through the English line, rolling over it in an unstoppable wave.

But the charge stuttered. Militia ran to the front, firing then falling to ground to reload, as was their custom. The French advance broke upon itself as the regulars clambered over their comrades. The charge became ragged, not one great wave but a series of them sputtering forward, their momentum lost.

"First rank, kneel!"

The scarlet soldiers dropped to one knee.

"Present!"

The drums rolled and two thousand guns took aim.

Suddenly Wolfe was propelled into the air. He came down half on Nashe's shoulder, half on his own feet. Blood oozed in gouts from his groin. Nashe tried to lay him down.

"No." The agonized voice choked out the words. "The men must fire. Give the order to fire. Front rank, shoot!" shouted Wolfe. His drummers took up the command. The drums rolled like thunder, then stopped. And in that instant, the first rank's fire shattered the air—smoke and flame and deafening blast. And the air was opaque, filled with smoulder and hints of colour through gunpowder grey.

Men were blinded, fumes stuck in their throats, the clouds of war palled the once rolling green of the Abraham Plains. Wolfe collapsed to the ground, his chest suddenly spewing blood. He had been hit yet again; his scarlet jacket glistened with blood, the gold lace discoloured by blood, his eyes were wide with shock.

A colonel beside him leaned down to his lips then quickly stood, sword in the air, shouting wildly: "Second rank...Fire!"

And again the deafening, ghastly thunder and more of the blinding, stinking smoke. Men swam in smoke. Ears rang from the noise. The great long lines became little groups surrounded by noxious clouds. Townshend stepped forward to take command.

"Advance! Reload and advance!"

The drums took his command and the lines surged forward, a disciplined whole.

"Advance and fire at will!"

The rattle of rapid fire replaced the two deadly volleys. The army rumbled forward. As the smoke lifted, Nashe witnessed a sight so horrendous he could hardly believe his eyes.

Where once had been proud ranks of men was a slaughterhouse. All along the sweep of the Plains the French were decimated. The white and grey lines were a shambles now, wounded men crawling, moaning, and pouring out blood.

The English advanced in perfect order. The French faltered, fired wildly, then broke. One brief spasm of 'Brown Bess' blew Montcalm's army to ruin. Five short minutes and a nation began to change hands. The French ran in terror from Wolfe's martial demons.

And Wolfe lay behind his men now, on the knoll where he was carried for safety.

An officer shouted from atop the rise, "See how they run!"

"Who runs?" Wolfe gasped weakly.

"The enemy, Sir! Egad, they give way everywhere!"

Wolfe's long fingers grasped the coat of an aide, his last breaths harsh and desperate. "Call the charge, man. Then go to Colonel Burton; tell him to march Webb's regiment with all speed down to the Charles River, to cut off their retreat from the bridge. Do it now, Sir. That is the way they must go."

He turned on his side then, his delicate hands gripping the soft grass of New France. He gazed long and strangely up at Nashe, then sighed softly: "Now, God be praised, I will die in peace."

Nashe heard the charge of the Highlanders, the skirl of the bagpipes as the Scots threw down their guns in favour of claymores. Nothing would stop them now.

Nashe left his general then; his mind found a different place, many places. They came upon him in flashes of memory. For Nashe this should have been the culmination of years of work within Quebec: seasons of disguise, months of lies, moments of deception leading to this climax. But the past was more powerful now. It played upon him in glimpses of remembrance and regret, of what had brought him here and what would bring him to fight his own war, the one that began four years before in the stinking alleys of Marseilles, the one that was not yet finished.

Nashe did not stay to watch James Wolfe die. He sprinted toward the brink of the cliff, then up through the trees passing the 35th Foot as they cleared the woods of French snipers. Once he felt his coat tear. A bullet had passed. He kept running.

Soon he caught up with French stragglers and the men who chose to fight the rearguard. He ran with them a while then passed them, ignoring the shooting pains in his leg. Through narrow pathways, once pleasant lovers' walks, he made his way quickly and with deft purpose. Luck was with him.

As he passed a poplar thicket, he decried a horse's neighing. Within the trees, he found a frightened bay tethered to stump. At its base, a French officer lay dead, shot through the face. He had come here to die.

The horse was skittish. Nashe calmed the animal, and then mounted. His sudden weight sent the horse into new spasms of panic. Nashe settled it, stroking its neck, and letting it pace, then turned it through the trees and onto the plain. French soldiers were running everywhere. The defeat became a rout.

Nashe guided the plunging animal toward the city. He was not long in arriving, the horse fast and spurred by fear. Near the St. Louis gate a number of officers were trying to turn their men toward the St. Charles to join the main body of the army. They only partly succeeded.

At the gate itself, Nashe found chaos. Troops of men crammed through the opening ignoring commands, racing to safety within the walls. Men fell and were crushed beneath the tide. Others wandered blankly. Nashe pushed his horse through the mass of men into the city just before the huge gates were closed. Vaudreuil had ordered his own men shut out of the city.

Once within the walls Nashe dismounted to be less conspicuous. As he turned down Rue St. Louis, he caught sight of a familiar black horse. Upon it slumped Montcalm, conscious but mortally wounded. The horse's flanks were bathed in his blood. De Vergor rode beside the general, holding him in the saddle. They passed down St. Louis. The streets were in an uproar. Shouted alarms and rolling drums called every man to the walls. The militia struggled through congested byways trying to reach their positions.

Nashe followed the trail of Montcalm's entourage keeping far back. He knew where they were going. He knew where Montcalm would choose to die. As the party swung off St. Louis onto Rue du Parloir, Nashe took a different route. In front of the house on du Parloir the gallant general was lifted from his mount and carried into the house.

As this happened, Nashe clambered over the shattered walls of the Ursuline Convent and picked his way toward the rear of that house. A mile to the north, the scarlet ranks advanced as inevitably as a storm. Further behind, at its source, another general lay already dead.

There is no improvising death.

## 94

Near the gate at Rue du Parloir, the wall remained intact. A donkey cart lay just inside the portal. By standing on the cart, Nashe could reach the wall's crest. One quick spring brought him onto the wall. On the other side lay a familiar courtyard, to his left the kitchen and servants' quarters, squatting grey and heavy on the yard's cobbles, to his right was the stable. In the house that rose above its courtyard was where Montcalm would be, no longer the charming master of rapiers, now a defeated, dying soldier.

Nashe dropped into the yard. As he landed, his bad leg crumpled beneath him. Nashe tested the leg placing his weight on it. There was pain, but it held.

The house was like a tomb. Nashe made his way along deserted corridors. He entered the foyer. It too appeared empty. It was not.

"May I help you, Monsieur?" a little voice came from above.

On the stairway leading to the second floor, a frightened girl peeked from between the banister's shafts. She looked like a startled fawn, her eyes wide, her breathing a flutter.

"Are you a servant here, child?" Nashe uttered softly.

"I am, Monsieur," her voice trembled in reply.

"Where is your mistress?"

"Mme. Beaubassin is in the upstairs salon, Monsieur. She is with the general."

"I see. And how is the general, girl?"

"I think he is dying, Monsieur. I could not watch so Madame sent me here. What shall become of us if the general dies?"

Tears welled in her eyes. Nashe stepped to the base of the stair and held out his arms. In an instant she had flown to him and buried her face in his chest. Nashe calmed her, stroking her hair.

"Will you take me to them, child?"

"I...cannot, Monsieur. Madame has told me to turn away any visitors."

"Who else is in the room with her?"

"The doctor, Monsieur Bigot, Monsieur de Vergor and two officers I don't know, and Mademoiselle Duchesnay."

That she was here stunned him. It was the last place he would have expected to find her. And the fact of her presence changed him. His plan for revenge disappeared and he made a new one then, in a new direction...in the direction he had been going almost without knowing.

"I must see them, child."

"My mistress would turn me out."

"I don't wish to enter the room, only to look inside. No one need know I am here."

"Do you promise, Monsieur?" the little girl snuffled.

"I do." He smiled. "I shall be quiet as a mouse. And I would like you to do me a favour."

"I'm not supposed to leave the stair."

"It will take but a moment. I want you to fetch me some paper, a pen and ink. Tell no one I'm here. Just bring me those things quietly and I'll give you this."

He offered a silver coin in his fingers. The girl stopped sniffling immediately.

"But, Monsieur, this is a petit louis. It's far too much for a girl like me."

"Nevertheless, the mission is important to me. Go now. I'll find my own way."

"Please be quiet, Monsieur."

"I shall. But you must be quick, and equally silent."

He patted her cheek and she ran off. Nashe climbed the stairs cautiously, making his way unobstructed to the salon. Heavy curtains were drawn to separate the room from the corridor. Nashe distinguished muffled voices within. He parted the curtains just slightly, enough to peer through with one eye. Inside was a sorry sight.

Montcalm lay on a couch dappled with his own blood. He was conscious but white as alabaster. His head rested on the lap of the good Beaubassin. She stroked his hair softly, her face a mask of anxiety. De Vergor peered out a window to the street below. Bigot stood at the foot of the couch. He was speaking quietly.

"... And so Vaudreuil is out of the city. He has gone to the St. Charles to join Bourlamaque. There are hopes, apparently, of a counter attack."

"Then you must command the defence of the city yourself, Intendant." Montcalm's voice was throaty. The man remained stoic. He would not show his agony to Beaubassin.

"I know little of fighting, General," Bigot whispered, "but I'll do my best."

"Go now, Monsieur. You'll be needed."

Bigot turned, taking the officers with him. As he walked toward the curtained doorway Nashe stepped quickly across the hall and into a narrow alcove. The Intendant and his men passed. For a brief second, Nashe thought of killing Bigot. It was obvious now Ledrew's plot had failed. And yet in that moment, revenge seemed an empty vessel. Trémais was long dead; Ledrew had regained himself; the Intendant was trapped within the city. He would pay for his crimes. And there were other things now on Nashe's mind. He returned to the curtain.

Montcalm's surgeon was doing his best to stem the flow of blood. The task was too painful for the patient. He ordered the doctor to cease his attempts.

"How long have I to live?" he uttered hoarsely.

"A few hours. I can't be sure."

"But you are certain of my death."

"I am sorry, General..."

"All the better." The pale face turned to gaze on Beaubassin. "I will not see the English in Quebec."

Just then Reine Marie entered the room by another door. She carried a steaming kettle. Nashe glimpsed her face for a moment as she took towels and placed them gently, until they cooled, on Montcalm's ghostly forehead.

"That is good, Mademoiselle," he murmured. "You have the touch of an angel. You show me the way I must go. I thank you for it, child. Do not cry. I go to safe haven and the end of wars. A good thing, you see, for I never wished to be a soldier."

A spasm took him then, his body suddenly rigid, his face beaded in sweat. Nashe heard the little maid at the top of the stairs. Quietly he closed the curtain and joined her. Taking paper and pen he wrote a brief note, handing it to the girl and offering her the coin.

"You must give this to Mademoiselle Duchesnay, girl. Be sure you give it only to her. Let no one see you do it, and tell no one I have been here. Understand?"

"Yes, Monsieur. I'll take it now."

"No. Wait till she is alone. I thank you, child, with all my heart."

Nashe returned through the house and across the courtyard. He entered the double door of the exercise hall. The place was cold, the huge hearth empty. Foils and rapiers hung above its mantle. A single table stood near the fireplace surrounded by a litter of chairs. Nashe chose one facing the door. He sat resting his aching leg on another. He placed a pistol on the tabletop and waited.

The stable was a hollow place now. Each movement he made echoed sadly. He recalled vividly the clash of steel, the cheerful laughter of Beaubassin and Bougainville, the crackle of apple wood in the hearth. That was gone now. All hollow. It was a fitting place for him now.

An hour passed. Then another. He was as alone as a man could be, the ticking of his watch his companion, his only light the sun coming through the door he'd left open.

Then a shadow crossed the opening. Nashe leaned forward his hand near the pistol butt. The shadow paused a moment as though its owner were deciding something. When she entered, she was blinded momentarily by the interior dark. It gave him the chance to look at her. She seemed tired, older, yet still possessed of that breathless beauty that made her a wonder. Then she discovered him and came down the long polished floor like a dream.

"Alan." Her voice was like dust.

"Reine Marie," he murmured softly.

"If you've come to assassinate the general, save your strength. He will die before the day ends."

"I didn't come for that."

"What other reason has a spy for coming here?"

"You must know, Reine Marie."

"I do not."

"For God's sake stop this sham!" he cried. "I'll do anything you wish, Reine Marie. Anything! I'll surrender if you command it."

"I won't have you surrender, Alan. They would shoot you."

"I love you," he whispered.

"Please don't say that."

"You think I'm blind? You think I can't see it in you?"

"You are mistaken," she said bitterly. "You see only weakness."

"How can that be? Let me explain myself, Reine Marie. Let me tell you how much I meant everything I said. I need you, Reine Marie, more than anything I have ever wanted or needed in my life. Without you I am lost."

"Then you must be lost, Alan. To me, you are already. I will remember the man I loved as a widow recalls her husband. I am a widow now, without benefit of a marriage. I shall never want marriage."

"You can't see how much I need you?"

"Victors need no one, Alan, but the defeated must turn to each other for succour. So I turn to the hands of my people for comfort, their tongues to mend my spirit. If your victory is your defeat, then I'm sorry for you. But only sorry. My love belongs to those you have trampled."

"Quite touching," a voice enjoined behind her. In the doorway stood de Vergor. "But the victor at times can still lose his head! Still playing the lover, Nashe? Draw your sword and prepare to die. And know this, you English bastard, that you die before her eyes. Draw your sword, damn you! This meeting is long overdue!"

## 95

In the half light de Vergor's rapier glittered as it rasped from its sheath. "For the love of God let there be no more murder!" the girl cried desperately.

"God has little to do with it, Mademoiselle," the Frenchman hissed. "This is between men."

"If you love me, either of you, stay your swords!"

"I'm afraid this has gone beyond you too, my dear. You weren't there on the Abraham Plains. You have no idea what this moment means. This spy here, this double man with his swift tongue and subtle manners, is the one who led us to this. You've lived too long, Nashe. You should have died on that beach with Trémais. And now things will be set to rights."

"I'll not fight you. Leave me with her for just a moment, then I'll surrender myself to you."

"Draw your sword you motherless dog! I'll have the satisfaction of your blood! Draw your sword or I'll kill you where you stand!"

He slashed wildly. Nashe stepped back avoiding the cut.

"I will not fight."

Again the Frenchman thrust. Nashe dodged sideways putting the table between them.

"Then die for your foolishness. Pray your end is quick, Nashe. If it's left to me, you'll die in pieces!"

The sword whipped up and across the table. Too late Nashe heard its deadly whisper. But the table was wide. Only the razor tip ripped his chest. A flesh wound, but it bled profusely.

As his eyes went to Reine Marie, he noticed a rapier in her hand. She had taken it from above the mantle. Her face was a myriad of confusions, yet beneath it, there in her eyes, was the thing he remembered.

"I can't see you die, Alan. Not for me." She walked to the table between the two men and set the weapon upon it. "Defend yourself. You have no other choice."

Then the rage of two years swept into him and centred on de Vergor—the rape of the girl, the murder of Trémais, the man's corruption...his own corruption...flooded his mind. He gave himself to the one passion he could fulfil.

There would be no quarter. And as they began de Vergor advanced recklessly stabbing, slashing, reaching each time for his vitals. Nashe's leg was a disadvantage and de Vergor noticed and pressed upon him, driving him backward to trap him against a wall. Yet Nashe felt no fear of the man. He parried and thrust and slowly retreated beneath the furious blows. De Vergor could not touch him. The deftness of Nashe's flickering steel weaved a silver net about him. De Vergor grew desperate. It was not the fight he'd thought it would be.

Then De Vergor stopped, retreated a step, and pulled a pistol from his belt. As he cocked the hammer he fumbled slightly. Nashe charged. The Frenchman was open to him. Nashe thrust forward extending to the full and pushed the needle tip of his sword just under the ribcage and up, into his rival's heart.

De Vergor's eyes went wide. His hand gripped the offending steel. That hand began to bleed. Then the cruel mouth opened in a last dying grimace. He fell, his blood spattering the polished floor making red stars against the sheen. De Vergor died as he had never lived, in silence.

Nashe felt nothing then, no triumph, no satisfaction. Hollow. He turned to the girl and dropped his weapon. It clattered to the floor, echoing in the hall.

"I didn't want this, Reine Marie..."

"What did you expect? You came here. What do you want?"

"Come with me. We can make a new life without lies. I promise!"

"How like a man you talk, Alan."

She drew a letter from her sash.

"This is for you. From Antoine de Bougainville."

Nashe unfolded the parchment to discover his friend's neat script. As he read, his blood dripped onto the page.

'My old friend,

I write in haste. I am leaving for my new post as commanded by my general. I know not when you will read this, so for reasons as unfortunate as they are obvious, I will not inform you of my whereabouts.

I knew somehow you would try to see her. I have spoken to her as I handed her this. She has read it. I find in her, as I always have, the best of women. I cannot but help feeling badly for having so disrupted her life. After all, it was I who introduced you. She has said she has forgiven me.

Needless to say I have discovered your identity. At first I disbelieved it. But the evidence was overwhelming. I admit for a time I was enraged. I felt a complete fool: used, played upon, my trust ground to nothing. It is not a good feeling to have been so totally duped. I realized then what an innocent I am. I have never looked for shadow, preferring always to seek the light of knowledge. Now I have learned in hard ways my own identity. You have taught me that much.

As to you, Alan, as to you... I hardly know where to begin. Your complexity astounds me. I recognize you had a duty as I have mine. You performed admirably. I salute your skill. Even now, despite all, I have seen in you a worthwhile man. And I have enjoyed your friendship. I will not believe, I cannot, being who I am, that all was sham. Perhaps it is the times. Perhaps another time would have given us each other as friends and given you her as the best of wives. This is a strange time to be living. The world about us alters so quickly and we are at our wit's end to keep with it. I suppose that may be said by any man of any time, but I live in this, and I am troubled.

I said she has forgiven me. She has forgiven you as well. I know this. And thus, I too extend my indulgence. I must. I am a soldier as are you. If I cannot understand, who will?

Yet I cannot clear the slate, Alan. I hope as a man you will recognize this, and understand it. Too much has happened, too deep are the wounds to ever completely heal. I love you as a man, yet you are my enemy.

I began this message, "My old friend," for that is what you are. In another time, another place, perhaps it might have been different.

It is as it is. We have little to do with it.

Goodbye, Alan. May our wars end soon.

As a man,
Bougainville'

"You've read this?" he murmured.
"I have. His thoughts are mine."

310

"Yes."

"I'll always love you, Alan. Love the man within. But I could never again be with the other."

"I understand."

"Goodbye, Alan. God be with you..."

She turned in the doorway, a silhouette in the dying sun. It reminded him of a thing Bougainville had once said.

"When I look at the moon, wherever I am, I'll remember you."

She was gone.

***

Alan Nashe left maison Beaubassin. He meandered through the narrow byways of Quebec. He was not noticed. Many uniformed men wandered about in the shock and confusion of that day. But there came a point when he could wander no further. He reached the edge of the Cap, resting there on a balustrade, peering out over the river's grey depths criss-crossed now by English ships. A soft breeze touched his face. It came from the west. He turned into it.

He could see the Plains of Abraham, still alive with scarlet columns. He could see the city's walls manned by its defenders. Far off to the north along the St. Charles shore the French brought their artillery forward. They would make their stand at the river.

But these machinations no longer held him. His attention wavered, and dissipated. He looked west again, beyond the Plains and toward the rolling, blue horizon so mystic and fine in the brightness of daylight. The guns on the St. Charles opened up, the French nation's salvoes raining more death on its brother humans.

But he could not hear them for the beating of his heart.

# EPILOGUE

On September 18, 1759, the British took possession of Quebec after the city surrendered. Brigadier Townshend was given the honour of accepting the city's capitulation. But the French army escaped, bypassing the English, and joined Bougainville's forces marching, too late, to the city's defence.

Admiral Saunders did not dare keep his ships on the river through the frozen Canadian winter. He and Townshend departed on September 26th leaving Murray in command of the English regiments.

De Levis escaped with a squadron of French ships and travelled to France to beg assistance from Versailles. The court refused his entreaties. He returned to New France in early spring and, gathering his remaining forces, attacked the British and besieged Quebec. On May 9, 1760, British transports appeared in the St. Lawrence Basin. De Levis was left no alternative. He ordered his troops to burn their colours so as not to have them fall into the hands of the conquering British. Almost a year had passed since the fatal meeting of Wolfe and Montcalm on the Plains of Abraham. A continent had changed hands.

Bourlamaque and Bougainville were shipped home with their fallen army. Vaudreuil remained in Quebec, co-operating with his new masters.

Louis Antoine de Bougainville became an explorer-scientist in the years that followed. One of the Solomon Islands is named for him, and a lovely sub-tropical flower. He died a senator in the reign of Napoleon.

Joseph Cadet and the other members of the Grande Societé were brought to trial in France and imprisoned for corruption. Francois Bigot too was brought to trial. He was fined the paltry sum of one thousand livres and exiled to Switzerland. He lived the rest of his days in luxury.

Antoine Duchesnay retired to his estate on the Beauport. He took no part in the English reconstruction, preferring to remain isolate. His daughter, Madeleine, went to Paris where she married into nobility. She was executed during the Reign of Terror in the revolution of 1789.

# The Betrayal Path

Reine Marie Duchesnay joined the Ursuline sisters. Her patience and selflessness became legend amid a conquered people rebuilding their lives from war.

Brigadiers Monckton, Murray and Townshend continued their careers in the British army. Murray intended to write a book on the fall of Quebec. If Murray did so, his papers were lost.

Offingham and Saunders both retired from active service soon after the surrender of New France. Guy Carleton, however, returned to Quebec in the ironic position of commanding general defending the city from American invaders during the War of Independence. He routed an assault on the Cap, his lessons well learned from previous experience.

Captain James Cook became an explorer-navigator who circumnavigated the globe. Natives in the Sandwich Islands killed him.

George Washington became a revolutionary. But he did not hang for it as Offingham prophesied. He became, instead, the first president of the newly formed United States of America.

Jeff Ledrew's body was found in Quebec after the British entered the city. It appeared he had shot himself.

The day after the British assault on the Plains of Abraham, Alan Nashe disappeared: a man who altered history, and was changed by it; as are we all.

******